GRACE UNDER FIRE

GRACE
UNDER
FIRE

JULIE GARWOOD

BERKLEY
NEW YORK

BERKLEY
An imprint of Penguin Random House LLC
penguinrandomhouse.com

Library of Congress Cataloging-in-Publication Data

Names: Garwood, Julie, author.
Title: Grace under fire / Julie Garwood.
Description: New York: Berkley, [2022]
Identifiers: LCCN 2021053270 (print) | LCCN 2021053271 (ebook) |
ISBN 9780593546291 (hardcover) | ISBN 9780593546307 (ebook)
Subjects: LCGFT: Novels.
Classification: LCC PS3557.A8427 G73 2022 (print) | LCC PS3557.A8427 (ebook) |
DDC 813/.54—dc23/eng/20211029
LC record available at https://lccn.loc.gov/2021053270
LC ebook record available at https://lccn.loc.gov/2021053271

Printed in the United States of America
1   3   5   7   9   10   8   6   4   2

Book design by Kristin del Rosario
Title page art: Bullet © Elegant Solution / Shutterstock.com

To my brilliant and beautiful granddaughter,

Macy Elyse Garwood,

may your future be as bright

as the light that shines within you.

GRACE UNDER FIRE

ONE

ISABEL MACKENNA HAD A HUNDRED THINGS TO DO TODAY. KILLING someone wasn't one of them.

She had such high hopes this morning when she dragged herself out of bed at the ungodly hour of five A.M. She had made detailed plans for the day that lay ahead, and she would have sailed through them if two unfortunate incidents hadn't waylaid her. The first was an irritating inconvenience; the second, a terrifying nightmare.

Scheduled to take an early flight on a no-frills, but supercheap airline to Boston, she arrived at the airport in plenty of time to go through security. She was dressed for comfort in a pair of snug jeans and a light pink T-shirt. Her long blond hair was up in a ponytail, and she wore a Red Sox baseball cap her brother-in-law, Dylan, had given her. She checked her luggage, which was packed for a trip to Scotland the following week, and carried her backpack that held everything she would need for the next few days. It was so stuffed she was pretty sure it weighed more than she did. The first time she attempted to swing it over her shoulder she nearly did a backflip. Fortunately, once she was on the plane, another passenger helped her lift it into the overhead compartment.

She had been assigned a window seat, and she planned to go to sleep as soon as the plane took off. In hindsight, perhaps her expectations were naive. From past experience she had learned that there was never anything smooth or easy about flying, and today was no exception. Once she boarded, she was trapped, and a flight that should have taken a little under three hours ended up taking seven and a half, thanks to the fly-by-the-seat-of-their-pants airline and the mechanical problems they were sure maintenance could fix in no time at all. The captain made the passengers sit on the plane for two full hours before they were allowed to go back into the terminal to continue their wait while repairs were completed. After another grueling hour passed, they were told a relief plane was being flown in to take them to Boston. Apparently, the fix-it-in-no-time-at-all plane couldn't be fixed.

It was a miserable flight. It began with Isabel plastered up against the window while two overly friendly college students in the seats next to her took turns hitting on her. They seemed to be in some sort of competition to hold her attention and get her phone number. One was in his seventh year at a college in Arizona. In the course of his monologue he sheepishly admitted he still didn't have enough credits to graduate. The other one was in his third year at Colorado State and had changed his major so many times he couldn't remember what it now was. Isabel thought maybe there was a little something extra baked into the cookies he was munching on. She was pretty sure he was stoned.

Being polite to the nonstop talkers took effort, for exhaustion was pressing down on her . . . and no wonder. She had gotten only three hours of sleep the night before, and the last several weeks had been brutal, with papers due and finals to study for, not to mention packing up almost everything she owned and shipping it back home to Silver Springs, South Carolina, leaving only some of her clothes and personal items. Finally, graduation. She had hoped both of her sisters would be there for the ceremony, but Kiera, the older of the two, was in the middle of a demanding medical residency and couldn't take time off from work to attend. Her other sister, Kate, and her husband,

Dylan, were there to see her walk across the stage and get her diploma. She was on her way now to meet them at Nathan's Bay, Dylan's family home just outside Boston. Judge and Mrs. Buchanan, Dylan's parents, were celebrating their anniversary, and their big family was gathering for the occasion. Isabel was happy to be invited to the festivities. The Buchanans were so warm and welcoming, and she looked forward to a week of fun and relaxation.

Then she and Kate were off to Scotland to see Glen MacKenna, the property she would soon inherit from her crusty and—she had it on good authority—horribly mean great-uncle. The land was located in the Highlands, and Isabel was anxious to see it. Kate and Dylan had given her the trip as a graduation present.

After she returned from Scotland, her plans were uncertain. Maybe the trip would give her some insight into what her future would be.

Once the plane was in flight to Boston and the incessant chattering of her seatmates had died down, Isabel rested her head against the porthole window. She was feeling horrible. She had thrown up—a couple of times, as a matter of fact—as soon as she'd rolled out of bed, and now her head was pounding. She closed her eyes and tried to sleep, but the drummer banging away on the inside of her eyelids wouldn't let up.

She had no one but herself to blame for her misery. She shouldn't have gotten hammered last night. It was unlike her to overindulge, and yet, if she was being completely honest, it had been totally worth her aches and pains today. Leaning back against the headrest with her eyes still closed, she thought about how much fun she'd had with her friends at Finnegan's, their favorite hangout a couple of blocks from campus.

It had been a fantastic night. Damon, her friend since freshman year, had banged on her door at nine o'clock, and for once in her life she was ready. Since this was the last time she and all of her friends would be together, she had decided to get dressed up, and because she was in the mood to look sexy, she wore her new royal blue, V-neck dress that showed a little cleavage. Her only jewelry was a bracelet of stacked multicolored beads and a pair of gold hoop earrings. Instead of using hair clips to hold the thick curls away from her face, she had let them fall around her shoulders. No muss, no fuss.

She opened the door wide for Damon to enter. As usual he looked gorgeous. She often told him that he could be a model because of his perfect physique and profile. He was tall and lean with broad shoulders and enough muscles to fill out a T-shirt. When he smiled, women melted into pools of lust, and yet, as handsome as he was, Isabel had never felt a single spark of sexual attraction. As to that, she was beginning to think there might be an issue. In her four years at Winthrop College she had never gone head over heels for any of the men she'd dated. They were all fun to be with, and some were quite good-looking, but there was never any electricity. Without some kind of sexual connection, she had refused to go to bed with any of them, which earned her a couple of unflattering nicknames. None of them fazed her. Some, in fact, made her laugh.

Damon gave Isabel the once-over and nodded his approval. "I can't believe you're on time."

Isabel grabbed her phone and keys, tucked them into her bag, and said, "I'm always on time. You're just always early."

Laughing, he gently nudged her out the door. After making sure it was locked, he followed her outside to his car.

"Are we going to pick up Lexi and Owen?" she asked, referring to two of their closest friends.

"No, they're already at the club."

Once they were on their way, she turned and put her hand on his arm. "We're all going in different directions tomorrow. I'm really going to miss you, Damon. You've been such a good friend. I don't want you to forget me."

He shook his head. "That's not possible. You're unforgettable, Isabel."

She could feel the tears coming and didn't want to become melancholy tonight, so she rushed to talk about something else. "Want to hear a secret?"

"Sure."

"We've known each other for a long time, and I've never told you my real name. On my birth certificate I'm Grace Isabel MacKenna. I'm told my father won an argument. He wanted Grace, and Mother wanted Isabel. I was a baby when my father died, and that's when Mother started calling me Isabel."

"Grace is a beautiful name," Damon said, "but I like Isabel better."

"There's something else I've never mentioned. On my next birthday, which is coming up soon, I'm going to inherit land in Scotland from my great-uncle, Compton. A lot of land, I'm told. It's called Glen MacKenna, and I'm going to go see it next week."

"Land in Scotland! That's amazing. What are you going to do with land in Scotland?"

"I'm going to sell it."

"Maybe after you see it, you'll want to keep it."

"No, I won't. I'm going to sell it and use the money to do something good. I've already received several calls from a man who wants to buy the land. He's really persistent. He told me he represents the Patterson Group, and they'll pay a fair price. I'm not going to do anything until I see it, though. I will inherit it from my great-uncle on my birthday, and there are stipulations he would like me to follow."

"What are they?" he asked.

"I don't know. They're in a sealed envelope in the solicitor's office in Dunross, which is in the Highlands. I'm supposed to open the envelope in front of witnesses."

"On your birthday."

"Or after, but not before."

"Your great-uncle sounds eccentric."

"Not just eccentric. He was cruel and mean, and he's the reason I'm selling it. I would never keep anything from a man who treated my family the way he did. I was still a baby when my father died, but my aunt Nora told me later what my great-uncle had done to him and my mother. My father had a large inheritance, but Compton blocked it. He was furious that my father defied him by marrying my mother, who Compton thought was beneath him. He had chosen another woman for my father to marry. My parents didn't care about the money, and, according to Aunt Nora, they were very happy. Then the accident happened. My father was critically injured, and the medical bills piled up before he died. Compton refused to release any of the funds, which would have relieved the burden from my mother. So that's why I could never take anything from him now, unless I can do something good with it."

"I don't get it. If he hated your family, why did he leave you an inheritance?"

"It was in his will. He said he hadn't expected us to turn out well, but that he was surprised to discover we were well educated and cultured despite our mother. He also noted that all three of us had gone to private schools and were hard workers. I think he attributed our successes to his bloodline. Even the inheritance was a sign of his vanity."

"I'm surprised you've never mentioned this before. What other secrets do you have?"

She wondered how he would react if she told him her great-uncle had left a fortune worth well over a hundred million dollars to her sisters, Kate and Kiera, and that they gave it away to build a wing at the hospital where their mother spent her last days. The addition would have their mother's name on it, not exactly what their great-uncle had in mind.

"Nothing I want to talk about."

"You must have had it rough as a child."

"Quite the opposite. I had a happy childhood. I always felt safe and loved. We were a normal family. We still are, even though it's just my two older sisters, Kate and Kiera, my brother-in-law, Dylan, and me now."

"I'm not so sure you're normal," he teased.

"Yes, I am, and I'm not the only one with secrets. You have secrets, too."

"Yeah?" He glanced at her and said, "Name one."

"Mia Davis."

His hand tightened on the steering wheel. "What about her? We dated for a while, then it was over and we moved on. No big secret there."

She shook her head. "Damon, I'm your friend. You can be honest with me."

"I am being honest with you."

"You know what I think? I think you're still in love with her."

"Maybe I was. I'm not anymore."

"Yes, you are." Before he could argue or get angry because she was pushing him to admit something he'd kept buried, she rushed on. "You could call her, take her out and apologize."

"Why would I apologize?"

"Because you were wrong."

"How do you know that?"

"A calculated guess."

"Based on?"

Smiling, she said, "Based on the fact that you're a man."

The mood lightened with her outrageous remark. Damon laughed. "I love all women, Isabel. Especially you."

The drive to Finnegan's took longer than usual. The streets were filled with students in a celebratory mood after the end of the term. Damon turned and took another route through the campus to avoid the crowd.

"It's open mic night," he suddenly remembered. "Finnegan's is going to be packed."

"I hope Crowley isn't there. He's very nice, but he gets up onstage and tells his lame jokes, and it's almost impossible to get him to let someone else take a turn."

"He wants to be a professional stand-up comic."

"But he's terrible. I hope he has something to fall back on."

"The Trio's playing, too. They start at ten . . . if they can get Crowley off the stage."

Isabel had always thought the three graduate students' naming themselves the Trio was rather unoriginal, but who was she to judge? It worked for them. The three musicians would occasionally play backup for anyone courageous enough to get up in front of a crowd and sing. One played guitar; another played the keyboard, and the third played drums. They were quite talented and could pick up a melody quickly and play just about anything.

Isabel and all of her friends had been going to Finnegan's since freshman year. Isabel had used a fake ID at first. She didn't feel she was doing anything illegal because she didn't drink alcohol, and yet she knew in a court of law her reasoning wouldn't stand up. Dylan, who just happened to be the chief of police in Silver Springs, wouldn't approve, either, but then she wasn't about to tell him. Besides, once she'd turned twenty-one it really wasn't an issue.

In all the times she had been getting together with friends at Finnegan's she had never gotten up onstage. Damon and the others believed it was because she was shy and would be too embarrassed. It wasn't the truth, but she let them think it.

As if reading her thoughts, Damon said, "Think you'll get onstage and tell a joke or sing a song tonight?"

"Probably not."

"You've said those exact words every time I've asked you that question. It's never going to happen, is it?"

Since tonight was their last night together the answer was obvious. "Probably not."

Damon turned into the lot next to Finnegan's. Eyeing the perfect parking space, he shot forward to get it before anyone else could.

She looked around at all the cars and said, "You're right. The club's going to be crowded tonight."

He wasn't paying much attention to her now, concentrating on backing his beloved Porsche between two cars, leaving enough room so the doors wouldn't get dinged when they got out. Satisfied, he put the car in park and carefully opened his door. "Yes, it's going to be crowded and loud inside, so if you want to have sex with me tonight, now would be the time to tell me."

"What would your girlfriends say?"

His grin was downright salacious. "They'd understand."

As they walked side by side across the lot, she slipped her arm through his. "Do you think you'll ever settle down and get married?" she asked.

"Doubtful. What about you?"

"Doubtful."

"Have you figured out what you're going to do when you get back to that tiny town you live in?"

"Silver Springs isn't tiny," she protested. "And to answer your question, I still don't know what I'm going to do, and no, I don't want to talk about it. Not tonight."

She couldn't stop thinking about it, though. Now that her education was over, it was time to settle into a career. She knew she should take the next step, but there was an intangible force holding her back. She was torn between what she knew she should do and what her heart wanted her to do. The last four years had been ones of internal torment, and yet she had shared her feelings with no one. Not her teachers, not Damon, nor any of her other friends. Ever since she'd entered college, Isabel had stayed focused, working toward a degree in history. She even took the required education courses to become certified as a teacher. She had always loved history, and she truly enjoyed her classes, but history wasn't her passion. What filled her soul and gave her absolute joy was music.

As a high school student, she'd had such big dreams. Every waking minute seemed to be filled with music in one way or another. When she wasn't singing, she was playing the piano or the guitar, and when she wasn't playing, she was writing songs. She performed in public several times—small events with no more than thirty or forty people—and the reaction was always positive, the reviews glowing. Everyone seemed to love her songs. Plans for her future were centered on music, and college was going to give her the training that would set her on the path to a music career. Her senior year at Assumption High had begun with exciting possibilities and hopes, but then everything changed when her mother got sick.

Once the horrible disease grabbed hold of her mother, it wouldn't let go. Isabel would never forget those painful months going back and forth to the hospital, holding her mother's hand during chemo, being so scared, and all the while silently praying for a miracle.

God didn't give her one. During the final days in the hospital, the three sisters kept watch by their mother's bedside. Kiera and Kate would periodically leave to attend to responsibilities, but Isabel never left. She was holding on to every precious moment with all her might. Her mother was so weak, she could barely speak, but she had so much she wanted to say to her girls, especially Isabel. On one of the occasions they were alone together, her mother reached for Isabel's hand and made a request that would change Isabel's future. Telling her how proud she was of her, her mother then asked Isabel to make a promise. She knew her daughter had grand dreams of becoming a songwriter and performer, but she was afraid of the heartache and struggle such a path would bring, and so she asked Isabel to forgo her dreams until she finished college. She insisted it wasn't because she didn't have any faith in Isabel—though Isabel doubted she was telling the truth—but her mother wanted security for her daughter, and so she asked her to put aside the music and major in a subject that was more practical, one that would give her something to support herself if her dream fell through and she didn't succeed. Her mother wouldn't rest until Isabel gave her word.

After her mother died, Isabel felt she had lost her bearings. For a brief time she rationalized that she could still study music. Maybe make it part of her minor degree. But then her mother's words came back to her, and she knew that was not what was asked of her, nor what she had agreed to. Even though her world seemed so unsettled, there was one thing Isabel was sure of. She had made a vow and she would keep it.

She didn't tell her sisters about it. They might try to interfere. This was something between Isabel and her mother.

As difficult as it was for her, Isabel stayed true to her promise. The music was still inside her, but once she was in college, she silenced it. The only time she sang her songs was in the shower when she knew no one else was around, and even then she didn't belt it out the way she wanted. None of her friends knew she could sing or that she wrote music. It was another one of her secrets.

Somewhere along the way her game plan and her confidence vanished. If her own mother didn't believe in her, why would anyone else? Maybe it was all part of growing up, or maybe it was just time for her to abandon her foolish dreams.

She didn't have the faintest idea what she was supposed to do now. Her grand plans had been demolished. At least she had her degree in history, and it was a subject she truly enjoyed. She would never regret that. Maybe someday she'd be able to teach it and make others appreciate it as much as she did, even travel to some of the great historic sites she'd read about. It was time for her to make some decisions.

She might be heading in a different direction than she had planned, but that didn't mean she couldn't still make music a part of her life, did it? Even though she didn't sing publicly, she still continued to write songs. She had notebooks filled with them. More were on her laptop taking up memory. Before she began saving them to the cloud, she had saved them on flash drives. She used whatever she could get her hands on when a lyric or melody came to her. One of these days she'd take the time to put them all together. Then what? Once the busy work was done and she had them all in one place, what would she do with them?

She was pulled from her thoughts about the future when Larry, the bouncer for the club, called out to her. He stood in front of the double doors. Only those he allowed got inside. The others stood behind a corded velvet rope. On Friday and Saturday nights the line went halfway around the block. Larry was a big man with an even bigger smile for those he liked, and Isabel was at the top of his list.

His eyes lit up when he saw her. "Hi, darlin'. Ready to have fun tonight?"

Damon slapped a folded twenty-dollar bill in his hand and responded, "Yes, darlin'. I'm ready."

Grinning, Larry held the door open, and as Damon walked past, he whispered, "Smart-ass," and then laughed.

The club was packed and so loud, people had to shout at one another to be heard.

Their friend Owen stood and waved, then gave a shrill whistle to let Isabel and Damon know where their group was seated. They'd scored a wide half-circle booth on the upper level. The dance floor was below them and the booth faced the stage. A popular DJ was running the show now, playing one song after another. The floor vibrated to the beat. The club routine was always the same. It would get quiet during the break at ten while the Trio set up, and then the racket would begin again. A happy racket, Isabel thought, because everyone would pour onto the floor.

There were three other couples in the booth, and after greeting everyone and trying not to laugh at JoAnn's platinum blond hair—her freshman-year roommate changed the color of her hair at least once a month—Isabel sat on the end across from Damon and ordered a beer. Damon was the designated driver tonight. He'd already told her he had to get on the road early tomorrow and didn't want to be hungover. Besides, it was her turn to have a few.

After a couple of hours of laughing and reminiscing about their years together, Isabel was beginning to feel light-headed. She should have stopped after two beers and switched to a nonalcoholic beverage, but she didn't. The air conditioner wasn't keeping up with the gyrating bodies on the dance floor, and the cold beer tasted wonderful. In between sips she pressed the icy bottle against her cheek.

The Trio had set up on the stage. So far, four brave souls—all men— had taken turns standing in front of the crowd and singing. None of them was any good. There was some halfhearted clapping after each was finished. Then Crowley demanded to take a turn. Everyone near the stage tried to stop him. He wasn't the least bit talented, but he was certainly tenacious, and he all but clawed his way up the steps. Some of the regulars obviously recognized him and began to moan and groan quite loudly before he even began his routine. Others outright booed him. Their reaction didn't faze him. He told one awful joke after another.

Isabel lost count of the number of beers she drank, and by the time Crowley was being pulled off the stage by management, vowing he was only taking a break, she was feeling no pain.

"Can you believe that guy graduated? He's such a moron," Owen commented.

"I can't believe all of us have graduated," Damon said.

A small voice in Isabel's head whispered something to her beer-soaked brain. She had graduated. *Graduated.* There was so much meaning in that single word. For the last four years, she had kept her vow to her mother. No singing. No music. The promise had been fulfilled, and now she was free of the obligation. Had she done the right thing? Isabel didn't know if she should be happy or sad.

She glanced at the smiling faces that surrounded her and decided to focus on the happy. She would deal with any sad thoughts another time. Tonight was a night to celebrate with her friends.

After several more people tried to win over the crowd, Lexi announced she was going to take a turn onstage. She slaughtered an old Taylor Swift song. Then Owen and the others started nagging Isabel to give it a try.

"All of us have humiliated ourselves on that stage, and this is our last night together," Owen reminded.

"You should give it a go," Damon insisted.

They waited for her to decline, just as she had every other time any of them had asked.

Isabel set her beer on the table. "Okay. I'll take a turn."

All of them looked stunned for a brief second. Then they laughed. They obviously didn't believe her until she stood up, swayed a bit, got her balance, and headed to the stage.

"You're bluffing," Lexi shouted as Isabel zigzagged her way around the crowd.

She put her hand on the wall to steady herself as she climbed the four steps to the stage. Her heart was pounding, and she wasn't at all sure she was going to have the courage to perform. Finally, reaching the center of the stage, she turned to the three musicians and asked to borrow a guitar, telling them she would like to sing a song she'd written. The guitar player handed his to her. After she'd played several chords, the Trio picked up the melody.

"We've got this," they assured her. "You sing. We'll catch up."

Nodding, she handed the guitar back. Then she walked to the microphone, waited while the drummer adjusted it for her height, took a deep breath, wiped her hands down the sides of her dress, and began to sing. Her voice was soft and low. Few people could hear her due to the noisy crowd packed into the room, but that didn't matter. She wanted to sing. She closed her eyes and let the music that had been inside her for the last four years soar. She sang one of her favorites, a bluesy tune with a sensual beat. It wasn't a quiet love song couples could slow-dance to, but a powerful lusty song that made you want to move. With each chord her voice became stronger and more seductive. At the end of the second chorus she noticed the crowd was getting quiet. She opened her eyes. Most had stopped their chatter and were staring up at her. They looked spellbound. Some were beginning to sway to the music. By the time the song ended, a hush had fallen on the whole crowd, and all eyes were on her. For Isabel the silence seemed to last a full minute, and then the crowd suddenly erupted into cheers. The sound was deafening. Bewildered and feeling a bit dizzy, she couldn't understand what was happening. She turned to the Trio and didn't know what to think, for all three were standing and clapping and cheering. Her head spinning now, she slowly walked down to the dance floor, where the crowd swamped her, tugging and pulling to get her attention.

Damon met her in the middle of the dance floor and got her back to their friends by arm-blocking the way. By the time she scooted into the booth, her adrenaline was fading, her hands were shaking, and she was feeling limp.

Everyone seemed to be gawking at her as though she'd just grown another couple of heads. "What? What's the matter?"

"What's the matter?" Owen asked with a good bit of incredulity. "Are you kidding? Did you know you could sing?"

"Of course she knew," Lexi argued. "How could she not know?"

"Isabel, you brought the house down," JoAnn said as though she were announcing the most astonishing news.

Isabel shook her head, but that only made the dizziness come back. Everything was being obscured by the fog that enveloped her. She remembered the crowd screaming but believed her friends were exaggerating.

Damon seemed the most thunderstruck of all of them. He was frowning at her like someone who had never seen her before and couldn't quite decide who or what she was.

"Are you angry?" she asked, and when he told her no, she smiled and said, "I think I drank too much. I should go home."

"No, not yet," Owen argued. "It's only a little past midnight."

After some coaxing from the rest of the table, she decided she could stay a bit longer, and so she ordered another beer.

Her friends continued to stare at her in such an odd way, it made her uncomfortable. What was the matter with them?

"You have a dynamite voice," Lexi blurted.

"It's so husky and sexy," Owen added.

Embarrassed, she said, "Thanks. Now can we talk about something else?"

That was easier said than done. People kept stopping by the booth to tell her how great she'd sounded. An older man in a sports coat—obviously not one of Finnegan's usual patrons—handed her a card and told her not to sign any contracts without gaining legal advice first. He was an attorney, and he would be happy to represent her when all the offers started pouring in.

Offers? Offers for what? She couldn't imagine what he was talking about, but she thanked him all the same.

For the next two hours, the friends continued to reminisce about all the fun times they had shared, but by two A.M. the crowd had thinned out, and it was time for them to separate. They hugged one another tightly and promised to stay in touch.

Damon walked Isabel to his car, taking very slow steps just to make sure she wasn't going to throw up when he poured her into the passenger seat and clipped the seatbelt.

Once back at the tiny apartment she shared with two third-year students, he helped her climb the stairs, then kissed her on her forehead and said, "If you ever need me, all you have to do is call or just show up at my door."

"All the way to Los Angeles?"

"Yes. All the way there. I'll text you my code to get in. I'll be your safety net. Okay?"

"That would be nice."

He laughed. "I doubt you'll remember any of this. Now get some sleep."

And he was gone.

TWO

ISABEL HADN'T HAD MUCH TIME TO THINK ABOUT DAMON SINCE last night, but now, sitting in a cramped plane on her way to Boston, the emotions were swelling up inside her. Damon was her dearest friend, and she loved him like a brother. She was going to miss him. A tear slipped down her cheek and she quickly wiped it away. It wouldn't do to start crying in front of the other passengers. Fortunately, the aspirin she had taken earlier was finally kicking in, and her headache was beginning to ease. She pulled her baseball cap down low on her forehead, curled up against the window, and slept hard until something jarred her awake. She thought about asking the eternal student with the goofy smile sitting next to her what that clunking sound was, but she didn't want to engage him in conversation because she knew, once he started talking, she'd never get him to stop.

And then it dawned on her. The sound she heard was the landing gear. They were arriving in Boston. She couldn't believe how long and how hard she'd slept. She didn't feel rested, though. Remnants of her hangover were still streaming through her head. She felt grimy and thought she probably looked like an extra on the set of *The Walking Dead*. After exiting the plane, she hurried to the ladies' room to freshen up. She washed her face, brushed her teeth, then applied makeup so she would look human again. Feeling a little bit refreshed, she headed to baggage claim, where Kate would be waiting.

Uh-oh. Her cell phone. She had forgotten to turn it on, and as soon as she did, she saw thirty-eight texts. The first one was from Owen telling her that several people had posted her singing at Finnegan's on YouTube and that she had gone viral. From the number of exclamation points peppering his text, she knew he was excited by his news. But then, so were Lexi and JoAnn. They left voice messages, and both were downright giddy with their news. Viral? What was the big deal? Maybe a hundred people would see the video. Then again, maybe not. Here now, gone in an hour.

Scrolling through the texts she found one from Kate telling her that a car would pick her up and take her to the Hamilton Hotel. She and Dylan were running late, but one or both of them planned to meet Isabel in the hotel lobby and drive her over the bridge to Nathan's Bay. They should be there by five, six at the latest, and suggested that Isabel sit in the lounge and have a beverage.

More sitting? She inwardly groaned.

Too late she realized she should have rented her own car, then she wouldn't have to depend on others to drive her around. Kate and Dylan had talked her out of it, using the excuse that Boston was one of the worst cities for traffic and gridlock. She knew that wasn't the real reason they didn't want her to drive, though. They thought she was— as Dylan put it—"a lunatic behind the wheel." Granted, she had had a couple of near misses, and it just so happened that Kate and Dylan were in the car with her at the time. She had swerved her way out of both messes—or "near-death experiences," as Kate called them—and she didn't have a single ticket on her license. As far as she was concerned, they had nothing to complain about.

She quickly went through the rest of her texts and read another one Kate had sent telling her that she had reserved two rooms at the Hamilton just as a precaution, in case all eight bedrooms at the Buchanan house were filled. Isabel remembered there was also a coach house on the property with two large bedrooms, and she wondered if those would be occupied, too. Were all the Buchanan brothers and sisters going to be home for their parents' anniversary celebration? It was a big family. Six boys—four were married now. And two girls—one was married, the other still single. If they were all back home with their spouses and children, it would be quite a crowd.

They were such a fun family. She loved all the Buchanans . . . all but one, anyway. Michael Christopher Buchanan, or Bonehead as she secretly called him, was the exception. He was rude, and if there was anything she couldn't abide, it was rudeness. He was also insensitive, impatient, and obnoxious. Yes, he was good-looking, but then all the Buchanan men were. Michael was tall, dark, and handsome, and she imagined there were a lot of dim-witted women who would fall at his feet. She wasn't dim-witted.

He didn't particularly like her, either. He never said so, yet it was obvious all the same. She knew she was being judgmental, but she couldn't seem to care. As long as she kept her unkind opinion of Michael to herself, she didn't think she was committing a sin, at least not a big one. True, she had spent only one weekend with him, when he and the rest of the Buchanans came to Silver Springs for Dylan and Kate's wedding. That was over four years ago, but it was long enough to form a strong opinion of the man. He had seemed pleasant at first. She had assumed he had good manners and was as charming as his brothers. Big mistake. He didn't have a charming bone in his body.

Kate had paired her with Michael for the wedding ceremony, which meant she had to walk down the aisle to him. Since Kiera was the maid of honor, she was paired with Dylan's best man, his brother Alec. Isabel begged Kate to let her trade Michael for one of the other brothers, but her sister wouldn't let her. She insisted Michael had a great sense of humor and was fun to be around.

After only a few hours with him she wondered if maybe he showed his good side to others. Most of the time he seemed oblivious to her.

It was a fact, she wasn't used to being ignored by men, but in his eyes she simply didn't exist. The man looked right through her.

During that monthlong weekend, every time Michael saw her, he had to be reminded what her name was. He couldn't be bothered to remember it. If she didn't immediately respond to his question, "What's your name again?" he called out, "Hey, you there." And if she continued to ignore him, he shouted, "Hey, kid." Oh yes, he was real fun to be around.

The insults didn't stop there. At the wedding dinner there was assigned seating, and she was forced to sit beside Michael. Once again he snubbed her by spending the entire meal with his back to her, talking to an older woman wearing way too much makeup and sporting such big breasts Isabel was amazed she could stand upright. The woman couldn't keep her hands off Michael, and he seemed to be thoroughly enjoying the attention.

Then there was the whopper of insults. When it was announced that all the bridesmaids and groomsmen were to take the floor for a dance, Michael grabbed the wrong bridesmaid and swept her onto the dance floor, leaving Isabel to stand alone. She quickly scanned the room for another groomsman without a partner, but there weren't any nearby. She couldn't tell if the blood rushing to her face was from anger or embarrassment.

Trying to appear unfazed by the slight, she nonchalantly turned and headed toward the open French doors to go outside on the terrace for some fresh air. She had just made her way through the first row of tables when she was intercepted by Dylan's friend Noah.

"May I?" he asked as he held out his hand.

Assuming he was taking pity on her, she hesitated. But when Noah said, "Please? This is my favorite song and I don't want to waste it," she took his hand and let him lead her to join the rest of the wedding party on the dance floor. In no time at all Noah had her smiling and enjoying herself. Every time Michael and his partner glided past them, however, her smile vanished and her eyes shot daggers of disdain.

Isabel would never forget dancing with Noah. The fact that he was a gorgeous, sexy man might have something to do with that. She had a terrific crush on him for a while, but that wore off shortly after the wedding when she learned that Noah and Dylan's sister Jordan had fallen in love and were getting married. Now Noah and Jordan were two of Isabel's favorites in the Buchanan clan, and she couldn't wait to see them again. She certainly wasn't looking forward to seeing Michael, though. She hadn't forgiven him and imagined he was still a rude boor. If luck was on her side, he wouldn't be at Nathan's Bay. He was a Navy SEAL, and surely they never got time off. Besides, he lived in San Diego or somewhere in Virginia, didn't he? And hadn't he been deployed? Or was he already back from that stint? Isabel couldn't ask Dylan about his brother because he might want to know why she was interested.

Since she wasn't in the mood to put up with Michael's rudeness, the Hamilton was the answer. She quickly texted Kate and told her she didn't want to put anyone out, and so she was going to take one of the rooms Kate had reserved.

She immediately perked up. She absolutely adored the Hamilton hotels. They were a chain of luxury hotels owned by the family of Kate's sister-in-law. When Isabel was in high school, she had stayed at the Chicago Hamilton while she checked out a couple of universities in the area, and she'd also stayed one night with Kate at the Hamilton in Boston. They were five-star hotels with their own unique personalities. No matter the location, you knew you were in the Hamilton the second you walked through the doors. Everything about them was aesthetically pleasing. If any hotel was suited for a special occasion, it was the Hamilton. The beds were fabulous, the staff catered to their guests' every need, and the food was outstanding. So were the fitness center and spa. Tomorrow she would go up and check out all the machines. Not today, though. She was determined to go outside and take a long walk to get in sync with the city she so loved. Boston was expensive, but if she had the money, she would move there in a heartbeat.

Okay, time to focus on the here and now. Be in the moment. That's what her sisters were constantly telling her to do. She hurried to baggage claim, retrieved her checked luggage, spotted her driver holding up a sign with her name on it, and headed in his direction, all but dragging her backpack behind her.

The driver introduced himself and collected her luggage. His name was Woodson, and on the way to the limo she chatted with him, or rather listened as he launched into his concerns about his new girl-friend flirting with other men. Isabel wasn't the least surprised or caught off guard to hear the man's personal problems. The truth was, she expected it. Strangers unloaded their worries on her all the time, usually within five minutes of meeting her. Being a sounding board was a peculiar trait, she supposed. At least that's what she had often been told by family and friends, but she was used to strangers pouring their hearts out and sharing intimate details of their lives with her. She never offered advice and they never asked for any. She took it all in stride, figuring they simply needed someone to listen to them.

At her request Woodson placed her backpack on the seat beside her, and while he continued to talk, she pulled out her navy blue windbreaker. The thin-as-air nylon jacket had a hood and zippered pockets. She put her wallet in one pocket and her cell phone in the other. Continuing to nod every now and then so Woodson would know she was paying attention to what he was telling her, she stuffed her purse and her baseball cap in the bag and zipped it closed.

Traffic was a snarled mess. There must have been an accident on I-90, she thought, until she checked the time and realized they were in the middle of rush hour. The plane trip had seemed interminable, and now the ride to the hotel was taking forever. She had been sitting so long she was surprised she didn't have bed sores.

Woodson's voice cracked. He sounded as though he was about to cry, which she was sure would embarrass him, and so she tried to help him think about something other than his girlfriend.

"How long have you worked for the Hamilton?" she blurted.

He paused for a few seconds and then answered, "Oh, I don't work for the hotel. I'm employed by a service the Hamilton sometimes uses when their limos are busy." He added, "The more good reviews I get, the better my chances are to move up in the company I work for now."

She took the hint and promised to give him a rave review.

"The thing with my girlfriend . . ." And he was off again, pouring his heart out. He finished unloading all his worries just as they were pulling up to the hotel's circular drive. He opened her door, took her hand, told her how much better he felt, and thanked her profusely. Since she hadn't said a word during his heartfelt soliloquy, she simply smiled and said she was happy she could help.

Woodson went inside with her luggage and her bag and gave them to the bell captain while she explained that she had a room reserved and that she would check in after she went for a brisk walk.

The bell captain pulled up the reservation on his computer and confirmed that the rooms were already paid for and one was in her name. She asked him to put the suitcase she was taking to Scotland in storage. Since she and Kate were scheduled to leave early Monday morning, they would be staying at the Hamilton Sunday night so they wouldn't have such a long drive from Nathan's Bay to the airport. Assuring her that her bags would be taken care of, he handed her a card for room 1612.

"You should walk along the Freedom Trail," he said, deciding for her. "It's real scenic and chock-full of history."

Might as well, she thought. Thanking him, she tucked the room card he'd given her in her back pocket and headed outside. She stopped on the sidewalk and was immediately asked by a valet if he might be of assistance.

"No, I'm going for a walk . . ."

"Freedom Trail, miss. Walk the Freedom Trail. Everyone does."

Getting directions to the trail turned out to be quite a challenge. The valet was a rather violent hand-waver, and she had to keep dodging his arm while he pointed every which way. Because of his thick accent the only words she understood were "Washington Street."

Just as soon as he paused to take a breath, she asked, "You want me to turn on Washington. Is that correct?" And before he could answer, she asked, "Which way on Washington?"

He pointed to the sky. She had no idea what that was supposed to mean.

Before she could leave, he launched into directions again, and she swore he wasn't making any sense. It was as though he were suddenly speaking a foreign language she wasn't familiar with, and he was talking so fast she didn't have any idea where he was sending her. She didn't want to ask him to slow down or start over because she didn't think it would matter. She still wouldn't understand him. She thanked him for his help and hurried down the drive while he continued to give directions.

Starting out in a pretty area with redbrick sidewalks and beautiful old buildings mixed in with modern apartments, she walked down one street after another. It felt good to be outside. She hated being cooped up on a plane. As she walked, she hummed a tune. Before long the music took over and she began to create a new song in her head. She wished she had her notebook with her so she could write it down. She knew she would remember the tune, but she wanted to record the lyrics so she wouldn't forget them.

After a while the humidity started to get to her. Her T-shirt felt as though it was stuck to her skin. The air was thick. She looked up at the sky and dark clouds were hanging low. She imagined that, if she reached up on tiptoes, she could puncture one, and like a heavy water balloon, rain would pour out. She stopped and checked her watch. No wonder she was hot. She had been walking at a fast clip for over an hour. She was also good and lost. Looking around, she saw that she had wandered into an area that was being renovated. Some of the old apartment buildings had already been restored, and others were still under construction. Gone for the day, the crews had left behind scaffolding, piles of bricks, and other signs of their trades. When she scanned the buildings that had already been completed, she couldn't help but appreciate the effort that had gone into restoring their original beauty. Instead of being torn down, they had been re-paired and scrubbed and still retained their history and charm.

She kept walking, trying to get her bearings so she could return to the hotel. She thought she heard someone behind her and eagerly turned to ask directions, but there wasn't anyone there. A couple of blocks farther, she walked past a soon-to-open coffee shop, according to the sign in the window. No one was inside. Where in God's name was she? Admittedly, she hadn't been paying attention to street signs. Her head had been in the clouds, as her mother would often say. Isabel was lost because she had gotten distracted. Lyrics had been flying through her mind, and it wasn't until she had a melody locked in her brain that she noticed her surroundings.

At the corner she turned around and headed back. Once again she thought she heard someone behind her and turned to ask directions, but no one was there. Three blocks later she stopped and looked around. She didn't recognize anything. Had she walked past this street?

Lightning lit up the sky and was quickly followed by a loud crack of thunder. She put her jacket on and was unzipping all four pockets looking for her cell phone so she could get accurate directions back to the hotel when she heard a loud pop, the sound very like a fire-cracker exploding. Then another pop and another and another. She looked to the sky, half expecting to see a dazzling fireworks display.

No . . . no. Those were gunshots, and they were coming from right around the corner.

It all happened so fast. There wasn't even time to run. Isabel was the only one on the street now. She turned and saw several men and women looking out their windows from the apartment building across the street. She was still holding her breath when a man staggered around the corner. His shirt was covered in blood, and there was even more blood streaming down his right leg, soaking his pants. He had a gun in his hand and a badge clipped to his waist. Before she could react, he lurched forward, reaching out to her. He was trying to say something, but she couldn't make out the words. His voice was a tortured whisper. He was mumbling the same word, over and over again. She was so shocked, she froze. Throwing himself into her arms, he clawed at her jacket. She wrapped her arms around his waist, stumbled back, then went down to her knees, trying desperately to protect him from crashing to the ground.

He was such a big man and so heavy. She tried to ease him to the pavement, but his weight pulled her forward. He hit his head before landing on his back. She landed full length on top of him. He still had a death grip on her jacket and was pushing his gun between them. Did he want her to hold on to it for him? He kept thrusting the gun at her until it was firmly in her hand.

The weapon was sticky with blood. She gripped it tightly with her finger on the trigger. She was lifting up when out of the corner of her eye she saw a man running toward her, coming fast. She didn't see his gun until he fired at her. Two shots. The first bullet went wild, but the second bullet grazed her upper arm and burned like the blazes. She reacted without thinking.

She shot him between the eyes.

He fell backward and landed with a loud smack on the street. Still holding the gun with her arms out straight, her left hand balancing her right, she braced herself, waiting to see if there were any more shooters out there.

Keeping her attention on the corner, she carefully moved off the injured man and laid the gun next to her. When she dared to look down, she saw he wasn't moving. She put her hand on his chest to find out if he was still breathing. Frantic, she spun in all directions looking for help, but the street was eerily quiet.

The wound on the man's shoulder was seeping blood in an even trickle, but his pant leg was completely saturated now. Oh God, there was so much blood. She had to do something. The bullet must have nicked an artery. Blood was coming so fast it was pooling on the sidewalk and streaming across the curb into the street. She pressed the palm of her hand against the opening, one palm on top of the other, hoping she could stem the flow. She glanced up, and that's when she saw a man standing at the corner a block away. He was big and had shocking red hair. She started to call out to him to come help her, but he suddenly disappeared. Had she imagined him? Oh God, she needed someone to help her.

Time stood still, and then suddenly chaos exploded around her in a blur. Everything was happening with lightning speed, and she didn't have time to react. People were screaming; sirens were blaring, and men and women were rushing toward her. Police cars and an ambulance arrived at the same time. Three police cars blocked the street and the ambulance was right behind them. She didn't know how many policemen there were, but it seemed as though a whole squadron was running at her. A very young officer had his gun drawn and was shouting at her. There was so much noise she couldn't understand what he was saying. A wave of nausea hit her. The metallic smell of blood was making her sick. She closed her eyes, continued to press against the wound, and took deep gasping breaths to keep from throwing up.

Just as the paramedics reached the injured man, the young policeman holstered his gun and shouted something. Was he reading her her rights? There were so many people yelling she couldn't really be sure.

One of the paramedics put his hand on top of Isabel's. "Okay, good job," he said. "You can let up now. We've got this." As she pulled away, he looked her over. "Are you injured?"

She shook her head.

"You're covered in blood."

"It's his blood." The words echoed in her head as though they were coming from a deep tunnel.

"Do you know this man?"

She shook her head again.

"He's with the police," she told him, shocked her voice was so weak. She knew no one had heard her, and so she tried again. "He has a badge."

The young officer, jumping to a false conclusion, grabbed Isabel's upper arm and jerked her up. His grip was tight and painful. Then he pulled out handcuffs, and all hell broke loose.

A crowd poured out of the apartment building across the street, and they were incensed. They shouted at the policeman to leave her alone as they pushed forward to try to protect her. The sound of their voices became a deafening roar.

"That girl saved that man," a woman yelled.

"Get away from her," another demanded.

"She saved him. Now leave her alone."

"She could have run, but she didn't. She stayed to protect him."

"Take your hands off her," an angry man in the back of the growing throng bellowed.

A riot was brewing. Within a minute, two at the most, the crowd had grown to three times the number. Men and women were rushing toward her from every direction, and all of them were fighting mad.

The shouting was getting angrier, and Isabel, in a daze, tried to focus on the poor injured man, but the instinct to panic was nearly overwhelming.

"Let go of her, Officer Morris," an older policeman shouted, clearly exasperated. He had to repeat the order more forcefully before the young officer obeyed the command. Isabel staggered back and suddenly found herself in the middle of a thick circle of strangers at least five deep. Several patted her shoulder and her back. Confused and disoriented at first, Isabel suddenly realized the group was trying to shield her.

A heavyset woman wearing a brightly colored muumuu and a matching bandanna handed her phone to the older policeman and said, "I got all of it on my phone. Watch it and you'll see this girl wasn't doing nothing wrong unless saving someone is a crime."

"He's wearing a badge. He's a cop," a policeman called out as he moved closer to the paramedics preparing their patient for the gurney.

Someone had finally noticed the badge, Isabel thought. She glanced at her watch and blinked. It didn't seem that any time had passed. It was crazy. Or she was crazy. At this point she couldn't tell.

A woman with long blond hair nudged her, asked her for her cell phone number, and then sent her a video. "Send this to as many people as you know before the police have it. You'll have your own proof of what happened."

The woman obviously had trust issues with the police. Isabel didn't argue. She pulled her phone from her pocket, but her hands were so bloody, and she was shaking almost violently now. Texting was impossible. The only thing she would accomplish would be getting blood all over her phone. She decided to wait until later to send the video.

Now that the trauma was sinking in, her shaking increased. Was she a criminal now? Morris, the policeman who had shouted her rights at her, thought she was . . . and she *had* killed a man.

"What happens now?" she asked the person standing closest to her, a middle-aged man wearing a T-shirt with a faded Marine insignia across the front.

"They'll take you to the police station to question you. I'd have a lawyer there before you talk about what happened."

A teenager with low-slung pants and tattoos across his bare chest chimed in. "I think she ought to get out of here now while she can."

Another youth next to him agreed with a nod. "Yeah. That's what she should do."

The woman in the muumuu put her hands up to calm the growing tension. "She hasn't done anything wrong. Let the police sort it out."

An elderly man leaning on a cane edged forward. "Young lady, I haven't seen you around here. Are you new to our neighborhood?"

"No, uh . . . ," she stammered. "I'm visiting Boston. I'm staying at the Hamilton."

"My word, that's a long way from here," the old man said.

"I wasn't paying attention," Isabel admitted. "And I got lost."

Glancing at the officers who had turned their attention to the victim, the marine said to her, "Hurry and tell your family where you're going before they take you in."

Nodding, she called her sister. She was still so rattled she didn't know how she was going to explain what had happened.

Dylan answered. "Where are you? My brother's at the hotel looking for you. You didn't rent a car, did you? Oh God, you didn't . . . did you?"

"No . . . I didn't. Dylan . . . I . . ."

"Yes? What's wrong?"

"I just killed a man."

THREE

ONE WOULD THINK THAT NOTHING COULD BREAK UP A CROWD—
even a crowd in the mood to riot—faster than a torrential downpour,
but that didn't happen. Every man and woman was out for blood,
and their main target was the young, loathsome Officer Morris, who
had shouted gross and incendiary profanities at them when a couple
of men told him to leave Isabel the hell alone. She didn't think Morris was going to be a policeman long, for in her expert opinion he was
really stupid. She had taken two psychology courses in college and
had learned how to spot an idiot—though, in truth, she had acquired
that ability years ago—and Morris definitely fit the bill.

As quickly as the rain started, it stopped, but the heavy clouds
and the rumble of thunder in the distance indicated another deluge
was coming. A kind officer had thoughtfully held an umbrella over
her during the downpour, so she barely got wet. Loathsome Morris,
she noticed, was soaked through.

The older and more experienced policeman who had ordered Morris to stand down told her his name was Officer Patrick Field. He was
an average-looking man of medium height with a receding hairline.
Lean and lanky, he had a runner's body except for the slight bulge at
his belt. A dimple creased his square chin, and there were wrinkles at
the corners of his eyes that indicated he was a man who laughed often.

Field was obviously the officer in charge and seemed to know what he was doing.

"I was the first on the scene," Morris shouted. "I should take her in."

"Oh, for God's sake," Field muttered. Then he shouted back, "No, you were not first on the scene, and you are not going to take her in. Go back to your vehicle." He leaned closer to Isabel, and in a conspiratorial whisper said, "That rookie needs to find another line of work. He's not cut out to be a policeman. Doesn't have the temperament. Don't judge the rest of us by his behavior."

Field was trying to put her at ease. It wasn't working. She was still trembling from head to foot.

"What is your name?"

"Grace Isabel MacKenna." She thanked God she could remember. "Everyone calls me Isabel."

"I watched the video, Isabel. You just went through a terrible ordeal, didn't you? How are you holding up?"

He looked sympathetic and sounded sincere. "Who are you?" she asked. "I'm sorry. I forgot your name. I know you told me . . ."

"I'm Officer Field." Frowning now he said, "I think you should see a doctor. You're pale and you're shaking. You could go into shock."

She shook her head. "I'm all right. I don't need a doctor."

He didn't press her. "Do you live around here?"

"No, I live in South Carolina. I'm staying at the Hamilton Hotel, and I wanted to go for a walk."

Field couldn't fathom it. "Do you know how far away you are from the hotel?" The whole situation was incomprehensible to him: a young woman going for a walk all alone in a strange city. Not paying attention to her surroundings or the people she passed, a pretty girl like her . . . any number of terrible things could have happened to her. And yet, instead, she saved a man. "I know you're scared, but you're safe now."

A man with an unlit cigar hanging out of his mouth put a protective hand on Isabel's shoulder.

She looked at the crowd surrounding them and said, "I know I'm safe. These good people won't let anyone hurt me."

Every man and woman nodded. She could tell Field didn't know what to think.

"Rain's coming any minute now," he said. "And you should sit down. Come with me, please."

He latched on to her elbow and was trying to get her to his police car before the downpour started again. It was a long, arduous trek due to the fact that the volatile crowd kept pressing in on him. They were determined to make sure he treated Isabel with respect, and they kept yelling just that as he tugged on her elbow to keep her moving forward.

"I feel like I'm walking through a minefield," he said. He spoke in a bare whisper, but she heard him all the same. The atmosphere was explosive, and she realized he was avoiding anything that would exacerbate the situation.

"I've been on the force seventeen years," he said, "and I've never seen anything like this."

"Like what?"

"Such a large group of men and women, young and old, united so . . . forcefully . . . to protect a young lady. It really is remarkable."

He might have been impressed but he was also nervous. Isabel could tell by the way he watched the crowd. He was on guard. Was he worried he would be the person to ignite the powder keg?

As they made their way through the people, she saw quite a few holding their phones up and continuing to take videos of what was going on. The woman who had asked for her phone number earlier leaned close and told her she would make sure to hang on to her video in case Isabel's phone was taken. Isabel responded with appreciation. Another of her champions lifted the hood of her jacket over her head. She stopped to thank him also. Still another patted her as she walked past. Several called out words of caution.

"Don't let them bully you," a teenager shouted.

"Not a word without a lawyer. Don't say one word."

There were also shouts of encouragement. "You stay strong," a woman called out.

"I'll try," she promised.

"Remember what you did today, girl. You saved a man's life."

But I also took a life, Isabel thought, *and the man I saved could be dying right this minute on his way to the hospital.* That was such a grim thought she tried to push it aside.

Officer Field had asked her name and wanted to know why she was in the area, but he hadn't asked her any other questions. She thought that was strange, and the way he kept glancing at her was a worry. He looked so perplexed, like he was trying to solve an intricate puzzle.

There was a man with a flashlight slowly scanning a brick wall to her left. Isabel slowed her pace and asked, "What is that man doing with the light?"

Field looked where she pointed and said, "He's part of the crime scene team. He's most likely looking for bullets."

"Do they have to find every bullet that was fired?"

"That's the goal."

"What is that other man doing with the tape?"

"He's measuring blood splatter."

Field must have seen her blanch because he grabbed her elbow again. "Don't pass out on me."

"I won't."

Blood splatter. All she had wanted was to take a little walk, to stretch her legs, to get in touch with the city. She guessed now she was going to get in touch with the criminal justice system, too. Did they have private cells at the police station? Crazy thoughts raced through her head. She was really losing it and knew she needed to get a grip on her emotions.

Just as they reached the police car, a nondescript beige sedan pulled up next to them and two men got out.

Field perked up when he saw them. "Detectives."

Isabel thought they both looked weary and perhaps even a little bored. Had they seen so much violence and death that they had become immune to it? Then she noticed the dark circles under their eyes and realized they were probably sleep-deprived from working hard, long hours. Her attitude toward them softened.

"You're in good hands with Detective Samuel and Detective Rayborne," Field told her. "Samuel has been on the job awhile now, so he'll probably take the lead."

Detective Rayborne was surveying the scene and shaking his head. She assumed he was much older than he looked. He was wearing a suit now, but in casual clothes he could easily pass for a man in his early twenties. She couldn't discern what he was thinking because he had a poker face. He wasn't giving anything away. He reminded her of a robot, and she wondered what it would take to get him to react or show some emotion.

Detective Samuel was more interesting to her. He was tall and thin, and his extremely stiff posture reminded her of a priest who had taught theology when she was in high school. No student ever slumped around Father Mahoney or she'd get a prod between her shoulder blades with the ruler he always carried. Even though he was a strict disciplinarian, the priest, she remembered, had a nice smile, and so did Detective Samuel. He actually managed a quick smile when one of the policemen said something to him. Then he looked at her and his expression changed.

Guessing what he was thinking, Field called out, "It's not her blood, Detective Samuel." He waited until both detectives were close enough and quickly made the introductions.

The policeman who had held the umbrella over her stepped forward and handed his phone to Samuel. "You're going to want to see this."

Isabel waited by Field's side while the detectives watched the video. She was feeling queasy; her arm burned, and all she wanted was a hot shower to wash away the blood. She wanted to burn the clothes she was wearing, too. She'd keep her jacket, though, because her mother had given it to her, but she planned to wash it at least a dozen times. One quick look down at her T-shirt was cringe-worthy. Blood everywhere. His blood. Then she noticed the tear in the left sleeve of her jacket near her shoulder. Had the man she was trying to help done that? He was clawing at her jacket, she remembered. Or did it tear when the bullet whizzed by her? The fabric was nylon and the jacket didn't cost much at all, but she treasured it and vowed to find a way to patch it and make it almost perfect again.

Field was getting nervous. His grip on her elbow tightened, and he watched the crowd with a worried look on his face. The detectives seemed mesmerized by the video. No, she thought. Samuel was mesmerized, but Rayborne was expressionless, giving no hint of a reaction to what he was seeing.

The crowd was edging closer.

Field turned his back to them and spoke to Samuel. "I think you should get her out of here as quickly as possible."

"Yes, all right," Samuel agreed without looking up from the video, which he was now watching for the second or third time.

"I'll be happy to take her in," Field offered.

"What's the hurry?" Rayborne asked.

"I don't think you understand what's going on here." Field nodded his head in the direction of the crowd. "These people have become her protectors." He couldn't explain how it had happened. Maybe it was because of her act of heroism or the fact that she looked so vulnerable now.

Samuel handed the phone back to the policeman. He didn't have to look at the people to read their mood. He put his hands up and said, "Everyone step back. Give us some room."

No one moved.

"Hey, Detective Samuel," a policeman called out. He lifted the large cloth that had been placed over the dead man. "Right between the eyes. Perfect shot."

Isabel didn't need to hear that. She bowed her head and tried not to gag. If she had any food in her stomach, she would have lost it by now. Thank God she hadn't eaten all day.

"Let's go," Field said. When he took hold of her arm, she cried out in pain. He quickly let go.

A man in the growing crowd shouted, "You leave her alone." Several others chorused their agreement.

"We aren't going to let you hurt her." A woman shouted that promise.

"I'm going to go ahead and take her in," Field said. He didn't suggest or ask this time.

A couple of minutes later Isabel was in the backseat of Field's vehicle and on her way to the station. The air inside the car smelled of kielbasa, sauerkraut, and Old Spice aftershave. Another wave of nausea engulfed her. To calm her nerves, she stared out the window and concentrated on the passing landscape. They turned a corner and drove by a park that had also been renovated. There was a brand-new playground with swings and slides and a huge jungle gym. The thick grass had been freshly cut, and there were a few tall trees providing shade to benches on the edge of the property. Any other time she would have stopped to watch the children laughing and playing, but not today. Today she was sitting in a police car on her way to being interrogated about a shooting. The whole scene was almost too absurd to believe.

Fortunately, it wasn't a long drive. But by the time she was helped out of the car and walked into the station with Field at her side, she felt like a criminal again. She kept her head down until she heard a deep voice calling her name. She looked up and inwardly groaned. Standing just a few feet away from her was Michael Buchanan.

FOUR

MICHAEL WASN'T PREPARED FOR THE SIGHT IN FRONT OF HIM. Isabel was covered in blood and was so pale she looked as though she was about to pass out.

The policeman with her stepped forward to introduce himself. "I'm Officer Patrick Field," he said. "And who are you?"

"Michael Buchanan," he answered, but his attention remained on Isabel.

"And you're here for Miss MacKenna?"

"Yes." His answer was curt.

Field was pretty sure he knew what Michael was thinking, and so, for at least the fifth time, he wearily said, "It's not her blood."

Relieved, Michael said, "Good. That's good."

"She wasn't injured," Field insisted.

Isabel remained silent. She was having difficulty getting past the surprise. Dylan had sent Michael to help her. Wasn't he supposed to be in Afghanistan or somewhere else halfway around the world? Apparently not, since he was standing a foot away from her. Her reaction to him was quite strange and not at all rational. Instead of getting her back up because he was such a bonehead, she had the almost overwhelming desire to throw herself into his arms and plead for him to get her out of there as quickly as possible.

They stared at each other for a long minute, or so it felt to her. She really couldn't tell the difference between minutes and hours. Ever since the shooting, time seemed to stand still.

Michael hadn't changed much. He could still make her shiver and irritate the dickens out of her at the same time. Nothing new about that. He was one attractive man in an outdoorsy way, even when he was frowning. He had a little more muscle now; his hair was longer, and there were fine lines around his eyes that hadn't been there before.

He gave her a slow once-over, and she knew he had to be appalled. Probably couldn't believe what he was seeing. Admittedly, she looked as though she had jumped into a vat of blood. Not a pretty image to anyone but a vampire. She knew there was dried blood on her face and neck. And everywhere else, she supposed. Even the tops of her tennis shoes were saturated. God only knew what she smelled like. Maybe iron. It was not a perfume she would have chosen.

"Are you okay?" Michael asked.

The sympathy in his voice almost unhinged her. "Yes," she answered. She wanted to yell, *No, I just killed a man! How do you think I am?*

Michael was doing a good job of hiding his reaction to her. He didn't seem to be the least bit bothered. She couldn't say the same for everyone else they passed. It had been noisy when they entered, but as soon as they started across the crowded office, where a large number of detectives, police officers, and staff members were working, everyone stopped what they were doing and gawked at her. No one made a sound. It was mortifying.

Their poor manners were a reminder to her. She looked up at Michael and said, "How are you, Michael?"

He didn't smile, but he came close. "I'm good."

"I'm sorry you were dragged into this. You don't have to stay."

"I'm not leaving you."

There was a thread of steel in his voice that actually was comforting, and she immediately felt a tinge of relief. She wasn't going to have to go through the rest of this nightmare alone. Unless they decided to lock her up. As soon as the horrid thought popped into her head, she blocked it. Now was not the time to panic. She could handle this.

When they reached the hallway, Field turned to her and said, "I'm going to put you in one of the interview rooms. You can wait there for the detectives."

Until now she hadn't made a fuss. In fact, she'd been extremely cooperative and had done whatever was asked of her. All that was about to change.

"No, I'm not going to do that."

"What?" Field asked. He was sure he hadn't heard correctly.

"I'd like to wash my face and hands, and then I'd like to leave."

"That's not possible. You have to answer questions before you can leave."

"Am I being arrested?"

"No, but you—"

"If I don't get this blood off my face and hands, I'm going to start screaming."

Michael didn't think it would be a good idea to tell her she was already screaming.

Field wasn't at all diplomatic. "Ma'am, you're yelling at me."

She looked at Michael for help. Maybe he would know what to do to get them out of there. If she weren't so tired, she'd try to run, but even as emotionally exhausted as she was, she knew that was a bad idea.

Michael could see that Isabel had clearly reached her breaking point, and after the god-awful time she'd had, he was surprised and proud that she'd lasted this long. She was a lot stronger than she looked.

He took over. Turning to Field he said, "First things first. Where can she clean up?"

Field led the way to the bathroom, and while Isabel went inside, Michael waited in the hall.

"While you're waiting, you might want to take a look at this," Field said, handing Michael a phone. "One of the neighborhood women got a video. It's taken from across the street, but you can see what happened pretty clearly."

Field tapped the phone, and the video started. There were loud voices of shock and outrage from whoever was standing nearby, but the view in the distance was clear enough to recognize Isabel and a wounded man throwing himself into her arms, then together falling on the sidewalk. He was grasping her hand and pushing a gun into it when suddenly another man sprinted around the corner, a gun raised. He fired twice. Isabel instantly took aim and shot, then dropped the gun and turned her attention back to the victim at her side. The video ended there.

"Wow," Michael uttered, shaking his head.

"Understandable why she'd be a little shaken," Field said, taking his phone and heading back to the interrogation room.

Now knowing what Isabel had gone through, Michael's protective instincts kicked in. He stood outside the door, his arms folded across his chest, his stance menacing. He wasn't going to let anyone get past him until Isabel came out.

Isabel was taking her time. She glanced in the mirror and gasped. She looked horrible. It took a while to scrub the blood off her face and neck. Her arms were next. She unzipped all the pockets of her jacket and removed the few items inside, placing them on the shelf above the sink. Besides her phone and wallet, she found an old peppermint that had come out of its wrapper and was covered in lint, a couple of folded tissues, and an old flash drive. The tissues had blood on them, and so did the flash drive. She tossed the peppermint and tissues into the trash, then carefully wiped off the flash drive and tucked it into one of the front pockets of her jeans. She put her wallet in her back pocket with her hotel room card.

The blood on the phone was beginning to dry, and as she cautiously cleaned the screen, she remembered the video the woman on the street had made. She activated her phone and found the text waiting for her, but she couldn't bring herself to open it. Instead, she forwarded it to Dylan. He would know what to do with it. She didn't have the stomach to relive those horrific moments.

Next, she carefully took off her jacket and examined the tear. "I can get this fixed," she reminded herself.

She draped it over the sink and turned her attention to her arms. The right arm was clean, but the left was a bloody mess from the scrape. It took ten wet towels to wash the blood away. She finally got a good look at her upper arm. Then she groaned, "Oh, damn." She wet another paper towel and patted the skin around the wound. It still burned like the devil. At least it had stopped bleeding. She was going to have to let a doctor look at it, she supposed. And she'd need an antibiotic so it wouldn't get infected. Yet a little more misery to put up with—all because she wanted to go for a walk.

Once she'd finished the ordeal of cleaning up, she forced herself to put on her jacket even though she knew the inside of the left sleeve was bloody. She threaded her fingers through her hair in an attempt to make some sort of order out of it, then finally gave up.

Standing outside when she opened the door, Michael quickly stepped back and tried not to stare at her. He had always been attracted to her. Hell, any man would be. He remembered telling his sister at Dylan and Kate's wedding that Isabel was the whole package. She had a great body, a pretty face, and she was damned sexy, but he also remembered she was young, just starting college, and he had no business messing with her, which was why he went to such great lengths to ignore her.

He couldn't ignore her now. Man, had she changed. She'd filled out in all the right places and, even covered in blood, was stunning.

Michael knew he couldn't let his lecherous thoughts get away from him. He was here to help her, not seduce her.

"Feel better?" he asked, his voice gruff.

"Yes," Isabel answered. It was a lie. Right this minute she wanted to take an hour-long hot shower, then crawl into bed, pull the covers up over her head, and let out a good long scream. Since she couldn't do that, she decided to try to have a more positive attitude now that the danger was over. Telling herself to toughen up, she asked, "Why did Dylan send you? He and Kate were supposed to pick me up . . . at the hotel."

"They are two hours away in Charlemont, Massachusetts. Their meeting was just finishing up. I convinced Dylan to go on back to Nathan's Bay and that I had this covered."

"'This' being me?"

He smiled. "Yes."

He looked at Field and said, "Let's get this done."

"The detectives are on their way. They should be here anytime now."

Isabel nudged Michael and whispered, "Shouldn't I have a lawyer with me?"

"I'm a lawyer," he answered.

"When did that happen?"

"When I finished law school and passed the bar."

No one ever told her anything. She supposed it was her own fault. She made it a point not to ever ask about Michael. She thought about him, though, not all that often, she qualified, just every now and again.

"I thought you were a Navy SEAL."

"I am a Navy SEAL, but my active duty is over."

Field led them into a room that resembled what she surmised a cell at Alcatraz must have looked like. The walls were gray, the ceiling was gray, and the floors were gray. There was a square glass window looking out at the hallway, but blinds covered it. A ceiling light shone on the gray metal table and chairs. She imagined this was the kind of room that encouraged a depressed person to kill himself. Having to stay here long would be suffocating.

As soon as Field left and the door closed behind him, she said, "Let me get this straight. You went to college, graduated at, what? Twenty-three? Twenty-four?"

"Almost twenty," he corrected.

He pulled out a chair for her to sit, but she ignored it. Hand on hip, she said, "I'm almost twenty-three, and I just graduated. No one graduates from college at twenty."

"I did, and so did Dylan."

"How is that possible?"

"We took a lot of courses when we were seniors in high school and took summer classes in college."

"I didn't do that."

"You had a lot to deal with when you were a senior in high school."

"Oh." Then, "You went to law school and graduated at twenty-three?"

"Yes."

"Then you took the bar and decided to become a Navy SEAL. Who does that?"

"Apparently I do."

"How old are you now? Forty?"

He laughed. "Twenty-eight," he answered.

"Are you going to stay in the Navy?"

"No," he answered. "Isabel, why are you asking all these questions?"

She shrugged. She didn't have the faintest idea why she was grilling him or why all of his answers made her mad.

There was a knock on the door, and a man walked in who introduced himself as the captain. He was a rather heavyset man with silver-tipped hair and a leathery face from years spent outdoors.

"That was some mighty fine shooting today, young lady. The man you protected is in surgery now."

"Will he make it?" she asked.

"We're hoping he will."

"Do you know who he is?" she asked.

"Not yet," he answered. Before she could ask any other questions, he turned to Michael and shook his hand. "I heard you were here. How's your brother?"

Michael smiled. "Which one?"

"Dylan, of course." He turned to Isabel and explained. "He used to work for me." He chuckled as he added, "Actually, I think he thought I worked for him, and some days I did. We were sorry to lose him."

Isabel responded, "Lose him? Dylan didn't die. He moved to South Carolina and married my sister."

"I know," the captain said. "I'm still hoping he'll come back here to work."

"I don't think that's going to happen," Michael said.

The captain continued to chat with Michael for a few more minutes, asking about his family, and then, as he was opening the door, he said, "I know your brothers, Alec and Nick, are both FBI agents. What about you, Michael? What are your plans? Are you going to join them?"

Michael grinned. "The Buchanans are an FBI family. I'm thinking about it."

"Oh, come on," Isabel whispered. She all but fell into the chair. Now he was thinking about joining the FBI? He graduates from college at twenty, then becomes a lawyer, then a Navy SEAL, and now is thinking of being an FBI agent. What's next? Astronaut?

And what was she doing with her life? Oh sure, she had a college degree. But did she have a plan, a goal? No. She had a few ideas, but no real direction. She was suddenly feeling quite stupid. Tears began to fill her eyes.

What was happening to her? She could be emotional at times, but this was over the top. Why did everything suddenly seem like an insurmountable problem? Why were Michael's prospects for the future so upsetting to her? When she glanced up at him, he gave her such a sympathetic look she wanted to weep. And that made her even more angry.

Her lack of control had to be because of everything that had happened in the last few hours. She was emotionally exhausted. She just needed some time to think, to put everything into perspective.

Detectives Samuel and Rayborne walked into the interview room just as the captain was leaving. Instinctively, seeing Samuel, she sat up ramrod straight. Father Mahoney would be proud.

Staring at Isabel, Samuel said, "What were you doing walking around by yourself? The city can be dangerous. You should always be aware of your surroundings, Isabel. Isn't that right, Rayborne?"

His partner agreed with a nod.

"Do you know what could have happened to you?" Samuel asked, and before she had a chance to answer, he continued. "She's damned lucky. Isn't she, Rayborne?"

Without a hint of expression, Rayborne agreed. "Damned lucky."

Isabel wasn't in the mood to argue with them. But lucky? Were they out of their ever-loving minds, or had they forgotten she killed a man? She was definitely not lucky.

Michael took the seat next to her, and for the next forty-five minutes she answered all of the detectives' questions. They kept circling around to the same ones, though. Had the dead man or the victim spoken to her? Had she met either one of them before today? What was she doing in that area so far away from the hotel? And how did she learn to shoot a gun with such accuracy?

Isabel had been operating in a rather numb state since she'd killed that man, but now every muscle in her body ached and her nerves were raw. She was more than ready to leave.

Michael finally called a halt to the interrogation. "You've got our cell numbers, and you know how to find us," he said. "If you need to talk to Isabel again, I want you to go through me. You don't talk to her without me."

Detective Samuel nodded. "Isabel," he asked, "will you be spending the night at the Hamilton, or will you go on to Nathan's Bay?"

"The Hamilton," she quickly answered before Michael could tell him he was taking her to Nathan's Bay.

"And you're going directly there now?" Detective Rayborne asked in his characteristic deadpan manner.

"Yes," Michael said.

"No," Isabel said at the same time. "We have to make a stop first."

"Why?" Michael asked.

Calmly, as though commenting on the weather, she answered, "I need to get this bullet out of my arm."

FIVE

OKAY, SO TELLING THEM ABOUT THE BULLET WAS A BAD IDEA. SHE should have waited until she was in her hotel room and then called the concierge for help in finding a doctor.

Michael and the detectives didn't exactly freak out, but they came close. Michael had her jacket off and was looking at her injury before she could tell him to leave her alone. Then the detectives had to look at it—she noticed Samuel winced at the sight—and of course the captain heard about it and he had to take a peek, too.

Isabel insisted she could take care of the problem without their help. But that wasn't how it was done, according to Detective Samuel. He was determined to accompany her to the hospital. As soon as the bullet was removed, it would be placed in a plastic bag, sealed, and wouldn't leave Samuel's possession until it was in the lab. It all had something to do with procedure, but she honestly wasn't paying much attention, so she really wasn't sure what he meant.

She was distracted because Michael had taken hold of her hand and wasn't letting go. Then he pulled her into his side, and she didn't know what to think about that.

"I'm going to get dried blood all over your shirt," she told him.

"Are you listening to me, Isabel?" Samuel asked.

"Not really," she admitted.

Michael shook his head. "I know you're tired and want to get out of here, but try to concentrate on the task at hand."

"The task at hand?"

"Concentrate. Detective Samuel asked if you understood why you needed to go to the hospital."

She wasn't an idiot. Of course, she knew why she needed to go to the hospital. She had a bullet in her arm. "Yes, I understand. I need to get this bullet out and you need to take it to the lab."

When all was said and done, the ordeal took a full two hours from the minute she walked into the emergency room and saw the giant digital clock flashing the time on the wall above her until she walked back out.

A plastic surgeon, who looked as though he hadn't slept in a year, was on his way out the door when he was called back in by the emergency room physician who had spotted him trying to sneak by. The surgeon wasn't happy until he saw Isabel. He perked up then and did a bit of harmless flirting, though, Michael noticed, Isabel didn't do anything to encourage his behavior.

The surgery wasn't a big deal. According to Dr. Alberts she was hit by a fragment when the bullet struck something nearby. The fragment was resting just under the skin, but it was entangled in muscle. She was x-rayed and brought back to one of the cubicles in the emergency room. After her T-shirt was removed, the nurse did a surgical drape, which would keep the area sterile. Dr. Alberts, gowned, masked, and wearing gloves, numbed the area and quickly removed the piece of bullet. Michael stood back, but as soon as the bandage was wrapped around her arm, he walked to her side and took hold of her hand again. She wasn't sure if he was offering her comfort or making sure she wouldn't bolt. It was an unnecessary gesture, though to be completely honest, she had been considering an escape.

She didn't need all that many stitches, but she did need an antibiotic to protect her against infection. She was offered pain medication but declined, certain regular old Tylenol would take care of any discomfort. Nevertheless, the surgeon wrote a script just in case she changed her mind.

Samuel motioned to Michael to step outside the cubicle to have a word. Isabel could see them through the opening in the curtains. Both men looked somber. Samuel was doing most of the talking, and every now and then Michael would nod. From their expressions, she knew the topic was grim.

Isabel wasn't about to wear the bloody T-shirt again and asked the nurse to throw it away. She put on her nylon jacket and zipped it closed. While Dr. Alberts wrote notes in her chart, she watched Samuel shake Michael's hand and leave.

"All right, you're as good as new," the doctor said. "The stitches should be removed in eight days."

"Thank you, Doctor," she replied, sitting up and swinging her feet over the side of the examination table.

Speaking to Michael, the surgeon said, "Isabel will have a scar, but it will be so thin no one will notice it. We can't let anything damage this lovely young lady. You know—with her golden blond hair and her brilliant blue eyes, she looks like a Greek goddess, doesn't she?"

Dr. Alberts walked out of the cubicle after his comment, so he didn't see Isabel roll her eyes.

Michael did and grinned. "Let's go, goddess."

"Not funny, Michael."

He thought it was and had a good laugh. Ignoring him, she scooted off the table and headed for the doors, stopping to thank the nurse on her way out.

"What was that about with Detective Samuel?" she asked as Michael opened the car door for her.

"We'll stop at a pharmacy to get the antibiotic filled and buy some Tylenol."

"So you're not going to tell me?"

He shook his head.

"You're rude."

The insult obviously didn't bother him. "Yes, I am," he agreed, closing the door.

His smile could be lethal, and she had to remind herself that he was not only rude, he could also be irritating. Regardless, she was thankful he stayed with her. She wondered how he would react if she told him he had it in him to occasionally be nice. He'd probably argue with her.

"Did you rent this?" she asked, glancing around at the interior of the BMW. "It's awfully elegant."

"Elegant, huh?"

She shrugged.

He explained. "It's my brother's car."

"Which brother? You have a bunch of them."

He laughed. "There aren't that many, and you've met them all."

She counted off their names. "Let's see. Theo is the oldest, then Nick, Alec, Dylan, you, and Zachary."

"And two sisters," he reminded. "Jordan, your sister's best friend, and Sidney. Nick picked me up at the airport, and I dropped him off at his house. He'll drive out to Nathan's Bay tomorrow with his wife. I'll keep his car while I'm here."

"And how long will that be?"

"I don't know yet. What about you?"

They stopped at a red light, and he glanced over at her, waiting for an answer.

"I'm not sure what I'm going to do." She noticed his duffel bag was in the backseat and asked, "You were on your way to Nathan's Bay when Dylan called you?"

"That's right. I wasn't out of the city yet, so I turned back."

There was a CVS a couple of miles away, and it didn't take any time at all to get the script filled and purchase Tylenol. The rest of the ride to the hotel was silent. When they arrived, Michael let the valet take his car while he went inside with Isabel. She looked straight ahead as she walked through the lobby. At this point, she was used to people staring, appalled by all the blood she was wearing on her clothes.

Michael followed her with the expectation of collecting her bags for the trip to Nathan's Bay, and she didn't correct him. She waited until they were in her room to tell him she was staying at the hotel. While he outlined all the reasons he was going to have to insist she go with him, she picked up her bag, carried it into the bathroom, then stripped out of her clothes and got into the shower. It was heavenly. She was certain the guests could hear her sigh all the way down in the lobby. The hot water streamed down her face, and she willed it to wash away this horrible day as the muscles in her shoulders and legs began gradually to unknot. She couldn't get her hands to stop shaking, though.

She was alone now, and it was safe for her to let go. Besides, she couldn't keep it inside any longer. No one would bother her, and no one would know. She began to cry. In seconds she went from silent tears to gut-wrenching sobs.

Yet another reason she wasn't in any hurry to go to Nathan's Bay. She needed to get past today's nightmare before she saw Kate and Dylan. It would be humiliating to fall apart in front of them.

Standing outside the bathroom door, Michael could hear her crying, and it was tearing him up. He didn't know what to do about it. If she were dressed he'd probably pull her into his arms and hold her, but she wasn't dressed; she was stark naked, and if he pulled her into his arms in the shower, he sure wouldn't be thinking about comforting her. The least he could do was knock on the door and ask her if he could help, or maybe ask if everything was all right. Fortunately, he was saved from going through with his awkward plan when Dylan called.

Isabel spent a long while in the bathroom to get herself under control, even taking the time to blow her hair dry. She emptied the pockets of her jeans and tossed everything into a makeup bag. The clothes she'd worn went into a plastic laundry bag. She looked around the large bathroom to make sure she'd picked up everything, then grabbed her laptop and opened the door, ready now for the argument she knew was coming.

Michael was on his cell phone, talking to Dylan and pacing around the bedroom. He came to a dead stop the second he saw her. He thought he was still breathing, but he couldn't be sure. Isabel was wearing a pair of hot pink pajama shorts and a tank top that was all but glued to her chest. The word *voluptuous* came to mind, along with several other descriptive words. Damn, but she was sexy. He tried but couldn't stop staring at her.

Dylan yanked Michael from his salacious thoughts about Isabel. "Michael, did you hear me? I want her to come to Nathan's Bay, too, but if she insists on staying at the hotel, let her. She's an adult. She can handle herself. Listen, you need to know . . ."

"Yes?"

"She likes to drive, but—"

Michael interrupted him. "She's been through a hell of a time today. I don't think she should be alone."

"She's a big girl, and like I said, if she needs some time to herself, that's okay. Don't make it complicated."

"Yeah, well . . ."

"What?"

Staring at Isabel, he said, "It's already complicated."

Michael disconnected the call before his brother could ask him to explain. How in God's name was he going to be able to stay away from her?

"What the hell, Isabel. Don't you have any regular pajamas?"

"These are pajamas."

"I'm taking you to Nathan's Bay."

"No."

"No?" His voice was firm, as though he wasn't accustomed to anyone challenging him.

Isabel wasn't in the mood to argue. Was he trying to intimidate her? If so, he was failing. She wasn't going anywhere. "Oh, I'm sorry. I meant to say, 'No, thank you.'"

When he turned away and didn't respond, she accepted her small victory and sat down on the bed. Propping the laptop on her knees, she opened it. She tried to look relaxed but couldn't get her mind to settle down. The bedroom seemed to shrink with Michael in it. He was such a big man and so muscular. She wasn't attracted to big, muscular men, she told herself. Too bad she couldn't sell that lie.

When had it happened? When had she changed her mind? Had Michael caused this sudden reversal? She was still furious with him over his rude behavior at Kate and Dylan's wedding. Or could it be possible that she was angry simply because he had ignored her? Had she been attracted to him even then? What a conundrum.

Conundrum? One of her aunt Nora's favorite words. Isabel decided she had spent way too much time with the elderly woman who had moved in with them after her mother got sick. She was beginning to think like her aunt, and that couldn't be good.

Why had her aunt suddenly popped into her head?

She closed her laptop and set it on the nightstand. "Are all Navy SEALS as big as you are? And you're, what? Six-two? Six-three?" Now, where had that question come from? She couldn't seem to hold on to a coherent thought for more than ten seconds.

Michael stared at her, puzzled. What the hell was going on inside that mind of hers? For a minute she had spaced out, and now she wanted to talk about the Navy SEALS?

"Get dressed," he repeated, ignoring her question.

If he wasn't going to respond, she would do the same. "I read that the training is intense. It is, isn't it?"

He stood over her, his arms folded across his chest, studying her, trying to figure out how to get her moving. "I know you're tired and you've had a bad experience today . . . ," he began.

"A bad experience? Killing a man was a bad experience?" She started to laugh, then stopped, fearing she sounded hysterical. Wouldn't that be the icing on her sucky cake.

Michael decided to reason with her, and he would be diplomatic. He moved her legs out of his way, taking time to notice how smooth and golden her skin was, and sat on the bed, facing her.

"I'm not going to leave you here alone."

"Why not?"

"You're kind of a mess." So much for diplomacy.

Isabel folded her arms and looked at him indignantly. "That's a mean thing to say."

"Put your hands out."

She did as he demanded before she thought better of it. They were still shaking up a storm. If she had a pair of bongo drums, she could really go to town. "It's just the aftermath of . . . today," she said, not wanting to put words to the horrible incident. "Besides, I haven't had anything to eat since yesterday . . . or was it the day before yesterday? Then I threw up this morning because I foolishly got trashed last night."

"You got what?"

"Trashed," she repeated. "You know, sloshed, soaked, hammered . . . I had way too much to drink. I should probably order room service. Once I eat, my hands will stop shaking."

"If you don't go with me, I'm staying here in this room with you." He waited for a horrified reaction. He didn't get one.

"Okay." She nonchalantly picked up the room service menu.

"Hell."

"I think I could eat a sandwich. What about you? Are you hungry?" Switching subjects abruptly, she asked, "What did you and Samuel talk about? You both looked so intense."

"Stop trying to redirect me."

"Caught on, did you?"

Michael noticed a dimple appeared on her cheek when she smiled.

The woman was damn near irresistible. "Okay, have it your way. We'll stay here."

Ever so slowly he reached across her to get to the hotel phone on the other side of the bed. The back of his hand brushed against her breasts. She didn't think the intimacy was deliberate until he looked at her and she saw the laughter in his eyes. He was having fun, trying to rattle her. No way was she going to let him know how much his touch affected her.

"There's another phone on the desk across the room," she pointed out.

He was sitting so close to her she could feel the heat radiating from his body, and if she reached out, she could run her fingertips down the side of his face and feel the day's growth of whiskers that made him look a little more dangerous than sexy.

So this was what being aroused felt like. Since she'd started dating, she had never had this kind of physical reaction to any man. She'd read about it, heard about it from her girlfriends, but she'd never experienced it. She had thought there was something wrong with her, perhaps something missing in her DNA.

Until Michael.

The discovery didn't make her happy. In her mind there was a huge difference between being attracted to someone and being aroused by someone. She had been attracted to Noah Clayborne before he married Michael's sister Jordan, but she hadn't been aroused by him.

Okay, so now she knew how it felt. She also knew she didn't like it. And the fact that it was Michael made it all the more alarming. Her hormones finally decided to kick in, but with Michael? She couldn't catch a break. Isabel was a person who needed control, and Michael was snatching that away from her.

Trying to clear her head, she asked, "Who are you calling?"

"Bell desk."

She listened as he requested that someone get his duffel bag out of his car and bring it up to Isabel's room. Then he handed her the phone so she could order from room service.

"I'm sure there are rooms available, or you could take the other room Kate reserved."

"Oh no. You want to stay here. I'm staying with you."

She was sure he was bluffing. She ordered club sandwiches for both of them, a beer for him and a Diet Coke for her, along with large bottles of water. He added a double cheeseburger to the order before she hung up.

She had a plan. She would be patient, even if it killed her. He would eat with her, then realize his bluff wasn't working, and he would leave. She just had to stay strong and not fold before he did.

Michael's cell phone rang. He saw who was calling but waited until he was across the room before he answered. His voice was so low she couldn't hear whom he was talking to or what he was saying. Probably one of a dozen women he was currently seeing, she guessed. His bag was delivered, but he left it in the alcove near the door, which she believed was an indicator that he was indeed bluffing and had no intention of staying with her.

The food arrived twenty minutes later. Isabel ate half of her sandwich. Michael ate every bit of his and the rest of hers. She went into the bathroom, brushed her teeth, and got back into bed. Doing her best to ignore him, she pulled up her emails on her laptop but found it impossible to focus on any of them. She wondered how she was ever going to calm down enough to go to sleep. The events of the day popped up like slides clicking through her mind . . . the man throwing himself into her arms, clawing at her, then falling, taking her with him, next—gunshots, the maniac shooting at her, watching the bullet strike him between his eyes. He seemed to fall back in slow motion. All the images appeared, one after the other, and then the slides started all over again. God help her, she couldn't get them to stop.

Her stomach felt queasy again. She took several deep breaths and that helped, but she didn't know what she could do about her hands. They were once again shaking almost violently. She pictured herself trying to put on lipstick and smiled. It would be all over her face.

She knew she had to stop thinking about . . . What had Michael called it? Oh yes. Her bad experience. What she needed was a distraction.

Michael unwittingly provided it. He held the door open while the dining cart was being removed, then locked the door, picked up his duffel, and went into the bathroom. No big deal, right? Until she heard the shower running. She had to admit that did freak her out. So maybe he wasn't bluffing.

But then, neither was she. There was a cozy sitting area in front of the windows with a sofa, coffee table, and an overstuffed easy chair and ottoman. Michael was too tall for the sofa, but he could sleep in the chair and put his feet up on the ottoman. Problem solved.

Michael walked out of the bathroom, and her ability to concentrate went out the window. He wasn't wearing much, just a pair of khaki shorts. He was built like a Greek god, perhaps Apollo, or maybe even Zeus. His chest and upper arms were all muscle, his stomach was flat, and his skin was bronzed.

Get hold of yourself, she inwardly scolded, looking down at the computer screen so he wouldn't see her staring. How could she dislike a man so much and be attracted to him at the same time?

She glanced up again when he turned to reach for his navy T-shirt. She saw the three surgical scars on his back then, two near the center and one lower near the base of his spine. The scar tissue didn't look all that old, and she was pretty sure she knew what the cause was.

"You were shot in the back."

"Yes," he answered, not turning around.

"Three times?"

"Yes." His tone was curt, indicating he didn't want to talk about it, which she completely ignored. "Were you shot in the line of duty, or was it an ex-girlfriend? I'm betting on an ex-girlfriend."

He didn't respond, but even from behind she could tell he wasn't frowning any longer.

She sighed with relief when he unfolded the T-shirt and put it on. What was wrong with her? Had she hit her head when she was helping the man on the ground? If only . . . She didn't think she had, but it would be a great excuse for the indecent thoughts that were suddenly racing through her mind. She had a choice to make. Slide show that would undoubtedly give her nightmares, or erotic thoughts about sex with Michael that would make sleep impossible?

Although she was loath to admit it, Michael was right. She really was a mess. She was still shocked that she had cried. It had been years since she'd last had a good cry. Five, to be exact—when her mother died. Isabel prided herself on being able to keep it together, and she'd succeeded . . . until tonight. She had really wailed in the shower. She was certain Michael hadn't heard her because he would have said something if he had. Only a sensitive man would have pretended he hadn't heard her crying, and Michael wasn't the least bit sensitive. Still, it was mortifying, losing control like that.

"It's late and I've been up since dawn," Michael said. He stood at the foot of the bed. "Are you ready to go to sleep?"

"I doubt I'll be able to sleep," she said. "I'm too revved up. Will it bother you if I keep the television on?"

"No, I can sleep through anything." He looked over his shoulder at the chair, then the bed again. "If it's okay, I'm going to sleep in the bed with you. I'll sleep on top of the covers; you sleep under."

"I don't know if that's a good idea."

"Sure it is. We'll both get a good night's sleep."

Before she could come up with a polite way to tell him absolutely not, he turned off the light, stretched out on top of the covers, stacked his hands on his chest, and closed his eyes. She could have sworn he fell asleep seconds later.

At least now she knew that, of the two of them, she was the only one plagued with lustful thoughts. He obviously didn't think about her the same way. He was quite blasé about sleeping with her. Her libido took a nosedive.

Too late, Michael realized getting in bed with her was a mistake. He told himself he had enough discipline to get through anything—even the night with a beautiful woman. Damn, she smelled good. He tried to block the images rushing through his mind, all involving Isabel, of course. In every one of them he was taking her clothes off. Yeah, big mistake. He should move to the chair or sleep on the floor. That's what he should do. But what he did do was stay right where he was. He could reach out and pull her to him. He blocked that thought, too.

Isabel turned the television off and hoped she could quiet her mind in the dark. She pulled the blanket up to her chin. The room seemed to be getting colder. She vowed she would think about only pleasant things until sleep took over.

It was a stupid plan. She came to that conclusion after ten minutes of trying to come up with a pleasant memory. The man she'd shot kept getting in her way. What she needed was another plan. She had too much energy to sleep now. Then it came to her. She would get dressed, go up to the fitness center, and get on the treadmill. She would run until she dropped.

As quietly as possible, she pushed the covers back, sat up, and tried to stand. Michael stopped her. And oh, was he quick. Before she could blink, he had his hands on her hips, holding her still.

"What are you doing?" he asked, his voice a sleepy whisper.

"I'm going to get dressed and go upstairs to the fitness center."

"You want to work out?" He was slowly pulling her toward him.

He had to think she was crazy, and she couldn't blame him. Who in their right mind would work out in the middle of the night? She put her hands on top of his and tried to push him away so she could get up.

"Your hands are freezing," he said.

"It's cold in here."

Michael didn't think it was cold at all. "You're shivering."

He made it sound like an accusation. "Yes."

"I can fix that."

He rolled to his side and pulled her down next to him. Her backside was pressed against his groin, the backs of her thighs were plastered to his, and her arms were crossed over her chest with his arms wrapped tightly around her, hugging her to him. All of a sudden she was toasty warm. The heat radiating from him felt wonderful.

"This is all wrong," she said. Yawning, she whispered, "You don't have to stay. I'm okay now. You can leave."

Another long yawn and she was gone.

SIX

FOR THE FIRST TIME IN YEARS MICHAEL SLEPT UNTIL ALMOST NINE in the morning. He was usually up and dressed by six, seven at the latest. He had slept hard. Sometime during the night he had let go of Isabel, and she had turned toward him. She was still in his arms, cuddled up against him. Her face was pressed into the side of his neck, and he could feel her warm breath on his skin.

Barely awake, he realized he had a beautiful woman in his arms, and damn, he wanted her. Fortunately, his mind cleared, and he gently pulled away from her, got out of bed, and went into the bathroom to take a cold shower.

By the time he was dressed, his mind and body were back to normal.

"Isabel, time to get up, babe."

"I'm up," she said, facedown in the pillow.

"Come on. Wake up. We need to get going."

"I'm up," she said again but didn't move a muscle.

It took three more tries and a threat to carry her into the shower to get her moving.

Groaning, Isabel rolled herself off the bed and staggered into the bathroom, the marble tile floor cold under her feet. Propping her hands on the vanity, she looked at her reflection in the mirror. Her hair hung over her left eye, and there was a slight crease in her cheek, a sign she had slept through the night without moving much. She splashed water on her face and brushed her teeth, then dug through her bag for something to wear. She decided on a short, straight khaki skirt, ballet flats, and a blue short-sleeve T-shirt. It was a bit snug across her breasts, but it was soft and comfortable, and after yesterday's fiasco she was determined that today would be laid-back and stress-free. After she brushed her hair, she looked in the mirror, gave herself an encouraging smile, and opened the door.

Michael was pushing a room service cart to the table. He looked up when she returned to the bedroom. Her hair was down around her shoulders, and he remembered how silky it felt. Her legs were simply sensational, long and perfectly shaped. Her skin was soft and smooth. He knew because she'd had one leg draped over him most of the night. He remembered stroking her . . . Oh hell, he was at it again, conjuring up all sorts of inappropriate but thoroughly satisfying ways he wanted to make love to her. He really needed to get away from her before he completely lost his mind.

Halfway across the room she stopped. "Is something wrong?"

"No." His voice was curt.

"Then why are you glaring at me?"

"I was thinking about something . . ."

"Anything I can help with?" she asked.

He laughed.

"You're in a strange mood."

She sat at the table and reached for a glass of orange juice, and he noticed drops of blood on her bandage. "Where's the sack with the supplies to change your bandage?" he asked.

"In the bathroom on the counter, I think, or maybe on top of my bag."

He found the sack, placed it on the table next to her, and sat down.

"Do you want some coffee?" he asked.

"No, thank you. I've tried to like coffee," she remarked, "but it's too bitter for me, no matter how much sugar I add. The lattes look so good with caramel and foam, but they taste awful. I've tried almost every combination."

"If you're going to drink coffee, you should learn how to drink it black. It's an acquired taste."

"Did you acquire a taste for it?"

"I had to. There were some days I needed it to stay alert."

He didn't go into detail. She assumed he was referring to his time with the SEALS, but she didn't ask. He had turned away without an explanation.

Michael moved his chair closer to her, and while she ate yogurt and blueberries, he carefully removed her bandage. "You shouldn't have gotten this wet," he admonished.

Her shrug indicated she wasn't concerned, as though her shower was more important than any other worry. Michael understood. He would have done the same thing. Washing away any traces of the blood from the shooting would have been his first priority, too.

He cleaned the area with the antiseptic she was given, then opened the package of gauze and tape. "Does it hurt?" he asked. The injury was swollen and angry-looking.

"Yes."

Her honesty made him smile. He was used to tough women, like his sisters, Jordan and Sidney, who could be bleeding to death and would swear their injuries didn't hurt a bit. He liked the fact that Isabel told the truth.

"Want a Tylenol?"

"Yes, please."

"Did you take your antibiotic?"

"Not yet."

He got the Tylenol and one of the giant-size antibiotic pills, waited until she had swallowed both of them, and then finished wrapping the gauze around her upper arm. He tried to be gentle as he applied the tape to hold it in place.

"You're doing a nice job," she said. "Let me guess. After college and after law school you went to medical school, then specialized, then went into the Navy SEALS. Right?"

The dimple in her cheek reappeared and was interfering with his concentration. He laughed and shook his head. "Are you suggesting I'm an overachiever?"

"Ouch."

He had pushed too hard on the tape. "Sorry," he said. "Theo and Michelle are at Nathan's Bay. They got in yesterday. We'll ask her to check your stitches."

"She's a surgeon, isn't she?"

He nodded. The gauze was beginning to bunch up, so he undid his work and started over. Isabel watched him. "On second thought, you didn't go to medical school," she said when she saw the difficulty he was having.

It seemed the most natural thing for the two of them to discuss mundane topics. As they ate breakfast together, Isabel was surprised by how comfortable she was becoming with him. The only other men she had ever really been comfortable with from the moment she met them were Michael's five brothers, Noah Clayborne, and Damon. None of them had the ability to make her crazy, though, like Michael did. He could make her want to kiss him and scream at him at the same time.

Did he think about kissing her? Doubtful, she thought. She was sure she wasn't his type. He probably only went for women who had triple degrees and carried guns.

They had slept together and he hadn't tried anything. But then, neither had she.

"Michael . . ."

"What?"

"When we were in bed . . ."

"Yes?" he prompted, wondering why she was suddenly blushing.

"What would you have done if I had tried to seduce you?"

To say she caught him off guard was an understatement. He didn't let it show when he answered. "I'd let you seduce me. So now I gotta ask. How come you didn't make a move?"

Smiling, she said, "I didn't want to embarrass you."

"I would be embarrassed?" he asked, trying to understand.

Isabel suddenly realized she was wading into dangerous territory. She hadn't intended for their conversation to turn racy, but now that she had ventured in, she couldn't turn back. The last thing she wanted Michael to think was that she was a prude.

"I would be too much for you to handle, and that would embarrass you." She brushed her hair over her shoulder. "I'm pretty incredible."

"In bed."

"Yes, in bed," she agreed. "It makes sense that I would be superior."

"Superior to me?"

She slowly nodded. Michael stared into her beautiful blue eyes, saw how they sparkled, and knew she was having fun teasing him. "Want to explain it to me?"

"All those years while you were going to different schools, studying day and night, and then learning how to be tough, carrying a thousand pounds over your shoulder and holding your breath under water for eighty minutes or so, I was home perfecting my technique. So you can understand why I left you alone. I was being kind."

Michael was speechless. She pushed her chair back, got up, and went to the phone to call housekeeping to ask for someone to pick up her laundry. He couldn't take his eyes off her. He shook his head as though that action would get rid of his raunchy thoughts. Hell, he was going to be thinking about what she'd said for the rest of the day.

"That isn't funny, Isabel," he said.

Laughing, she said, "Yes, it is. If you could see your expression . . ."

"You shouldn't taunt a man about sex," he said. "I might take you up on it."

"I wasn't offering," she said nonchalantly.

"Sure you were," he countered with a grin.

"And I'm not worried," she continued as though he hadn't said anything. "The last time I saw you, you made it abundantly clear that you didn't like me." She put her hand up so he wouldn't interrupt and added, "It's all right. I didn't particularly like you, either."

He laughed as though her comment were ridiculous. "It doesn't matter if we like each other. Sex is . . ." He stopped himself before he said something crude.

"Sex is what?"

His mind raced for an explanation that wasn't gross and would make sense to her. "A pleasurable activity. Yeah, it's a pleasurable activity. Sometimes it's extremely pleasurable. And that's all it is," he added with a shrug.

"Oh, come on. I would never have sex with someone I didn't like."

He stared at her for several seconds, then slowly looked her up and down. "I would," he said. "You might want to keep that in mind."

She opened her mouth to respond, then stopped herself.

He grabbed his duffel bag and zipped it closed. "Come on. Pack your things and check out."

"I'm not checking out. I'm going to keep this room," she said. "I'll ride with you to Nathan's Bay to see everyone, but there won't be room for me to stay there. Besides, I want to stay here."

He wasn't going to argue with her. "Have you talked to Kate about this?"

"I don't need my sister's permission."

"I know you don't," he said. "But have you talked to her or Dylan since you . . ."

"Since I killed a man?" she asked, and before he could answer, she continued, "No, I haven't spoken to either one of them since I called Dylan from the street. They've called quite a few times, and they've texted, but I let their calls go to voicemail, and I didn't text back."

"Why not?"

"I'll see them soon enough," she said. "And I don't want to talk about what happened over the phone."

"Yeah, okay. I get it."

She rushed to change the subject. "When is the celebration?"

"The family dinner is Wednesday, and the party with friends and relatives is Saturday night. That will be a real blowout."

"When I return to the city later today, I'll rent a car through the hotel and drive back and forth."

Michael's cell phone rang just as housekeeping knocked on the door. Isabel handed the man the plastic bag with her laundry to be washed and dried. She explained about the tear in the jacket and asked if it could be repaired. After thanking him, she shut the door. Gathering her purse, room card, and cell phone, she was ready to go.

Michael gave her the bad news. "Change of plans. Detective Samuel wants you to come back to the station."

"Why?"

"More questions," he explained. "He thinks, now that you've had a good night's rest . . ."

Hands on hips, she demanded, "He thinks what?"

"You'll maybe remember something you forgot to mention yesterday." He shook his head. "Hell if I know what he really wants. He's got the video. It's all there."

"I can't turn him down, can I?"

Smiling, he said, "He's not inviting you to lunch, so no, you can't turn him down. Come on. Let's get this done."

Isabel suddenly felt guilty. Michael hadn't signed up for any of this. He had come to Boston for a celebration and a vacation, and she was interfering. "You don't have to go with me. You've done enough. You should go on to Nathan's Bay."

"For now, I'm your attorney. I'm going with you."

He opened the door, stepped back, and waited for her to go ahead of him. She stopped an inch away from him, put her hand on his chest, and tilted her head back so she could look into his eyes. "How much is this going to cost me?"

He leaned down and whispered into her ear, "Later, babe. I'll tell you what I want later."

It wasn't what he said as much as how he said it that gave her goose bumps. Time for her to stop flirting with him before she got into trouble. As satisfying and as fun as the playful banter was, she had a feeling he was a pro at this sort of thing. She didn't want to get into a competition with him, knowing full well he would make mincemeat of her. Fun time was over.

ONCE THEY WERE IN THE CAR AND ON THEIR WAY TO THE STATION, he said, "I should call Dylan. He could meet us."

"No, absolutely not." Her voice was emphatic. "He's on vacation, and I don't want to bother him. I'll see him soon enough. Besides, I only need an attorney with me, and I've got one of those."

He glanced over at her. "What's going on? Why haven't you talked to Kate? And Dylan could be a big help. There's more to this than your not wanting to explain over the phone."

She shook her head. She didn't tell him the truth, that she didn't want her sister and brother-in-law to think she had lost track of where she was because she had been distracted. She had, but she didn't want them to know it.

"Why haven't you called them?" he asked again. The man was relentless. No wonder he became an attorney. Arguing to get his way seemed to be second nature to him.

"You're a nag."

He wasn't giving up. "Why?"

"Because they'll know I zoned out."

"You what?"

"Zoned out," she repeated.

He looked puzzled by her confession. "How did you zone out?"

"I got distracted. I do that . . . sometimes," she said hesitantly. "I write songs in my head. A thread of a lyric or a phrase comes to me, and I have to finish it before I can think about anything else. I'm kind of obsessive-compulsive, I'm told."

"You write songs and you sing, don't you? You sang a song at Dylan and Kate's wedding. I remember you didn't want to, but your sister got you to change your mind."

"Yes."

"Okay, so you got distracted . . . nothing wrong with that."

"I walked for over an hour, maybe closer to two . . . I don't know . . . I didn't look at any street signs. I got lost because I wasn't paying attention to my surroundings. I turned around and started back . . ."

Michael pictured her naively wandering around the city, and every muscle in his body tightened. Did she have any idea what could have happened to her? He got mad thinking about it.

Isabel could see his jaw clenching. When he looked at her, she swore there were sparks in his eyes.

"I'm usually very aware of my surroundings," she said, trying to placate him. "And I don't take chances."

"But you got distracted."

He made it sound like she'd committed a grave sin. "Yes."

"You're damned lucky."

"Yes, I am."

A minute passed in silence, and then he said, "And you saved a man's life."

"Maybe I did. He's critical."

"How do you know that?"

"Detective Samuel. He arranged for me to be put on the list so nurses in ICU can talk to me and give me updates."

"How many times have you called to check on his progress?"

"Just three times."

Before he could tell her she was a neurotic mess, Isabel quickly moved to another topic. "What's our strategy going to be with the detective?"

"Strategy?" he said, trying to hide his smile. She sounded so earnest. "Samuel will ask questions and you'll answer them."

"What if he wants me to come in so he can arrest me?"

"On what charge?"

"Murder."

Glancing over at her and seeing the genuine worry on her face, he softened his tone. "Are you seriously thinking you could be charged with murder?"

"I killed a man," she reminded.

"The man was trying to kill you and the man you were trying to help."

"Yes, that's right. Be sure to mention that if Detective Samuel brings out the handcuffs." The mere possibility gave Isabel the shivers.

"That's not gonna happen," Michael assured her, but he could tell she didn't believe him.

Isabel wanted to be calm and in control when she sat down with Samuel. She wasn't sure how she was going to accomplish that goal, though. Right now her mind was a riot of emotions and crazy thoughts, all because of Michael. She had enough to think about. She didn't need to have Michael on her mind, too.

He was simply doing a favor for his brother. Otherwise he wouldn't give her the time of day. As impossible as it seemed, she had to stop fantasizing about what it would be like to be with him. He was, as the saying goes, way out of her league. Michael was so much more sophisticated, far more worldly. The women he liked were probably worldly, too, and didn't have any expectations of a future with him, wanting pleasure for one night or maybe a week and then moving on without any deep emotional connection.

Isabel knew she couldn't handle a relationship like that. She needed the emotional commitment.

Did it make her a fool that she wanted to be in love with a man before she slept with him? In this day and age, it probably did, but she didn't care. Her dear friend Lexi felt the same way. They'd talked about it at length one night and decided they were dinosaurs.

God help the woman who would want to marry Michael and settle down. She would have an uphill climb for sure.

Now that she had sorted it all out and had come to the conclusion that for self-preservation she should get as far away from Michael as possible, she could move on to more important matters.

Then she turned to take a long look at him. He was driving, so he wouldn't notice she was staring. What was so great about him anyway? Sure, he was tall and very fit. And, no question, he was handsome . . . in a rugged sort of way. He obviously was very intelligent and had done some heroic things in serving his country. And even though her original opinion of him had not been favorable, she had to acknowledge he could be thoughtful at times. He didn't have to stay with her or help her through this disaster, but he hadn't hesitated.

Okay, so what? Lots of men were handsome and smart and thoughtful. That didn't mean she would want to have sex with any of them. Michael got roped into this situation, she reminded herself. He wasn't anything special. He had plenty of flaws. She had seen them firsthand. She was simply getting carried away by their circumstances. And once she parted ways with him, she would be rational again.

Her sigh at finally figuring all of this out must have been audible because Michael turned. His eyes sought hers and his mouth curled into a smile. Her heart began to race.

Oh yes, she definitely needed to get away from him. When she was around him she couldn't think straight. She had important decisions to make, and she couldn't afford to have anything . . . or anyone . . . interfere.

"I'm going to Scotland," she blurted. She couldn't get much farther away than that, now, could she?

"When are you going?"

"I'm spending a week in Boston, then Kate and I leave next Monday. But my plans could change because of the shooting. The detectives might keep me here." The fear of being detained by the police resurfaced, and she quickly shook it off. "But I'll go soon," she insisted. "I have land there."

"Where?"

"In the Highlands."

"Where exactly in the Highlands?"

"I don't know."

She was about to explain that, yes, she knew where Glen Mac-Kenna was, but she couldn't give him an exact location unless she had a map in front of her. The look of disbelief on his face changed her mind. He seemed so astounded that she could be that clueless, she decided to have a little fun.

"You don't know where your land is?" he asked.

She had to bite her lower lip to keep from laughing. "That's right. I don't know."

They had arrived at the station. Michael parked and walked around the car to open her door. He took her hand to help her out and didn't seem inclined to let go.

"So you're just going to wander around until you find it?"

With a shrug and a smile, she said, "That's the plan."

Samuel met them at the top of the steps and led them into yet another interview room. Same color, same depressing atmosphere.

She straightened her back and sat down. Folding her hands in her lap to create the impression that she was completely relaxed, she asked, "Detective Samuel? The man that I helped. Do you know who he is?"

"Yes," he answered. "His name is Craig Walsh. He's a detective out of Miami. He has an impressive record."

"What was he doing in Boston?" Michael asked the question.

"We don't have that information yet. We're working on it."

Michael nodded. He could tell that Samuel was being evasive, but he didn't push him. He could get all the information they had from his brother Nick or Alec, who were both FBI agents, or from Dylan, who knew just about every detective in Boston.

Isabel wanted to get this behind her. "What questions do you have for me today, Detective?"

He cleared his throat. "I thought we could watch the video and go over the sequence of events again. I'm hoping you'll remember something more."

"I'll be happy to go over the sequence of events, but I'm not ready to look at the video."

"You still haven't watched it?" Samuel asked. His surprise was evident. "I can't tell you the number of times I've watched it. Why haven't you?"

"I don't want to."

"I think you should," Samuel said. "Seeing it might trigger something."

Isabel looked at Michael, who said, "She'll watch it when she's ready."

Samuel agreed reluctantly. "All right. Let's get started."

No matter what, Isabel was going to remain patient, she told herself, and she would go over the event as many times as Samuel wanted. Cool and calm. That was the objective.

Michael pulled out one of the metal chairs and sat down next to her, draping one arm across the back of her chair.

Isabel took a second to settle her nerves and then proceeded to describe in detail what had happened from the time she stepped outside of the hotel to go for a walk until the moment the police showed up. Samuel took notes, and as soon as she finished, he began asking the same tired old questions again.

"I know we've been at it awhile, but would you mind going over it one more time?" he asked.

Would he mind if she started screaming? Probably, she thought.

"I'll be happy to," she lied, and once again she went through what Samuel was now calling "the event." She thought that was an odd name for what had happened, but then Michael called it her "bad experience," which she thought was odd, too. She had her own special name for what happened. *Nightmare.* A frickin' nightmare.

"Isabel?" Michael said. "Focus on the task at hand. Samuel asked you a question."

She had zoned out. "I'm sorry. What were you wanting to know?"

More questions followed. They were a bit different from the ones asked several times yesterday. Samuel was more interested in knowing what the injured detective had said to her. She thought she had gone over it yesterday. Maybe he forgot.

Samuel studied his notes for a few seconds, then said, "Now, Isabel, when Detective Walsh was reaching for you, he was whispering something, wasn't he?"

She tried to remember. "He was mumbling . . . I think. I don't know. If he was whispering something, I didn't hear it clearly. There was blood everywhere, and I was thinking that he must be in terrible pain and I needed to help him. I doubt he was making sense."

He nodded. "Our technicians are examining the video. They'll slow it down and try to determine what Detective Walsh was saying." He put his notepad on the table and leaned back in his chair. "I think most people would have tried to run away, but you wanted to help."

She couldn't let him believe she had done anything heroic. "It all happened so fast, and I couldn't have gotten away even if I wanted to. He had a fierce grip on me. I do believe most people would want to help. I think you might be a bit cynical."

Michael began to stroke her upper arm. It felt nice. "And you might be a bit naive," he said.

"I've been at this job a long time," Samuel said. "I've seen the worst in people." Nodding to Michael, he added, "I'm sure you've seen things you won't ever forget. You were in Afghanistan, weren't you?"

Michael nodded but didn't want to talk about past experiences, so he said, "How is Detective Walsh doing? Any change in his condition?"

"No, he's still listed in critical condition," Samuel answered. "He may never wake up."

"What about the man I shot?" Isabel asked. "You told me that, as soon as you knew anything about him, you'd tell me. I'd like to know who he was."

"As soon as I know something, I'll share it with you."

She had a strong feeling he wasn't telling her the truth, and she couldn't understand why he would lie to her. Why wouldn't he give her the man's name, at the very least?

Michael could see how dejected she looked. "Are we finished here?" he asked.

Before they could leave, Samuel once again wanted to know where Isabel would be in case he needed to talk to her. How many times was he going to make her come back to the station to ask her the same questions? Did he think she was holding something back? The poor injured man had whispered something to her, but she hadn't understood what he was saying. What more could she add to the investigation? She had told them everything she remembered.

When they were finally allowed to leave the station, Isabel voiced her concern. "Michael, why won't Detective Samuel tell me anything about the man I shot?"

"He's gathering facts. Give him time."

Isabel didn't want to go to Nathan's Bay. She wasn't in the mood to be chatty today. "Would you mind dropping me off at the hotel? I think I'll hang out in my room. I'm tired, and I won't be much fun. I might go up to the spa," she added.

He shook his head. "You're going with me."

"I need to decompress," she insisted.

"You can decompress at the house. Everyone's waiting for you."

He remembered Dylan had commented that Isabel liked to drive, and he thought that might cheer her up. When they reached the car, he handed her the keys.

"You want me to drive?" She sounded thrilled.

"Yeah, sure."

Those were the last coherent words Michael spoke until they were parked in the drive on the side of his parents' home. Most of the words he shouted didn't make sense; the rest were obscenities. He wasn't a screamer, but she'd pushed him to his limit.

Five or six times on the endless drive he thought they were going to die. The last time he might have welcomed a quick death. He lost count of the near misses. Crossing the bridge he was sure they were going to fly off into the ocean. He grabbed the wheel and got them back into the right lane before the car was launched over the rail. And did she appreciate him saving their asses? Hell, no. She slapped his hand away and yelled, "I've got this," when, in his opinion, she clearly didn't.

By the time he got out of the car, he was shaking. He'd been in plenty of firefights, surprise attacks, and every other kind of gunfight while in Afghanistan, and he'd never been unnerved. But then he'd been working with competent men and women who knew what they were doing. Isabel, on the other hand, was a maniac behind the wheel.

Dylan and Kate were sitting at the kitchen table reading a report on Dylan's laptop when Michael stormed in, slammed the door shut behind him, and roared, "Son of a bitch!"

Kate jumped and grabbed hold of her husband's arm. Dylan didn't flinch. He took it all in stride because he knew exactly what had happened. Michael's face was bright red, and there was murder in his eyes.

Dylan calmly looked up from his laptop and with a grin said, "You let her drive, didn't you?"

SEVEN

MICHAEL GRABBED A WATER BOTTLE OUT OF THE REFRIGERATOR, opened it, and gulped down half the bottle, then leaned against the sink, trying to slow his racing heartbeat. He wanted to fight, and Dylan seemed to be the likely target. "You told me she likes to drive. I specifically remember—"

"Yeah, but you didn't let me finish. I was trying to tell you she likes to drive, but if you value your life, don't let her. You cut me off before I could warn you."

Michael rubbed his brow. "Dear God, how did that woman ever get a license?"

Kate thought she should defend her sister. The problem was, she felt the same way Dylan and Michael did. "Isabel just needs a little more practice," she said halfheartedly.

"I'm never riding with her again," Dylan said. "And neither are you, sweetheart."

"Where is my sister?" Kate asked.

"You didn't do anything to her, did you?" Dylan asked. "Like lock her in the trunk?"

"She's outside talking to Jordan and Noah," Michael said. Glaring at his brother, he added, "I didn't do anything to her except take the car keys."

"Try to calm down before you talk to her," Dylan suggested.

"I am calm," he snapped. "And I don't plan to talk to her. I'm staying as far away from her as possible."

"She's sensitive," Kate said.

Michael snorted.

"She is," Kate insisted. "And you watched the video. You know what she's been through since she got off the plane. Give her a break."

Dylan was trying to be sympathetic. God knows he'd been in Michael's place. "Listen. You're here now, and you're in one piece, so take this as a win and move on."

"It was god-awful."

Dylan and Kate both nodded.

"Dylan, if you laugh I'm gonna put my fist through your face," Michael muttered.

The door opened and Isabel walked in. She ran to Kate and hugged her, then hugged Dylan and kissed him on the cheek.

"How are you feeling?" Kate asked.

"I'm fine. Don't look so worried, Kate. I'm okay. Finish what you're doing," she said, pointing to the laptop. She was hoping they were too busy to ask about the shooting.

But of course they did ask. They started out easy. She folded her arms and completely ignored Michael while she answered questions about her flight and her decision to stay at the hotel. Isabel thought she was being quite agreeable until they asked her about the shooting. Then she shut down.

"We'll talk about the . . . incident later," Kate told her.

"Now it's an incident? Detective Samuel calls it 'the event' and Michael calls it my 'bad experience.' I guess 'incident' works."

"What do you call it?" Dylan asked.

"A nightmare."

Isabel was clearly rattled. She picked up a half-empty bottle of water from the table, then put it back. Kate got her a cold bottle from the refrigerator and handed it to her.

"Come sit down," Kate suggested.

Isabel shook her head. She walked over to the island and stood there, facing Michael. She still refused to look at him until she got her temper under control.

"Did you hurt yourself?" Dylan asked.

"No."

"You've got a bandage on your upper arm," he pointed out.

"Oh, that." She had forgotten it was there.

The body language between Michael and Isabel was amusing Dylan. Michael was glaring at Isabel, but it was wasted effort since she wouldn't look at him. "Yes, 'oh, that,'" he replied. "What happened?"

"I got shot."

"You what?" Kate exclaimed.

Isabel let out a loud sigh. *Here we go again*, she thought.

"Oh my God," Kate whispered.

"Do you have stitches?" Kate asked, alarmed.

"Yes," she replied. "Five or six stitches, I think. Nothing to be concerned about."

"Why didn't you answer any of our phone calls or our texts?"

Isabel knew that look. Kate was getting angry. "I didn't want to worry you. Besides, there wasn't anything you could do. I sent the video, and I think that said it all."

Dylan put his arm around Kate but kept his attention on Isabel. "Okay," he agreed. "Anything else new?"

"Yes."

Because she was smiling so sweetly, Dylan was unprepared for what she said.

"Your brother is a mean, pompous, egotistical jerk."

Kate was shocked. Her sister always took politeness to the limit, no matter what the circumstances were. She was kind and considerate of others' feelings, so to hear her say anything critical about Dylan's brother was shocking.

"Isabel, you shouldn't criticize—"

Isabel shot a warning look at her sister. "Don't defend him, Kate. You weren't in the car. You didn't hear the gross profanities he was shouting at me."

"Isabel." Michael said her name in a smooth, even voice. "I shouldn't have shouted at you. I'm sorry about that."

She was so surprised by his apology she didn't know what to say. She was also suspicious. "You're sorry?"

"Yes."

"Okay, then." She still didn't believe him but decided not to make an issue out of it.

"I would like to mention a couple of things," Michael said. His voice was mild now, almost pleasant.

"I'm listening."

He took another drink of water. "The speed limit here isn't a suggestion. If the sign posted is forty-five miles per hour, you shouldn't double it."

"I don't think I—"

He put his hand up to stop her. "Another thing I'd like to mention. We drive on the right side of the road here."

Isabel's face was turning pink, and Michael's voice was getting grittier.

"Anything else?"

"Yes," he answered. "The yellow light isn't a dare. You're not supposed to honk the horn and slam on the gas to make it across before the light turns red."

"Are you finished?"

"Just about."

"Okay. What else would you like to tell me?" It was killing her not to shout at him. He was acting like an obnoxious know-it-all.

"On the bridge did you happen to notice the 'no passing' sign? And before you answer, let me explain that, like the speed limit sign, the do-not-pass sign isn't a suggestion. They really don't want you to pass when driving on the bridge, which is why they posted the do-not-pass signs." He leaned down close to her, and in a hard, clipped voice said, "Do . . . not . . . pass means do . . . not . . . pass."

Dylan had turned toward the wall and was rubbing the back of his neck so Isabel wouldn't see him smile.

Kate stared at her sister and looked horrified. "Grace Isabel Mac-Kenna, did you try to pass a car on the bridge? Oh my God, what were you thinking? Didn't you see the signs? Passing on that narrow bridge . . . Did you get distracted?"

Kate used Isabel's full name only when she was furious with her, and Isabel hated when that happened. She was feeling horrible now. She could have caused a disaster. The truth was, she hadn't noticed the signs, but she wasn't going to admit it.

"You could have killed someone," Michael said, straining not to lose his temper.

She scowled at him. "I've already done that," she countered.

"Let me guess. You were writing another song in your head. Right?" Michael asked, caustically.

She was suddenly just as angry. "As a matter of fact, I was. The song was all about you, Michael. I even came up with a title."

"Yeah? What's that?"

She poked him in the chest. "Dumbass."

EIGHT

DESPITE THE FACT THAT SHE'D TRIED TO KILL THEM NUMEROUS times on the way to Nathan's Bay—it wasn't on purpose, but it counted all the same—and despite the fact that she was a giant pain in the ass, Michael couldn't seem to stay away from Isabel. He kept checking on her to make certain she was okay, which really was ridiculous because she was surrounded by people who loved and cared about her.

The house was overflowing with Buchanans. With all the commotion, Isabel didn't think anyone, not even Michael, saw her slip out the back door to go for a long walk around the island. It was a beautiful afternoon, and she wanted a little time to herself to clear her mind and think. She had just started down the path to the shore when Kate caught up with her.

"Isabel, wait up. I need to talk to you."

With a sigh Isabel turned to her sister. Time alone was becoming a precious commodity. "I was just going for a walk," she said.

Kate didn't ease into her news. "We can't go to Scotland Monday. We're going to have to put off the trip for a while . . . maybe a month or two."

"I'm supposed to meet with the solicitor of the estate at Dunross and sign papers that will transfer the land to me. I don't want to put it off for a month or two. Why can't you go? What happened?"

"The scented oils for my new line of candles didn't arrive, and my company has orders to fill. Everything will come to a halt if I don't go home and fix this. I'm so sorry. I know how much this trip meant to you."

Isabel's first reaction was disappointment, but her attitude quickly changed. "We don't have to put the trip off. You can't go, but I still can. I'll go ahead like we planned, and when your crazy workload eases up, we'll go together another time." She expected Kate to argue with her but was surprised by her response.

"I can't say when I'll be able to get away, but I promise I will see Scotland and Glen MacKenna with you someday," Kate assured her. She thought for a second, then said, "I don't like the idea of you going alone. Isn't there someone you could take with you?"

"I suppose I could ask one of my friends," Isabel answered, knowing full well her sister would object if she didn't agree.

"Good." Kate sounded relieved.

Isabel didn't like misleading her sister, but the idea of going alone and taking her time actually appealed to her. She knew she was going to love Scotland. She had read so much about the beautiful rugged land.

After fifteen minutes of going over the details of the itinerary and giving her sister advice on traveling to another country, Kate left Isabel to continue her walk.

Okay, Isabel had a new plan. Swim, sail, and party until next Monday, and then off to Scotland on her own. Of course, this plan was all contingent on Detective Samuel allowing her to leave Boston. After their last meeting, she couldn't imagine why he wouldn't, but still, she needed to be sure. She'd ask Dylan for his advice. She would prefer to discuss the matter with Michael, but at the moment they weren't on speaking terms.

There was another worry she wanted to address. She had to find the courage to look at the video of that poor detective falling into her arms. She was hoping she would remember what he mumbled to her.

It was probably nothing more than him pleading for help, but she needed to be sure, didn't she? And how was she going to be able to watch herself killing that man without throwing up?

She walked for a long while then stopped and stared at the waves lapping against the rocks below her. She wondered how life had become so complicated. It was most likely her own fault. She never should have gone for that walk in Boston. Of course, if she hadn't, Detective Walsh would be dead. As it was, his life was now hanging by a thread, according to the latest report she'd gotten from Nurse Terry, who was now on a first-name basis with Isabel because she'd called so often. Isabel knew she wouldn't stop worrying about the poor man until he improved, and she absolutely refused to think that he might not make it.

As much as she hated to admit it, Michael was yet another worry. A big worry. She hated being attracted to him, and wanting him to want her. How pathetic was she? He had made it obvious that he didn't like her much, and maybe that was the reason she kept trying to irritate him. Was it possible to be furious with someone and still be drawn to them? At the police station she should have sent him on his way and hired her own attorney. Michael had only been doing a favor for his brother, and now he acted as though he were stuck with her.

Was she wallowing in self-pity? Of course she was.

She decided then and there to stop mentally whining and concentrate instead on how fortunate she was to have such a great family. Kate and Dylan and Kiera would do anything to protect her, and she would do the same for them. It was unconditional love, which Isabel knew was a rare and beautiful thing. She could count on them, no matter what.

Okay, time to adopt a new attitude. From now on she would think only about positive things that were happening in her life. She loved being on the island. That was a positive. To her, Nathan's Bay was a paradise. She strolled along the shoreline to the gently winding path that led the way to the Buchanan home. The three-story clapboard house had recently been painted a light gray. The shutters were black, as was the front door. It was pristine, but she knew that in a couple of years, with the windstorms and the ice and snow, the weather would take its toll, and it would need to be painted again. Facing the shore, a wide porch spanned the entire length of the house and welcomed anyone who wanted to sit and take in the beauty of the bay. The lush green lawn was about the size of half a football field. To the south was a large rectangular pool, and to the north was a coach house that had been converted to a guesthouse. The rest of the island had been left in Mother Nature's care.

Isabel thought it would be fantastic to own her own island. Nathan's Bay, tucked in its own cove but looking out on the wide expanse of the Atlantic, was a perfect hideaway that provided privacy, space, and safety. It was so peaceful and quiet, yet less than thirty minutes away was Boston. There was such energy there. On Nathan's Bay you could have both worlds.

Dylan told her that developers had tried for years to buy the island or at least a chunk of it, but Judge Buchanan, the patriarch of the large family, wouldn't sell. To him the island would always be a safe haven for his six sons and two daughters.

Isabel strolled across the lawn and entered the house, which was still buzzing with the activity of a large family. She had met all of the Buchanans, but the only ones she knew well were Dylan and Jordan, and now she was learning a bit about Michael.

Theo was the oldest and was married to Michelle. Theo worked as an attorney for the Justice Department and also had a law practice where he and his wife lived, in Bowen, Louisiana. They had left their nine-month-old twin boys at home. One of the babies was getting over an ear infection, so Michelle's brother, John Paul, and his wife, Avery, moved in to watch and spoil the little ones. Michelle's father was on rocking chair duty. No one had seen much of Theo or Michelle since they'd arrived. They were both so sleep-deprived, they had been taking continuous naps.

Nick, the second oldest, and his wife, Laurant, were also there without their children, Samantha and Tommy. They lived nearby in Boston but decided to leave their little ones with their nanny and have several days and nights of peace and quiet on the island. Jordan told Isabel that none of the brothers wanted to miss any of the celebration. It had been a long time since they had all gotten together.

Noah and Jordan also lived in Boston, but they, too, had moved in for the weekend. When Noah Clayborne married Jordan Buchanan, he was immediately accepted by the rest of the family, which meant he was treated like one of the brothers, and that sometimes translated into "every man for himself." So the moment he and Jordan arrived at Nathan's Bay they quickly snagged one of the large bedrooms on the second floor with a king-size bed.

Dylan and Kate grabbed the other premium-size room.

Alec, the third Buchanan son, and Regan had flown in from Chicago the night before. They got stuck sleeping in one of the smaller bedrooms with a queen-size bed. Even sleeping at an angle, Alec's feet still hung over the bed, but he didn't mind, as long as his wife snuggled up next to him. The fact was, Alec could sleep anywhere, anytime. He'd been accused by his brothers of falling asleep during a speech— a speech he was giving.

Sidney, the other daughter, was working in L.A. and wasn't going to be able to make it back to Nathan's Bay for the festivities. She needed to finish her documentary before the deadline. Although she would miss seeing her brothers and her sister, she had spent a long weekend at home with her parents just the month before and was able to have her own celebration with them.

Zachary, the youngest, also couldn't make it. The Air Force owned him. He'd graduated from the academy and was now somewhere in Iceland, flying those sleek jets he was crazy about.

Judge and Mrs. Buchanan were away on a short and well-deserved vacation and would be returning home soon. They rarely had time to get away, but their children had encouraged them to take a few days for themselves. Besides, with their parents away, the siblings could prepare for the party.

The judge had reached retirement age; however, his dedication to the law had kept him an active member of the court. Because of his example, most of his sons had taken up professions in the law as well. Theo was a federal attorney. Nick and Alec were FBI agents. Dylan was a police chief in South Carolina. Zachary, thus far, seemed to be headed in a different direction because of his passion for flying. And that left Michael. With his service in the military and his education in the law, he could choose any number of careers, and yet no one except Michael knew what his future would be.

Even without the younger siblings there, the house was bursting at the seams.

As the family had grown over the years, so had their home. Their parents had expanded and remodeled the kitchen and had added a master bedroom suite on the first floor. A long hallway separated it from the rest of the house, which gave them more privacy when their big family was visiting. And it seemed there were always a few children or grandchildren staying with them. There were five bedrooms on the second floor and two small bedrooms on the third floor that were rarely used.

The guesthouse with a living room, kitchen, and two bedrooms was just across the lawn. It was reserved for a few relatives and friends who were coming from out of town. And that left the two bedrooms on the third floor of the main house. Michael was assigned one of those, and Isabel was expected to take the other—assuming she could be persuaded to leave the Hamilton.

It was getting on in the evening, almost eleven, and all the women were in the kitchen, sitting around the table, catching up on one an-other's lives. Isabel sat quietly next to her sister Kate. She was relieved and thankful to have the distraction. The chatter took her mind off the events of the day before. She loved hearing all their stories and wondered if they realized how lucky they were. They had careers that fulfilled them. They were surrounded by a loving family. And they had found their soulmates.

When there was a lull in the conversation, Isabel asked the women to tell her how they had met their husbands.

"Laurant, you've been married the longest. Why don't you start and tell how you met Nick," Kate said.

"Just a minute. Does anyone want ice cream?" Laurant asked, heading to the freezer. Earlier she had opened a bag of potato chips, poured them into a bowl, and put them in the center of the table. She then proceeded to eat most of them.

She didn't wait for an answer but pulled out a container of chocolate chip, then grabbed some spoons and put them on the table.

"Lately I'm always hungry," she explained. She opened the container, helped herself to a spoonful, and then between bites told a harrowing tale of a madman who had threatened to kill her.

"My brother called his best friend, Nick, who was an FBI agent, for help. He stayed with me until the psycho was caught," she said. She went on to tell the details, and when she was finished, she added, "It was pretty awful at the time, but in the end, you might say it was the best thing that ever happened to me because Nick and I found each other."

Kate picked up a spoon, but it was too late. Laurant had already claimed the carton of ice cream for herself, so she put the spoon down. "It was Jordan who introduced me to Dylan. I'd never have found him if it weren't for her," Kate said. "She and I became friends when we were in a European history class in college and discovered that the MacKenna and Buchanan clans both lived in the northern Highlands of Scotland. Our ancestors can be traced all the way to the Middle Ages. I'd like to think our families were connected even back then and that it was destiny that brought Dylan and me together."

Everyone agreed her theory was possible or, at the very least, terribly romantic.

Isabel sat engrossed as Jordan and Regan described their first impressions of their husbands next.

Michelle was the last to tell how she met Theo, and her version of their introduction made Isabel laugh.

"I had to attend a mandatory hospital party at a hotel with other doctors, and I had spent a fortune on a beautiful Armani dress," she began, and then took the time to describe the garment from neckline to hem, ending with, "And the love of my life appeared out of nowhere and threw up all over it."

"What did you do?" Isabel asked.

"I removed Theo's appendix," Michelle said, smiling. "And I decided to keep him."

Michelle beamed when she said Theo's name, and Isabel felt a brief pang of envy. She knew that true love existed, but she believed it was rare. Her sister had found it with Dylan, and it was evident that all the women at the table were madly in love with their husbands. She wondered if she would ever feel that way someday.

"What about Michael and Sidney and Zachary? Who do you think will be the next one to get married?" Laurant asked.

"I'm guessing Sidney," Kate said. "But not for a couple more years. She's so busy filming documentaries, she hasn't had time to think about marriage."

"And she hasn't met the love of her life yet," Michelle added.

"I don't think Michael will ever get married," Jordan commented.

"What about Amanda Foley? She'd marry Michael in a heartbeat, and they have a lot in common," Kate remarked.

"How so?" Isabel asked, trying to sound nonchalant.

"They're both attorneys, and they both graduated at the top of their class."

"Is she in the military?"

Jordan answered. "No, she works for a firm here in Boston."

"What's she like?" Isabel asked.

Jordan had to think about her answer for a minute. "She's sophisticated and polished and a bit standoffish, but then we Buchanans tend to overwhelm people when they first meet us."

"Do you like her?" Isabel asked.

"I really don't know her," she hedged. "And I've only been around her a couple of times."

"But?" Kate prompted.

"But . . . no, I don't like her. I haven't seen her with him in a long time. I don't think he loves her."

"If she's as uptight as Michael, it would be a good match," Laurant interjected.

Jordan nodded. "He is uptight, isn't he? He didn't used to be that way."

"Getting shot in the back three times will definitely change a person for a while," Michelle said.

Kate turned to Isabel. "He's lucky to be alive. He was in Afghanistan when it happened."

"We tried to get more information, but no one is talking," Jordan said. "Our father knows the details, but he's the only one, and Michael acts like it never happened."

"It did change him," Kate said.

Jordan agreed, then added, "I miss the old Michael."

Laurant reached for the bowl. "Hey, who ate all the potato chips?"

Everyone pointed at her and started laughing.

The men could hear their laughter all the way in the sunroom where they were camped out. It was quiet now because ESPN was showing highlights of last year's football games, and the footage was riveting. Noah and Nick were sprawled in easy chairs with their feet up on ottomans, and Theo was half-asleep at one end of the sofa. Alec was sound asleep at the other end. Dylan walked over and nudged him awake when he started snoring.

Michael had just checked on Isabel once again and now stood in the doorway, drinking a Pepsi while he watched highlights of the Notre Dame–Michigan game.

At a commercial break Dylan pulled his phone from his pocket and punched in the number to hear the voice messages on his home landline in Silver Springs. It took several minutes to get through them all, and when he was finished, he turned to Noah. "Can you pull up YouTube on the television?"

"Sure. What do you want to see?" Noah asked as he reached for the remote on the table next to him.

"Isabel singing a song she wrote. It's causing quite a sensation. According to most of the messages on my phone it's gone viral and has really taken off."

It took only a couple of minutes for Noah to find it. No one said a word while they watched Isabel hypnotize her audience with her voice. She captivated all of them. Michael could barely catch a breath. It seemed that every cell in his body reacted to her, and he didn't have any idea what he could do about it. He thought he should turn around and walk away, but he didn't.

As soon as the song ended, Nick whispered, "Wow."

Noah nodded agreement. "Wow" summed it up.

"She's incredible." Theo made the comment.

Michael couldn't keep his irritation from showing. "Look at how the crowd is grabbing and pulling at her."

"Play it again," Alec requested.

And so they all watched and listened to Isabel once more. The reaction was the same.

"She really is amazing," Alec said. "I remember her singing at your wedding, Dylan, but her voice is much stronger now, more mature."

Dylan dropped down into a chair. "The numbers are skyrocketing."

"You mean the number who have watched the video?"

"It's over two million now," Dylan answered. "This isn't going to go away. I hope she's ready for what's coming."

"What are you saying?" Nick asked.

"They're already trying to get to her."

"Who's trying to get to her?" Michael demanded.

"People who want something from her."

"To hell with that," Michael snapped.

"Meaning?" Theo asked.

"Isabel isn't ready for all that," Michael said.

Everyone looked at him. "How would you know what she's ready for?" Nick questioned.

"She just killed a man," Michael reminded. "She needs time to get through that." He took a breath and then said, "Ah hell. The shooting isn't on YouTube, is it?"

"Everything's on YouTube," Alec remarked.

Noah did a quick search, and sure enough, someone had posted the video of Isabel. Fortunately, her name wasn't there. They all watched the video without making any comments. When it ended, no one needed to see it again.

"That video should have been taken down by now. I'll make sure it is," Nick said. He picked up his cell phone, found the contact he was looking for, and started texting.

Noah turned to Dylan. "Did you teach her how to shoot?"

Dylan nodded. "She liked going with me to the shooting range. It was the only time it was just the two of us and she could talk things out." Shrugging, he added, "I've become her big brother, I guess, and Kate tends to lecture her instead of listening. When Isabel went off to college, we were all she had. Their mother had just died. Kiera, the oldest, wasn't available. Getting through a grueling residency had to be her focus."

"Isabel didn't take a gun to college with her, did she?" Nick asked.

"Of course not," Dylan said. "But every time she came home on break she wanted to go to the shooting range, and since I've got to keep my skills up as chief of police, I took her. That's when I would find out what was going on in her life," he added. "Funny thing is, she hates guns, but she knows how to take them apart, clean them, put them back together, and shoot. Man, can she shoot," he praised.

"I also taught her how to defend herself, and I encouraged her to take a couple of self-defense classes. I kind of pushed her. I mean, come on," he continued. "Look at her. Men are gonna hit on her. She needed to know how to protect herself."

"All girls should know how to protect themselves," Nick said. "I dread the day Samantha wants to date."

"When will that be? When she's forty?" Noah asked.

"That's right," Nick agreed.

"That gives you thirty-five years to worry about it," Noah remarked.

Everyone laughed. Then Theo said, "I'm glad I don't have to think about that. My biggest worry is how to get the twins to sleep at the same time."

"I'm gonna tell you something, but you've got to keep it down. No cheering." Nick made the statement. "Noah knows, but I haven't told anyone else."

"Okay, what is it?" Michael asked.

"Laurant's pregnant."

Everyone took turns congratulating him. Then Michael said, "That's great . . . isn't it?"

"Yes," Nick said, smiling. "She had a hard time with the last pregnancy, and she knows I'll worry, so she hasn't told me yet." He laughed then and said, "I'm not sure she's ever going to tell me."

"How did you find out?" Dylan asked.

"I'm an FBI agent. I'm trained to find the truth."

"So, who told you?" Theo asked.

"I heard her on the phone. She was telling her brother, Father Tom. She thinks I'll overreact and try to coddle her."

"Will you?" Dylan asked.

He smiled. "Yes."

"I thought you were gonna say something like, 'FBI agents don't overreact,'" Michael said.

"What about you, Michael?" Theo asked.

"What? Overreact?"

"You know what I'm asking. Are you going into the FBI? I could use you in my office. You'd make a great federal attorney," Theo said.

"Screw the attorneys," Alec said. "FBI. Great benefits."

"Such as?"

"Sometimes you don't have to wear a suit, and they give you those cool jackets with big FBI letters on the back." Nick grinned as though he had just sealed the deal.

"That'll clinch it, all right," Noah drawled.

"I took the exam," Michael announced.

"And?" Nick pressed.

"Did all the interviews."

"So? Are you or aren't you?"

Michael smiled but didn't answer. Although he had made his decision, he wasn't ready to talk about it. His brothers understood what it meant to fight evil. They all fought it in their own way, but there were experiences he would never be able to share with them. Only his brothers in combat would ever know about those.

All his life he had followed a set path. His focus was razor-sharp. First college, then law school. After taking the bar exam he had several offers. Any of them would have set him up for life, and yet his sense of duty led him in a different direction. Others might have thought he was being idealistic, but he couldn't shake the notion that he had an obligation to contribute to a country that had given him so many blessings, and so he enlisted in the Navy and applied to become a SEAL.

The training was brutal, but it was exactly what he needed for what awaited him: villages turned to rubble, families torn apart with no hope of being reunited, death and destruction everywhere. The missions he was sent on showed him a side of humanity that enraged him and at the same time almost tore his heart out. He had learned to do his job without emotion, and yet it was his last mission that threatened to destroy his soul.

His full-time military life was behind him now, but he would never get the scenes of that day out of his head. In the hospital he'd had a lot of time to think about his future, and he decided that the FBI was a good fit for him.

Theo pulled him out of his dark thoughts. "Leave him alone," he ordered the other brothers. "He'll tell us he's going to work in my office when he's ready. He's not gonna waste his law degree."

"I do have an announcement, a serious announcement," Michael said.

"Yeah? What's that?" Alec asked.

"Under no circumstances are any of you to give Isabel your car keys."

Everyone, including Dylan, laughed.

"What's so funny?" Michael asked.

"Dylan told us about your drive here," Noah explained.

"She wants to rent a car in Scotland," Dylan announced.

"God help the Scots," Nick said. "Maybe someone should warn them."

"She should be all right," Michael said. "They drive on the left side of the road over there, don't they? Isabel already does that, so there won't be any learning curve."

After they stopped laughing, Noah said, "She can't be that bad."

"Go for a ride with her and find out," Michael suggested.

Changing the subject, Nick asked, "Has anyone talked to our parents? When are they getting home? I'm assuming they'll want to be here for their party."

"Early tomorrow," Dylan answered. "Not sure when the cousins will get here."

"Which cousins?" Theo asked.

"The MacAlisters."

A collective groan rolled through the sunroom.

"There goes my liver," Nick said.

Dylan shrugged. "It's a fact that any one of them can drink all of us under the table."

"How many are coming?" Theo asked.

"Just four. Sebastian, Gavin, Hunter, and Gabriel."

"Better lock up your women," Michael warned.

"Our women?" Alec laughed.

"If one of them goes after Laurant, I'll have to shoot him," Nick said.

Noah shook his head. "That will just piss him off."

At that moment Jordan appeared in the doorway. "Isabel is ready to go back to the hotel. Who wants to drive her?"

Everyone was quiet as all heads turned to Michael.

"No way!" he protested.

"You got her here. You can take her back," Nick said. "Besides, you're the only one of us who hasn't had a drink, so you're the designated driver."

Reluctantly, Michael had to give in.

Thankfully, Isabel's reaction to him had cooled down a little, but she still wasn't inclined to forgive him just yet. As Michael walked her to the car, she veered away and headed to the driver's side.

Seeing his life flash before his eyes, Michael rushed after her and took hold of her shoulders, turning her around and steering her to the other side. He deposited her in the passenger seat before letting go.

Disaster averted, he closed her door and went around to the driver's seat. Her crossed arms and the fiery glint in her eyes as she stared straight ahead told him it was going to be a silent ride back to the Hamilton, and yet he heard her mutter something under her breath. It was a whisper, but he heard it all the same.

"Dumbass."

NINE

MICHAEL WAS EASY TO RILE. ALL ISABEL HAD TO DO WAS OFFER TO drive again.

"Not funny, Isabel," was becoming his mantra.

"I wasn't trying to be funny," she argued. It was a lie, but she was sticking to it.

She couldn't get another word in for a good ten minutes while he vented.

As soon as he wound down, she said, "You're in a mood, aren't you? And by the way, when we left the house, I was simply offering to drive by walking over to the driver's side of the car. You could have said, 'No, thank you,' but instead you dragged me to the passenger side—"

"I did not drag you."

Ignoring the interruption she continued, "—and proceeded to lecture me while working yourself into a lather reciting the rules of the road. What did you do? Memorize the driver's manual? And yes," she continued before he could interrupt again, "I do know a rolling stop isn't a stop, and I also know that *yield* doesn't mean I get to squeeze into the lane no matter how many cars are in my way."

When Michael began to laugh, she realized she was the one getting all worked up now.

"Okay, no more lecturing," Michael conceded. "I'll even change the subject. Are you planning to stay at the hotel tonight, or will you pack your things and drive back with me?"

"I'm staying at the hotel."

"Then you'll check out in the morning." It was a statement, not a question, and he expected her to agree.

"I don't know what I'm going to do yet."

"What do you mean, you don't know yet? You came to Boston to have some fun, didn't you? And then you're going to Scotland, right?"

Isabel's cell phone rang, halting the conversation. She saw who the caller was and pushed the decline button. Then she answered his question. "Plans have a way of changing, Michael."

Her cell phone rang again. It was the same caller and she once again declined.

She said, "He's very persistent."

"Who?" Michael asked.

"James Reid. He was calling me nonstop for a while, but I haven't heard from him for several days, so I was hoping he had given up. He's with a company called the Patterson Group, and they want to purchase Glen MacKenna. That's the name of the land I'll own soon," she explained. "Or have I already told you that? They offered what they insist is a good and fair amount. Those were Reid's words in the multiple messages he left. He even suggested that their attorney would be happy to get the papers ready for my signature."

"And?" He was determined not to tell her what to do. She should make up her own mind. Still, he wasn't going to let her do anything crazy.

"And I'm going to get my own attorney."

"Good girl."

"My great-uncle, Compton MacKenna, was a very peculiar man. He wrote a letter to me. It's in a sealed envelope, and I'm not supposed to open it until my birthday, not a day before, in the solicitor's office."

"Before you sign anything, you'll want your attorney to go over all of it, too. Right?"

"Of course."

She waited, and when he remained silent, she asked, "Aren't you going to say 'good girl' again?"

"No, you only get one of those a night. You'll have to wait until tomorrow."

Feigning surprise, she said, "Why, Michael Buchanan, I think you might have a sense of humor."

"But I'm still a pompous jerk?"

"A pompous, arrogant, obnoxious jerk," she corrected, ". . . with a sense of humor."

"Don't forget dumbass."

"I won't," she assured him with a grin.

When they arrived, the Hamilton was teeming with people. On one side of the lobby a dozen or so women, surrounding another woman decked out in a pink boa and a plastic crown, were headed toward the bar. On the other side a group of men in business attire were shaking hands and exchanging business cards. And at the front desk a team of college-age athletes stood in a cluster waiting to check in. From the size of them, one would conclude they played rugby or football.

Michael waited until they had made their way through the noise and hubbub and were in the elevator to ask Isabel to explain why she wanted to stay at the hotel.

"The house is already crowded," Isabel explained. "There won't be room for me."

"There's room."

"I'm not fit company."

"Sure you are."

"I've got a lot on my mind."

"Like what?"

She wasn't sure how to say what was at the top of her list and so she settled on what Michael had called it. "My bad experience."

"What about it?"

"I want to find out the name of the man I killed. Did he have a family? Did he shoot people for a living? Was that his occupation?"

"You want his résumé?" he asked, trying not to laugh. "You can't interview him. You killed him."

Isabel's whole demeanor withered, and Michael immediately regretted his words.

"I'm sorry, Isabel," he said. "That wasn't funny."

"I'm just saying . . ."

"That Detective Samuel has the information you're looking for but won't share it?"

"Exactly so. Detective Walsh is still in critical condition."

"How many times did you call to check on him today?"

"Just a couple of times." *In the last two hours*, she silently added. In all, she'd pestered the nurses at least six or seven times. "I'd like to go see him."

He didn't know what a visit to the hospital would accomplish, but Michael could see how important it was to her, so he didn't argue. "Okay. I'll go with you."

"You will? Thank you. I don't know anything about Detective Walsh except that he came to Boston from Miami. Why was he here and what was he doing on that street? He had a reason, and by now Detective Samuel should know what it was."

"You shouldn't worry about this. You aren't part of the investigation now. You just happened to be on the street when the gunman tried to kill Walsh. You saved his life, Isabel, and you should be proud of that."

"I did stroll right into the middle of it, didn't I?" she asked, and before he could respond she said, "Aren't you at all curious to know what Detective Walsh was up to?"

"Eventually we'll find out. After Samuel finishes his investigation, he'll tell us."

"You think?"

"Yes."

"I know Walsh is still unconscious. I just wish I could grab him by his shoulders and shake him until he wakes up."

"I don't think it works that way," he said. Then he asked, "What else is on your mind?"

"A couple of things. I won't bore you with the details."

"Go ahead. Bore me." He took the room card she handed him and opened the door.

Isabel walked in ahead of him, and as the door closed behind them they stood facing each other in the alcove. It was dark, but neither one of them reached to turn on the lights. Her back was against the wall, and he was close enough for her to feel his heat.

"Isabel?"

She realized she'd zoned out and said the first thing that popped into her head before he could tell her to focus on the task at hand. That seemed to be one of his favorite expressions. "I wish I weren't a video on YouTube."

"The singing or the shooting video?"

Startled, she asked, "What did you say? The video of me shooting that man is on YouTube for everyone to see?" She felt a sudden chill down her spine.

"Yes, but—"

"Oh my God . . . People see me killing a man . . . and with all that blood . . ."

"Your name isn't attached. No one knows who you are."

"Yet," she said. "They'll find out."

She took a shaky breath, and when she tried to take her room card from him, Michael saw her hands were trembling again. He reached for her and pulled her close, wrapping his arms around her and holding tight. Isabel put her head on his shoulder and leaned into him.

Intense sensations began to course through Michael's body. He knew he needed to put a stop to them before things got out of hand and it was too late to turn back. Gently letting go of her, he lifted her chin to look at him.

"Nick is getting it taken down," he promised.

"You also saw the video of me singing? I don't suppose you can take that down, too? I didn't intend for lots of people to see that, but someone posted it."

"I'm afraid it's too late for that one," he said. "Once it's gone viral, you can't take it back. You were wonderful, Isabel."

Embarrassed by the compliment, she said, "I was drunk."

"You were wonderful," he repeated. "Now you say, 'Thank you.'"

"Thank you."

"Who was the guy with his arm around you, pushing people out of the way to get you across the floor after you sang? The guy with the blond hair. Did you know him?"

"That was Damon. He's a good friend."

Friend. Not likely. Whoever filmed the video had scanned the audience, and Michael noticed the look on good old Damon's face as they crossed the room.

"How good a friend?" he asked.

"He's like a brother to me."

He must love that, Michael thought.

Something about this Damon fellow annoyed him. But why did he care if the guy wanted her? And from the look on his face while she was singing, it was obvious that he did. Michael felt a hint of resentment beginning to swell up inside him. What was wrong with him? That was probably the tenth time he'd asked himself that question, and he still hadn't come up with an answer.

The temptation to pull her into his arms again was becoming almost impossible to fight, and damn it, there was a bed just a couple of feet away. He wasn't made of iron, for God's sake. Didn't she understand that?

"I should get back." He knew he sounded desperate.

"Okay, leave."

She didn't understand. She wouldn't have sounded so annoyed if she realized what was going through his mind.

"I'll leave in a minute. You said there were a couple of other problems you wanted to figure out. The video of you singing was one. What's the other?"

Isabel wondered what he would do if she told him the truth: *You. You're the other problem.* "I can't remember. It must not have been important."

He threaded his fingers through his hair. He thought his frustration must be obvious to her. "Are you going to be okay here . . . alone?"

"Of course."

"You won't go up to the spa and work out in the middle of the night?"

Isabel thought it was sweet that he was worrying about her. She still didn't think he liked her much, but she could tell he was physically attracted to her. The way he looked at her told her so. He must hate that.

"I have no desire to work out tonight."

"Okay," he said. "I'll come get you in the morning."

"You don't need to do that."

"Noon. I'll be here at noon."

He grabbed his duffel bag, and he was out the door.

Isabel walked into the bedroom and noticed her laundry had been returned. Her windbreaker was neatly folded on top of her other clothes. She checked the sleeve and was impressed because she could barely see that there had been a tear.

Glancing around the empty hotel room, she realized she was finally alone, and she didn't like it one little bit. She was used to Michael being around. Granted, they had had a couple of squabbles, but there had been a sense of security when he was with her. Nothing to worry about, she told herself. She was fine without him. After she changed into her pajamas and settled in, she would enjoy the peace and quiet. She wouldn't miss him at all.

She went into the bathroom to get ready for bed and spotted Michael's shaving kit sitting on the vanity. Quickly reaching for her phone, she called him.

"Yes, I need it. I'll come up to get it," he said.

"No, I'll meet you in the lobby."

Had he wanted to argue, he was too late. She'd already disconnected the call. Slipping her room card into her pocket, she grabbed the kit and went downstairs.

The lobby was still crowded with guests coming and going, but because he was so tall, he was easy to find. He had just walked back into the hotel.

Michael spotted her right away. How could he not? She was the most beautiful woman in the lobby. He was walking toward her, thinking she had a great smile when, quick as a blink, her expression changed to one of sheer panic.

Isabel had heard shrill laughter and turned toward the sound. There was a group of ladies clustered together near the atrium, and all of them seemed to be talking at the same time. They were a happy group, she thought.

Several older businessmen deep in conversation were inadvertently pressing in on her. She stepped back, and that was when she noticed him. A man with red hair and an angry expression etched on his face was staring at her and coming fast, weaving his way through the crowd. Seeing him triggered the memory of the redheaded man standing on the corner watching her as she tried to help Detective Walsh. Oh God, was it the same man? And if so, why would he be following her?

He looked like the same man . . . didn't he? She shook her head. She'd seen him on the street for only a few seconds, and he was too far away for her to get a really good look.

Suddenly Michael was there, reaching for her and pulling her into his arms, blocking her view.

"What's wrong?" he demanded.

"Did you see him?" Isabel was so frantic, she could barely get the words out.

"See who?"

"There was a man . . ." She pulled away from Michael and searched the lobby, but she couldn't find the man anywhere. How had he vanished so quickly? "He's gone," she said.

The color had left her face, and Michael worried she'd pass out. He put one arm around her shoulders and led her to a chair. Whomever she'd seen had scared the hell out of her.

"I think I saw him there," she said as she sat down, still searching the lobby for some sign of the man. "He was on the street at the corner . . . at the shooting . . . but he didn't help me. He just disappeared. Now he's done it again." Michael squatted next to her and she grabbed his arm. "How is that possible? And what does he want with me?" She didn't give him time to answer. "He had such a hateful look on his face."

Michael pulled her to her feet. "Come on. We're going to pack your things and get out of here. I'm taking you home with me."

She thought that was a wonderful idea. "I'll be safe there."

"I'm going to make sure you'll be safe." He knew how arrogant he sounded, but he was telling her what he believed to be true. He would kill anyone who tried to hurt her.

Before they went upstairs to gather her things, they stopped at the front desk to check out. Michael made one call to his brother Alec and then tried to hurry Isabel along. She was still so rattled she would have forgotten her cell phone and charger if he hadn't seen it on the bed and taken it. He carried her bag and held her hand as they left the hotel. Walking through the lobby, Isabel attempted to look self-assured and at ease, but on the inside she was fighting the urge to run.

She furtively scanned in all directions in case the redheaded stranger was still there, lurking in the shadows.

Once they were back in the car and pulling away from the hotel, Isabel could breathe again. "If that man hadn't looked so angry, I might have waited until he reached me and talked to him to find out what he wanted, but he was scowling as he rushed toward me in the lobby." She stopped to shake her head as if to clear her thoughts. "*If* he was running to me. He could have just been in a hurry. I feel so foolish now. I overreacted, and just because I saw a man with red hair, I jumped to the conclusion that he was the guy on the corner watching me help Detective Walsh. And so what if he was?" She turned to Michael and admitted, "It was his hostile expression that freaked me out. Maybe because it triggered a memory."

Michael held his patience and tried not to sound frustrated when he asked, "How come you didn't mention this guy at the station when Samuel was questioning you?"

"I forgot all about him."

He nodded. "You said he was on the street?"

"Yes, at the corner," she explained. "I remember now. I was kneeling next to the detective, and I was trying to stop the bleeding. I looked up and saw him watching me. I remember him because he had red hair." She added, "I needed help. I don't know if I called out to him or not. I didn't think about him after that because I was focused on Walsh."

"You didn't call out to anyone."

"How do you know . . ."

"I watched the video."

"Right," she said. She looked out the window and stared at the passing lights, wondering if there was anything else she had forgotten. "I need to watch it, too," she admitted finally. "Maybe I'll remember something else. That man . . . He was there for an instant and then gone. Still, I should have remembered him."

"Samuel needs to know, Isabel."

She groaned. "Know what? That there was a man standing on the corner for a second? And maybe or maybe not the same man was in the lobby?"

"Yes."

"I could call tomorrow and tell him. The man in the lobby is probably long gone by now. And it's late," she pointed out. "Although . . ."

It was the way she drew the word out that made Michael ask, "Although what?"

"I have an attorney," she said, looking at him expectantly. "Don't you think he should talk to Detective Samuel?"

"Okay, I'll call him," he said. "And Alec should have the video by now."

"What video?" she asked.

"There are security cameras in the lobby. Hopefully the redhead's face will be visible."

"Wouldn't it be great if we had a photo of his face?"

They pulled into the driveway a half hour later. The Buchanan house was dark except for a light shining from the kitchen window. They found Alec in front of an open refrigerator drinking milk out of a carton. His hair was sticking up every which way, and Isabel was certain Michael's call had gotten him out of bed.

"The security recording is on my laptop," Alec said. "Isabel, you looked like you were seeing a ghost."

He pulled out a chair at the island for Isabel, then opened his laptop and touched the screen. Michael stood behind Isabel with one hand on her shoulder while they watched. The cameras were scanning the lobby, and she was disheartened because she couldn't find the man anywhere. It was when she saw Michael with his arm around her that she spotted him.

"There," she said, pointing to the screen. "He's looking down. All you can see is the top of his head."

"He certainly was in a hurry," Alec commented.

Isabel didn't want to think about this any longer. Everything from the past few days was overwhelming. She had to keep reminding herself that, when she was on that street, she hadn't been given a choice. The man she killed would have killed her and Detective Walsh if she hadn't been quicker. He chose death the second he raised his gun.

She was eager to get on a plane to Scotland and put the shooting behind her. Eventually Detective Samuel would find out why Walsh had come to Boston. He had told her that Walsh was a detective. The obvious conclusion was that he was working on a case, and whatever he had uncovered had gotten him shot. Isabel was certain, by the time she returned from Scotland, the investigation would be sorted out, and Detective Samuel would have all the answers.

"Where am I sleeping?" she asked Alec.

Michael answered her. "You and I are both on the third floor. Come on, I'll go up with you."

He picked up her bag and followed her up the stairs. They climbed to the second floor and then to the third. She was thinking she could get a nosebleed this high up. He was thinking what a great ass she had.

There were two sconces on either side of the narrow hallway, barely lighting their passageway.

"It's so quiet and private up here," she remarked.

The bedrooms were across from each other with a bathroom in between. Michael opened both bedroom doors. "The rooms have queen-size beds."

"Is that big enough for you?" she asked, smiling.

He shrugged. "I can sleep anywhere."

Michael placed her bag on a chair adjacent to the window. Banging his head against the ceiling when he turned around, he muttered an expletive. "I can't seem to remember the ceiling slopes up here."

"I think it's cozy."

"Let me know if you need anything," he said as he was walking out.

"Good night, Michael."

Isabel looked around at her room. The walls were a pale blue with matching curtains, and there was a quilt on the bed that had all the colors of the ocean. It was charming. It wasn't the Hamilton. It was better. She felt safe here.

While she unpacked and changed into her pajama shorts and top, Michael showered. She waited until he'd gone into his bedroom before she went into the bathroom to brush her teeth and wash her face. She was just about to shut her door and get into bed when she remembered she needed to charge her phone. Neither the phone nor the charger was in her duffel bag. She checked every pocket twice, then dumped everything out of her purse and searched through all the clutter. Not finding it, she stuffed the things she never left home without back into her bag, muttering all the while, even tossing in a few unladylike blasphemies, then decided to ask Michael if he knew where they were. After all, he had helped her pack.

She turned around, and there he was, leaning against the doorframe with her phone and charger in his hand. He hadn't made a sound, and she wondered how long he'd been standing there. And oh, did he look good. He wore a pair of khaki shorts he hadn't bothered to button and a white T-shirt that was molded to his body. The man was all muscle and heat, and she had the insane impulse to run to him and throw herself into his arms.

Michael didn't budge from where he stood. He couldn't take his eyes off her. God knows he tried. He knew that if he walked into her bedroom he wouldn't be leaving. He tossed her phone and charger on her bed, then crossed his arms so he wouldn't reach for her.

The same question nagged at him again. What the hell had happened to him? This time he knew the answer. Isabel had happened. His discipline and control vanished whenever he was around her. All he wanted to think about was touching her, and how messed up was that? She was all wrong for him, and he was definitely all wrong for her. Isabel was young and unaware of the treachery in the world; he was hardened by what he had seen and done and very familiar with treachery. His cynicism would wear her down and eventually destroy the goodness and joy inside her. Being together would end in disaster.

Michael knew she couldn't handle a casual affair. And with Isabel, neither could he. She was so different from all the other women he'd known. She looked at the world the way he wanted to, and maybe that was yet another reason he was drawn to her.

There was also another deterrent, the fact that she was Dylan's sister-in-law. Michael knew he'd never hear the end of it if he got involved with her. And yet he was in the mood to ignore all of his reasons to leave her alone.

Isabel couldn't imagine what was going on in his mind. He looked angry and perplexed at the same time. "Michael? What are you thinking about? You look so serious."

He didn't hesitate answering her. "I think you're probably the sexiest woman I've ever known."

Astounded, she whispered, "Oh." Then, "But you've never even kissed me." Frowning now, she walked over to stand in front of him. "I think you should."

Michael loved that she was blushing. Damn, she was sweet. "Yeah?" he said.

She slowly nodded. "Then you'd know."

Smiling, he said, "Yeah, then I'd know."

Staring into his eyes, she slowly put her arms around his neck. He didn't seem to be in any hurry, but she was suddenly impatient. She pulled on his hair so he would tilt his head toward her. She kissed the pulse at the base of his neck, using her tongue to tickle his skin, then kissed his chin, and with a sigh she tugged on his earlobe with her teeth.

Michael's heart felt as though it were slamming against his chest. He wrapped his arms around her and pulled her tight against him as his open mouth came down on hers. Her mouth was so warm; her lips were incredibly soft, and her tongue rubbing against his drove him crazy. He couldn't seem to get enough of her as his mouth slanted over hers. No other woman had ever affected him like this. He kept trying to bring her closer. His hands cupped her backside, lifting her up until her pelvis was pressed against him, and he growled low in his throat when she moved.

The kiss went on and on and kept getting hotter.

Michael knew he was losing control and abruptly drew back. "We've got to stop this," he said, and then he kissed her again, longer, harder, until both of them were shaking.

He came to his senses before she did. His hands had moved under her pajama top, and he was stroking the sides of her breasts. If he didn't stop, he would rip her clothes off and take her right then and there. It took all his strength to pull away from her. He saw the passion in her beautiful eyes and knew he'd rattled her, but then she'd done the same to him.

"I like kissing you." She whispered her confession and waited to see what he would do.

He didn't say a word. He simply stepped back into the hallway and pulled the door closed behind him.

Isabel stared at the door for a while, then walked to the window and gazed out at the night ocean. The moon cast a silver light on the water. It was churned up tonight, and the whitecaps looked like fat marshmallows. She smiled over the silly comparison.

Her mind wouldn't settle. She didn't know how long she stood there while she tried to make sense of what was happening to her, but she knew she couldn't avoid the truth any longer. She was actually beginning to like Dumbass.

God help her now.

TEN

THE FOLLOWING MORNING MICHAEL BROKE UP WITH HER, WHICH she thought was extremely odd since they hadn't even been dating. Honest to Pete, he took her aside right after breakfast to tell her they needed to go their separate ways.

Her reaction wasn't what Michael expected. She told him she thought he was out of his ever-loving mind. Then she laughed, which he didn't appreciate.

They went for a walk—his suggestion, not hers—so they could have some privacy for the scene he was sure she was going to make. But, as it turned out, he was the one who made the scene, not her.

They strolled along the shoreline in silence for a few minutes, and then he stopped to face her.

"I need to stay away from you," he said, his declaration sounding more like a reprimand.

"Then stay away," she said. "And the problem is solved."

When she smiled up at him with those big beautiful eyes, Michael clasped his hands behind his back to keep from taking her into his arms. He didn't dare look at her sweet mouth, or he'd lose the battle he'd been fighting since he'd kissed her last night.

"And you need to stay away from me."

"Okay."

"Isabel, I'm serious."

She didn't argue. She simply shrugged nonchalantly and said, "I know you are."

He felt he should explain his reasons, but at the moment, standing so close to her, he couldn't come up with any. Damn, she smelled good.

"This is lust between us, not love, and I worry you won't be able to tell the difference. I don't want you to get hurt." He pulled his gaze away from her face, looking past her shoulder at the waves hitting the rocks. "It would never work."

Isabel was reeling from his lust-not-love comment. Did he think she was an idiot? That she wouldn't know the difference between love and lust? Fortunately, she wasn't afflicted with either. Still, she wasn't a robot. She had feelings, and it hurt knowing he didn't want to have anything to do with her.

"I want you to understand—" he began.

She interrupted. "Are you going to list all the reasons we should go our separate ways, or would you like me to?" she asked.

"Go ahead."

She wasn't smiling now. "You have all sorts of degrees. You graduated from university at the top of your class, and you graduated from law school at the top. Then you took the bar and, according to your father, who told Kate who told me, you got the highest score. All of this suggests that you're very smart, Michael. I, on the other hand, took four and a half years . . ." She paused, took a breath, and then said, "Actually, it was five years because of all the extra classes I took. Yes, five to graduate from college, and I assure you I wasn't at the top of my class. I was somewhere in the middle, which would suggest that I'm pretty average."

She put her hand up when he looked as though he was going to interrupt. "All right, then," she continued. "So the first reason is that you're smart and I'm not." She turned and walked ahead of him as she continued. "You're also sophisticated, and you believe I'm naive. You've been all over the world, speak several languages, and have had all sorts of experiences, good and bad. I speak a little French and a little Spanish, but not well, and I haven't been anywhere."

"Are you finished?" he asked.

"Not quite," she said. "You're cynical, and I'm too trusting. I look for the good in others, or at least I try to, and you have been trained to look for the bad."

She was walking faster now, heading back to the house. "Oh, one last and probably least important reason. I assume you've had sex with a lot of women. You have, haven't you?"

He almost laughed. Man, had this conversation gotten away from him. "Yes, I've had sex with a few women."

She stopped to face him, waiting for him to ask her about her sex life. He remained silent. It obviously wasn't important to him. She was about to point out that he was experienced and she wasn't, then changed her mind. Turning back, she continued on her way to the house with him by her side. "And those, Michael, are just a few of the reasons we would never work."

Isabel didn't wait around to hear his rebuttal. When they reached the steps to the porch, she hurried inside, letting the screen door swing shut behind her.

Noah was walking past the dining room just as she was racing through. He spotted her and asked, "What's wrong?"

She forced a smile. "Nothing's wrong."

He didn't believe her but didn't pry. "Alec and I are going sailing. You want to come along?"

"Just the two of you in that big boat?"

"Michael's also going."

Oh, hell no, as Dylan would say. "It sounds fun, but I've already made plans." Her voice was strained, and she was sure he picked up on it. "Thanks for asking."

She turned and hurried up the stairs to her bedroom before Noah could insist she tell him what was bothering her. She would have to explain that Michael had broken up with her. Noah would be surprised, of course, and would say that he didn't know she and Michael were together. She would then respond, neither did she. How wacky was that?

A few minutes later she was sprawled out on the bed replaying the ludicrous conversation she'd had with Michael when it occurred to her that she was actually hiding in her bedroom until he left to go sailing.

"Enough already," she muttered. She wasn't going to hide from anyone.

Her cell phone rang then. It was Detective Samuel, who had a few questions about the man she'd seen on the street corner.

When she explained that she had glimpsed at the man for only a second, Samuel asked, "And you saw him again last night at the hotel?"

"I couldn't swear it was him," she admitted. "I saw a man with red hair coming toward me. The lobby was crowded but he seemed to be staring straight at me. Maybe I imagined him to be the same man."

"We've studied the hotel security tapes. We did see the man you describe, but he turned and left the hotel. He appeared to be in a hurry."

"I'm sorry if I've complicated things."

Samuel was sympathetic. "Don't be. This has been a traumatic experience for you. It's important that we look into every detail that you think you remember."

"*Think* I remember? What's that supposed to mean?"

"Under severe stress the mind can play tricks on us."

Isabel didn't disagree. Maybe she was overreacting and confusing her memories with reality.

Samuel went on to share some information about the investigation. "We've identified the man you shot. His name was Jacoby, and he has a criminal record a mile long. We've talked to the Miami police, and they've told us that Detective Walsh was in Boston on personal business but he mentioned something about helping a friend. We believe he was after Jacoby. We haven't sifted out the particulars yet, but with the Miami police involved now, we'll get to the bottom of this soon. We won't need you any longer, at least not for the time being, but I would appreciate it if you would keep us informed of your whereabouts just in case something comes up."

"I will," she promised.

"I want to thank you for your cooperation and your patience, Isabel," he said. "You're a very brave young lady."

She didn't agree. "I'm not so sure about that."

"I am," he insisted. "I'll let Michael know what we discussed."

"Actually, Michael won't be available. He isn't my attorney any longer. His brother Nick will be handling any legal issues from now on." She added, "He lives in Boston."

She hoped Nick was agreeable. She knew he was an attorney, and if he declined, she would ask Theo. Assuming she needed an attorney at all.

She had just ended the call when another came in. She didn't recognize the number but decided to answer anyway.

"Is this Isabel MacKenna?" There was something oddly familiar about the man's deep, baritone voice.

"Yes," she answered. "And who is this?"

"My name is Xavier O'Dell. I'm hoping you're familiar with my work and that you like it."

"Xavier . . . Did you say . . ."

She heard a long drawn-out sigh over the phone, and then he said, "I'm better known by my initials, XO."

She nearly dropped the phone. Even though she recognized the voice now, she couldn't believe it was really him. She burst into laughter. "No, you're not XO."

Did he honestly think she would believe the man she was talking to was XO, the most famous singer in the United States . . . perhaps even the world? And the hottest?

"Isabel?"

Snap out of it, she told herself. "Yes?"

"It really is XO, Isabel," he insisted. "I prefer Xavier, but it seems my fans prefer my initials. I'm not sure who started it, but it quickly caught on."

It took another five minutes to convince her. By then she was shaking from head to toe.

"I love your voice," she blurted.

"And I love yours," he replied. "I've watched your video at least a dozen times, and when I found out you were in Boston, I decided to call and ask a favor. I also have a business proposition for you."

"How did you find out I was in Boston? And how did you get my number?"

"I have a large staff. They've been looking for you."

"Oh," she said. She was so excited she could barely think. "What's the favor?"

"I'm performing at The Garden Friday night."

She knew The Garden. She'd been there before. It was a huge arena with maybe twenty thousand seats. It was an older facility, she remembered, but it had been updated and the acoustics were surprisingly good.

Xavier's concerts were always sold out just minutes after tickets were offered for sale. The Boston concert was no exception. She was hoping that XO would offer her tickets, but as it turned out he offered her much more.

At the end of XO's call Isabel thought her heart was going to explode, it was beating so fast. She ran down the steps. She found Nick and Dylan in the kitchen. They had architectural blueprints spread out on the table.

Nick was in the middle of asking a question but stopped when he saw Isabel's face. Her cheeks were flushed.

"What's the matter?" he asked.

"You're not going to believe . . . I mean, I can't believe it . . . It's crazy," she stammered. "Completely crazy . . ."

"Take a breath," Dylan suggested. He pulled out a chair next to him for her to sit.

She inhaled deeply, then said, "It's good news. But first things first. Michael's out. You're in, Nick, if you'll agree."

"Agree to what?" he asked.

"Agree to be my attorney if I need one to talk to Detective Samuel. It makes sense since you live in Boston. I know you travel for work, but you're based here," she hurried to add so he wouldn't ask her why Michael had been booted.

"Sure, I'll do it."

She sat down, took another deep breath, and tried to slow her racing heartbeat. "Do you know who Xavier O'Dell is? He's known as XO."

"Isabel, we aren't that old," Dylan said, exasperated. "We know who he is. Everyone knows him."

"Laurant loves him," Nick said. "She swears she'd leave me in a heartbeat for the man she calls a sex god."

Dylan laughed. "Sex god?"

"I can see that," Isabel said, nodding. "He kinda is a sex god. The man oozes sex appeal."

"What about him?" Dylan asked.

"He just called me."

"The sex god called you?" Nick looked astonished. "Are you sure it really was XO?"

"He prefers to be called Xavier," she said. "And yes, I'm sure it was him."

Dylan leaned back in his chair. "What did he want?"

"He told me he watched the video of me singing, and he liked it."

She appeared to be dazed, and Dylan laughed in reaction. "Of course he liked it."

"He said he watched it over a dozen times." She paused to shake her head. "I can't imagine why. It's not my best work."

"I thought it was pretty good," Nick told her.

"Isabel, you're sounding like Kate now," Dylan remarked. "Whenever she's excited or nervous about something, her voice takes on a thicker Southern drawl. Try to calm down before you pass out. Your face is bright red."

Calming down wasn't possible, but she did take a couple of long deep breaths. They actually helped. She finally got her mind to stop whirling and said, "He's performing at The Garden Friday night. This Friday night."

She looked at both of them and waited. She seemed to think they should know something she hadn't told them yet.

"And?" Nick prodded.

"Did he give you tickets? Is that why you're so excited?" Dylan asked.

"No. He wants me to be part of his concert. That's what he told me."

"Hold on a minute. Are you saying he wants you to sing onstage with him?" Dylan asked, trying to clarify.

"He wants me to sing my song from the video . . . alone . . . in front of thousands of people, and he also wants me to sing another song with him. Oh, and he wants to buy my song, and offered to pay me a heap of money."

"What's a heap?" Nick wondered.

When she told them the amount, they were both speechless. Their stunned expressions made her laugh.

"That much?" Dylan asked.

She nodded. "That much."

"Hell, that is a heap of money," Nick said.

"Xavier said he's going to email phone numbers, and my people are supposed to contact his people . . ."

Her voice trailed off while she thought about selling her songs.

It had always been her dream, and now it looked like it was coming true.

Dylan could tell from the look in Isabel's eyes that she had spaced out.

"Isabel, snap out of it."

"Yes?"

"What did you tell him when he asked you to have your people contact his people?" Nick asked.

"I told him I didn't have any people."

"Yes, you do," Dylan said. "Nick and Theo and Michael are all attorneys—"

"She needs an entertainment attorney," Nick suggested. "I'll find a good one for you, Isabel. Don't sign anything yet."

"I won't," she said.

Nick and Dylan spent a few minutes discussing the next steps to be taken, and when they finally turned their attention back to Isabel, she seemed to have deflated. She was leaning her elbow on the table with her chin in her hand, staring into space.

Dylan brought her back to the moment. "Isabel?"

"I don't think I can do it," she said, sitting up and shaking her head. "Xavier said he's sending a car Thursday. He's on tour now and will arrive in Boston late Wednesday night, and Thursday afternoon from one to three is the only time we can rehearse."

She couldn't be still another second and began to pace around the kitchen. Her mind was racing again. She took a bottle of root beer out of the refrigerator, opened it, and handed it to Dylan. Then she got another one out and gave it to Nick.

"Guess we're drinking root beer now," Nick whispered to his brother.

Dylan nodded. "Guess we are."

They were both watching Isabel pace.

"I should have said no right away. That's what I should have done.

I'm not ready to be a performer. I'm a songwriter." She was really starting to freak out, now that it was all sinking in.

"You got up onstage and sang. I watched the video," Nick said. "You didn't look at all nervous."

"I was drunk," she admitted. "Are you saying I'll have to get drunk every time I want to sing onstage? I can't do that . . . can I?"

"No, you can't," Dylan said.

"For God's sake, Isabel." Michael was standing right behind her.

She nearly jumped out of her skin when she heard his voice. She whirled around and demanded, "How long have you been standing there?"

"Long enough to hear you say you have to get drunk to sing." He shut the door behind him and looked at Dylan and Nick. "What's going on?"

Michael joined his brothers at the table, and Isabel continued to pace while Nick caught him up on the latest news. When Isabel opened the refrigerator, Dylan said, "Michael, you're getting a root beer."

"I don't want—"

"Just go with it," Dylan suggested.

Isabel walked over to the table, shoved the bottle into Michael's hand, and pulled a chair out. She didn't sit, though. She stood gripping the back of the chair. "Michael doesn't need to know what's going on. No one but you, Nick, and Dylan need to know. I don't want the rest of the family involved. This week is a celebration for your parents. I don't want anything to take the attention away from them."

"Yeah, okay," Dylan said. "The thing is . . ."

"Yes?"

"Nick just told Michael everything."

"Why did you do that?"

Nick shrugged. "He asked."

Isabel hadn't looked directly at Michael since he walked in. That bothered him more than he wanted to admit.

"You're going to tell Kate, aren't you?" Dylan asked.

"Absolutely. I tell her everything." That wasn't exactly true. There were things she didn't want to share with her sister—like kissing Michael and then getting dumped by him—because it would only upset her. There was also the fact that Kate loved to lecture. She must, Isabel thought, because she did it so often.

Emotionally exhausted, she fell into the chair and reached for Michael's root beer. She took a drink, then handed it back to him. She finally looked directly at him. "Why aren't you sailing?"

"I changed my mind."

An awkward silence followed his reply. Not wanting to give the impression that she cared one way or the other, Isabel turned to Dylan. "What are these blueprints?"

"Kate and I want to remodel the house. The electrical is shot, and the pipes are old and corroded."

"Why not sell it and build somewhere else? Or tear it down and start over if you and Kate like the neighborhood."

Dylan looked thunderstruck. "You wouldn't mind selling your family's house?"

"It isn't my house. It's yours and Kate's."

He started to disagree, but she stopped him when she put her hand on top of his and said, "I know I'll always have a place to stay if things don't work out for me. But I don't have any emotional connection to the house now. My connection is with you and Kate and Kiera."

Dylan nodded. "Yes, you'll always have a home with us."

Nick wanted to talk about XO. "Xavier is sending a car for Isabel Thursday to rehearse," he told Michael.

"She's not going alone," Michael stated as though he had the last word on the matter.

"Of course I'm going alone," Isabel protested, making no effort to hide her irritation. He had no right to order her to do anything.

"I don't think you should," he countered. "The man running toward you in the hotel is still out there."

"Detective Samuel watched the surveillance video. He believes the man was just in a hurry. He also thinks my mind was playing tricks on me because seeing the man triggered the memory of the redhead standing on the corner when I was helping Detective Walsh. I'd forgotten all about him until I saw the man in the lobby. The memory came back then."

"You shouldn't go anywhere alone," Michael insisted.

Michael's frown could ignite a fire, yet it didn't faze her. "You needn't worry about this, Michael. You're no longer my attorney."

"You're out. I'm in," Nick said, grinning. "You're going to have to catch me up on the investigation. You know, background information in case Isabel is pulled back in by Samuel."

"Why am I out and he's in?" Michael asked Isabel.

Because you're a bonehead, and he isn't. If they had been alone, she would have said exactly that, but they weren't alone, and so she said, "It's complicated, and I'd rather not go into it now."

"Like it or not, I'm back in, babe," Michael told her.

"I don't like it."

"Too bad."

"Michael, you're such a pain."

"And you're not?"

"I'm trying to be polite."

"It's not working."

Nick felt as though he were watching a tennis match. "You see what I'm seeing?" he whispered.

Dylan nodded. "Yes, I do. I'm not sure I like it."

Nick agreed. There were sparks flying all over the kitchen.

"I'm through discussing this," Isabel said, then turned to Dylan. "Xavier is interested in buying some of my other songs. I'll download what I can, and I have a few on an old flash drive here, but it's saturated with blood. Do you think a technician could clean it without wiping the songs?"

"How did your flash drive get blood all over it?" Nick wanted to know.

"It was in my pocket. When that poor Detective Walsh fell into my arms, there was blood everywhere."

"I can get a technician to clean it for you," Nick said.

"Thank you."

Her mind was suddenly racing again. "There's so much to do. Xavier wants to hear some of my songs, but I'll have to organize them first and put them all in one file."

"And make a couple of copies," Dylan suggested.

"Yes, I will," she agreed. "But getting all my songs together will take time."

"What about copyright?" Michael said.

"Taken care of."

"That's smart thinking," Nick said.

She wished she could take credit. "Dylan made sure I protected each song."

"With everything going on, you aren't still planning to go to Scotland next Monday, are you?" Dylan asked.

"Everything is scheduled. I can't see any reason to cancel."

"Who's going with you?"

She didn't want to answer because she knew all three brothers would try to stop her.

"I haven't decided yet."

"But you will take someone with you?" Dylan persisted.

Here we go, she thought. She might as well get the storm over with now. Bracing herself, she said, "I thought I'd go by myself."

"Someone should go with you. Someone who can drive," Dylan said. Turning to Nick, he explained, "Kate was going to go with Isabel, but a problem at work needs her attention, and she can't put it off."

"I'm perfectly capable of going by myself. In fact, I much prefer it. I can go at my own pace, take detours if I want, and I . . ." She stopped when she realized Dylan's and Michael's minds were set, and so she decided to humor them, which meant telling a little lie. "Oh, all right. I'll ask Damon. He'll go with me."

"Oh, hell no," Michael blurted.

Isabel pushed her chair back and stood. Hands on hips, she frowned at him and demanded, "What is wrong with you?"

Michael also stood, towering over her. Looking just as irritated, he snapped, "Hell if I know."

ELEVEN

ISABEL WATCHED MICHAEL WALK OUT OF THE KITCHEN AND FELT like throwing her hands up. "He is the most aggravating man."

She didn't expect Michael's brothers to agree with her and was pleasantly surprised when they both nodded.

Determined to put him out of her mind, an almost impossible feat, she ran upstairs to get the bloody flash drive, then placed it in a Ziploc bag and handed it over to Nick.

"I've got to go into the office for a little while this afternoon. I'll drop it off then," he said. "If they're slammed—and they usually are—it might be a few days before anyone can get to it. Are you okay with that?"

"Of course. You're doing a huge favor for me, and I really appreciate it."

While she was still in the kitchen, Dylan showed her the blueprints for the remodel. He had included a large bedroom for her. It was a comfort knowing that Kate and Dylan included her in their plans; however, by the time it was finished, she'd hopefully be making enough money to be out on her own.

Dylan and Nick made sandwiches and then headed out. As soon as she was alone, she started cleaning the kitchen. Lucy, the housekeeper, had taken time off but would be back late this afternoon. Isabel wanted the kitchen to be spotless when she arrived, which was no small feat with the brothers constantly digging through the refrigerator and the cabinets looking for food. They acted like bears getting ready to hibernate.

The family dinner was tomorrow night, the actual date of their parents' marriage. The menu was set with all of their favorite dishes, and it would be only the immediate family . . . and her. Isabel didn't think she should attend because she wasn't part of the immediate family, but Dylan was insistent. Helping any way she could made her feel as though she was contributing and wasn't taking advantage of the Buchanans' kindness and generosity.

She was scrubbing the countertop when Judge Buchanan and his wife walked in. Thrilled to see them, she dropped the sponge and ran to greet them.

Mrs. Buchanan—Elizabeth to her husband and friends—was an elegant lady. The sparkle in her eyes gave her a youthful appearance. The only sign of her years was the short silver hair that framed her face. She was the kind of woman who could wear anything and be the most fashionable woman in the room. Her smile, so warm and genuine, made her even more beautiful. It was obvious to Isabel that both Jordan and Sidney had inherited their grace and elegance from her.

Judge Buchanan was an older version of his sons. He was as tall as they were and just as handsome as Michael, even at his advanced age. The wrinkles on his face from years of sun and wind while sailing his boat didn't detract from his appearance. In fact, they made him look even more handsome. There was such dignity about him in the way he walked and the way he spoke, and there was kindness, too. She felt she could talk to the judge about anything, just as she could with Dylan. Well, almost anything. There were probably some things even the judge wouldn't want to discuss. Like her sex life. That would probably be a topic to avoid. She could never talk to him or Dylan about that. The mere thought made her shudder.

Isabel realized her head was in the clouds again and forced herself to pay attention to what the judge was telling her. Or as Michael would say, she needed to focus on the task at hand.

She made iced tea with mint for them and sat in the living room while they told her all about their mini vacation. Isabel noticed they smiled at each other often. The love flowing between them was enviable, and she hoped that one day she would experience the same.

"Now it's your turn, Isabel. Catch us up on your life," the judge insisted. "Anything exciting going on?"

If he only knew. She smiled but was saved from answering when Mrs. Buchanan said, "You'll soon be on your way to Scotland, won't you?"

"Yes. I'm going to see the land my great-uncle left me. I talked to the solicitor in Dunross, Scotland, who is handling the inheritance, so I'll be meeting with him. I really don't know much about it except that it's a very large piece of land in the Highlands. I'll be going next week as long as there aren't any setbacks. I guess you could say there have been a few glitches . . ."

"Glitches?" Michael laughed after repeating the word as he strode into the living room.

"That's code for 'not wishing to discuss this now,' Michael," she said through a clinched smile. "Your parents just returned home. It's a festive occasion, you . . ." Dear God, she'd almost called him a jerk in front of his parents. What was the matter with her? From the way Michael was looking at her, she was pretty sure he had guessed she'd almost blurted out something inappropriate about him.

"If you'll excuse me, I need to attend to something upstairs." She didn't give anyone time to ask her questions but rushed up to the bedroom she now thought of as her hideaway.

As lovely and kind as all the Buchanans were, Isabel changed her mind about not staying at the Hamilton. There she wouldn't face the risk of running into Michael all the time. Even being in the same room with him made her nervous. Michael would have a good laugh if he knew how easily he rattled her. One kiss and she was ready to rip her clothes off . . . and his. She was in over her head. And Michael? He couldn't care less about her. That little kiss hadn't fazed him . . . the big jerk.

Enough already. She didn't want to think about him any longer. Keeping busy was the solution. With that notion in mind she opened her laptop and began to answer her emails. It took a long while and she was about to close up when another email appeared. This one was from Xavier. She was almost afraid to open it. Her immediate thought was that he had changed his mind and no longer wanted her to sing, which would have been a disappointment but also a big relief. Just thinking about getting up onstage in front of thousands of people terrified her. There was another worry, too. What if he changed his mind and no longer wanted to buy her song? That would be devastating.

"Just open the thing," she whispered.

The message Xavier sent was upbeat, telling her how eager he was to meet her. He also included a clip of him onstage singing the song he wanted Isabel to sing with him. He thought she might want to work on it, and Thursday they'd sing it together as many times as necessary to get it the way he wanted. He also explained that he had reserved a suite overlooking the stage for her family and friends. His assistant just needed to know the number of tickets Isabel would need. He added his assistant's email address and ended his email with his full name.

Her thought to keep quiet about Xavier and let the focus be on the parents' celebration wasn't possible now. Isabel would tell all of them tonight, she decided.

The next order of business was for Isabel to "man up," as Dylan would say, and watch the video of her shooting that horrible man.

She found the text the woman on the street had sent and activated the video. As she watched it, she paid close attention to Detective Walsh stumbling into her arms. Just as she suspected, he was mumbling something to her, but she couldn't make out what he was saying.

"Isabel?" Michael knocked on her door and said her name again. "Come in."

He opened the door and said, "Do you still want to see Detective Walsh?"

"Yes, I do. Now?"

"Yes, now."

She didn't know why Michael was suddenly being accommodating, but she wasn't going to question his motives if it meant he'd take her to Walsh.

"Give me five minutes. I'll meet you downstairs."

It took her fifteen minutes to change. At her request, the bell captain had put her suitcase for Scotland in storage, and most of the clothes she had brought in her backpack were meant for a casual visit to Nathan's Bay, but thankfully she had thought to pack a couple of dresses. She quickly changed into a yellow cotton sundress and hurried downstairs.

Michael had changed, too. Instead of jeans he wore khaki pants and a button-down shirt with the cuffs turned back. Even when he didn't try, he looked gorgeous.

When they reached the hospital, they cut through the emergency waiting room to get to the elevators. The ICU was quiet. A nurse wearing the name tag "Terry" was behind the desk. The second Isabel introduced herself, the nurse's face lit up. As she led them down the hall to Walsh's room, she gushed, "I took your advice, and you were right," she said. "I did overreact. John and I had a long talk, and we've decided to keep the dog, slobber and all."

"I'm glad you worked it out," Isabel said.

A uniformed policeman stood by Walsh's door. When they identified themselves, he told them Samuel had authorized their visit, and he let them pass.

A multitude of tubes and wires were hooked up to the poor man. The nurse explained that the breathing apparatus had been removed, and he was breathing on his own now. There were other improvements as well, but he was still unconscious, and everyone was anxious for him to open his eyes.

Isabel thought he looked peaceful in sleep, and yet she still wanted to shake him to help him wake up. She didn't give in to the temptation, thank goodness, not only because it would be wrong to manhandle a patient, but also because the guard was giving her suspicious looks. Later that same guard was telling her how he was drowning in debt. All she had done to elicit such a lengthy declaration was to thank him for watching out for Detective Walsh and ask him if this was his usual duty.

Isabel listened to his worries for a good ten minutes before he finished. She shook his hand, wished him well, and was ready to leave, but then one of the orderlies wanted to chat with her. Michael guessed it was going to take a while, so he leaned back against the wall with arms crossed and waited. He couldn't figure out why people were so prone to unload their problems on her. She didn't hand out any wisdom. As to that, she didn't say much of anything. She usually engaged them in conversation, chatting amicably about mundane things. Once they started talking, she just listened and nodded every now and again. Michael noticed that everyone who talked to her walked away smiling. It was, in his opinion, the strangest thing he had ever seen, and it kept happening. People were drawn to her . . . just like he was, though he sure as certain wasn't going to pour *his* heart out to her.

He had to drag her out of the hospital or they never would have left.

"Why are you in such a hurry?" she asked, trying to keep up with him as they walked down the hospital corridor.

"I have things to do," he said.

She checked the time and then said, "Do you have plans tonight?"

"Yes."

No further explanation, just a simple "yes." She guessed what that meant. He had a date. Probably with that lawyer, Amanda Something-

or-Other. She wasn't going to grill him. If he didn't want to tell her, she wasn't going to nag.

"That nurse . . . ," Michael began, as he turned the key in the car's ignition.

"What nurse?"

"The one behind the desk."

"You mean Terry," she said, turning toward him. "What about her?"

"When did you talk to her?"

"I've talked to her several times on the phone," she explained. "I'd called to check on Detective Walsh, and she answered. She's a lovely woman, isn't she?"

"Yeah, sure," he said. "She thanked you for all your advice, but you didn't give her any, did you?"

"I asked her how her day was going, and she told me."

He shook his head. "It's the damnedest thing."

"What is? That people need someone to listen to them? There are a lot of lonely people in the world who don't have anyone to turn to. You wouldn't understand because you come from such a big family. If you need anything, you can turn to your brothers and sisters, and you have parents who love you. I hope you realize how fortunate you are."

He glanced over at her and said, "Yes, I do realize how fortunate I am. What about you? Were you lonely growing up?"

"No, not at all," she replied. "I was very close to my mother."

"And your sisters?"

"Yes."

"But they weren't around all that much, were they? Kiera was away at college and medical school, and Kate went away to college, then got her graduate degree in business—"

"Okay, no, they weren't home all that often, but I knew they would be there if I needed them."

Several minutes passed in silence, and then Michael said, "Were they home when your mother got sick?"

"Off and on," she answered. "Toward the end our aunt Nora moved in to help."

He nodded. "I understand now."

"Understand what?"

"You have tremendous empathy for others, and that's why they're drawn to you."

"They? Who are you talking about?"

"Terry, the nurse," he said. "And the orderly. What was he telling you? He looked agitated."

"His name is Cruz, and he was upset. He told me he's one of six children, and their single mother raised them. Now she's sick, and none of them want to take her into their home and care for her. The more he talked, the more he realized that her children have an obligation to take care of her."

"What do you think?"

"Brothers and sisters and parents should be loyal to one another, no matter what."

He reached over and put his hand on top of hers. "I agree."

Michael was slowly beginning to realize how much he liked being with Isabel. When he first met her at Dylan's wedding and wasn't trying his damnedest to avoid her, he had thought her opinions were naive, but now he realized how strong her character was. He had learned not to trust anyone but his family and his SEAL team brothers. Trust was unconditional with all of them. Outsiders weren't to be trusted. In his past line of work, that was the reason he stayed alive.

"Do you trust Dylan unconditionally?" he asked.

"Yes, I do." There wasn't any hesitation at all.

"Do you trust me unconditionally?"

"Yes." Again, no hesitation. Before he could gloat, and Isabel was sure that he would, she added a caveat. "And I can't give you a reason why."

On one hand, Isabel aggravated the hell out of him, and on the other, she made him feel good. His only explanation was that his reactions to her were just plain crazy.

"I'm not going to ask if you trust me unconditionally," she continued, "because I know the answer. You're too cynical to trust anyone out of your core group."

He didn't disagree. Instead, he changed the subject. "There's the bridge to home. Notice the sign on that post?"

"Yes."

"What does it say?"

Here we go again. Isabel silently groaned. "Do not pass. The sign says, 'Do not pass.' Michael, are we going to argue again?"

Fortunately, her cell phone rang before he could get worked up thinking about their near misses while she was driving. She didn't bother to see who was calling. A minute later she wished she had. James Reid was on the line, and he was even more eager than the last time he'd called.

She decided to share the conversation with Michael and put Reid on speaker.

"You don't want to miss out on this fantastic opportunity, Miss MacKenna. Really, you don't. The price the Patterson Group will pay is quite high." He added, "Yes, it is. You won't get that much from anyone else, but you must act now. The deal could go away," he warned. "And we don't want that to happen."

Isabel thought Mr. Reid sounded like a spokesman in a late-night television infomercial.

"I can't make a decision yet. I'd like to see the land first."

His tone suddenly changed, and now he sounded sincerely concerned. "Miss MacKenna, it would be most awkward if you were to come. Most awkward."

She looked at Michael and rolled her eyes. James Reid was given to drama, she decided.

"And why is that?"

"You won't be welcome. To most of the people around Glen Mac-Kenna you're a pretender and don't deserve the land. They'll be hostile. Why would you want to be put in that situation? It could be dangerous for you. Sell it now and be rid of the worry."

She kept her voice pleasant. "You've given me quite a lot to think about. As soon as I make a decision, I'll let you know."

"When? When will that be?"

"As soon as I make a decision, I'll let you know. Bye now."

He was blabbering when she disconnected the call.

Arriving back at Nathan's Bay, Michael parked the car and rushed around to open the door for Isabel, but she was already heading to the house.

"See you later," she called over her shoulder.

Isabel had to get away from him. One minute she was arguing with him, and the next she was sharing her personal thoughts. She was suddenly feeling overwhelmed with frustration and confusion. She never should have come to Nathan's Bay. If she had had an inkling of how she would react to Michael, she would have gone home after graduation and flown to Scotland from there. Lust, she decided, was a terrible affliction, and she wanted no part of it.

Needing to get rid of some of her nervous energy, she changed into her workout clothes to go for a run. Unfortunately, she didn't realize how hot the weather was until she was out in it. The sun beat down on her, and she was drenched with sweat by the time she returned to the house.

A cold shower revived her. She put on a different pair of shorts and a tank top, found her flip-flops, and went downstairs. She found Kate on the front porch sipping iced tea. Her long hair was up in a ponytail and she was fanning herself with a magazine. The second she spotted Isabel, she started talking. "How long were you in the sun? You've got a sunburn. Did you use sunscreen?"

"Of course I did," she answered. "I want to talk to you about—"

It was as far as she got before Kate launched into her day. "I wish you had gone with us. I know you hate shopping, but you would have had fun with us. We stopped at the Hamilton for lunch, and there's this fantastic women's clothing shop in the back near the promenade. It's called the Madison," she added. "I swear I wanted every dress. There were several that Regan and I thought you would look stunning in, so Regan put a hold on them and added quite a few casual outfits for you to try on. We'll go Thursday afternoon. You need a new wardrobe now that you're out of college. I also deposited ten thousand dollars in your checking account this morning. You'll need it for your expenses."

"Kate, just because you and Dylan have money doesn't mean you should support me. I'm not going to be a charity case. I'm giving the money back."

"No, it's a gift, Isabel. You're my sister. Dylan and I want to help. Just say, 'Thank you.'"

Isabel couldn't get her back up because Kate was being so sweet. "Thank you," she said. "How long will the shop hold the clothes?"

"As long as Regan wants them to," Kate answered. "The Madison is owned by the Hamilton, and the Hamilton hotels are owned by . . ."

"Regan and her brothers," Isabel said. "I am going to need some clothes," she admitted then. "Most of my wardrobe is college grunge. I do have two nice dresses. I wore the blue one when I went to the club and sang."

"We'll have fun," Kate promised. "I've missed you, and the last couple of weeks have been crazy with work. It's nice to kick back and relax."

"Thursday isn't going to work for me. Any chance we could go tomorrow?"

"I could make it work. What's going on Thursday?"

Isabel got up from her chair and went over to the porch swing. It looked so inviting. "You aren't going to believe me, but I swear I'm telling the truth."

Kate frowned. "What'd you do?"

How like Kate to assume that Isabel had screwed up. Of course, the assumption was based on the fact that there had been more than a few times she had, in fact, screwed up.

"Do you know who XO is?" She didn't give her sister time to answer, but continued on. "He called me. I'm rehearsing with him Thursday afternoon, and Friday night I'm performing with him at The Garden." She laughed then and said, "Kate, your mouth is open, and you look like you just got tasered."

It took a full minute for Kate to react. Once it sank in, she shouted, she was so excited. "Oh, please let me be there when you tell Laurant," she begged. "She's going to die when she hears . . . and Regan will flip, and . . . oh my God, Isabel . . ."

Isabel patiently waited while her sister rambled on and on, and then blurted, "Kate, I'm so nervous about meeting him."

Kate didn't downplay or make light of Isabel's worries. "I'd be in a panic, too, I think, walking on the stage with thousands of people watching. Maybe you can figure out a way to block them and concentrate on your song. I wish I could come up with something better," she admitted. "And even though I know you won't believe me, I think you're going to be phenomenal. Mom would be so proud of you."

"I'm not so sure of that."

Before Kate could argue, she told her about the promise their mother had asked Isabel to make just before she died.

Kate became teary-eyed. "Oh, Isabel, why didn't you tell Kiera and me? You sang all the time, and I never could understand why you let it go when you went off to college. Now I realize what you sacrificed. I'm so sorry. Mother shouldn't have asked you to give up what you love. Music is part of who you are."

"Mother was worried I wouldn't be able to support myself. I don't think she had a lot of faith in me. I know she didn't want me in what she called a cutthroat business. Toward the end she was afraid, and I would have agreed to anything to give her peace." She took a breath and said, "It's been over five years and I still miss her."

"I miss her, too," Kate said.

The two sisters spent several minutes reminiscing about some of the happier times they'd had with their mother.

"We never could pull anything over on her," Kate said, a note of pride in her voice.

They were laughing over one particular plan Isabel had hatched, when Regan came out to join them. Her reaction to Isabel's news about Xavier was as enthusiastic as Kate's had been, and she agreed they needed to go back to the clothing boutique tomorrow for Isabel.

"Where's Laurant?" Kate asked. "She'll freak when she hears."

"She and Nick went home to be with the kids. They'll be back tomorrow with Samantha and Tommy for the family dinner."

Isabel sat quietly while the two women discussed what she should wear to rehearse with XO and what she should wear onstage. Every time Xavier's name came up Isabel could feel her stomach tighten. She wasn't sure if it was due to excitement or anxiety. When she wasn't worrying about XO, she was thinking about Michael. He'd been crowding her thoughts since she'd arrived in Boston. What was he doing now? she wondered, barely stopping herself before asking her sister. She really needed to get a grip.

Scotland was looking better and better. If she could, she'd leave tonight.

LATER THAT EVENING MICHAEL WAITED UNTIL ISABEL HAD LEFT the living room to talk to the others about safety concerns, and it was decided that Nick would accompany her to the rehearsal with Xavier. Noah would let Nick know their plan as soon as he called to check in. It was up to Michael to let Isabel know what was decided.

She was out in the sunroom, curled up on the sofa with her pen and notepad in hand. He stood just inside the doorway, watching her. He noticed every little thing about her. Her legs were a bit sunburned and so were her arms and her face. Her hair had white-blond streaks in it now, and he remembered how silky it felt.

Hell, he was at it again.

"Isabel." He said her name as he walked over to the sofa and sat down next to her.

She moved her feet out of the way in the nick of time. "There are other places to sit in this room."

"I like sitting here."

She refused to get into an argument over such a silly thing. "Did you want something?"

"Yes," he answered. "Nick is going to go with you to the rehearsal, and if I can move a couple of appointments, I'm going to tag along."

"Why?"

"We want to meet him."

"What's the real reason?"

"We decided that Nick would go with you because he carries a badge and a gun."

"Why is that important?" She was looking at him as though she thought he had lost his mind.

"We don't know anything about Xavier and his crew."

"His staff," she corrected.

"Okay, staff," he patiently repeated. "Better safe than sorry."

"In other words, if anyone tries something, Nick will shoot him or you'll punch him?"

That sounded good to him.

"Whose wacky idea was this?" she asked, and before he could come up with an answer, she guessed. "It was yours, wasn't it?"

He shrugged, then decided to justify his actions. "You don't know anything about these people, so yeah, I did suggest—"

"That you and Nick intimidate everyone?"

Okay, yes, that was exactly what he wanted to do. "I don't want anyone messing with you."

She couldn't make up her mind if he was being sweet or insulting. She placed her notepad and pen on the table and stood. Crossing her arms, she said, "I can take care of myself, Michael."

She turned to leave, then changed her mind. "And another thing. You told me to stay away from you, and you were going to stay away from me. Remember? So how come every time I turn around, there you are? You might as well stop trying to drive me crazy. Thanks to you, I'm already there."

With those parting words, she stormed out.

TWELVE

WEDNESDAY WAS A BLUR OF ACTIVITY. AS MUCH AS ISABEL HATED shopping, she had to admit she had fun with Kate and Regan at the Madison. She was sure she tried on at least a dozen outfits, and Kate insisted on buying most of them. Then Isabel was tugged and pinned by an exuberant alteration lady named Vera, who couldn't stop raving about Isabel's figure. And since she was a woman who liked to talk while she worked, she also told Isabel all about her cheating brother-in-law. While the woman confided her long list of worries, Isabel stood patiently with her hands folded, nodding every now and then. Once Vera had marked her last hem and aired her last complaint, she packed her pins and tape measure back into her sewing basket, but before she left, she gave Isabel a warm hug as though she was saying good-bye to one of her closest friends.

Kate took the scene in stride, but Regan was mesmerized. When Vera had exited and Isabel had stepped behind the curtain to change back into her own clothes, Regan turned to Kate, "Did you hear what Vera said?"

Kate was flipping through the store's catalog. Without looking up she said, "Yes, I heard."

"Isabel barely said anything at all."

"I know."

"Yet Vera hugged her."

"Uh-huh."

"It was . . . bizarre . . . wasn't it?"

"Uh-huh."

Regan began to laugh. "You're used to it, aren't you?"

Kate looked up from the catalog, smiling. "Oh yes. It happens all the time."

"Okay, I'm ready to leave," Isabel announced, stepping out of the dressing room.

"Have you decided what you'll wear onstage?" Regan asked.

Kate thought her sister should wear the hot pink top with a new pair of skinny jeans and stilettos.

The suggestion made Isabel laugh. "You want me to wear stilettos onstage? I'd fall on my backside in front of thousands of people."

Regan stepped in before the argument escalated. She suggested that Isabel consider the black suit. She could push the sleeves up on the fitted jacket and wear the brilliant blue sequined camisole with it to add sparkle. The skintight ankle pants would show off her long slender legs, especially if she wore the stiletto heels Kate wanted. She also suggested Isabel take a backup outfit and recommended the gorgeous silk dress she'd chosen for her. The low-cut neckline was a bit daring, but the top was so fitted it wouldn't slip or show anything inappropriate when she moved around, and the short, flared skirt swayed with each step she took. The color was stunning, a cerulean blue that brought out the exact color of her eyes. Barely-there nude high heels would be perfect. Although she had worn a blue dress onstage at Finnegan's, there wasn't anything similar about the two dresses. The new one was elegant, very sophisticated, and extremely sexy. Regan raved about it; Kate also loved it but worried it was a little too provocative.

"Spoken like a true big sister," Regan said. "Admit it, Kate. She looks incredible in the dress. XO is bound to lose his voice when he sees her." Turning to Isabel, she said, "The clothes will be ready tomorrow afternoon. I'll get them for you and bring them out. I have to be in the city anyway."

Isabel was astonished the alterations could happen that quickly, and she was most thankful. Thinking their shopping spree was over, she was ready to head back to Nathan's Bay, but Kate and Regan had other ideas. They took her to an intimate apparel shop to buy new undergarments and sleepwear, and when they were finished, all three of them walked out with bags filled.

There was more. Shoe shopping was next. That also took longer than Isabel wanted. Once that was done, Kate thought they should look at jewelry. Isabel had to put her foot down then. She was starving, and the only thing she wanted was lunch.

While they were eating salads, she noticed the look Regan and Kate exchanged, and she also saw them check their watches a number of times. She knew they had another plan in the works, but she didn't find out what they had conjured up until after they'd eaten.

"We thought it would be fun for you to get a haircut and makeover," Kate said.

"Just a trim," Regan explained as she signed the tab.

"Your appointment is here at the hotel in fifteen minutes."

"It shouldn't take much time," Kate assured her.

It was two against one, and not wanting to appear ungrateful, Isabel reluctantly agreed. An hour later she had to admit it was worth it. She left the hotel with yet another bag filled with makeup, hair products, and lotions.

Laden with their purchases, Isabel returned to Nathan's Bay exhausted. She wasn't used to so much fuss over her appearance. All she wanted was a few minutes to decompress, but when Dylan, Theo, and Michelle stopped her and asked her to go sailing with them, she changed her mind. It was hot and humid, and a couple of hours on the water sounded ideal. She rushed to change into shorts and a tank top.

A half hour later she was on the boat watching Dylan manipulate the sails to catch the wind that sent them flying across the bay into the open waters. It was like watching a beautifully choreographed ballet, and soon they were skimming the waves. Isabel stretched out on the deck and raised her face to the sun, letting the wind blow through her hair. For the rest of the afternoon there were no worries.

She was having a wonderful time, but unfortunately her escape from the world came to an end when Dylan checked his watch and announced they were heading back to shore. The family dinner was tonight, and no one wanted to be late.

Back at the house, Isabel passed the dining room and saw the table was set for dinner. The Buchanans were all being so gracious to include her, but she didn't feel comfortable. This was supposed to be a special occasion for the immediate family. She would rather join in the celebration when other friends and family came for the party on Saturday. Thinking she would grab a bite later, she went looking for her sister to explain.

She walked into the kitchen just in time to hear Kate call Mrs. Buchanan Mom. She was so shocked, she actually froze for a second. Both Michael and Dylan saw the look on her face, but before either one could say anything, Isabel turned around. Without a thought as to where she was going, she went out the front door, brushing past Judge Buchanan, who was coming up the steps. She stopped just long enough to tell him she was going for a walk, promising she wouldn't be gone long.

Isabel needed to be alone for a few minutes so she could figure out her crazy reaction to hearing Kate call another woman Mom. She felt as though she'd been hit hard in the stomach, and for that instant she'd been flooded with grief. And wasn't that ridiculous? Calling someone else Mom didn't make Kate disloyal. Their mother was gone now, and Kate's love for her hadn't diminished. Hearing the word had been a shock, that was all, and she was thankful she'd been able to hide her reaction from everyone.

She headed down to the shore, then changed her mind and made a detour to sit on the hill overlooking the water. There was a beautiful tree she fancied to be at least a hundred years old with thick branches that arched out and down halfway to the ground. From the distance it reminded Isabel of a giant umbrella. It was secluded and peaceful.

She sat down with her back against the tree trunk. Folding her hands in her lap, she closed her eyes and listened to the sound of the waves lapping against the rocks and tried to quiet her thoughts. It was lovely to be alone, away from the chaos for a little while.

Michael was suddenly standing over her. So much for solitude.

"What are you doing?" he asked.

"Relaxing," she answered, shading her eyes with her hand as she looked up at him. "I've decided this is my new favorite spot on the island."

"You can relax later," he said. "Come on. It's time for dinner."

"You go ahead. I'm not hungry."

He reached down, grabbed her hand, and pulled her up. She wanted to point out that it was a family dinner and that she wasn't family, but she thought that would sound childish.

She turned to the shore. "I'll just stretch my legs—"

"Good idea," he said.

She walked around him and continued on.

He caught up to her and anchored her to his side, putting his arm around her shoulders and turning her back toward the house. She was about to demand that he let go of her, but then she looked up and lost her train of thought. His smile knocked her off her game. Why did he have to be so sinfully sexy? When she was around him, all she wanted to do was grab hold and never let go. And if she did exactly that? He would eat her alive and then move on.

No, thank you.

"Nick and Laurant just arrived with Samantha and the Wild One. It's time for dinner," he told her.

"The Wild One?"

"Tommy's almost two. He's a handful. It bothered you when Kate called my mother 'Mom,' didn't it?"

He didn't miss anything, did he? No reason to lie because he'd know it. "Yes, and I can't stop thinking about it. It was a ridiculous reaction." With a shrug, she added, "It just surprised me, that's all."

They went up the steps together and stopped on the porch. Before she had an inkling of what he was going to do, he leaned down and, wrapping his big strong arms around her, kissed her long and hard.

For Isabel the kiss was mind-blowing. Her whole body went limp. She wanted to say something, but her pounding heartbeat drowned out any words. She prayed for a coherent thought.

"You . . . you . . ." She sounded like a blithering idiot.

He had the gall to smile at her. He knew how rattled she was, and he seemed to get a kick out of it.

"Now you've got something else to think about," he said.

He walked into the house and left her standing on the porch. Threading her fingers through her hair, she rushed after him. "You have to stop doing that."

She almost bumped into him when he turned around and looked at her. "Yeah, I probably should."

"Probably should what?" Dylan asked the question. He was standing just inside the dining room with all of the family behind him, gathered around the table.

Michael looked like he was going to explain, but thankfully, Judge Buchanan saved her from mortification.

"Dinner's ready. Come sit down," he ordered, pulling a chair out next to him.

There was no getting out of it now. Tonight Isabel was a member of the family.

THIRTEEN

ISABEL WAS A NERVOUS WRECK. BY THE TIME SHE HAD FINISHED dressing to meet Xavier, she was shaking in her flats. He'd told her to wear comfortable clothes, and she took him at his word. She put on her favorite pair of skinny jeans and one of her new blouses. The color was jade green and quite flattering, according to Regan, who picked it out. After she brushed her hair, Isabel added a touch of makeup, lip gloss, and a dab of her favorite perfume.

Panic was trying to grab hold. Her mind conjured up all sorts of horrible scenarios. She pictured herself walking onto the stage and her throat closing, making it impossible to sing. Or she would walk onto the stage, smile at the audience, and throw up. Wouldn't that be lovely? Crazy thoughts were tripping over each other. What if they hated her voice and booed her? What if she fainted? Worse, what if she slipped and went flying into the audience?

Kate and her sisters-in-law took Isabel's mind off her fears. Xavier's car wouldn't be there to pick her up for another forty-five minutes, so Isabel went into the kitchen to get something cold to drink. Laurant, Regan, and Kate were all sitting at the table. All three of them had makeup on and were wearing pretty sundresses.

"Are you all going out to dinner somewhere?" Isabel asked.

"No, we're just hanging out," Laurant answered casually.

Isabel was slow to catch on. "But you're all dressed up."

"We're a little bored," Regan told her. "And we thought it might be fun to go with you. You know . . . keep you company while you rehearse with Xavier."

Isabel started laughing. Then Michelle walked in. She also had makeup on and was wearing a lovely sundress and strappy heels. "That sounds like a great idea."

"Sorry to disappoint you, but no," Isabel said.

"Why should the men have all the fun?" Regan asked dejectedly.

Laurant nodded. "I'm the one who loves XO's voice, and yet Nick gets to go with you."

"And Michael," Regan reminded. "I could take his place."

"They are not going," Isabel said.

"They think they are," Kate told her.

Isabel wasn't laughing now. "Where are they?"

"In the sunroom," Kate said. "We just want to meet XO . . ."

"Friday night I'll introduce you. I promise," she said, adding the stipulation, "If he still wants me to sing with him."

They continued to plead their case, and she had to tell them no four or five times before they believed her. "Now, if you'll excuse me, I need to have a talk with the men."

With effort, she was able to keep her temper under control. "They are not going with me," she muttered. She marched into the sunroom and all but shouted, "Sit down and listen up."

Nick was sitting at the desk, going over some papers, and Michael was slouched on the sofa with his legs stretched out, one ankle crossed over the other, his arms folded across his chest, looking half-asleep.

"We are sitting down," Nick pointed out.

"Yeah, we kinda are," Michael agreed.

"I thought I made myself clear earlier when I told both of you that I was going by myself to rehearse with Xavier."

"We thought we should go with you," Michael said.

"You thought wrong," she snapped. She paused a second to gather

her composure and then lowered her voice. "Michael, when I needed a lawyer, you were there for me, and I appreciated your help. I know you like being in charge, especially in charge of me for some reason. I think you enjoy telling me what I can and cannot do, and I've tried to be accommodating. But that stops now. I'm going to make my own decisions. Got that?"

"Of course you can make your own decisions," Michael said. "But . . ."

"But what?"

"You don't know what you're walking into."

"You probably should have some backup," Nick suggested, and Michael nodded agreement.

They weren't kidding. If they didn't look so sincere, she would have laughed. "I'm not going to a brawl. Xavier's staff isn't going to attack me."

"No need to get upset, Isabel," Michael said. Leaning forward with his elbows propped on his knees, he looked very serious when he added, "You haven't seen what men are capable of. I have."

His patronizing tone irritated her. "I'll make a deal with you, Michael. If this rehearsal turns out to be an ambush, I'll be sure to call you."

"Okay, you're on your own," Michael warned. "But if you get into trouble, you damn well better call me."

She didn't dare roll her eyes. "Yes, I will," she promised, wondering how many times she was going to have to say it.

"Don't get distracted. Focus on the task at hand while you're there. When you don't pay attention, you become vulnerable."

For the love of . . . Did he think she would space out and write a song in her head while meeting Xavier? It was pointless to argue with him, she decided, because it wouldn't matter. Besides, the two men were giving each other a knowing look, and it made her wonder. Did she get distracted so often that even they noticed?

"Do you have pepper spray in your bag?" he asked.

"Do I . . . You want me to carry pepper spray to the rehearsal?"

"Yes, I do."

"You should always carry it," Nick told her.

"Should I hold it in my hand when I meet Xavier in case he tries anything funny?"

Laurant interrupted. "Isabel, your car is here. He's early, isn't he?"

Nick and Michael stood. Isabel put her hand up. "Stay," she demanded.

"We just want to meet the driver," Nick said.

"And show him your gun and badge?" Isabel asked.

Nick shrugged. "He'll probably notice it."

They both started for the door again. "Stay," she ordered, louder this time. She felt as though she were training dogs.

Nick's attention was diverted when Laurant appeared in the doorway. Staring at his wife inquisitively, he said, "You're all dressed up. Are you supposed to go somewhere?"

The question lightened Isabel's mood, and she was laughing as she ran outside.

She came to a quick stop. Noah was draped over the driver's open door, talking to him. Noah's gun was very noticeable. He opened the door for her with a devilish grin. She couldn't imagine what he'd been telling the driver.

She wasn't left guessing for long. The driver told her his name was Jax and then said, "I understand you have a federal judge, three FBI agents, a lawyer who works for the Justice Department, and a chief of police in your family. Did I get that right? Or was Agent Clayborne joking?"

She laughed. Talk about intimidation tactics. "No, he was telling the truth." She started to say "They're a," then stopped herself. "We're a law-abiding family."

"Should Xavier be worried about any of them?"

"No, of course not," she said. She didn't add the fact that Noah hadn't mentioned the one brother he should worry about. The former Navy SEAL named Michael.

Wanting to change the subject, she asked Jax if they were going to a recording studio to rehearse or to The Garden.

"Directly to The Garden," he answered. "Xavier wants to show you the layout. He has a large suite, and you'll probably rehearse there."

The closer they came to The Garden, the more nervous she became. Her stomach was doing flip-flops.

"The last time Xavier and I were in Boston, there was a huge snowstorm," Jax commented. He continued to talk about their trips to Boston until they were circling the street close to the entrance.

"When I pull up, two guards will accompany you to Xavier. Keep your head down and walk between them. You'll be all right."

"Why wouldn't I be all right?"

"Sometimes a few rabid fans get past security, and they can be pretty aggressive. Since the concert isn't until tomorrow night, there shouldn't be any problems, but better to be prepared. We aren't going in the front entrances."

The secrecy added yet another layer to her nerves. A few minutes later they stopped at either the side or back entrance—she couldn't tell which—and two big, muscular guards rushed forward to escort her. They wore black suits with white shirts and striped ties. The bulge under their jackets indicated they were armed. *Yikes*, she thought. Maybe she should have brought some firepower of her own after all. She wished now she had relented and let Michael come with her. He would get a kick out of all the security, and knowing him, he'd find ways to improve safety.

The guards nodded to her but didn't speak. They led her down a maze of concrete floors, fluorescent ceiling lights, and beige walls. They passed one door after another after another. By the time they stopped in front of Xavier's door, she had no idea where she was.

"I'm never going to be able to find a way out of here, am I?" she asked.

One of the guards smiled. "Probably not, but don't worry. We'll show you the way." From his accent she thought he might be a born-and-raised Bostonian.

A young man in jeans and a gray XO concert T-shirt opened the door, and when the guards who'd escorted her remained in the hall, she turned to them and said, "Thank you, gentlemen."

They looked surprised by her gratitude. Both nodded before the door was closed.

The suite was crowded with Xavier's staff. She counted four women and twice that number of men spread around the sofas, tables, chairs, and two desks that filled the area. It was a warm inviting space with plush beige carpet and white walls. Bold, contemporary paintings added color.

The suite consisted of two large rooms. She wondered how many more staff members were in the other room and if Xavier had arrived yet.

Everyone stopped talking and stared at her when she walked in. They all seemed frozen, and it was horribly awkward. She didn't know if she should introduce herself or wait for one of them to snap out of it.

She finally broke the silence. "Hello. I'm Isabel MacKenna."

That seemed to do the trick. A man in his thirties, wearing a sport coat over his jeans, jumped to his feet, nearly overturning the desk chair in his haste, and rushed over to shake her hand. "Yes. Isabel MacKenna. We've been waiting for you."

"Then why do you all look so surprised?"

Xavier O'Dell answered her question. He walked in from the other room and stopped just inside the doorway. "You're very pretty, Isabel," he said, his voice deep and husky. "You took their breath away."

Wow. Just plain old wow. Isabel didn't know if she was gawking or not, but she couldn't take her eyes off him. She could describe him in one word: *perfection*. He was tall and lean, yet muscular through his wide shoulders. He had dark hair, intense gray eyes, and a flawless bone structure the Greek gods would weep over. Even his lips were beautiful. She had seen him on the screen countless times, but he looked even more amazing in person. There should be a golden haze all around him, she thought.

Laurant was right. Xavier really was a sex god. The way he smiled and the way he moved . . . there was a definite bad-boy allure about him. And dear God, his voice . . . it was so sensual. His voice alone could seduce a woman. It was certainly having an effect on her.

But he was no Michael. Xavier didn't make her knees weak or her pulse quicken. He didn't make her want to kill him, either, the way Michael did.

Now, why had that thought entered her head? Why was Michael always interfering?

Xavier shook her hand and quickly introduced her to the men and women in the room. She didn't remember a single name, but at least she was able to stop staring at Xavier while she met each one.

An older gentleman stepped forward to shake her hand when Xavier introduced him. "This is Robert Davison. He's one of my attorneys and has papers for you to take with you. Have your attorneys read them over and then sign if you agree with the terms. If not, we'll negotiate. All right?"

"Yes, all right," she agreed, then asked, "What are the papers for?"

"The purchase of your song," he explained.

"Oh yes, of course." She could feel her face heating up.

"We'll rehearse first, and then I'll show you the stage. It's going to be a little overwhelming for you, I imagine."

"She's going to need a name, Xavier," a young man with freckles and a warm smile announced.

Confused, she said, "I have a name. Isabel—"

"Isla. It's spelled i-s-l-a, but pronounced 'Eye-luh.' That's catchy." He added, nodding, "Memorable."

"She's already memorable," another man said.

"What about El?" a woman with pink braces on her teeth suggested. "It's just as catchy."

Xavier raised his hand. "Isabel, these two are Calum and Amy. They're part of my creative team. They're always looking for an angle."

"Don't worry. We'll come up with some other nicknames if you don't like Isla or El," Amy promised.

Everyone started talking at the same time. Isabel was thoroughly bewildered. She couldn't make sense out of what was happening. She had a name. She didn't need another . . . did she?"

Xavier put a stop to their brainstorming. "Her name is Isabel. It's a beautiful name and we're not going to change it." He then took her elbow and pulled her into the other room, shutting the door and leaving the chaos outside. It was time to go to work.

It took a little while for Isabel to settle her nerves, but once she did, she was able to sing without messing up. She actually remembered all the words, which was quite an accomplishment considering the sex god was in the same room with her. Xavier was easygoing and that also helped. Once the song took over, she lost herself in her music, just as she always did, letting the melody flow through her.

They worked on two songs, one she would sing alone and one she would sing with him. After they finished rehearsing, they talked for a long time, and she was surprised by how comfortable she was becoming. Then he took her to the stage. He showed her the way she would enter, where she would stand, and where he would be if she needed him.

"The spotlight on your face will be filtered so you won't squint," he promised.

After they went over the plan for Friday at least three times, he told her not to worry about anything because there would be a staff member by her side at all times guiding her if she ran into a problem.

Isabel stood in the center of the stage and looked out at the thousands of seats. She wasn't filled with euphoria, nor was she thrilled by what was happening, probably because she was so scared. She still didn't know if she had the courage to step on the stage and sing. Guess she would find out Friday, she thought a little hysterically.

By the time they finished going over everything, the adrenaline was fading, and Isabel felt as though she'd just run a marathon. Xavier put his arm around her and walked by her side back to his suite.

"Isabel, are you seeing anyone?"

The question surprised her. "No. Are you?"

He grinned. "No."

She laughed. "Aren't we a pair."

"Maybe I could take you out sometime. It will involve a lot of planning," he explained, and then he sighed. "Weeks of planning to go anywhere without a mob scene. It will be a hell of a challenge."

"Maybe I could take you out sometime," she countered. "To an island, and I promise there wouldn't be a mob."

"Nathan's Bay."

"Yes."

"Will the FBI agents, the Justice attorney, the federal judge, and the chief of police be there?"

She laughed. "Jax told you."

"I already knew about the Buchanan family. When do your stitches come out?"

She came to an abrupt stop. "You know about . . ."

He leaned down and whispered into her ear, "The shooting? Yes, I know. I watched the video."

"But how . . ."

"I have ways of finding out things, Isabel," he said with a smile.

Still stunned, she said, "The video didn't identify me, how could you know . . ."

"Actually, I found out from one of my guards," he admitted. "He's an off-duty cop. He saw the video of you singing and connected it to the other one."

"Oh," she said. This was the last thing she wanted to hear today.

"Relax, Isabel. None of my staff knows, and if they did, none of them would leak it to the press." He shook his head and added, "That was one hell of a shot."

He nudged her along. When they turned down the last hallway, there were four guards waiting. While one of them stepped forward to speak to Xavier, Isabel walked into the suite to collect her purse and say good-bye to everyone.

"Amy, get a baseball cap or a scarf to put over Isabel's head," Xavier said. Turning to the guards, he instructed, "I don't want anyone to see her or take photos, and I want all of you to block her in on all sides until you've got her in the car."

"Is there a problem?" Isabel asked, knowing full well there was.

"Word got out that I'm here," Xavier said. "There's a crowd outside, front and back. Don't worry. You'll be okay."

He took both of her hands in his and kissed her cheek. "All your dreams are about to come true. Tomorrow night you're going to become a superstar. I hope you're ready for it."

He was wrong, but she didn't tell him so. Being a superstar wasn't her dream.

FOURTEEN

ISABEL GOT A TASTE OF XO MANIA WALKING THE GAUNTLET TO THE car. She likened the crazed fans surrounding the guards on all sides to an angry swarm of bees. Following instructions, she kept her head down and stared at the pavement while her unflappable escorts moved as a single unit through the shrieking crowd. It was sheer bedlam and a little bit terrifying. By the time she dove into the backseat of the car, she was trembling.

Once they were on their way and Jax called, "All clear now," she was able to breathe.

"Jax, I don't understand why they were screaming at me. Couldn't they see I wasn't XO?"

"It's impossible to understand the mindset of a mob. Maybe they figured you were a friend of Xavier's. Who knows?" He added, "I'll warn you now. This was nothing compared to what's coming."

"Oh my," she whispered. What had she gotten herself into?

She had never been so happy to see the bridge that would take her back to the island, and when Jax finally pulled into the drive of the Buchanan house, she was weak with relief.

"Did Xavier go over the schedule with you for tomorrow?"

"Yes," she said. "We tweaked it a little. He wanted me at the arena by one o'clock. I talked him into a later hour. The Hamilton Hotel is just fifteen minutes from The Garden. I wanted you to pick me up at six o'clock, but Xavier wouldn't hear of it. He said traffic will be horrible, and if there was an accident . . . so we settled on you picking me up at the hotel at four o'clock. I won't be late," she promised.

"Why the Hamilton?"

"Xavier didn't want me to stay on the island. It's too far away from The Garden. He suggested I stay at his hotel, but I'd rather stay at the Hamilton."

"The traffic around The Garden is going to be horrible," Jax said. "Fans like to get there early even though there is assigned seating, and there will be a long line at least three deep wrapped around the parking lot and the building by five o'clock. You need to understand what I call 'Xavier talk.' Picking you up at four means I'll be there at three."

"Okay, I'll be ready."

"Will you be bringing anyone with you?"

"I'll have some friends and relatives at the concert, but I wasn't planning on bringing guards with me. Do you think I should?"

"A few extra guards wouldn't be a bad idea. Tomorrow night's going to be chaotic." Then he laughed. "That's an understatement."

He insisted on opening the door for her. She thanked him and started up the drive.

"Don't worry about anything, Isabel," Jax called. "Xavier will take good care of you."

Dylan was rounding the corner of the house and was holding his tackle box and fishing pole. He propped both on the side of the steps and shouted to Isabel, "Hold up." He waited until she reached him and then said, "You look shell-shocked."

"That's how I feel," she admitted. "I need to talk to you, but I don't want the whole family there. Where is everyone?"

"Dad's in his office working," he said. "Theo and Michelle are upstairs. They said they wanted to call and check on the twins. Now that they've caught up on their sleep, I think Theo and Michelle are a little homesick. Everyone else is in the city. I've been fishing."

"Did you catch anything?"

He shook his head. "It's too hot. Fish weren't biting. When do you want to talk?"

"Let's meet in your father's office in an hour. He told me to interrupt him when I got back, but I've got to get this makeup off and change."

"You need a whole hour to do that?"

"I need time to decompress," she admitted.

"Are you okay?" he asked, worried now.

"I will be."

He took her at her word. "Okay. See you in an hour."

Isabel planned to take a few minutes to clear her mind and put her feet up, but that didn't happen. Because it was so beastly hot, she ended up getting in the shower, then changing into comfortable shorts, a sleeveless top, and tennis shoes. She thought she looked like a slob, but she was finally comfortable. She still couldn't unwind, though, not until she had tomorrow's schedule completely organized.

She went downstairs, knocked on the library door, and went in. Dylan was already there, sitting in a leather chair, talking to his father. Isabel told them about the rehearsal but didn't go into much detail until she got to the harrowing walk back to the car.

"There was this crowd . . . they acted crazy, screaming at me and pushing. I kept my head down, but I did see some of them. They weren't just teenage girls. There were also a lot of grown men and women. I can't imagine what it will be like tomorrow. There will be security, but it was suggested by Jax, the driver, that I bring someone with me. Xavier's guards are armed," she added. "And I'm sure he'll see to my protection . . ."

"You'll have guards with you," Dylan said.

The judge nodded agreement. "We have enough men in this family who can go with you."

"As long as it's not . . ." She stopped in time before she said Michael's name.

"As long as it's not what?" the judge asked.

"Too much of an inconvenience. Dylan, you're good at pushing back when someone pushes you, and I know Noah would do it."

"I'm good at pushing?" He laughed.

A commotion in the kitchen interrupted them.

"I guess everyone's back," Dylan said. "We'll figure out the details and go over it with you later. Don't worry about anything."

"That's exactly what Xavier said to me. Telling me won't change anything. I'm still going to worry."

She thought she sounded belligerent and apologized. Voices were getting closer, and she knew what was coming. Kate and the others would want to hear all about Xavier.

Dylan followed her into the kitchen. "I smell pizza."

"You're a Buchanan," Kate commented. "It's your superpower."

She and Laurant placed five giant pizzas on the island. Dylan didn't wait for an invitation. He opened a box and reached for a huge slice with pepperoni.

"We want to hear every word, Isabel," Laurant insisted. She pulled out a chair at the table and told her to sit. "Start at the beginning and don't leave anything out. I am so excited to hear what XO . . . I mean Xavier . . . is like."

"Hold on. I want to ask Isabel a question first. How many tickets can you get?" Kate wanted to know. "I thought it would be nice to invite Michael's girlfriend, Amanda, and a couple of Jordan's friends."

Dylan's eyes immediately darted to Isabel. "Absolutely not," he said. "Do not invite Amanda . . . or anyone else."

Kate looked surprised. "Why not?"

"It's taking advantage of Xavier to ask for more tickets," Laurant guessed.

Regan nodded. "It would be rude, Kate. Besides, I don't think she is his girlfriend. He never talks about her."

Kate walked over to Dylan with a puzzled look on her face and he pulled her into his arms. "Sometimes, honey, you're just oblivious," he whispered. And then he kissed her so she wouldn't ask any more questions.

Isabel was mortified. Dylan's reaction to the mention of Amanda was to immediately look at her. It was obvious he somehow knew she had feelings for Michael. Great. Like Noah and Nick and Alec, all FBI agents, Dylan didn't miss a trick. He noticed every little thing, so she figured the other men must know, too. She felt like such a fool. Running away to avoid Michael wasn't the answer. She needed to get over him.

Regan noticed she was staring off into space. "Isabel? What are you doing?"

Smiling, she looked up and said, "Writing a song about Scotland . . . and escape."

The women didn't let her mull over her problems long. They bombarded her with questions about XO. Michael walked in the door just in time to hear Isabel tell everyone how nice Xavier was to her.

"He's very handsome," she said. "But not vain. He's considerate, too," she added.

Michael took a bottle of beer from the refrigerator. He leaned against the counter and listened while the women grilled Isabel.

"Did he like you?" Laurant wanted to know. "I mean, did he like your voice?"

"Yes," she said. "Once my nerves cooperated, my voice got stronger." She added with a shrug, "I guess he thought it was okay."

She deliberately avoided looking at Michael while the barrage of questions continued.

"He wants to take me out on a date. He says it will take a lot of planning. I guess he gets hounded everywhere he goes. I can't imagine anything more awful. Being a superstar traps a person."

"That's the price you pay," Regan said.

Michael stood quietly listening to the conversation, and when there was a lull, he downed the last of his beer and turned to Dylan. "What time are the MacAlisters getting here?"

"In a couple of hours," he answered. "And yeah, I know. Time to lock up our women."

Michael nodded, smiling, as he walked through the kitchen. He tugged on Isabel's ponytail as he passed her. "Especially this one."

With a frown Isabel spun in her chair. What was that supposed to mean? Once again, Michael was doing everything he could to irritate her. She opened her mouth to retaliate, but decided against it. Now was not the time for an argument. She turned back to the table, where the women were making plans for her big night.

Regan offered her a suite at the hotel. Isabel was grateful but told her that wouldn't be necessary. However, she would appreciate having the same room she'd had before. Kate lined up a makeup artist and hairstylist to take care of Isabel. Jordan and Laurant weighed in on the issue of shoes. They insisted flats were out; heels were in. They would make sure the pair she decided on wouldn't slip when she walked across the stage. To accomplish that, Laurant ran upstairs to fetch a pair for Isabel to practice walking.

Isabel felt ridiculous wearing them around the house and down the drive to break them in. Thank goodness they weren't the six-inch stilettos Kate wanted to buy her, but the pair she had on were still awkwardly high. After about an hour she got used to them. In fact, they actually became comfortable. Who would have thought?

Once she was back in her room and alone, she began to organize her wardrobe. Because she was such a neurotic worrier, she tried to anticipate every possibility. She checked and then checked again to make sure both the suit and the dress were in the garment bag she would take to The Garden. She didn't plan to change into her performance outfit until an hour or two before she went onstage, and if anything happened to it, she'd have the other in reserve. She even packed an extra pair of shoes.

With all of those preparations completed, she moved on to her plans after Nathan's Bay. She needed to arrange for a driver to take her to the airport Monday, which meant she would spend Sunday night at the hotel. She felt guilty that she had misled Dylan by agreeing to ask Damon to go with her. While she would love to see her good friend again, she never had any intention of inviting him along. Besides, she was perfectly capable of going to Scotland alone.

As she was zipping her wardrobe bag closed for the last time, she heard voices coming from down below. She went to the window to look out. Everyone was outside by the pool, laughing and carrying on. The moon was bright, and when she checked the time, she was astonished by how late it was.

She could hear the shower running in the bathroom and knew Michael was still inside. When the water stopped, she waited until she heard him leave the bathroom and go through the door to his bedroom before she tried the door on her side. It was locked, so she tried to enter the bathroom from the hallway. That door was also locked. She was about to knock and ask him to unlock them, when his bedroom door opened and he stepped out. A towel draped around his neck and his hair still wet, he was dressed only in a pair of boxer briefs that rode low on his hips. She didn't need to see that.

"Please unlock the bathroom door on my side. I want to brush my teeth," she said, trying to act indifferent.

Even though he turned around and did what she asked, she could tell from his expression that something was bothering him. He was wound up tight tonight. After brushing her teeth, she flipped off the bathroom light and went back into her bedroom, closing the bathroom door behind her.

She had just pulled down the comforter on her bed when there was a knock on her door. She opened it to find Michael standing inches away.

"What?" She hadn't intended to sound surly, but it was too late.

"I was going to ask if you were going down to the pool, but from your appearance I'm guessing not."

"What's wrong with my appearance?"

She took a step back and looked down at herself. Oops. She was dressed for bed.

"Never mind," she said when he gave her his *are you kidding?* look. She folded her arms across her chest and continued. "I'm staying in. What about you? Are you going down to the pool?"

"Maybe."

"You should," she said.

He leaned against the doorframe. "Why?"

"Because you're angry tonight."

"The hell I am." Michael realized how foolish he sounded the second the words were out of his mouth. He sounded as angry as he felt. The problem he was trying to work out had nothing to do with her, and yet she'd somehow gotten right in the middle of it, and that didn't make any sense at all. "You shouldn't be walking around dressed like that."

She knew he was serious. "I'm not going to walk around. I'm going to bed." She couldn't leave it alone. "You know what, Michael? You're a giant pain in the backside, and I'm going to be very happy when I can get away from you."

"Yeah?" He walked her backward into her room, shoving the door closed behind him.

He was at it again, trying to intimidate her. He still hadn't caught on that it didn't work. She poked him in his chest. "Yes."

"Isabel, you're a temptation and a hell of a distraction I don't need."

Drawing back, she demanded, "Was that an insult?"

"You can't tell?"

She decided to be honest. "No, I can't."

He folded his arms and frowned. "I know you'll be going to Scotland Monday."

"And?" she prodded.

"I want to clear something up."

She waited, but he didn't say another word for a long minute. Why was it taking him so long? She suddenly thought she knew what he was going to say.

"Oh no, you don't. You'd better not be breaking up with me again. I'm not in the mood to hear it."

"What? No, that isn't it," he said. "I just need to tell you something."

"Yes?"

"You said I was smarter than you are. That isn't true, and it bothers me that you think it is. The fact is, you're a hell of a lot smarter than I am, and no, I'm not going to explain why."

He turned to leave, and as he headed to the door, she stepped up behind him. "Flattery isn't going to work on me. You're still a bonehead."

Michael started to laugh. Shaking his head, he spun around just as Isabel took a step forward and bumped into him. Instinctively, he reached out to her. With his arms wrapped around her, he responded. "It wasn't flattery."

"It sounded like it." For the next few seconds they stood pressed together, neither one of them moving, and then Isabel kissed the pulse at the base of his neck.

He flinched. "Stop that."

"You don't like it?"

"Stop fooling around, and let me get the hell out of here before I do something we'll both regret."

Michael let go of her and stepped back. The problem was, she wasn't letting go. He had to get out of her bedroom and away from her bed. The longer he stayed, the more difficult it became not to touch her. He admitted he loved being close to her. No other woman had this effect on him, but Isabel . . . all she had to do was walk past him or smile at him, and every part of him reacted. He kept telling himself it was nothing more than raw animal attraction, but that lie wasn't working any longer.

"Good night, then," she whispered. She leaned up and brushed her mouth against his. There wasn't anything wrong with a good-night kiss. It was . . . platonic, nothing more. But then he pulled her to him and kissed her, and it was anything but platonic. His mouth was hot, and his tongue made love to her as he lifted her, her pelvis pressed against his.

Michael had kissed her before but nothing like this. His passion ignited her own, and Isabel suddenly couldn't get enough of him. She moved restlessly against him, her tongue dueling with his, and when he abruptly ended the kiss, she all but collapsed against him.

Without a word, he pulled her hands away from him and walked out the door.

Isabel dropped down on the bed and closed her eyes. Michael was turning her into a slut, she decided, and he didn't even know it. Trying to blame him for her behavior didn't work. She had all but attacked him. Yep, it was official. She was headed down the road to Trampville.

She laughed out loud at the absurdity of it all, and she was beginning to accept the fact that she was letting her imagination get away from her, but then a line for a song came to her, and all she could think about was a melody. Unlike other times when she'd been inspired with an idea, however, she didn't let herself dwell on it long. She needed to get some sleep.

Isabel had no idea what tomorrow would bring, but there was one thing she was sure of: it was either going to be a catastrophe . . . or a miracle.

FIFTEEN

FRIDAY MORNING ARRIVED, AND ISABEL WAS FREAKISHLY CALM. NO one was more surprised than she was. She ate breakfast and kept it down. That was another surprise.

A little before noon Alec packed the car and drove her and Regan to the Hamilton. Ignoring Isabel's wishes, Regan put her in a large one-bedroom suite. It was quite beautiful and spacious, with a panoramic view of the Charles River in the distance. The living room was done in blacks and grays with upholstered furniture throughout, and it was separated from the bedroom by a pair of French doors. The bedroom was a mixture of muted grays. On the king-size bed was a soft plush down comforter and luxurious white linens. The bathroom, all in white marble, was almost as big as the bedroom.

"I don't need all this room," Isabel protested.

"People will be coming and going," Regan reminded. "Hair and makeup will be here shortly, and Vera is coming up in case you need something pinned or tucked, so yes, you do need this much room." She made the comments while she helped one of the maids hang up Isabel's clothes and unpack her bag.

Isabel wasn't used to being pampered. It was sweet and thoughtful of Regan to move her into a suite, and Isabel was grateful. "You didn't have to go to all this trouble, but I really appreciate it. Thank you, Regan."

"We're happy to help," Regan replied. "Aren't we, Alec?"

"Of course we are," her husband agreed as he took the empty bag Regan handed him and set it in the back of the closet.

Isabel watched Regan for a minute and then said, "You're so normal."

"Who's normal?" Alec asked.

"Your wife," Isabel answered. "She and her brothers own all the Hamilton hotels, and she's unpacking for me. It's just so . . . normal."

Alec laughed. "Regan's a lot of things, but normal isn't one of them."

"Hey . . . ," Regan protested.

"Darling, if you were normal, you never would have married me."

"Good save," she told her husband.

The couple was so oddly paired, Isabel thought. Regan was a beautiful, polished woman who felt at home in her elegant hotel, and Alec was rather scruffy-looking and admittedly a bit of a slob when he was off duty, neither of which bothered Regan in the least. Alec was growing his hair longer—it covered his ears now—for another undercover assignment, and with the beginning of a beard he could be downright scary if you met him in a dark alley. He was also a teddy bear, she knew, and he loved his wife with a passion. Oddly paired, but perfect for each other. They were so comfortable and so at ease, Isabel hoped some of their calm would pass on to her and loosen the knot that had a grip on her stomach.

Regan stopped what she was doing and glanced at Isabel, who sat on the edge of her chair, her back ramrod straight. She was so rigid she looked as though she were about to shatter.

"Are you okay, Isabel?" she asked.

"I'm fine," she insisted.

"Okay, Isabel, here's the schedule," Alec said. "Noah, Nick, and Michael are going with you whenever Xavier's driver gets here."

"Jax told me he's supposed to be here at four, but Xavier will probably send him early. Why do I need three men to go with me? Wouldn't two be enough?"

"Michael insisted on three," Alec said. "Actually, he wanted four, but I talked him down to three.

"Kate and the others will be here around five," he told her. "Dylan's driving them. They'll hang out in your suite until it's time to go. Regan and I will wait here for them."

There was a knock on the door, and Alec went to answer it. He came back in the living room with Michael, who was carrying his gym bag. Without comment, Alec took it from him and put it in the guest closet.

Isabel tried not to react to Michael. He was wearing a suit and looked even more handsome than usual. How was that possible?

Regan drew her attention. "Kate wanted to come with us," she said. "But she's very nervous about tonight, and she doesn't want her nerves to rub off on you."

"That's funny. She's usually the calm one," Isabel said. "I called Kiera and actually got through to her," she said to no one in particular. "Shocked the socks off my sister when I told her I was performing with Xavier. Turns out she loves him, too."

"It's too bad she can't be here," Regan remarked.

"It's okay. She'll be able to see me on YouTube."

"They're going to put the concert on YouTube?" Alec asked. "That can't be right."

"They'll put it on when I screw up. It will be all over the Internet."

Exasperated, Michael said, "You're not going to screw up."

She stood, then sat again. She couldn't remember what she was supposed to do now.

"What's wrong?"

"Do I get undressed now and then get dressed after makeup and hair, or do I get dressed first?" she asked, trying with all her might to sound composed and in control. "And I also wonder . . ."

"Yes?"

She leapt to her feet. "What in God's name am I doing?" Her voice escalated to a near-hysterical shout. "I can't go onstage and sing. I should never have . . ."

"You're going to be great," Alec promised her.

Regan nodded. "You'll sing your songs and everyone will cheer. You already have millions of followers on the Internet," she reminded. "Think of it, Isabel. Millions," she exclaimed dramatically. "You're a sensation, and everyone in The Garden is going to love you."

Isabel was frantically shaking her head. "I don't think I can do it. Twenty thousand people will be there, and I . . . I just can't." Panic was grabbing hold in a big way.

Both Regan and Alec tried to talk her down, but Michael went another way.

"Snap out of it, Isabel," he ordered.

Apparently Michael wasn't one to coddle.

"Oh, that's comforting," she muttered.

"You want comforting? Go to my mother. She'll comfort the hell out of you."

"Yeah, she will," Alec agreed.

They were serious. The idiots weren't joking. Isabel looked at Regan and then both of them began to laugh. Isabel was still laughing when she went into the bedroom and closed the French doors.

For the next two hours, the professionals transformed Isabel into a superstar. At least that's what Regan kept telling her they were doing every time Isabel tried to get the stylists to hurry up and finish.

Michael interrupted when he knocked on the door. "Detective Samuel is on the phone. He wants to talk to you."

Isabel, wrapped in a robe, ran to the door and opened it. "I can't go to the station for another interview now. Make him understand, Michael. I can't imagine what other questions he has. Surely he can wait until . . ." She finally noticed that Michael was shaking his head. "What is it?"

"He wants to ask a favor."

She took Michael's phone but held it against her chest as she whispered, "Did you tell him I can't go to the station?"

"Yes. I told him."

Frowning at Michael, she answered the phone. "Hello, Detective Samuel. What can I do for you?"

The detective hemmed and hawed, and she could hear what sounded like excited teenagers screaming in the background.

"I just found out that you will be performing with XO tonight. Is that correct?"

She automatically straightened her shoulders at the sound of his voice. "Yes," she answered, wondering how he had heard.

"I really hate to ask, but my daughters are big fans of yours, and when they heard that you will be singing with XO . . . Hold on," he said.

She could tell he'd cupped his hand over the phone because his voice was muffled, but she could still hear him ordering his daughters to quiet down.

"Are you there, Isabel?"

She decided to get to the point for him. "How many tickets do you need?"

"Three," he told her, relief in his voice.

"Okay. I'm sure Xavier has a few extras. They'll be at the will-call window for you. If you run into any problems, contact Michael. He's going with me, and he'll have his phone with him."

"Thank you," he said.

Before he could end the call, she blurted, "Wait. I'd like to ask you a question."

"Yes?"

"Have you learned why Walsh was in Boston?"

"We're working on it," he replied. "Walsh still isn't awake."

"Yes, I know. I talked to the nurse on duty this morning. She told me his stats are improving, and they expect him to wake up anytime now." She noticed Michael smiled when she told the detective that she'd talked to the nurse.

"I'll keep you informed," Samuel promised.

Isabel thanked him and ended the call. Handing the phone back to Michael, she said, "Please don't let me forget. Detective Samuel needs three tickets."

"Shall we get back to work?" Regan suggested. She pulled Isabel back into the bedroom, smiled at Michael, and shut the door in his face.

The transformation continued. The blue sequined top was more low-cut than Isabel remembered, but Vera made sure it wouldn't shift or slip, no matter how much Isabel moved.

Regan tried to ease her concerns. "It isn't a plunging neckline. It's just that you're a bit overendowed," she explained. "Now stop worrying about it. You're very decent. Why, you could wear that top to church."

Isabel laughed. "And get hit by lightning."

She was prodded back into the chair by one of the stylists, who insisted on wrapping a flesh-colored bandage around her upper arm to hide her stitches. Isabel didn't object, although she thought it wasn't necessary since she'd be wearing the jacket.

While they were working on her, she received three phone calls from the extremely annoying James Reid. She ignored all of them, sending the calls to voicemail. He wasn't giving up. If he thought he could wear her down and persuade her to sell Glen MacKenna land to his Patterson Group just to be rid of him and stop his harassment, he was mistaken. In fact, the opposite was happening. Each time he called, she became more inclined to sell the property to anyone but him.

"Isabel, the hairstylist wants your attention," Regan said when Isabel didn't answer a question.

Back to the business of trying to turn her into a superstar. "Are we almost finished?"

"Almost," Regan assured her.

Regan packed her heels and other necessities and carried the bag into the living room. Worried she had forgotten something Isabel might need, Regan paced in front of the windows while she went over the list again and again.

Nick and Noah had arrived, and they, along with Michael and Alec, watched her pace until Alec finally anchored her with his arm around her shoulders.

A few seconds later the hotel phone rang. Regan rushed to answer it. "Limo's here," she announced. "Should we hurry Isabel along?"

"No," Michael answered. "She'll come out when she's ready."

"Unless she makes a run for it," Alec said.

Michael grinned. "I already thought of that possibility, but this is the only way out of the bedroom, and the windows don't open this high up."

Ten minutes passed, then ten more, and finally the bedroom doors opened, and Isabel, transformed for the stage, walked into the living room.

Regan gasped when she saw her. "You're stunning, Isabel."

With all the work done on her, she should be stunning, she thought. "Thank you."

The men were gaping at her, and she immediately felt self-conscious. After a long minute of silence she decided to use everyone's favorite go-to command. "Snap out of it."

Michael spoke up. "Are you ready to leave? The driver's here."

Since he was closest, she handed him her room card and her cell phone. Nick carried the garment bag Regan had packed.

"We'll see you there," Regan called from the doorway. "If you need anything, text me."

Fortunately, the elevator was empty. When the doors closed, she turned to her three escorts. "Thank you for giving up your Friday night to help me."

"We're not giving anything up, Isabel," Noah told her. "We want to be here."

Flanked by Noah and Michael, Isabel crossed the lobby, and Nick followed behind.

Michael was proud of her. He knew she was scared, but she wasn't letting it show now. She walked like she owned the world. There was such attitude in the way she moved, and those hips . . . damn. Then he noticed he wasn't the only one appreciating Isabel. It seemed to him that every man in the lobby was watching her, and why wouldn't they? She was beautiful and desirable.

Great. Hell if he wasn't lusting after her again.

"Michael?" She whispered his name.

"Yes?"

"Stop glaring."

Her hand brushed against his. She didn't grab hold. He did. He slipped his fingers through hers and gave her a little squeeze.

"I've got your bottle of water," he told her, then turned to take the bottle from Nick. "This is all you drink. Understand? You don't drink anything anyone else gives you."

She thought he was being a little overprotective and suspicious, but then she noticed Noah was nodding agreement.

"You're going to be okay," Michael said. He leaned down and whispered, "I'm not going to let anything happen to you."

"I know." As annoying as Michael could be sometimes, she always felt safe with him. He would never let anyone hurt her.

Uh-oh. She could feel herself getting teary-eyed. She didn't dare cry, not with all the eye makeup she had on. She wasn't sure what to do. She liked Michael more when she was fighting with him, but he was being nice to her now—a rare occasion, to be sure—and that was why she was becoming emotional, she reasoned. Now was not the time to fall apart. She needed to put a stop to it before he said something really sweet.

Then it came to her. "Michael, you're going onstage with me when I sing."

His answer was swift. "The hell I am. Are you out of your mind? Why in God's name would you think I would go onstage with you?"

"But I thought—"

"Oh, hell no." He was glaring at her now.

And things were back to normal.

SIXTEEN

THE RIDE TO THE GARDEN SEEMED TO TAKE FOREVER.

"Jax, you weren't exaggerating. There's already a huge crowd in line."

"They're everywhere. Getting you inside is going to take muscle."

"I've got plenty of that," she said.

Her phone buzzed with a text. Michael pulled her cell out of his pocket and handed it to her. He noticed how her hands shook and opened the text for her.

"It's from one of Xavier's assistants telling you three tickets are in an envelope with Detective Samuel's name on it at the will-call window."

"I sent the text requesting tickets while my hair was being curled," she explained. "Now I have one less thing to worry about."

"Okay, here we go," Jax called out. He turned the corner and headed to the back entrance. The car was all but swallowed up by screaming fans, both male and female. There were so many the car actually rocked.

"They think Xavier is in here," Isabel said.

"Jax, you'd have a better chance of sneaking past the crowd if you weren't driving a limo," Nick said, stating the obvious.

Michael agreed. "This is a beacon."

"The windows aren't just tinted. They're also bulletproof," Jax told them.

"There is that," Noah said.

"If you want to get people out of your way, you should let Isabel drive," Michael suggested.

Noah, Nick, and Michael had a good laugh. Isabel wasn't amused. "That's not funny," she snapped, which only made them laugh all the more.

Jax ignored them. He continued to drive at a slow pace until they finally reached the steps to the doors. Isabel was amazed he hadn't run over anyone. Guards blocked fans from coming closer.

"I don't want to get out of the car," Isabel whispered.

Michael made her laugh then. "I don't, either."

"You're going to have to show identification because you're armed," Jax warned.

"We know the drill," Nick told him. "Are you ready to have some fun, Isabel?"

She nodded. "I'm ready."

Noah exited the car first and held the door open. Then Michael got out with Isabel, holding her close to his side. Nick led the way through the guards, who quickly surrounded all of them. The screaming and cheering had intensified, making conversation impossible. Isabel walked with her hands down at her sides. She wasn't about to hold on to anyone. Once inside, she strode down the hallway with her heels clicking against the concrete floor, following two guards leading the way to Xavier.

It seemed there were twice the number of staff members inside the suite this time, and everyone was busy on a phone. The room, with all the activity, resembled a call center. It was hectic, but happy, for everyone was smiling. Isabel could feel the energy. She couldn't remember anyone's name, so she said hello to all of them. Several waved to her; others smiled and nodded while they continued their conversations on their phones.

A young woman Isabel did remember rushed forward to greet her. "Oh my God, Isabel, you look gorgeous. Wait until Xavier sees you."

"This is Amy," she told her escorts. "She's part of Xavier's creative team, and she wanted to give me a nickname. Did you come up with a good one?"

"I did, but Xavier wouldn't hear of it."

"Is he here?"

"Yes, but he's on the phone doing an interview. He'll be out in a bit."

Isabel remembered her manners and introduced Michael, Nick, and Noah to Amy. She noticed most of the women in the room were staring at the men, and she couldn't blame them. They were mighty fine-looking. Who wouldn't stare? She was no longer the focus and that was just fine with her. It removed some of the pressure she was feeling. She even managed to smile, a real smile that wasn't forced.

An older gentleman who seemed to be in charge came forward to shake hands and introduce himself. His name was Paul Emerson, and he was Xavier's agent. He had a smooth way about him.

"Are all three of you FBI agents?"

Nick answered. "No, just Noah and I are agents."

Emerson turned to Michael. "I noticed you aren't armed."

"No, I'm not."

"But you're one of Isabel's guards tonight?"

"Yes."

Isabel couldn't resist. "Take a good look at him, Mr. Emerson. Do you think he needs a weapon?"

Nick laughed. "I can assure you he doesn't."

Emerson looked confused.

"You have no reason to be concerned," Isabel said to clarify. "He'll watch out for me."

Noah had a bit of the devil in him. "You'll be fine, too," he said. "As long as you don't piss him off."

"Yeah, he's got a temper," Nick drawled.

Exasperated, Isabel explained, "They think they're funny."

Emerson seemed to take it all in stride when he turned back to Isabel. "You forgot to take the legal papers for your attorney to look over. I have them here."

Isabel took the folder and handed it to Michael, who handed it to Nick to put in her bag.

Isabel thought she had hours to wait, but when she checked the time, she was shocked. There was less than an hour before the concert started. Nick and Noah left to get the lay of the land, and as soon as the door was opened, she could hear the audience chanting XO's name and stomping their feet in rhythm. She took a drink of water from the bottle Michael offered her and handed it back. She wanted to pace, but there wasn't room.

Xavier came out ten minutes later. He wasn't dressed in anything glittery, but then she didn't expect he would be. The mere thought was inconceivable. Glitter wasn't his style. He wore black pants and a crisp long-sleeve white shirt. It was unbuttoned at the neck, and the sleeves were rolled back at the wrists. His only jewelry was a watch, and even that wasn't fancy. His shoes were his signature. Xavier always wore white tennis shoes onstage, and tonight was no exception. He obviously chose comfort over the latest style, which made her like him all the more.

He spotted Isabel across the room and headed toward her. The way he looked at her, with such warmth in his eyes, made her heart skip a beat. They met each other in the middle of the room. When he hugged her, she was careful to turn her face away so she wouldn't get makeup on his shirt. After greeting her, he draped his arm around her shoulders.

"Paul, what do you think? Was I right?" he asked his agent.

"Yes, you were right," Paul called back from the other side of the room. "She really is lovely."

Isabel didn't like them discussing her as though she weren't there. She pulled away from Xavier and introduced him to Michael. The two men shook hands and started talking, and within minutes they acted like best friends. They both had the same twisted sense of humor. Watching them, Isabel had an epiphany. Michael could be charming.

Xavier acted as though he had all the time in the world to chat. Then Noah and Nick returned to the suite and joined the conversation. Isabel kept checking the time. She noticed Xavier didn't look at his watch once. She couldn't understand how he could be so relaxed. She went into the other room to warm up her voice, then reapplied lipstick and walked back to Michael and took a drink from the bottle of water. She couldn't pay attention to the conversation. She was too busy trying not to freak out about what was soon going to happen. *Almost twenty thousand people . . . Oh my God . . . twenty thousand . . .*

Michael leaned down and whispered in her ear, "You're going to be great."

She looked into his eyes. "You think?"

"I know."

She almost believed him.

"It's time, Xavier," one of the staff members called.

"Okay, then," Xavier said. "Are you ready, Isabel?"

He didn't give her time to panic. He simply took hold of her hand and led the way. He indicated with a tilt of his head for Michael, Nick, and Noah to come with them. Isabel couldn't keep up with his long-legged stride, and when Xavier noticed she was all but running, he slowed his pace.

"We're going to have a good time tonight." He saw the look on her face and laughed. "I promise."

The closer they got to the arena, the louder the chant, "XO, XO, XO," became. Xavier stopped at the entrance to the stage, let go of her, and winked at her. He was quickly fitted with a mic so that he could move around with his hands free. On cue the band started to play one of his songs, and the audience immediately quieted. The air was thick with excitement.

Xavier walked out, and the crowd went wild. They settled down as soon as he started to sing. He was, simply put, magnificent. He hypnotized the audience, held them in the palm of his hand, all with his amazing voice.

Michael stood beside Isabel and waited. And then it was her turn. Xavier surprised her. All of a sudden, a clip from the video of Isabel singing at Finnegan's appeared on the giant screen above the stage. The audience watched and cheered when Xavier said, "We all know her from the video that became a viral sensation this week. Now you get to meet her and listen to her sing for you." He put his hand out and simply called her name. "Isabel."

She took a deep breath.

"You've got this," Michael told her.

She nodded, accepted the mic from the assistant, and walked onto the stage.

SEVENTEEN

ISABEL BLEW THEM AWAY AND LEFT THEM BEGGING FOR MORE.
Xavier knew she was going to be wonderful, but even he was astounded by the crowd's wild reaction to hearing them sing together.

Just as they had practiced, she sang her song and another song with him, and then, with a smile and a wave, she left the stage. Xavier had asked her to stay by the entrance until he finished the performance, and she happily agreed. Michael stood behind her, and she leaned back against him. Until now Isabel's nerves had been coiled tight, and she was finally able to let go. Relief that she had gotten through the ordeal without a blunder made her all but euphoric. It was finally over.

Or so she thought. But Xavier had another little surprise in store for her. After he finished singing what Isabel assumed was his last song for the night, he crooked his finger at her and called her name. She quickly strode back onstage, believing that the two of them would take a bow together.

When the cheering died down, he asked Isabel if she knew the lyrics to one of his favorite songs. It was called "Wanting You."

"Of course," she answered. "I imagine everyone here knows the lyrics. I love that song."

Again the audience cheered and clapped.

"Let's sing it together."

"What? Now? You want to sing it now?" Her heart felt as though it were about to stop.

The crowd began to chant her name, louder and louder until she finally agreed. "Yes, okay." She moved closer to him and whispered, "I'm going to get you for this."

"Isabel, love, my mic is on."

She groaned, and the crowd roared their approval as a mic stand was placed in front of her. It was bedlam until Xavier raised his hand to quiet them. He began to sing, and she quickly joined in. To the audience, the way they looked at each other was like two lovers about to come together. When they finished the tender ballad, the crowd jumped to their feet, cheering wildly. Xavier smiled at her, then leaned down and kissed her. He didn't linger, but the kiss was still long enough to cause a near riot. He laughed when he saw that she was blushing. He waved to the audience, took Isabel's hand, and the two of them walked off the stage together.

The next hour was a flurry of activity. Laurant, Regan, Jordan, Kate, and Michelle, along with their husbands, were escorted to Xavier's suite. Nick had a good laugh when his wife became tongue-tied while shaking Xavier's hand.

Noah and Michael stood watching from across the room. Nick joined them.

"You're not at all jealous?" Michael asked him.

"Hell, no. She's in my bed, not his."

"You didn't like it when Xavier kissed Isabel," Noah remarked to Michael. "And before you ask, it was the look on your face."

"Yeah? How'd I look?" Michael asked. He couldn't keep the hostility out of his voice, which, of course, didn't faze Noah.

"Like you wanted to punch him."

"That's exactly what I wanted to do, and hell if I know why," Michael admitted.

"Hey, Nick," Noah said.

"Yes?"

"When did your brother become so clueless?"

Nick grinned. "He hasn't been himself since he let Isabel drive him home."

Michael ignored their ribbing. He shook his head, then said, "We've taken enough of Xavier's time, and Isabel looks tired."

The throng of people around Isabel finally dwindled, and she was talking to Emerson, the agent, when Xavier interrupted. He took Isabel aside and talked to her for several minutes, then walked with her to the door.

"You've got the schedule. I'll see you when you get back."

Michael nudged Isabel out into the hallway before Xavier could kiss her good-bye. Nick and Noah followed.

There were only two of Xavier's guards outside the door. Isabel looked around and asked, "Where did Kate and the others go?"

Michael answered her. "Jax is driving them back to the Hamilton."

"Are they all coming up to the suite before they go home?"

"No," Nick answered.

"Oh, good." Too late she realized she'd said the thought out loud and rushed to explain. "I'm sorry. It's just that it's been so loud and chaotic . . ."

"Isabel, you don't need to apologize," Michael told her.

"Okay," she said. "How are we getting back to the hotel?"

"We've got that covered," Noah said. "Let's go."

Nick and Noah started down the hallway with Michael and Isabel behind them. They hadn't gotten far when she stopped. "My garment bag. We forgot it. It's in Xavier's suite . . . the closet . . ."

They backtracked and waited until one of the guards carried out the bag and handed it to Noah.

"Want to try this again?" Nick asked.

"Okay, but I'm telling you, we're never going to find a way out of here. It's a maze," Isabel said.

Nick and Noah knew what they were doing, and it didn't take long to reach the back entrance.

"Here we go." Nick had to shout because the noise coming from outside was ear-piercing.

"They're waiting for Xavier," she insisted.

"They're calling your name, too," Noah said.

As soon as they stepped outside, the screaming intensified. The barricade couldn't hold the fans back, and they ran to Isabel. She waved to them, but she didn't dare stop. There were so many. Had she been alone, it would have been scary. She didn't think they meant her any harm, but their enthusiasm could mow her down. With one arm around her and the other extended to ward off the crowd, Michael wouldn't let anyone get near her. She felt like a football tucked in his arm as they hurried to the car parked in a "No Parking" zone at the side of the building. A policeman had his pad out and appeared to be writing a ticket. When he spotted Noah, he nodded and hurried to open the doors. The four of them were in the car and on their way in seconds. Isabel could finally let go of some of the tension she'd been holding in all night. She was so thankful it was over.

"That was a hell of a thing you did tonight, Isabel," Nick said. He turned in his seat to look at her and noticed how she leaned into Michael.

"Now you're a superstar," Noah said.

"Oh God, I hope not."

She had sounded so appalled Noah and Nick both laughed.

"It will get easier," Nick said. "Just look at Xavier. He's at the top of the music world, and he couldn't be any more laid-back."

"He's had a lot of practice with crowds. I looked at his bio. He's been doing this since he was a teenager in Ireland."

"The guy's got a superpower," Nick said.

"How's that?" Noah asked.

"He raises his hand, and the audience quiets down. Think I could learn how to do that with Samantha and Tommy?"

Nick got a call from the concierge at the Hamilton, ending the discussion. He was only on the phone for a minute. "There are reporters with cameras in front of the hotel. They don't know where Xavier is staying, so they're covering the five-star hotels, hoping to get a shot of him."

"We're going up in the service elevator," Nick said.

Isabel was impressed with how organized Nick and Noah were, and their steady self-assurance was a relief. The pressure was finally loosening its grip when it suddenly dawned on her that they should have reached the hotel by now. She looked out the window and didn't recognize any streets.

"Where are we going?" she asked.

Michael answered. "We're taking the scenic route back. Are they still following us?" he asked Noah.

"I think I've lost them," Noah answered. "Just want to be sure."

Twenty minutes later, after a meandering route through Boston streets, Isabel was back in her suite.

"You can relax now," Noah told her. "No one gets on the elevators without showing a room card."

Both he and Noah took off their ties and stuffed them into the pockets of their suit jackets before heading to the bar refrigerator for a beer. Nick tossed one to Michael, who had already taken off his jacket and hung it in the closet. He grabbed his gym bag and dropped it in a chair by the bedroom door. Then he uncapped his beer and took a long drink. Ready to take a breather, Noah and Nick sprawled out in the chairs, and Michael leaned against the bar. It wasn't until then that Isabel drew their attention.

After circling the room several times, she went to the sofa, sat, and then jumped right back up. "I'm so happy it's over. I think it went well. Didn't it go well? Maybe it went well. Does it matter now? It's over, thank goodness. Did Kate have a good time? I hope so. My sister works hard." She was talking so fast her words were tripping over one another.

Michael looked at Nick and said, "Treadmill."

"Treadmill? What does that mean?" Nick asked.

Isabel didn't give Michael time to explain but continued rambling. "Did you see how happy Laurant was when she shook Xavier's hand? I can't believe I'm not tired. I should be exhausted, but I'm not. I've got an abundance of energy."

"An abundance?" Michael said.

"That means 'a lot,' Michael," Nick explained.

He shot his brother an annoyed glance. "I know what it means."

Isabel paced in front of the chair with the gym bag and stopped. "Why do you have your bag?" she asked.

He answered with a question. "Are you going to stay here tonight?"

"Yes, I am."

"Then I'm staying with you. I'll sleep out here on the sofa."

"Why are you staying?" she asked.

"Because I know what's going to happen. In the middle of the night you're going to want to go to the fitness center and get on the treadmill, aren't you?"

She decided to admit the truth. "I might."

"Ah, treadmill," Nick said, finally understanding.

"Has she done this before? Get up in the middle of the night . . . ," Noah began.

"She tried. I didn't let her."

Isabel started speed-talking again. She bounced from one thought to another.

"Nick, when are you going to get my flash drive back from that technician? I promised Xavier I would put my songs together soon, and I should probably gather them all. Thank God I don't have to sing in front of a huge crowd like that again. Promise me, none of you will ask me to sing at the party tomorrow night. Okay?" She didn't give them time to agree. "I'm just so happy I didn't mess up. I didn't, did I?"

Since she was looking at Michael, he answered. "No, you didn't mess up."

Her smile was radiant. She looked like he had just given her the highest praise ever.

"Would you like something to drink, Isabel?" Nick asked when he could get a word in.

She went to Michael and took his beer. "No, thank you," she said. She took a drink and then handed the bottle back.

"What you're experiencing is a surge of adrenaline, Isabel," Noah told her.

Nick nodded agreement. "In a little while you're going to crash, then you'll be able to sleep." Turning to Michael he said, "I think it's a good idea for you to stick around."

"We should get going," Nick said.

"Yeah, you should," Michael told them. Just as Noah was about to stand, Michael said, "No, wait. Stay until I get out of the shower. She might take off while I'm in there."

He picked up his bag and had his hand on the bedroom doorknob but turned when Isabel began to protest. "I'm perfectly capable of taking care of myself. I'm . . ."

She stopped arguing because he disappeared into the bedroom and shut the door. She looked at Nick and said, "That was rude, wasn't it? Yes, it was rude. Some of the fans tonight were overly enthusiastic, but I don't think any of them were rude. They were just excited. Right? Weren't they excited?" Once again she didn't give them time to answer. "I'll admit I would have been scared if Michael and you two weren't there. They could have rolled over me. They'd push like they did when we were hurrying to the car. I don't believe I could push that many people out of my way." She shivered, picturing the mob scene, and whispered, "I just never expected anything like that. Thank God you were with me."

"It's over now, Isabel," Noah said. His voice was kind and soothing.

She nodded. She sat on the sofa again, her hands at her sides. "Did you have a nice time tonight?"

Thinking she would keep talking, neither one answered her for several seconds, but when she looked at them expectantly, Noah said, "Yes, it was fun tonight. I like Xavier."

She smiled. "I like him, too."

Nick frowned. "How much do you like him?"

"What's that supposed to mean? You either like someone or you don't. I do like him. That's all there is to it. I like a lot of people."

Noah, blunt as always, asked, "What about Michael? Do you like him?"

"Sometimes."

Noah and Nick exchanged a look as though they found her answer amusing.

Isabel settled back against the sofa pillows. "I'm not going anywhere," she told them. "You should take off."

"We'll wait," Noah said.

Now that she had quieted down, Nick answered one of her earlier questions. "About your flash drive—I was promised I'd get it back Monday or Tuesday."

"Thank you."

"Are you going home tonight, Nick? Is Laurant home with the children?"

"Samantha and Tommy spent most of the day and early evening on the island with my parents. They're back home now with the nanny. Tomorrow's a busy day for them. Sam has a play date and a birthday party to attend, and Tommy has a clean house he'll try to destroy."

Noah laughed. "He's not even two years old yet, and already giving you fits. I love that kid."

The talk turned to the MacAlisters. "After the party tomorrow, no matter how late it is, you know they're gonna want to play poker," Noah said. "Are you in?"

"Sure. Are you?"

"Wouldn't miss it."

"Until Jordan drags you to bed," Nick said.

"I like it when my wife drags me to bed." He grinned after making the comment.

They continued talking about the relatives until the bedroom door opened and Michael walked out. He was barefoot and wore a white T-shirt and gym shorts. His hair was still wet. "Okay, Isabel. It's your turn," he said.

"Are you sure you don't want to go back to the island tonight, Isabel?" Nick asked. "We'll help you pack up."

She shook her head. "I want to wind down, and this is the perfect place. It's quiet, and I can order room service."

She thanked them for taking such good care of her tonight and then walked into the bedroom to get ready for bed. She paused at the doors, turned back, and said, "Please take Michael with you. I'm fine, and I really want to be alone." Thanking them once again, she closed the doors.

She spent a long time in the shower. She had to wash her hair again because of all the product the stylist had insisted on, and it took even longer to get all the makeup off. By the time she dried her hair and put on moisturizer, she was wiped out. She went into the bedroom, opened a room service menu, and sat on the side of the bed, flipping through the pages of the menu to find something she wanted to eat. Finally coming to the conclusion that she wasn't really hungry after all, she turned down the comforter but didn't get into bed. The tension of the day had left her drained and all she could do was stare into space. She was still sitting there in a silent stupor when Michael walked into the bedroom. Adrenaline was suddenly flowing through her veins again. It didn't matter what he was wearing, a business suit or shorts and a T-shirt, he was one fine-looking man, all right. He was also a pain in her backside, she reminded herself.

"Why are you still here?"

Ignoring her question, he said, "Let me get that bandage off your arm. It's wet."

Michael sat down beside her, so close his thigh rubbed against hers, and it was almost impossible to concentrate on what he was doing. After several attempts he finally got the bandage off and tossed it in the trash can. The pad that had covered the stitches kept them dry.

"How does it look?" she asked. She was so close to him she could feel his heat.

"It's healing," he answered. Michael told himself to get up, and yet he couldn't make himself move. He desperately wanted to lose himself in her. He needed to think about something else—anything else—and then he noticed she was holding a leather binder opened to the room service menu. "Did you want to order something to eat?"

"I don't know. Do you?"

They stared at each other a long minute without saying a word. The silence was heavy with anticipation.

She stood, thinking she should shoo him out of the room and get into bed and try to sleep. It wasn't what she really wanted to do, though. Since Michael had walked into the police station, she had this indescribable need to be with him, and she simply didn't want to resist any longer. She knew it was crazy and that a relationship with Michael could never go anywhere, but right this minute she didn't care about consequences or being reasonable, and she wasn't going to worry about what she would do if he rejected her. Whatever happened tonight, she was a big girl, and she could handle it.

"It's been a long day. You should get some sleep," Michael said, reaching over to turn off the bedside lamp. He was about to force himself to get up when she sat down on his lap, put her arms around his neck, and rested against him. Her head was tucked under his chin, and he could feel her heartbeat. "What are you doing? Get off me, Isabel."

"I will . . . in a minute." She decided to make up an excuse so she could hug him longer. "I'm cold and you're nice and warm."

He wrapped his arms around her and pulled her tight against him while he again ordered her to get the hell off him. His actions contradicted his demand, but he wanted her too much to care. What was the harm of holding her for a few minutes? He was comforting her after her long stressful day and evening. Yeah, that was it.

He let out a long sigh. *Comfort, my ass.*

EIGHTEEN

MICHAEL BEGAN STROKING HER BACK AND IT FELT WONDERFUL. Isabel closed her eyes and let thoughts ramble through her mind. She wondered how he would react if she told him she was determined never to fall in love with him. He was too dangerous. He'd probably jump with joy, she imagined, for he definitely wasn't into personal commitment now. He had too many new careers to conquer, and settling down would be the last thing on his mind. She wasn't sure she ever wanted to settle down, either. She had too much to do and see. And if she ever changed her mind, she would choose someone who would love her passionately and be true to her. Someone just like Judge Buchanan. The way he looked at his wife, after all these years together . . . with such love. Yes, that's what she wanted . . . eventually.

It was lust controlling her now, she decided. They were two consenting adults, and she wanted to know what it would feel like to give in to desire. Was that a sin? To give in to temptation? She couldn't seem to care if it was.

"What are you thinking, Isabel?" Michael asked. She'd become tense in his arms.

"That I'd like you to kiss me."

She leaned back, looked deeply into his eyes, and that was all it took. His hand went to the back of her neck, and his mouth came down on top of hers in a scorching kiss that let her know how much he wanted her. His tongue rubbed against hers, teasing a response. The kiss was wet, wild, and incredibly hot. She had the softest lips and tasted so good. He couldn't seem to get enough of her fast enough. One kiss, and intense desire he'd never experienced before knifed through him.

Isabel wasn't passive. Her tongue was every bit as wild as his. Her fingers threaded through his hair, and she let out a low groan when he ended the kiss. She wanted another and another.

The bedroom was cast in shadows, the only light spilling in from the living room French doors. The only sound that of their harsh breathing. She never wanted to let go of him.

He kissed her again, a long, slow kiss that made every nerve in her body tingle. She couldn't stop caressing him. Her hand slowly slid across his shoulders and upper arms. She could feel his muscles under his skin. There was such power and strength in him, and yet he was so gentle with her. Leaning in, she kissed the side of his neck. She was suddenly feeling shy and vulnerable but was determined to make her intentions clear.

Her voice quivered when she said, "I want you, Michael."

There was a hint of amusement in his replay. "I know."

His arrogance didn't bother her. "Do you want me?"

"Yeah, I do."

She quit hiding from him and leaned back. Trailing her fingertips down his cheek, she looked into his eyes and said, "Remember. Sex is just a pleasurable activity tonight."

Oh God, had he really said that? He couldn't come up with anything better?

Michael was frowning and Isabel wasn't sure he understood what she was telling him. Should she remind him? The first time they were in the hotel together, he had told her that a man didn't need to like the woman he took to his bed, and he had said very matter-of-factly that sex was just a pleasurable activity, sometimes an extremely pleasurable activity. She didn't want him to feel guilty or have regrets tomorrow, though, in truth, she doubted he would.

Isabel decided she didn't want to go into a long explanation now. If he didn't recall the conversation, that was on him. "Sex is just a pleasurable activity," she repeated.

Michael could hear the tremor in her voice, and he could see how tense she was, though she was obviously trying to hide her insecurity. He knew she wasn't scared—he wouldn't touch her if she was—she was just a little nervous. But then, so was he. He had fought for so long not to touch her, but lately it was all he could think about, and now that it was finally happening, he didn't want to overwhelm her. If he went at the warp speed he wanted to, they'd already be done . . . the first time. He'd make love to her all night long if she'd let him. Isabel made him feel whole again. It was the only way he could explain it.

It would be all over for him if he didn't pace himself. He kept picturing all the ways he wanted to make love to her, and though he tried, he couldn't block the image of her naked body writhing beneath him. Yeah, he had it bad, thanks to his wild undisciplined thoughts. Then it came to him. He'd get her talking and, come heaven or hell, he'd force himself to listen.

"Isabel?"

"Yes?"

"Are you going to show me how incredible you are in bed?"

Uh-oh. "Oh God," she groaned. She had forgotten all about her outrageous boast that, while he was busy training to become a lawyer, then a Navy SEAL, and only God knew what else, she was perfecting the art of seduction. It had been a silly lie. Did he actually believe her? Of course not. She could see the mischief in his eyes and knew he was teasing her.

He lifted her off his lap, and she stood between his legs facing him. She watched as he pulled his T-shirt over his head and tossed it aside. The sprinkle of dark curly hair on his chest tapered at his navel. She wanted to kiss every inch of him.

Isabel had a sexy-as-sin body, and Michael was about to tell her so, but then she removed her top, and he lost every thought in his head. Never taking her eyes off his, she slowly slid her pajama shorts down over her hips and let them drop to the floor. Michael forgot how to breathe. She was perfect. It seemed that all he had to do was look at her or think about her and he became aroused. She had that much power over him, and he wasn't fighting it any longer.

Her boldness pleased him. He reached out to caress her breasts, marveling at how soft and smooth her skin was, and then he slowly trailed his finger down to her hips, smiling over the goose bumps he caused her. He lifted her away from him so he could stand, then quickly stripped out of the rest of his clothes.

Michael pulled the sheets back, then turned to her. She moved into his arms, squeezing her eyes shut in absolute bliss because his body felt so good against hers. He kissed her again, long and hard, and fell into bed with her. He rolled her onto her back, then stretched out on top of her, bracing his weight with his arms. He nudged her knees apart so that his pelvis could press against hers. His groan was loud and freeing. "God, you feel good."

She sighed. "So do you."

Wanting to make their coming together perfect, he forced himself to take his time. Her breasts were pressed against his chest, and every time she moved at all, her pelvis rubbed against him. Taking his time was the most difficult thing he had ever done, but he was determined. She moved again, and the pleasure she gave him was so intense he clenched his jaw. He could feel his composure disintegrating.

Overwhelmed now, he made love to her with his mouth, his tongue mating with hers, sliding in and out while his hands caressed her breasts.

Isabel had no idea how sensitive her breasts were until he kissed them and stroked them with his tongue. He slowly moved down her body, teasing and tormenting her. He kissed the valley between her breasts, then her navel, then moved lower between her thighs. She nearly came off the bed when he touched her so intimately. She tried to get him to stop. The pleasure was so exquisite, it scared her, yet at the same time she clung to him and demanded more. His tongue was magical. Her hips moved against him, and her moans told him how much she loved what he was doing to her.

When it was Isabel's turn, the pleasure she gave him shattered Michael's control. She was a little awkward, and that made it all the better. He couldn't let her torment him for long. He pulled away long enough to get protection, and when he returned, he reached for her and rolled her on her back again, rougher now with his need to be inside her. He knew she was ready for him. He wasn't gentle as he pushed her thighs apart. His mouth covered hers as he lifted her hips and thrust inside her. He didn't expect her to be this tight, this hot, this perfect. She cried out when he entered her, and he immediately stopped until she arched up against him.

"Isabel, am I hurting you?" He was panting and his voice was harsh.

"Please . . . please don't stop." Her nails dug into his shoulders again, a demand to move.

It was all the encouragement he needed. He couldn't take his time now, but thrust deep, withdrew, and thrust deep again. She moaned with pleasure, begging him with whispered words that didn't make any sense.

Passion controlled both of them, and when he felt her tighten around him and whisper his name, he knew she was about to come apart.

"Let it happen, love. Let go. I'll keep you safe."

Isabel had never had a climax before, and what she was feeling scared her because she had no control over it, but when Michael promised to keep her safe, she stopped fighting and let the euphoria overtake her. Her orgasm consumed her, and it was the most exhilarating and frightening thing she had ever experienced. She felt as though she were flying among the stars and ever so slowly floating back into Michael's strong arms.

He was there with her, climaxing while she was in the throes of her orgasm. She shouted his name and squeezed him inside her. He whispered her name, then groaned low in his throat and tightened his arms around her, pulling her up against him as wave after wave of ecstasy consumed him. His release was pure rapture, and it was all because he was with Isabel. His head dropped down in the crook of her neck, his breathing harsh against her ear. He noticed she was having as much trouble recovering as he was and that made him inordinately pleased.

Their bodies were slick with perspiration. Michael was so content, he never wanted to move, but then he knew, once he got his strength back, he would make love to her again. With Isabel he was insatiable.

What the holy . . . Those were the first words Isabel wanted to shout, but she thought she caught herself in time. She was still reeling.

"It's called an orgasm, sweetheart."

Oops. So much for being sophisticated about it all. She shivered when he kissed the side of her neck. Then he rolled to his side, got out of bed, and went into the bathroom. Isabel was shocked how her body was trembling and reached for the sheet to cover up. Was it the aftermath of what she had just experienced? She took a deep breath and slowly let it out. Having sex with Michael was the most amazing thing.

It didn't take any time at all to want him again. Good God, Michael had the power to turn her into a sex maniac. But only with him, she qualified. She couldn't imagine being this free and letting any other man touch her the way Michael did.

What was the protocol after sex? What should they talk about? Or should they not talk at all and just pretend to go to sleep? No, of course not, she decided. They were adults. She knew Michael was going to be very laid-back about it all. He had probably been having sex since he hit puberty. He was a pro, though she doubted he would want to hear that. He certainly had perfected his technique. He had her melting as soon as he touched her.

By now he knew how inexperienced she was, and she hoped he didn't say anything about it. She knew she had pleased him. The way he held her and called her name, and all the nonsensical words he whispered into her ear told her so. She wondered if he said those words to the other women he'd taken to his bed. She blocked the thought. She didn't want to think about the other women now. She was still feeling wonderful and didn't want to move.

Closing her eyes, she let her mind wander. It had been an amazing day. Her thoughts drifted to the concert tonight and how incredible Xavier had been. Talk about charisma. The man had an abundance. Xavier had loads of personal charm. Until tonight she hadn't thought Michael had any charm at all, but then she saw him talking to Xavier and some of his staff and he had been quite charming and pleasant. What a revelation that had been.

Her mind then went to the crowd and the craziness outside and how it took three strong men and a carefully thought-out plan to get away safely. The screaming got to her, she admitted. Had she been alone she would have been terrified.

Michael returned and walked into the living room to get her cell phone from his jacket pocket. He put it on the charger and then got back into bed with her.

"How come you're frowning?" he asked as he pulled her into his arms. "What are you thinking about?"

He wasn't prepared for her answer.

"I was thinking I never want to do that again."

She'd stunned him speechless. The condition didn't last long. "What the hell, Isabel? I know you had at least one orgasm. You came apart in my arms, and you were yelling my name. If I hadn't been in such a hurry, you would have had two, maybe three, more. In fact,

I'm going to make sure . . ." He stopped ranting at her when she put her hand over his mouth.

"I was talking about the concert," she explained. He looked so upset she didn't dare laugh. "I was thinking about it, and I made up my mind I'm never going to do that again. Even though Xavier made it easy, I still hated being onstage. As for the other . . ." She deliberately left him hanging.

"Yes?" he demanded, and before she could answer, he said, "Stop toying with me."

"It was nice, Michael. Very nice," she whispered.

The impish twinkle in her eyes encouraged him. "Next time I'll do better than nice," he promised. He began to nuzzle the side of her neck. Every time he got near her he got hard. It was her smile . . . and her sass.

"Isabel?"

"Hmm?"

"Guess when next time is?" He gently nudged her on her back, then stretched out on top of her. Lifting up on his elbows, he stared into her eyes while he waited for her answer.

She traced his lower lip with the tip of her tongue and whispered, "Now?" a second before his mouth covered hers. By the time he ended the kiss she was begging him not to stop.

"You're going to love this," he promised.

The man was nothing if not truthful. She could barely keep her arms around his waist when he finally gave in to his own need and thrust inside her. Though it didn't seem possible she climaxed again when he did.

Could making love kill her? With Michael it just might, she thought.

He turned her and pulled her close, her head on his chest as he gently stroked her back. Even though there weren't any sweet loving words, his caresses were enough. Isabel considered herself a realist. She knew that down the road, if she ended up with a broken heart, it wouldn't be anyone's fault but her own. She didn't want to think about the future now. She wanted to savor every minute of the night with Michael.

She tried to get out of bed to get something to drink, but Michael wouldn't let her move. He got both of them bottles of Coke. He even poured hers into a glass with ice. Like a man who had just taken a brisk walk through the desert, he guzzled his drink, and when it was empty, he drank most of hers.

"Oh, that's lovely," she said. There was less than a sip left in the glass.

His response was to laugh. He got her another Coke, then sat back against the headboard, looking perfectly content to be stark naked. He was such a distraction she couldn't concentrate on what he was telling her, so she pulled the sheet up.

"I'm sorry. What did you say?" She scooted up and sat next to him, leaning into his side.

"I said your cell phone is charging," he repeated.

"Thank you."

"That son of a bitch called you three times while you were on-stage."

"Which particular son of a bitch are you referring to?" she asked sweetly.

"James Reid," he said. "I let the calls go to voicemail."

"His sales pitch is turning into harassment. He must be getting a big commission."

"Want me to talk to him?"

"No, I can handle it."

"Tell me about this land you're going to inherit."

"Why would I do that? You don't share anything personal with me."

He leaned down and kissed her forehead. "Baby, I just shared my body with you. Can't get any more personal than that."

He had her there. "You know what I mean. You always close up on me whenever I ask anything about your personal life."

He didn't argue. "What do you want to know?"

"How did you get those three bullets in your back?"

"I was shot three times."

He was being flippant, but she wasn't going to push him. If he didn't want to tell her, she would let it go. He was proving her point, though. He closed up whenever she asked anything personal.

"It's like talking to a tree stump," she remarked on a sigh.

He laughed. Another minute passed, and then he said, "I was on a mission. That's when I got shot."

"Navy SEALs?"

"Yes."

"You were in Afghanistan, and before you ask, I heard your father talking to you."

"What else did you hear?"

"That's all. I know you can't and won't talk about your time as a Navy SEAL. There's a code, isn't there? You only talk to your other team members about your missions, but no one outside the SEALs?"

"That's right."

"Were your injuries the reason you didn't stay with the SEALs?"

"No, the mission was my last. My tour was over and I didn't re-up."

"You could have died," she whispered, a tinge of fear in her voice.

He nodded. "I was lucky."

Michael could see that Isabel wanted more from him, but he couldn't give it. The details of the mission were in a classified file, and that's where they would stay for the time being, or at least until the Navy released them, but the memories from that day would be with him as long as he lived.

The team had been sent into a village that was nothing more than a tiny dot on the map of Afghanistan. A band of insurgents had swarmed into the area and set up camp. By the time the SEALs arrived, almost half of the inhabitants had been slaughtered, including women and children. Michael would never forget the horrific scene when they arrived. Carnage and bloodshed everywhere. Innocents gunned down where they stood.

The town was eerily quiet as the team went from house to house, searching for the men who had done this. In some, they found nothing, and in others they found terrorized victims too frightened to speak. Finally, a young boy, no more than nine or ten, whom they discovered huddled with his mother in the corner of a bedroom, timidly stepped forward and told them he saw the insurgents going into the house of one of the village elders. With some coaxing and despite the pleas of his mother, he agreed to show them the way. He then led them toward the edge of the village and pointed to the house, a traditional mud-and-timber structure surrounded by a low wall.

Reconnaissance and surveillance equipment revealed there were eight insurgents holding a man, a woman, and a young girl inside. The SEALs waited for the right moment, and then they stormed the house. The enemy put up a fight but were no match. Leading the way, Michael found the man and woman cowering by the door, but he didn't see the child. He rushed the couple outside and ran back in. With gunfire all around him, he searched, finally spotting the top of the little girl's head behind a stack of pillows on the floor. He snatched her up in his arms and raced out. Protecting the child with his body wrapped protectively around her, he sprinted to get her away from the house and the flying bullets. He almost made it to safety, but one of the insurgents, in a final blaze of glory before collapsing from his own wounds, took aim and fired at Michael's back, hitting him three times.

The next thing Michael remembered was waking up in a field hospital with his SEAL brothers around him. The first words he uttered were, "Is she okay?"

"Thanks to you, yes," his commander assured. "She's with her family."

Now every time images of his last mission returned to haunt him, Michael saw the devastation, the death, and the terror in that little girl's eyes. He had seen enough brutality and its aftermath to last a lifetime. There was no way he could put an end to all the evil he had witnessed, but maybe the solution—at least for him—was to stop the terrorists before they could execute their plans. After weighing his options, he decided the Counterterrorism Division of the FBI would be the best place for him. He realized it would be naive to think he could save the world, but at least he could try to save a small part of it.

Isabel pulled him from his thoughts when she said, "Please answer one more question. Did that mission make a difference in anyone's life?"

Michael remembered the family he'd helped escape. At least they were safe now. "Yes," he answered. "The mission made a difference."

He tucked a stray strand of hair behind her ear and said, "Okay, it's your turn, Isabel. Tell me about the land you're going to inherit."

"I'm going to sell it. I'm getting it from my great-uncle, Compton MacKenna, who amassed quite a fortune. Kate and Kiera and I never met the man. Compton was mean-spirited. He disowned my father when he married my mother. He made a video outlining the changes to his will. Like I said, he had amassed a fortune and his brother's grandsons thought they were going to get it all. Kate and Dylan went to the attorney's office and watched the video Compton made to go with his will. In it he defamed our mother. He said horrible things about her. He also said he believed his great-nephews were all useless and they didn't deserve to get much of his money. He liked us three girls, he said, because in spite of our mother, who he said was no better than a street beggar, we had all made something of ourselves. Kate and Kiera received the bulk of his estate, close to one hundred million dollars."

Michael smiled. "They didn't keep it, did they?"

"No, they didn't. All the money went to build a new cancer center at the university hospital complex. It's called the Leah MacKenna Cancer Center. That ought to make that mean old man roll over in his grave."

"And he gave you Glen MacKenna."

"Yes," she said. "I don't know why. Perhaps the letter he wrote to me will explain his reasons. Compton MacKenna was given to drama. Kate brought the DVD home of Compton spelling out the terms of his will. It was difficult to watch and listen to him slander my mother. He looked down on her because she wasn't born with a title or high social status. Her family didn't have money, and they weren't blue bloods, so Compton deemed her unworthy to join his family."

"Did Compton have a title? Was he a blue blood?" he asked.

"No. He was a hypocrite."

"Sounds like it," he agreed. "Your mother raised all three of you without any help, didn't she?"

"No, she had help. She went to work at a private school, and when Kiera and Kate became students there, the tuition was free. My aunt Nora moved in to take care of me." She laughed and added, "She had quite an influence on me. Sometimes I sound just like her."

Michael tilted Isabel's chin up and looked at her with a concerned expression. "There's something we need to talk about."

Was he going to bring up her inexperience in bed? Wouldn't that be great? She wouldn't be feeling so insecure if she hadn't bragged about being such a sex goddess. He'd known she was teasing, hadn't he? Of course he had, but her mind still raced to come up with an explanation if he brought it up.

"Yes?"

"You said you never want to go onstage again."

Relief surged through her. "Yes, that's what I said, all right."

He seemed puzzled. "Did you mean it?"

"Of course I meant it. I wouldn't have said it if I didn't mean it."

He took her empty glass and set it on the table next to his drink, then fixed his eyes on hers. "Do you understand what happened tonight?"

"I was there, Michael, so yes, I know what happened."

Isabel really didn't have any idea how fantastic she was. She had become a superstar tonight, and he was shocked to learn she didn't want it.

"I'm a songwriter," she said. "I'm not a performer."

Isabel didn't want to talk about the concert any longer. She knew she would have to figure out what she was going to do, but that could wait until tomorrow. She had other ideas now. She surprised Michael when she kicked the sheet down and turned to straddle his lap. She got up on her knees and kissed him. Then she leaned back.

"I was thinking I would seduce you."

The sexy smile in his eyes made her shiver. "Yeah?"

She nodded. "And then I'm going to write a song about it."

He was totally unprepared for that statement and burst into laughter. "Sweetheart, that would be an X-rated song."

She trailed her fingertips down the stubble on his cheek. He was such a rugged-looking man, and oh how his scent appealed to her. It reminded her of worn leather and the woods after a rain, but also it was male . . . so Michael. There was just something about him. When she got near him, every part of her reacted.

Isabel put her arms around his neck. "I'm going for triple X."

Those were the last coherent words she spoke for a long while.

Later . . . much later, they fell asleep wrapped in each other's arms.

NINETEEN

MORNING DIDN'T BRING ANY REGRETS. OKAY, MAYBE THERE WERE a few, but they came much later.

Isabel slept until after eight, and when she opened her eyes, she was alone in bed. She heard movement in the other room and surmised that Michael was an early riser, just another trait she was discovering about him. Last night had proven he was indeed a man of surprises. Groaning, she slowly stretched, then went into the bathroom to get ready for the day. When she moved, she was astonished at how tender she was, but then she had used just about every muscle in her body. How many times had they reached for each other? How many times had she reached for him? She was pretty sure she even nudged him awake once or twice. She had been that ravenous. But then, so had he.

A shower helped revive her. By the time she dressed, she was wide awake. And starving.

While she was drying her hair, she noticed Michael's shaving kit wasn't in the bathroom, and when she walked out through the bedroom she realized Michael wasn't in the suite. She thought he might have gone downstairs for something until she noticed his gym bag was gone. He had packed up and taken off.

"That was rude," she whispered. "Damn rude." She thought of

quite a few expletives she could shout just to vent her frustration, but then she came to her senses and realized how futile they would be.

Then she spotted the envelope with her name on it on the desk. She dreaded opening it. If he said, *Thank you for last night*, she might just let some of those expletives fly. Did he sneak away? No, of course not. Michael wasn't the sneak-away kind of man. Still, he was gone. Didn't he want to face her in the morning light? Why didn't he wake her and tell her where he was going?

Isabel held the envelope in her hand for a good five minutes before she finally opened it. The note was short. Michael had a long drive to get to a meeting he couldn't miss, and he wouldn't be back until early evening. Regan was in the city and would drive Isabel back to Nathan's Bay. Michael's last line was anything but affectionate. *See you at the party.*

Couldn't be more lovey-dovey than that, now, could he? What had she expected? She knew what she was doing last night. She had all but begged him to make love to her, and she wasn't at all sorry about it. She just wanted to be with him for one beautiful night. No strings attached. She knew he didn't love her, and she had to remind herself to be okay with that.

Having reasoned it out, she could move forward. She ordered breakfast and opened her laptop to read her emails. One email was from Damon, and what he wrote lightened her mood. He'd run into Mia at Starbucks, took her out to dinner, and found himself apologizing. He still didn't know what their argument was about, but Mia decided to forgive him. He didn't think it would be a good idea to ask her specifically what he had done. He ended the email with a disclaimer: he wasn't in love with her. Isabel interpreted his denial to mean just the opposite. Another email was from Lexi, who suggested that Isabel check out several celebrity sites. According to her, at the moment Isabel was the It girl.

Isabel bounced from one gossip site to another and was shocked.

Overnight, rumors had started flying. Her face was everywhere, and the reports about her were outrageous. Two different sites wrote that she was engaged to Xavier; another suggested they were already married. There was also a story that she had signed with one of the top recording labels for millions of dollars. How could they make up such blatant lies and print them? She knew there were people who believed whatever they read. She couldn't stop them, so she decided the only thing she could do about all the misinformation floating around out there was to ignore it.

There was a knock on her door, and Isabel rushed to answer it. Maybe Michael's meeting had been canceled or rescheduled and he'd come back. When Regan walked in, Isabel turned away so her friend wouldn't see how disappointed she was.

Isabel was disgusted with herself. She was not going to let herself turn into a lovesick, needy woman. The possibility of that ever happening turned her stomach.

Forcing a cheerful voice, she said, "Thank you again for letting me stay in this beautiful suite. I'll hurry and pack—"

Regan interrupted. "No, the suite is yours until you leave on Monday."

Although grateful for Regan's generosity, Isabel refused to take advantage. "That's too much," she said. "I'll move my things—"

"The suite is yours until you leave for the airport Monday," Regan repeated. "I've already done the paperwork." She added with a smile, "Besides, this particular suite is scheduled for a complete makeover, and it won't be booked again until it's finished. If you don't use it, it will just sit empty until the middle of next week. That's when the crew will start the remodel."

"Regan, I appreciate all you've done for me, but I want to be responsible for the room charges. I gave my credit card to the front desk."

"There won't be any charges," Regan insisted. "This is your graduation present from Alec and me. We want you to pamper yourself. Order whatever you want and take advantage of the spa."

"I was planning to stay on Nathan's Bay tonight," Isabel said. "But coming back here is very tempting."

"Just leave your things here until you're back . . . whenever that is."

Room service arrived, interrupting the discussion. The waiter wheeled in a table laden with enough food to feed a large family. Lifting the silver domes he revealed fresh fruit, yogurt, bagels, cream cheese, and an assortment of Danish and toasts with jam. Crystal pitchers were filled with two kinds of juice, and a sterling pot of water was steaming hot for the variety of teas next to it.

"Oh my," Isabel said when she saw the feast. "Have you had breakfast, Regan? Will you stay and eat with me?"

"As a matter of fact, I left Nathan's Bay early, and I was going to order something when I got here. This is perfect." As she poured orange juice into a glass, she asked, "Are you in a hurry to get back to the island today?"

"Not at all, but I'll leave whenever you're ready."

"I'd like to get some work done, and it's going to take time. Kate called and told me it's a madhouse on the island. The men went sailing to get out of the way while the catering companies get the place ready for the party. They're expecting around a hundred people, and there's even going to be a dance floor and music. I think we should also stay out of everyone's way. Don't you?"

Isabel laughed. "I'm all for that."

"I brought my dress with me for tonight. I'll come get you around five."

"What time does the party start?"

"Six," she said.

"Why so early?"

"Some of the guests are quite elderly and will want to leave by nine. That's when the party will really get started. You'll have the rest of the day to relax. Why don't you get a massage and a facial?"

The talk eventually turned to the concert, and Regan admitted she was a little starstruck.

"Xavier is wonderful, isn't he?" Isabel said.

"Yes, he is, but I was talking about you. When you walked on-stage, you . . ."

"I what?"

"You took over. Isabel, you were fantastic, and you looked so at ease. The audience loved you."

Isabel shook her head. "At ease? I was worried the entire time that I would throw up."

Isabel was glad she had been able to convince people she was totally comfortable onstage, but their perception couldn't be further from the truth. Singing with Xavier in front of thousands of people had been a thrill of a lifetime; however, it wasn't a thrill she wanted to repeat. And after all these years of suppressing music, this was a revelation she would never have expected. Maybe she was finally discovering who she was.

After breakfast Regan left to go down to the business office, where it was quiet and she could get some work done without distractions. Having the rest of the day to herself, Isabel decided to take Regan's suggestion. She spent a long while at the fitness center, even did some laps in the pool, then showered and ordered a snack. In the mood to pamper herself, she then put on baggy sweats and went down to the spa. She was hoping she could beg someone to do her hair and makeup, but she didn't have to beg at all. Everyone there knew who she was, and the same stylist—a sweet man about her age named Curtis, who had applied her makeup for the concert—couldn't wait to get his hands on her again.

The hairstylist got hold of Isabel first, and while he washed and dried her hair, he told her all about his wife's interfering sisters. Then Curtis stepped forward to do her makeup. He wasn't as heavy-handed as he'd been for the concert, and as he worked, he confided in great detail that his fiancée's mother didn't approve of him. He continued his narrative about the woman for a while, then paused and stepped back with a makeup brush in hand, silently pondering his situation

and finally nodding to her. "Right, Isabel. Maybe I should stop calling her a bitch."

Isabel was pleased he agreed with her suggestion.

By the time Curtis finished with her, a crowd surrounded her,
and all of them wanted to know every little detail she could remember about Xavier. Answering all their questions took another hour,
and she didn't leave the salon until late afternoon.

With all the distractions, Isabel lost count of the number of times
she checked her phone to see if Michael had called. She guessed she
wanted some kind of acknowledgment that their night together had
been memorable. But then, for Michael, maybe it hadn't been.

Since it was a dress-up affair tonight, she decided to wear the black
fitted dress Regan and Kate had insisted she get. The crossover straps
at the neck and racerback showed off her tanned shoulders. If a dress
could be both modest and sexy as hell, this was it. She slipped into
her high-heeled sandals and dabbed on her favorite perfume.

Regan arrived promptly at five. She had changed into a soft peach
dress that looked lovely on her. With her dark hair, the color was
spectacular.

"We're going to take the service elevator to the garage," she explained.

"Why?" Isabel asked. She took her phone and room card from
the table and put them in her small wristlet with her lipstick.

"It's quicker," Regan told her.

Isabel accepted the explanation until she opened the door and
saw two security guards dressed in black suits, waiting for them.

"What's going on, Regan?"

"There were some photographers out front. Security has ordered
them off the property, but if we go out the circle drive, we'll be trapped.
There are also quite a few young men and women hanging around."

"They must think XO is here."

"Don't be so sure he's the one they're waiting for. You've become
quite a sensation yourself. It could be your autograph they're wanting."

Isabel was shocked. She couldn't comprehend why anyone would wait just to get her autograph.

"You should go without me," Isabel said. "They might surround the car . . ."

"Oh, I'm not driving. Alec is waiting downstairs for us. All we have to do is step off the elevator and get in the car." She took Isabel's hand and pulled her along.

Once they were in the elevator with the guards in front of them, Isabel asked, "What about your car?"

"I rented it through the hotel, so no worries. I've already given the keys to the concierge."

"I've made this such an inconvenience for Alec and you. I'm sorry."

The elevator doors opened, and there stood Alec. When he saw his wife, his eyes lit up. "Wow, babe, you look incredible." He then pulled her to him and gave her a long kiss.

Isabel didn't want to stand there and watch the two lovebirds, so she moved out of the way and let one of the guards open the back door of the car for her.

When the kiss ended, Regan, looking a bit dazed, was led around the car by her husband, who tucked her into the passenger seat. He then leaned down at the open back door and said, "Hi, Isabel. What are you doing there? You're supposed to get in the trunk." Getting the startled reaction he was seeking, he laughed as he shut the door and went around the car to get behind the wheel.

"Your husband has a warped sense of humor," Isabel told Regan.

"Yes, he does," she replied cheerfully. "Doesn't he look handsome tonight?"

Alec did look good, Isabel thought, even as she watched him tug on his tie. He wore a conservative navy blue suit with a white dress shirt and a blue-and-white-striped tie. He still looked a bit scruffy for his next undercover case, but there was no denying he was a Buchanan male, which meant he was an extremely handsome devil.

"Yes, he does," she agreed. "Alec, is it really crowded outside the hotel?"

"It's not bad. Just look straight ahead. We'll be out of here in no time."

This was just plain crazy, she thought. Surely the crowd outside thought XO was at the hotel. They wouldn't be waiting for her, would they? How long had she been onstage last night? Ten, fifteen minutes at the most. Her face was plastered on the gossip sites along with Xavier's, and now bedlam? She was certain this would all die down soon enough, and the notoriety would fade. Once she was on her way to Scotland, she could escape this madness.

They drove out onto the street and were immediately surrounded by screaming fans. Most were chanting Xavier's name, "XO, XO, XO," over and over again. But there were a few yelling her name, too. She noticed that some of the more frantic fans were shouting at every car that pulled out.

Alec, every bit as skilled as a Grand Prix driver, quickly and effortlessly got them on their way. Traffic was congested as usual, yet once they reached the highway, Isabel began to relax. A half hour later they were on the bridge to Nathan's Bay. No one would bother her there.

Isabel, who used to have a carefree attitude, had become quite the worrier.

No matter what, she was going to concentrate on the positives. It was going to be a beautiful night. Nathan's Bay was ready for a party. Every light in the house was on, and when darkness fell, it would become a beacon for everyone on the island. A huge square-shaped dance floor had been laid near the center of the manicured lawn. There were posts at least twelve feet high at each of the four corners. A net of tiny white lights attached to the top of the posts became a sparkling ceiling. It looked like a thousand twinkling stars.

The valets were setting up to park cars. Alec waved them off and drove around to the back of the house, next to the garages.

"Who organized this celebration?" Isabel asked. She took Alec's hand and let him help her out of the backseat. Before he could answer, she guessed, "Never mind. It was Jordan, Kate, and Regan. Right? I'm right, aren't I?"

Alec laughed. "I was going to try to convince you that my brothers and I planned the party, but you'd never buy it, so, yes, our wives did all the work."

All three of them came to a quick stop as soon as they entered the kitchen. The catering company had taken over the space, and their staff, dressed in white shirts, black pants, and black loafers, were rushing back and forth with silver trays laden with delicious-looking canapés. The aroma was heavenly. Alec popped a couple of shrimp into his mouth on his way through.

Isabel maneuvered through the pandemonium and hurried up to the third floor. Michael's bedroom door was open and his gym bag was on a chair near the window, which meant that he was back. He must have changed and gone outside to join the party. She could go looking for him but decided not to. Just in case she returned to the hotel tonight, she'd changed the sheets on the bed and made sure the room was ready for other guests. The thought of sleeping in Michael's bed tonight crossed her mind, but she quickly rejected it. The way he left without saying good-bye and without trying to contact her all day after what she thought was a mind-blowing night together made her feel like a piece of meat, or in this case, a piece of ass. Is that what she was, a one-night hookup? She thought about calling Damon and asking him what the proper term would be.

Why would she want to be with a man like that, anyway? A man who had the sensitivity of a hedgehog. Isabel realized she was getting worked up without knowing the facts. There might have been a good reason he didn't wake her up to say good-bye or call her all the damn day long.

Guess she would find out soon enough. It was time to say hello to Michael and hopefully get an explanation she could believe.

When she returned to the first floor, the party was in full swing. Judge Buchanan and his wife were in the living room greeting old friends, so Isabel went to them and once again thanked them for their hospitality. She was in the middle of answering a question the judge had asked when they were interrupted. A woman took hold of the judge's arm, kissed him on the cheek, and told him how happy she was to see him again. After a quick and dismissive glance in Isabel's direction, she turned her attention back to the judge.

The woman was tall, thin, and very attractive. She had looked right through Isabel. She was definitely a force to be reckoned with. Isabel was embarrassed, though she wasn't sure why.

Being a gentleman, the judge listened to her chat about the evening's festivities for a minute and then, gently removing her hand from his arm, he brought Isabel forward and said, "Isabel, I'd like you to meet Amanda Foley. She's a friend of Michael's."

"Oh, more than a friend," Amanda replied with a sugary-sweet smile.

"Amanda," the judge continued, "this is Isabel MacKenna. She's Kate's sister."

Amanda finally gave Isabel her full attention. "Isabel MacKenna. Aren't you the singer? I heard some people outside talking about you." With that, she gave Isabel a cool once-over.

So this was the infamous Amanda. Isabel couldn't blame Michael for being attracted to her. She was beautiful.

Isabel's response was polite but brief. "I guess I am." She wasn't going to lie and say that it was a pleasure to meet Amanda, so she gave a curt nod and turned to go outside.

Kate intercepted her just as she was about to open the door. She took Isabel's hand and pulled her into the sunroom to meet more Buchanan relatives. They were eager to talk to her, for they had heard that she had performed with XO—Kate had told them—and they had all sorts of questions besides the usual *What was he like?* Isabel patiently answered them, and finally, after discussing Xavier for a good twenty minutes, was able to excuse herself and go look for Michael. She knew the only way she could get rid of her anxiety was to talk to him, and God help him if he didn't have a good reason for his rudeness.

Walking from the sunroom to the front porch turned out to be quite a challenge. She kept getting stopped by friends and Buchanan relatives who had heard about XO. By the time she stepped outside, she wanted to put a gag in Kate's mouth to keep her from boasting to anyone else about the concert. Isabel knew Kate was proud of her, but she wished her sister would be a little less exuberant about it tonight.

There was quite a lively crowd out on the lawn. The band was playing an upbeat popular song, and the dance floor was already filled with couples gyrating to the electrifying beat. Noah and Jordan drew her attention. They were glued to each other, slowly swaying to their own love song, and ignoring the pulse of the music and the men and women dancing wildly around them.

The lawn looked beautiful. There were round tables with white linen tablecloths that touched the ground, and candles, each glowing softly as night rapidly approached. Servers with silver trays of tempting canapés threaded their way through the guests. A buffet was being set up at the north end of the lawn, far enough away from the dance floor that people could carry on a conversation.

Isabel stayed on the porch while she scanned the crowd for Michael. Alec, Dylan, and Nick were standing near the pool. They all looked as though they were having a good time. Finally, there was Michael. He was crossing the path to join his brothers. Amanda was with him. She wasn't holding on to Michael, but she was walking so close to him her arm repeatedly rubbed against his. She kept looking up at him and smiling, but Isabel didn't think the smile was all that sincere.

She realized she was looking for reasons to dislike the woman. The fact that she and Michael had been together should have been enough. Isabel had assumed their relationship was over. Now, where had she come up with that idea? Jordan, she decided. Jordan had put the notion in her head when she said that Michael would never marry Amanda because he didn't love her.

Michael and Amanda certainly looked friendly now, didn't they? While the brothers talked and laughed, Isabel noticed Amanda leaning into Michael with her hand on his arm. It was a disgusting display of ownership. If they were still involved—and it was apparent they were—why did Michael spend the night with Isabel? She knew the answer, just hated admitting it. She had thrown herself at him. He had tried to leave the bedroom, but she had shamelessly seduced him. She remembered exactly what she'd said to him: "I want you." Was that before or after she removed her pajamas?

Michael wasn't a cad, but he was human, and she had been relentless. She would have left him alone if he'd mentioned he was still involved with Amanda. Why hadn't he mentioned it?

Isabel was blatantly staring at the couple when Michael looked across the lawn and saw her on the porch. He started to walk toward her but was stopped by Amanda when she took his arm and said something to him. He turned back to her then.

It was time to have a talk with Michael. Isabel knew she had a bad habit of jumping to conclusions without knowing all the facts. She would find out the truth by simply asking him. And the sooner, the better.

She went down the steps and came to a quick stop. Sauntering toward her were four fit, gorgeous males. She knew who they were. These giant Texans were the MacAlisters, the Buchanans' relatives. The brothers had sandy brown hair, which was the only difference between them and the Buchanan men, who were just as tall and broad-shouldered, but with dark hair.

The air was brimming with testosterone. Noah joined them and quickly made the introductions. Sebastian, Gavin, Hunter, and Gabriel greeted Isabel with broad grins and hearty handshakes. There was no mistaking their intent. These gentlemen were there to have a good time. Maybe it was time for her to do the same.

Sebastian took hold of her hand. "Come on, darlin'. Dance with me." With the twinkle in his hazel eyes and his rascal smile, he was quite a charming fellow. He didn't have to coax her. Michael didn't seem in any hurry to get to her. He was still talking to Amanda. Isabel smiled at Sebastian and took his hand.

Once she started dancing, she let the music take her away. One song led to another and another, and then Gavin demanded a dance. She couldn't turn him down. Two more dances later, she was ready to take a break. But just as the band began to play a slow, romantic love song, Michael tapped Gavin on the shoulder, told him he was cutting in, and pulled Isabel into his arms. Pressing her body to his, he began to move to the music. Tilting her chin up so he could look into her eyes, he asked, "How was your day?"

Was he serious? That's what he wanted to talk about?

"It was busy. How was your day?" she asked, deciding to play along.

"Busy."

And that was it. Not one word about last night. She waited, thinking he might be working up to the topic of being hot, sweaty, and naked with her all night long, but he didn't say a word. He couldn't be that blasé, could he? Had Michael already moved on, or had he forgotten about last night? No, of course he hadn't. Perhaps to him sex was like having a beer in the evening. No reason to talk about it the next day because it wasn't significant. It was just a beer.

Not one word about Amanda, either. It was time to get answers.

God knows she tried, but it was impossible to ask him anything because they kept getting interrupted. First by Gabriel MacAlister, who wanted to cut in, but Michael wouldn't let him, then by Theo, who wanted to remind Michael that he and Michelle would be leaving early tomorrow morning. The song ended while the brothers talked. Michael didn't seem to notice when Isabel let go of his arm and turned around . . .

until she tried to walk away. He took her hand and drew her back to him, then draped his arm over her shoulder so she couldn't move.

"Isabel, are you going to sing for us tonight?" Theo asked.

"No."

He waited for an explanation, and after a couple of seconds he realized she had nothing more to say. He laughed and said, "Okay, then."

"Want me to drive you to the airport tomorrow?" Michael asked him.

"I'd be happy to drive you," Isabel offered.

The look on Theo's face was one of horror, but when he turned and headed back to the house, Isabel could see his shoulders shaking with laughter.

"My offer wasn't funny."

"Yeah, it was," Michael told her.

Isabel spotted Alec heading their way, and behind him was Amanda, watching Michael. Isabel would have to wait until later to catch Michael alone. She once again tried to walk away, but Michael tugged her back to him. The man didn't know his own strength and practically plastered her against his chest.

Michael stopped Alec's and Amanda's approach. "If you'll excuse us, Isabel and I are going to dance." Alec immediately nodded and turned back, but Amanda stood frowning at them for a second before retreating.

"Michael, I'm not a football," Isabel said, sighing. "Stop gripping me so tight. Dance like a normal person."

He gently pushed her head down on his shoulder and began to sway to the music. "I like your dress."

"You do?"

"It's very sexy," he whispered into her ear. "Can you breathe?"

"It has a lot of spandex. It isn't indecent, is it?"

"No, it isn't," he answered. "It's the way you fill it out, sweetheart."

The endearment flustered her, and she didn't know how to respond.

He smiled down at her and said, "You're blushing."

A couple of young men called out to Michael. Both he and Isabel turned in their direction, and Isabel caught a glimpse of Amanda standing at the edge of the dance floor, still watching, but this time her laser-sharp glare was directed toward Isabel.

Michael smiled and nodded to his friends, but when he turned his attention to her again, his expression had changed. He looked very serious when he said, "Isabel, we need to talk."

She leaned back. "Yes?"

"Last night was great," he said. "But it shouldn't have happened. I should have gotten up and walked out of that bedroom. You were . . ." He paused as if searching for the perfect words.

"I was what?"

"Inexperienced . . . and I feel I took advantage of you." He looked truly sincere when he added, "I'm sorry about that."

"You think having sex with me was a mistake?"

"Yes . . . but . . ."

"Wow. You sure know how to flatter a girl."

"Isabel, I'm trying to explain . . ."

"I'd rather you didn't," she whispered.

Before Isabel could utter another word, she felt a tap on her shoulder. She turned her head to find Amanda standing behind her.

"My turn," Amanda announced in a breathy voice. "I'd like to dance with my guy."

My guy? "Of course," Isabel said. She took a step away from Michael. "He's all yours."

Fighting back the tears, she walked away. Michael called her name. She ignored him. More than anything she needed a few minutes alone. She was angry and hurt and had no one to blame but herself. Michael had been brutally honest with her when he told her he regretted their night together. Isabel didn't want to know all of his reasons for wishing it hadn't happened. He'd said quite enough.

Isabel headed to the house. Her goal was to go up to the third-floor bedroom, shut the door, and take a few minutes to get her emotions under control. She was so close to losing it. Unfortunately, she was waylaid again and again by guests at the party who wanted to meet her . . . and yes, to know what XO was like. She almost made it to the stairs a second time when the MacAlisters got hold of her and dragged her to the dance floor again. Their flirting was so outrageous, they had her smiling in no time at all. An hour later, in a much better frame of mind, Isabel finally made it all the way to the stairs.

Just two steps up, she was halted by Amanda. "Isabel. A moment, please."

Isabel sighed. "Yes?"

"I've been wanting to catch you alone so I could ask you."

"Yes," she prompted again, trying her best to hide her irritation.

"Will you sing at our wedding? Michael and I would love it if you would."

Isabel's reaction was so swift, it even surprised her. She laughed. "No. I don't do weddings."

She didn't waste another minute discussing it. She now had only one thought in mind: to get away from Michael and his soon-to-be bride. She couldn't seem to stop laughing as she ascended the stairs to gather her things.

The laughter saved her from crying. Either that, or she was becoming hysterical. She got her wristlet with her phone and room card out of the credenza and hurried down through the kitchen to get to the back door. She was determined to get off the island as quickly as possible. If she had to walk to the Hamilton, then, by God, she would.

Regan caught up with her as Isabel was closing the door. She followed her outside and asked, "Where are you going?"

"I want to find a ride back to the Hamilton."

"Is something wrong? It's not even eleven."

"I'm very tired."

It was a lame excuse and she knew Regan wasn't buying it. She didn't press her, though, and Isabel was thankful she didn't have to make up a more elaborate lie. The truth was too painful to talk to anyone about.

"There are so many people here who wanted to meet you and ask you questions about XO."

"I think I've met everyone."

"And they all asked about XO, didn't they?" Regan asked, smiling.

"All but one," she replied, her voice trembling now. "Amanda Foley asked me if I would sing at her wedding. She said that she and Michael would just love it if I did. I told her I don't do weddings. Then I laughed. I'm not sure why I did that."

If Isabel hadn't been feeling so miserable, she would have laughed at Regan's flabbergasted expression.

"No," Regan gasped.

"Yes," Isabel insisted.

Regan didn't try to talk her into staying. "Theo hired a car service for those guests who have had too much to drink. You can get a ride back to the hotel whenever you're ready to leave."

"I'm ready now."

Regan motioned to one of the drivers, who quickly opened the back door of a black town car. "I'm going to call the hotel and have security waiting for you in the parking garage. They'll be in front of the elevators we used earlier, and they'll accompany you up to your suite."

"Is that necessary?"

"Better to be safe than sorry."

Desperate to get going, Isabel didn't argue. She could feel anxiety building, and she knew, if she didn't get it under control soon, she was going to have a full-fledged panic attack right there in the back of the town car.

Thanks to Michael she was an emotional mess. If it were possible, she would go to the airport right this minute in her fancy cocktail dress and her stiletto heels and catch the next flight to Scotland. All she wanted was to disappear for a while. She took a deep breath, leaned back against the plush leather seat, and closed her eyes. The weight of the last few days was bearing down on her.

First and foremost, there was Michael. She had to get as far away from him as possible. He'd hurt her, and it was going to take time and distance for her to heal.

Then there was the shooting and poor Detective Walsh. She'd killed a man and hadn't come to terms with that fact yet. There was a tiny part of her that felt tremendous guilt. She had taken a man's life, and she knew she would never be the same.

Becoming an overnight sensation, as Xavier said, was yet another reason to run away. There were fanatical fans out there who had transferred some of their love and mania onto her. Though she hadn't admitted this to anyone, they scared the bejeezus out of her. She pictured them crowding in on her and shivered at the thought. It was so claustrophobic. Escaping to the Highlands and Glen MacKenna was just what she needed.

As soon as she arrived back at the Hamilton, she had her suitcase for her trip to Scotland brought up from storage. She opened it, realized she'd overpacked, and took out more than half the number of outfits and put them in a box the concierge supplied. She also emptied her backpack and stuffed all those clothes in the box. When she was finished, she asked the concierge to mail the box back to her home in Silver Springs.

Too worked up to relax, she channel-surfed for a while, but she couldn't concentrate on any program. She wished she could get out of Boston now. The thought had crossed her mind earlier, and it had seemed an implausible idea. But why? Why couldn't she leave now? There really wasn't any reason to wait until Monday to leave for Scotland, was there? Maybe she could get an earlier flight.

It took only a couple of phone calls, and she was all set. In order to leave as soon as possible, Isabel had to make adjustments to her itinerary. Instead of flying to Glasgow, she was now landing in Edinburgh. A flight that had been scheduled to leave earlier in the evening was waiting for a new crew coming in from Los Angeles. The airline decided to reschedule, and the new departure time was five thirty Sunday morning, much to the disappointment and anger of quite a few passengers. Several canceled their tickets, which was a stroke of luck for Isabel. One of those cancellations made a first-class seat available. If she could get to the airport and through security in time, she would be on her way lickety-split. She didn't waste any time, quickly changing into comfortable leggings, a long black T-shirt, and her lightweight blue jacket. In a hurry to gather her things and arrange for a ride to the airport, she didn't book a hotel reservation, thinking she would find a place to stay when she arrived in Scotland.

Isabel was excited about the change. She couldn't wait to explore Scotland and see all the places she'd read about. Earlier in the week she had taken the time to pinpoint the location of Glen MacKenna. It was way up there, and she planned to make a lot of stops along the way. The attorney handling the estate was waiting to hear when she would arrive, and she would notify him in a couple of days to set up a meeting. Any other details she would address later.

She made it in plenty of time to board her flight. When she was going through security, one of the guards recognized her and called over three others to meet Isabel. They didn't make a scene, which she appreciated. They wanted an autograph, and each pulled out his cell phone to get a photo with her. All of them had the same burning question: What was XO like?

Once she was settled in her seat, she texted Kate and explained that she was on her way to Edinburgh. She asked her to tell Dylan that she was going alone and not to worry. She assured her sister that, as soon as she figured out where she was going to stay, she would let her know. It was five twenty in the morning, and she knew Kate was sound asleep. She wouldn't get around to reading her texts until much later in the day, which benefited Isabel because Kate couldn't call and argue with her about going alone.

Although Isabel was exhausted, it took time for her to quiet her mind. She kept going over the conversations she had had with Michael and with Amanda. Just by being honest with her, Michael had broken her heart. He couldn't have been more blunt when he told her having sex with her shouldn't have happened. *Lovely, just lovely.* And Amanda. Dear God, what a nightmare that woman was. What did Michael see in her?

For a good long while Isabel wallowed in anger and self-pity. Then she decided to be reasonable, once again reminding herself, Michael had never promised her happily ever after. She had seduced him, after all. Maybe she had expected more than he could give. She was the one with the problem, not him. She should have stayed away from him.

Vowing she wouldn't waste another minute thinking about Michael, she zipped up her jacket, pulled the hood up over her head, and finally fell asleep.

TWENTY

THE MORNING AFTER WASN'T PRETTY.

It was a little before noon Sunday morning when Nick, bleary-eyed from playing poker until dawn and drinking way too much beer, walked into the kitchen in search of caffeine. Noah and Michael were sitting at opposite ends of the table. Michael was reading an article on Dylan's laptop, and Noah was slumped over the table, guzzling orange juice. Feeling dehydrated, he had already gulped down two large bottles of water. Neither Nick nor Noah had showered or shaved yet. They both felt as bad as they looked.

Michael, on the other hand, looked as though he were ready for a photo shoot. He had showered, shaved, and wore crisp khaki pants and a dark blue polo shirt. Unlike Nick and Noah, Michael had on shoes. He was the only one in the room without bloodshot eyes. But then, he'd known when to stop drinking.

Nick found a clean mug, filled it with coffee, and took a drink. Then he leaned back against the island and said, "What in God's name was I thinking?"

Michael understood what he was asking and answered. "You thought you could keep up with the MacAlisters. A rookie mistake," he added, flashing a grin.

"If they stayed an entire week, we'd all need liver transplants," Noah said, his voice a scratchy whisper. "The last time I drank this much was when I was at the university, and that was a long time ago."

"Same here," Nick said. "I forgot how bad a hangover can be. This is brutal." He dragged a chair out and sat down at the table. "Where is everyone?"

Michael answered. "Laurant, Kate, and Jordan left a while ago with Mom and Dad."

"Where were they going?" Noah asked on a yawn.

"I don't know. I didn't ask. Michelle and Theo left for the airport real early."

"Yeah," Noah agreed. "I was going to bed when Theo was coming down with their luggage."

Nick sat staring off into space while he waited for the coffee and the two aspirin he'd taken to kick in so he'd start feeling human again.

"Good afternoon," Regan called from the doorway. She walked into the kitchen, looked at Nick and Noah, and started laughing. "Have a little too much fun last night?"

"Last night actually ended this morning," Michael told her.

"We all stayed up way too late," she said. "Isabel was the smart one. She left the party around eleven."

"Why so early?" Michael asked.

"I believe Amanda had a little something to do with Isabel taking off." She then told them about the conversation Amanda had had with Isabel.

"She said what?" Michael shouted. He was furious.

Regan patiently repeated, "Amanda asked Isabel to sing at your wedding. She said, 'Michael and I would just love it if you did.' According to Isabel those were Amanda's exact words."

"You're engaged now?" Noah asked. "If you are, I think you should know you're marrying a real bitch."

Nick nodded agreement. "You don't belong with her."

Michael was outraged. "I'm not marrying Amanda. We haven't been involved in a long while. Honest to God, I don't know what I ever saw in her."

"She obviously isn't ready to move on," Nick said. "Why did you invite her to the party?"

"I didn't." Michael shoved the chair back and stood, muttering an expletive.

"How did Isabel react to Amanda's question?" Nick asked.

"Yeah, what did she say?" Noah wanted to know.

"She said, 'I don't do weddings.' Then she laughed."

"That's our girl," Nick said.

"She's not your girl," Michael snapped.

"She sure as hell isn't yours," Noah retorted.

Dylan had been standing in the doorway listening to the conversation. Shaking his head, he looked at Michael and said, "Dumbass."

Michael surprised everyone when he nodded agreement. He needed to talk to Isabel as soon as possible. He owed her an apology. He knew she had to be angry and hurt. The look on her face when he stupidly told her he shouldn't have touched her said as much. Yeah, he really was a dumbass.

"As soon as she comes down, I'll talk to her," Michael said.

Regan shook her head. "She isn't here. She went back to the Hamilton last night."

Before Michael could react, Dylan asked, "How did she get back to the hotel? Did someone drive her, or did she borrow a car? Oh God, she didn't drive . . . did she?"

"Calm down," Regan said. "Car service drove her. Security was waiting for her, and after she was safely back in her suite, I was notified. She's fine."

"I've really got to go for a drive with this woman," Noah said. "She can't possibly be as bad as you say."

The men continued to talk, but Michael wasn't paying attention. He was thinking about Isabel. He needed to see her. His apology had to be given face-to-face. Hopefully, by the time he got to the hotel, he would find the right words to repair the damage he had done.

Regan was on her way upstairs to wake Alec and start packing for their trip back to Chicago when someone started pounding on the front door.

As soon as she opened the door, the young man blurted, "My name is Everett Redman. I'm a tech with the FBI lab, and it's urgent that I see Special Agent Nick Buchanan. Is he here? I was told he was staying until Monday. God, I hope he's here."

"Yes, he is," Regan said, and pointed the way. "He's in the kitchen. You can—" She didn't finish her sentence because the man was already gone.

Nick was surprised to see the tech. Everett was young and eager and brilliant in his area of expertise. He was usually laid-back, but not today. His face was red and he was panting.

Both Nick and Noah were wide awake now.

"What's going on, Everett?" Nick asked.

Dylan looked perturbed by the intrusion. "Who is this guy?"

"His name is Everett Redman," Noah answered. "And he's one of the best techs in the lab."

Everett was focused on Nick. "You need to see this, sir."

"You drove all the way out here to . . . ," Nick began.

"Sir, you need to see this now." The urgency in his voice was palpable. Everett held up the flash drive Nick had given him. "I cleaned this up, got all the blood off. There wasn't any corruption at all. When I was checking it, I thought I'd find some audio of Isabel singing. She's quite the rage now, and I love her voice."

Everett was talking so fast, Nick raised a hand to slow him down. "It's okay that you listened to her sing."

"But that's just it. There wasn't any singing. This doesn't belong to her," he said as he handed the flash drive to Nick. "But it's all about her, or it's all about Grace Isabel MacKenna. There are three full pages of instructions and information," he continued. "And there's a timetable.

It has a lot of personal information on her and her schedule, beginning with the day and time of her graduation, her stay in Boston, and her flight information to Glasgow, including a list of hotels where she'll be staying in Scotland. You'll notice a number in the left-hand corner of the first page. One hundred thousand. I think that's what they'll pay."

Nick inserted the flash drive into the laptop.

Everett scrolled down to the last page and pointed to the screen. "The last line is underlined. They want it done as soon as possible. There's a bonus if it's done before her birthday, June twenty-second."

"What the hell . . ."

"Sir, I think it's a kill order."

TWENTY-ONE

MICHAEL WAS IN A PANIC AND TRYING NOT TO LET IT SHOW. HE had to make sure Isabel was safe.

He had a plan. He was going to call Isabel, tell her to stay in her suite with the door locked, and not let anyone in until he got there. Once he had her, he wasn't going to let her go until the bastards out there who wanted to hurt her were apprehended or killed. At the moment, he was voting for the second solution.

It took only one phone call to find out she had checked out of the hotel in the middle of the night. Three o'clock in the morning, to be exact. One of the Hamilton limos had driven her to the airport.

Where in God's name had she gone? Isabel wasn't scheduled to leave for Glasgow until Monday. She had obviously changed her plans. She hadn't taken an early-morning flight to Glasgow. He'd checked. Had she gone home to Silver Springs and put the trip to Scotland on hold?

Dylan had the answer. He knew that Isabel wouldn't go anywhere without letting her sister know. He called Kate and asked her if she had checked her messages today.

"Not yet," she told him. "Why? We were in church, and now we're in a restaurant with your parents and some of their friends. I'll check them when I get back."

"I need you to check now and tell me if Isabel sent you a text."

Kate excused herself from the table and walked out into the restaurant's foyer. "Is something wrong?"

Dylan planned to tell her everything when she got back to Nathan's Bay, but not now. "Michael wants to know." He didn't mention why.

While he waited, Kate scrolled down through her messages. There was a text from Isabel that she had sent at five twenty that morning. Kate couldn't believe what she was reading, and she didn't take her sister's news at all well.

"Oh my God, she doesn't even have a hotel room booked. What could she be thinking?" she asked her husband. "Why couldn't she wait until Monday and fly into Glasgow? I had her schedule all set and her hotel rooms reserved."

A hotel room was the least of her worries, Dylan thought, but didn't say. "Send me the text. We'll talk about Isabel later."

He disconnected the call before she could ask any more questions. Kate sent him the text, and he read it out loud.

"Okay, that's good," Michael said. "Whoever wants her out of the way thinks she's still here on Nathan's Bay. Right? According to the instructions in that order, they think she's leaving for Glasgow Monday."

"Who the hell puts a plan like that on a flash drive?" Dylan wondered, shaking his head.

"Maybe someone who thinks others are less likely to see it," Nick speculated.

"I hope to God she hasn't called the attorney or anyone else. If that son of a bitch Reid calls her and she tells him where she is . . ." Michael stopped, took a deep breath, trying to get his anger under control, then said, "I'm going to go get her."

"I thought you might," Noah said. He pulled the laptop over in front of him and quickly looked up flights to Edinburgh. "There's one leaving this evening, but it's booked."

"Can you get him on?" Nick asked.

"Yeah, I can. I'll call Kemper." He picked up his cell phone and asked Michael, "Do you have your passport with you?"

"Yes." He never left home without it.

Dylan could see the anxiety on Michael's face, and said, "She's going to be all right."

"Yeah? How do you know that?"

"Do the math," he said. "Her plane took off at five thirty this morning, and it's a six-hour flight. She arrived in Edinburgh at eleven thirty this morning our time. So she's just getting off the plane. It's four thirty in the afternoon there. She hasn't been there long enough for anyone to get to her."

It was a prayer and a hope, but Michael wanted to believe the men who were after her didn't know she was in Edinburgh.

Nick held out his hand. "Dylan, give me your phone. I'll see if I can reach her."

Everyone in the room watched in silence as Nick held the phone to his ear. After several anxious seconds, he handed the phone back to Dylan. "Her phone isn't connected."

Isabel wasn't making it easy for them to find her. She had probably forgotten to turn on her phone when she got off the plane, and if that was the case, as soon as she did turn it on, Nick could track her.

Everyone believed Isabel wasn't in immediate danger—everyone but Michael—and each had a theory as to her whereabouts. Noah thought she might have checked into a hotel near the airport and was so exhausted she went to bed. With Everett's help he gained access to her credit card account but found no charges had been made yet.

Dylan was hopeful. He had given Isabel the name of the company that supplied drivers throughout Scotland and knew they had offices in Edinburgh. If she was being sensible, she had contacted one of them and was now with a responsible driver. Three phone calls later, however, his hopes were dashed when he found out she hadn't hired a driver. She had rented a car—a car without GPS—and had taken off for parts unknown. At that news, Dylan started praying for the people of Scotland, too.

Michael's outlook was even more pessimistic. He thought Isabel might have driven into the North Sea. Driving up into the Highlands all alone was just plain crazy. He pictured her trying to navigate those narrow roads in Scotland and shuddered. That wasn't his only worry. There were also the overzealous fans who all wanted a piece of her. If she was recognized—and there had been so much Internet exposure after her performance with XO, he was sure she would be—she'd be run over.

The Buchanan kitchen quickly turned into an operations room, each of the men making calls to anyone who could help locate Isabel. Nick and Noah even had the FBI's contacts in Scotland and England searching for her. With all of their resources, they were confident she would be found quickly.

When they had done all they could to reach her, they faced the biggest worry of all. Who was after her? And why? The bloody device was in her pocket, and she obviously hadn't known it was there. The only conclusion that made any sense was that Walsh had somehow put it there. A close examination of the video confirmed it. Nick had saved it on his phone and played it for the others. Rewinding and slowing the action proved their suspicion. Walsh was clearly reaching for her pocket with something in his hand.

So, who was Walsh really? And what did all of this have to do with the man Isabel shot? The detective lying in the hospital had the answers, and the Buchanans were determined to get him to talk.

Michael couldn't wait around for the answers to any of these questions. Isabel was in danger, and he had to get to her. He gathered his gear and took off for the airport. He didn't have any doubt at all that Noah would get him a seat on a flight. As he was striding into the airport, he received a text giving him the name of the airline, the flight number, and his seat assignment, 2A. Michael was also certain that by the time he arrived in Edinburgh, Nick and Noah would have found Isabel and gotten protection for her.

In the meantime, Nick had gone to his office and gathered a team of agents to aid in the search. He then called Detective Samuel and read him what was on the flash drive, followed by an emailed copy. Samuel was outraged on Isabel's behalf, but he was also furious with Nick because he hadn't checked the flash drive the minute he saw it. Nick didn't defend himself. Samuel was right. He should have checked it no matter how bloody it was. Isabel thought the flash drive was filled with songs she had written, so he had assumed the same. Why wouldn't he believe her? He wasn't investigating her, for God's sake. Still, no amount of justification made his guilt lessen.

On Nathan's Bay the atmosphere was tense as Dylan waited to get word that Isabel was safe. He had stayed on the island so that he could explain it all to Kate and be there when her sister finally decided to call.

ISABEL HAD NO IDEA OF THE TURMOIL SHE WAS CAUSING.

It had been a long twenty-four hours, and she was worn out. She had slept only an hour at the most on the plane. Then she went through quite an ordeal at the airport when she was recognized by a tour group of teenagers on their way to a football match. Why they needed to shriek was beyond her. It only drew more attention, as other travelers joined the spontaneous fan club. She signed autographs and hurried out of there as quickly as possible.

By the time she was seated in the car she had rented under Dylan Buchanan's name—the company had his credit card on file—her nerves were frayed. Fortunately, an hour outside of Edinburgh she found a charming hotel with available rooms. After she checked in and—due to an unfortunate little mishap—asked where the nearest auto body shop was located, she went up to her room and got ready for bed. It wasn't until she was plugging her phone charger in that she realized she hadn't turned her phone on. As soon as she did, she was shocked to see that there were at least twenty calls and just as many texts. There was even a call from Detective Samuel. She assumed he wanted to thank her for the concert tickets and put him last on her callback list. Barely able to keep her eyes open, she decided she'd read the texts and answer everyone tomorrow. She did take the time to text Kate and Dylan and tell them where she was staying tonight. Then she turned off her phone again and got into bed.

Could a person be too exhausted to sleep? Isabel's mind wouldn't quiet down, and she tossed and turned for a long while. When she did fall asleep, it was only for an hour or two. She finally crashed just as the sun was coming up, and she slept like the dead until noon. A hot shower revived her, and by the time she was dressed, she was ready for what was left of the day.

First on her agenda was to plan her route to Dunross and Glen MacKenna. She had picked up a travel guide at the airport and opened it to a map that highlighted all of Scotland's points of interest. She was looking forward to taking side trips to some of these places. Since she wasn't on a schedule, she could take her time exploring. At some point in her travels, she would call the solicitor for Glen MacKenna and let him know when she'd arrive. Until then, she was free to wander.

She called room service and ordered breakfast, then took a pen and pad from the bedside table and began to make a list of the sights she wanted to see. Just as she was reading about the history of Stirling Castle, she was interrupted by a knock on her door. Impressed that room service was so efficient, she put down her pen and went to answer.

Her mouth dropped open when she looked through the peephole. She couldn't believe what she was seeing and looked again. He hadn't vanished, and he wasn't a figment of her imagination. Michael Buchanan was standing there.

Speechless, she unlocked the dead bolt, removed the chain, and opened the door. She was so dumbfounded she could only stare up at him. When she finally found her voice, she didn't mince words. "There's just no getting away from you, is there?"

TWENTY-TWO

DAMN, BUT HE WAS HAPPY TO SEE HER. MICHAEL WALKED INTO the room, quietly shut the door, and leaned back against it. He was weak with relief. Thank God she was all right. No one had gotten to her. The tightness he'd been carrying around in his chest since he'd heard that she had left Boston was finally easing, and he could breathe.

Isabel backed away from the door. "Why are you here?" It was a reasonable question, she thought. She sat down on the side of the bed and waited for him to answer. And waited. He had such an intense look on his face. She couldn't imagine what he was thinking.

"Michael?"

"I'm here to take you home," he said with both relief and urgency in his voice.

The worry of the last few hours had been torture, but now that he was here with her, and she was okay, it was time for action.

"Why would I want to go home? I just got here."

He hated answering her because he knew he was going to scare her. "Something has happened," he began, slowly walking toward her.

She jumped to her feet. "Oh my God, did someone in the family get hurt? Is it Kate? Dylan?" Her mind raced with dire possibilities.

He put his hand up. "Everyone back home is fine. You're the one in trouble."

Before she could demand an explanation, he pulled her into his arms and hugged her. "I was . . . worried about you, but you're all right."

Isabel was utterly confused. Why was he acting so strange? It wasn't like him to be so emotional. And yet, she had to admit, after the shock of finding him at her door wore off, she really was happy to see him. Then her mind cleared, and she remembered he had broken her heart. She also remembered the lovely conversation she had had with Amanda. Broaching that subject was going to spark a whopper of a fight. She'd been building steam since she left the party, but it would have to wait until later. First, she wanted to know why she was in trouble. She hadn't been in Scotland long enough to do anything wrong.

She tried to step back, but he wasn't ready to let go of her, and if room service hadn't interrupted, she thought he might've kissed her. She decided she would let him, and after he explained what his sudden appearance was all about, she would give him hell.

Michael opened the door, and Brodie, the proprietor of the small hotel, wearing a white apron over his tweed suit, carried her breakfast tray in and placed it on the table. "Cook added another cup and saucer and a few more scones and such for your mister."

Her mister? Isabel didn't correct him. "That was thoughtful of her," she said. "Please tell her thank you."

Turning to Michael, he said, "Per your instructions I changed the name on the register and will use your credit card for the charge. Will you be staying another night?"

"I'm not sure yet," Isabel said, wondering why he directed his question to Michael.

At the same time Michael said, "No, we'll be leaving on a flight to Boston tonight."

"I'll keep the room available for you just in case."

Isabel followed him to the door. "Thank you, Brodie."

"No, no, I should be thanking you," he replied. "Your suggestions were spot on. I'll let you get to your breakfast."

Michael waited until she had closed the door, then asked, "What were your suggestions?" Before she could answer, he said, "You didn't give any, did you? I'm betting you didn't say anything. You just listened, didn't you?"

"Good guess," she said.

"Not a guess," he corrected. "I just observed your past behavior."

Isabel took a seat at the small table, lifted the cozy from the teapot, and poured the hot liquid through the strainer into her cup. She offered Michael a cup of tea, but he declined with a shake of his head.

"Sit down, Michael. You look so tense." When he was settled in the chair across from her, she said. "Now, are you ready to tell me why you came all this way, why you want to take me back to Boston, and why you think I'm in trouble?"

"Yes," he said. "But first I need to know if you have contacted anyone connected to Glen MacKenna."

"No."

"What about Donal Gladstone, the solicitor handling the estate? Or James Reid, the man harassing you? Have you talked to either one of them?"

"No," she insisted. "I spoke to Mr. Gladstone right before I went to Boston, but I haven't spoken to him since. I don't have to worry about Reid anymore."

"Why not?"

"I got a text from him yesterday. He apologized and told me he wasn't going to pressure me anymore. He hopes I'll let him bid against other offers. I guess he's finally convinced I'm not going to sell Glen MacKenna . . . at least not to him."

Nodding, he said, "Okay, so no one knows you're here." *Thank God*, he silently added.

"There were some teenagers at the airport who recognized me."

"How many?"

"I don't know. Fifteen or twenty. They took some photos and made a bit of a fuss. Why do you think I'm in trouble?"

He was about to ruin her day, and he was sorry about that. She had been so excited to see the Highlands. He felt as though he were snatching one of her dreams away from her.

"Remember the bloody flash drive you gave Nick to get cleaned up for you?"

"Yes," she answered. "Oh no, did the blood seep inside and ruin it? Is that even possible?"

"It isn't yours."

"It . . . I'm sorry . . . what? It was in my coat pocket. Of course it's mine."

"No, it isn't. Detective Walsh put it in your pocket before he collapsed."

She thought a long minute, recalling the details of the incident, and then said, "He was clawing at me. I thought he was trying to hold on so he wouldn't fall. What was on it?"

Michael had downloaded the flash drive to his computer, but he had also made a printout because he knew Isabel would want to read it over and over again—like he did—until she believed it.

"Everett, the tech, is calling it a kill order."

A kill order? Isabel looked up at Michael. He wasn't kidding.

He reached inside his jacket and produced the folded papers, handing them to her. Isabel put her teacup down and started reading. Michael waited silently, watching her eyes widen as the reality of what he had just told her began to sink in.

"The flash drive belonged to Detective Walsh?"

Before he could tell her what he and his brothers had learned, she said, "I won't believe it. I learned a great deal about Detective Walsh. He's a good and honorable man. He has received at least five commendations over the years, and his coworkers rely on him. He didn't come to Boston to kill me. I don't know where he got the flash drive, but I'm sure he was trying to protect me, and that's why he got shot."

"Isabel, no one—"

It was as far as he could get before she continued with her passionate defense of the detective. "He was happily married for twenty-six years, and he was devastated when his wife died, but he had to keep it together for their daughter, Kathleen. He flies back to Boston as often as possible. He grew up there and comes from a large family." She added, "He's going to move back there next year."

"How do you know all this?"

"Kathleen told me. It took the police a while to find her. She was visiting friends in San Francisco. She flew back to Boston and has been at her father's side almost every minute."

"No one thinks the flash drive belonged to Walsh."

"Then why did you let me go on and on—"

"I couldn't get you to stop," he said.

She decided to read the succinctly written kill order once again. Then she carefully folded the papers and handed them back to Michael.

"I don't want you to be afraid," Michael said.

Her back stiffened. "Afraid? I'm not afraid. I'm furious." She jumped up and began to pace. "Is James Reid behind this? Of course he is," she decided. "He's probably getting a whopping bonus if I sell to the Patterson Group, and he represents them, remember? Every time he called he sounded more determined. Right?"

Michael didn't answer fast enough. She stopped in front of him and asked, "Am I right?"

"No."

"Why not?" Now she sounded disgruntled.

"If you're dead you can't sign the land over to them."

"I realize that, but . . ."

"You get Glen MacKenna on your next birthday," he began.

"Day after tomorrow."

"What?"

"My birthday is Wednesday, day after tomorrow," she repeated.

He nodded. "We'll celebrate early on the plane."

"I'm not going to be on a plane tomorrow."

"You need to get back to Nathan's Bay," he insisted. "You'll be safe there until the investigators find out who's behind this kill order."

She shook her head. "No, that's not what I'm going to do."

And thus began a blistering argument that lasted a good twenty minutes. Unfortunately for Michael, Isabel made sense. There was also the fact that she was far more stubborn than he was, yet another trait he couldn't help but admire.

"I'm going to drive north toward Dunross, stay off the highways, and talk to people along the way. Once I get up into the Highlands, someone will know something about Glen MacKenna. There's a reason someone besides the Patterson Group wants the land, and I want to know what it is. I didn't come to Scotland just to turn around and run back home because of a threat, especially if I don't know who is making it or why. Besides, I know I told you I have to be present in the solicitor's office to sign papers to receive the inheritance. You just forgot."

"No, I did not forget. I know you have to wait until your birthday to sign papers and get the land. But does it have to happen on your birthday? I know it can't happen before, but what about after? Could you schedule to meet the solicitor a month later?"

She skirted the question. "I'm going to sign the papers on Wednesday."

Michael made one more attempt to reason with her but in the end reluctantly conceded. "Then I'm not letting you go alone." He waited for her to object and when she remained silent, he said, "No argument? Okay, then."

Isabel tried not to let her reaction show. Why was she so relieved he was going with her? She should be trying to get rid of him, shouldn't she?

"Yes," she said. "Whoever wants me gone will find out I'm here, but if we stay off the beaten path, and I don't tell anyone who I am, we should be all right . . . for a while."

God, she was naive. "You have millions of followers on the Internet," he reminded.

"I won't use my credit cards with my name—"

"You're gonna be recognized."

"Not if we only stop in small villages."

"Sweetheart, the people living in these small villages know how to use the Internet."

"Yes, of course they do. I'm still going to stop and talk to them. I'll just have to be cautious."

Cautious? He wasn't sure she knew what the word meant. She had crazy faith in people, and it was going to get her into trouble one day.

Oh, hell yes, he was going with her.

He hated that they had to stay until Wednesday, but he vowed he would make it as safe as possible for Isabel. He didn't care if the law was on his side or not, he would kill anyone who tried to hurt her.

Admittedly, he thought her demands were outrageous. Driving from village to village in the Highlands so she could talk to people was crazy, and yet he had agreed. Maybe he was crazy, too.

"Isabel, we need to establish some ground rules."

She was so thankful he was going with her she decided not to complain, unless, of course, his ground rules were unreasonable. "I'm listening."

He looked at his watch and then said, "After you pack, we'll check out and head north. You can have the rest of the day and evening to talk to people and ask questions. I'll drive you wherever you want to go. You can also have all day Tuesday and Tuesday evening, but Wednesday you and I are in Dunross meeting with your solicitor. Agreed?"

"But what if—"

"And Isabel," he continued as though she hadn't spoken, "this schedule could change in a heartbeat. If I feel there's going to be trouble or it becomes dangerous, we aren't stopping to talk to anyone. Agreed?"

"What if I need more time to—"

"Wednesday, Isabel. We're in Donal Gladstone's office on your birthday, which is Wednesday. Agreed?"

His tone was hard, and she knew he wasn't going to bend. "Agreed," she said. "Any other rules?"

"You don't go anywhere without me, and I mean anywhere."

"What about the ladies' room?"

"If it's empty, you can go in, and I'll stand outside the door. I won't let anyone else in until you come out."

She thought he was taking that rule a bit too far but didn't argue. "Okay. What else?"

"You don't tell anyone your name, and if you're asked any questions, all your answers have to be vague or you don't answer at all."

"Not answering at all would be rude, but if that's what you want, I'll do it. Anything else?" she asked, and before he could answer she said, "If anyone wants to know how we're related, I could say I'm your sister."

"Oh, hell no."

"It was just a suggestion. No need to get prickly. Okay, I'll be vague or just won't answer."

"Right," he agreed. "Let them think whatever they want."

"What happens when we check into a hotel?"

"I'll check us in," he said. "And wherever we stay, we're in the same room."

"I'm not sure that's a good idea, considering . . ."

"Same room," he repeated, his tone unbending.

She slowly nodded. "Okay," she said. In a whisper she added, "If you think you can handle it."

He heard her, of course. "I can."

Trying not to sound irritated, she asked, "Are there any other rules?"

"No. That about covers it."

The way Michael was looking at her now, as though he wanted to say more but was holding back, was making her very nervous.

Filling the silence, she said, "You should eat something." She poured a glass of orange juice and placed it in front of him. Then she took a scone from the basket and began to spread clotted cream on it. "I don't understand how you can go with me. Don't you have to be somewhere soon? With your rigid schedule, how can you take time?"

"My rigid schedule? I don't have a rigid schedule."

She slowly nodded. "Yes, you do. Would you like me to explain? I know how your mind works, Michael."

Scoffing at her boast, he said, "You do? Enlighten me."

She took a sip of tepid tea. "You're always going after the next difficult challenge, and you always finish what you start. Usually spectacularly. You stay the course, or as you love to tell me, focus on the task at hand, and you never allow deviation or distraction. You're inflexible when you want something, and you don't let anyone or anything get in your way."

"How would you know I'm inflexible?"

"Anyone who looks into your background would know you're goal-oriented. You set the goals and then you exceed them. You don't know what the word 'defeat' means."

"Of course I do," he argued. "I fail all the time, and I'm not inflexible."

"It's not a flaw," she said. "You're also inflexible in your values, and so are your brothers. I know what your next challenge is, and I know that you're going to do well and end up at the top because that's what you always do."

She set the tray aside, then folded her napkin and placed it on the table. "Do you wonder how I know all this?" she asked. "It's simple. There aren't any secrets in the Buchanan family. You know that. I heard Dylan telling Kate that you're going to Quantico soon to train to be an FBI agent, and you're hoping you'll be assigned to the antiterrorism department . . . whatever that is." She continued, "You told Dylan you'll stay with the Bureau until you retire, but Theo isn't giving up.

He wants you to work for the Department of Justice and put your law degree to good use."

Michael leaned back in his chair and looked amused. Then he said, "There aren't any secrets in the Buchanan family? Are you sure about that?"

"I'm sure."

"Then everyone knows that you and I had sex."

Mortified by the very thought, she said, "Absolutely not. I don't want anyone to know, and since you believe it was a mistake, I'm going to assume you haven't told anyone."

He didn't comment, and because he said nothing to deny it, she concluded he hadn't changed his mind. His obvious insensitivity hurt and embarrassed her. She pushed her chair back and stood. "Soon we'll forget it happened. In fact, I've already forgotten," she lied.

"I haven't."

Just sitting across from Isabel made Michael want her. She was so damned beautiful and sexy and loving, and he remembered how good it had been between them. Her next comment pulled him from his erotic thoughts.

To Isabel, changing the subject seemed safer than getting into a talk about sex. "I'm still feeling jet-lagged. What about you?"

"I'm okay. Listen, we can't leave just yet. I'm waiting to hear from Nick. He's gathering some information for me."

"Can't you talk to him in the car?"

"Not until I know you're going to be safe. That's when we'll leave."

What kind of cryptic answer was that? "Has he talked to the police here?"

"We both have."

Before she could ask him what, if anything, he had found out, his phone rang. That one call turned into six.

Isabel sat on the bed to wait and within minutes fell asleep.

It was close to two in the afternoon when Michael nudged her awake. "We can leave now."

Isabel sat up and stretched her arms over her head, feeling refreshed from her short nap. "I'll be ready in a few minutes," she promised.

Michael leaned against the door and waited with a resigned look on his face as Isabel got organized.

After looking for and finding her jacket with the hood, then checking to make sure she had her cell phone and charger, she slid her cross-body bag over her shoulder and said, "Let's go."

"Where's your car parked?"

He held the door open for her, and as she walked past, she said, "Down the street. I'm going to drive it to Henson's Motor Store and Smart Repairs. It's just a couple of blocks away, and the owner will see that the car is returned to the rental agency."

"Why are you taking it to a motor store?" He had asked what he thought was a normal question. Her reaction wasn't normal at all. Her face turned bright pink faster than a blink.

"I'm driving the car there because it's easier than driving back to the airport."

"Couldn't you just leave the keys at the front desk?"

She rushed down the stairs. "No."

What wasn't she telling him? She reached the front doors, but he grabbed her before she could go any farther. "When we're outside you stay close to me. Understand?"

"Yes."

They stopped by his car in the lot behind the hotel first so that Michael could put her bag in the trunk. It was a dark four-door sedan, big enough for him to drive. Then they walked on to her rental car.

"It's the red one, just down by the corner."

The closer he got, the more Michael wanted to laugh. The car was the size of a go-kart. With his long legs there was no way he could get behind the wheel. His concern for the dimensions of the car, however, was quickly erased when he saw the scratches. They etched the driver's door and spread in a winglike pattern across the passenger door in back. He had a feeling there were matching scratches on the other side. Curious, he walked around the car to find out if he was right. He was. There was a small dent in the fender as well.

Isabel stood on the sidewalk, hands folded, anxiously waiting for him to comment. She didn't want to fight, but she would if he said anything sarcastic.

"Did you leave anything in the car?" he asked.

"No."

"Doors locked?"

"Yes."

"Okay, let's leave it here, and we'll drive my car to the body shop and drop off the key."

"I could drive it over there."

God, no. "Let's leave it here," he said instead.

Something else wasn't quite right about the car, but it took him a minute to figure out what it was. In his defense, the deep scratches and dent had held his attention and had distracted him.

"Where are the side mirrors?"

She answered without hesitation. "In the backseat."

Since Michael didn't seem to have anything to say about that, Isabel felt she needed to explain. "The roads are extremely narrow up here."

As they walked back to his car, he draped his arm around her shoulders. "Good to know," he said.

TWENTY-THREE

DETECTIVE CRAIG WALSH FINALLY DECIDED TO WAKE UP.
Nurse Terry happened to be in his ICU room checking his IV when her patient suddenly opened his eyes, grabbed hold of her arm, and bolted upright. He called for Grace over and over again, his agitation increasing until he was gasping for air. His voice was raspy and raw from the breathing tube the doctor had removed the day before.

"Oh my goodness, you gave me a shock," Terry said, her voice soothing despite the fact that he'd all but scared the curl out of her hair when he'd jumped at her out of the blue. "We've been waiting for you to come back to us. Do you know where you are?"

Walsh fell back against the pillows and closed his eyes. He was desperately trying to clear the thick fog clouding his brain.

"No," he answered.

"You're a patient at St. Margaret's Trauma Center in Boston," she told him.

"Why?" he asked, genuinely confused.

"You were shot, and you've been unconscious for quite a while."

Frowning, he repeated what she had told him. "I was shot." He tried to pull up the memory, but it was beyond his grasp.

"Yes," she said. "You don't remember?" He didn't answer her. "You were calling for Grace. Who is she?" Terry asked as she tucked the cover around him.

"I don't know," he said, his frustration showing on his face.

She patted his arm. "Your memory will come back to you. Just give it a little time. Rest now while I page the doctor and tell her the good news. She's going to be very happy to hear you're back with us."

There were other people Terry had been asked to call: Special Agent Nick Buchanan; Boston Detective Samuel; the patient's daughter, Kathleen, who had just gone home to catch a couple hours of sleep; and Isabel MacKenna.

Terry was happy that Isabel had been added to the call list. She had shown so much compassion for Detective Walsh. Her call immediately went to voicemail, so, just to make certain Isabel would get the message, she also texted her.

Two hours later ICU was swarming with FBI agents, Boston detectives, and policemen. Because of the chaos they were creating, Walsh, along with his IV and monitors, was moved to a private room adjacent to the unit. Only Nick Buchanan, Noah Clayborne, and Detective Samuel were allowed in.

Nick thought Walsh looked pretty good, given all he had been through. His eyes were clear, and he seemed fairly alert, considering. The fact that he was lucid after his ordeal was amazing, though his memory of the event was spotty at best. It seemed he could recall only bits and pieces up to the actual shooting.

Nick stood on one side of Walsh's bed, with Samuel on the other side. Noah stood in front of the door and tapped his phone to record the interview.

Samuel began the questioning. "Your Captain Perez told us that you came to Boston to do a favor for a friend."

Walsh shook his head. "I was already in Boston. I fly back and forth from Miami whenever I get the chance. I'm going to retire in a couple of years, and I've been looking for a place close to my daughter."

"Your friend wanted a favor?" Samuel asked, trying to guide Walsh back to the important topic at hand.

"Yes."

Walsh closed his eyes and sighed as though speaking took more energy than he could summon. A long minute went by without a word being spoken. Then Walsh said, "Donal Gladstone is his name. We went to college together here in Boston."

They could all see that Walsh was struggling to remember.

"And you've kept in contact with this man?" Noah asked.

"Yes."

"Do you trust him?" Nick asked.

"Yes, absolutely." From the look on his face, they knew the question had surprised him. "He's a good friend."

"What was the favor he wanted?" Samuel asked again.

"I'm trying to remember," Walsh said. "May I have some water? My throat is dry."

Noah left the room but returned a minute later with Nurse Terry. She carried a small plastic cup filled with ice chips.

"No gulps of water just yet," she said. "Ice chips will have to do for now."

She helped him scoop a few chips into his mouth, then put the cup on the cart next to the bed.

"Have you remembered who Grace is?" she asked. She turned to Nick and said, "When my patient opened his eyes, he started calling for Grace. He must have said her name at least ten times, but when I asked him who she was, he didn't know."

"Her name is Grace Isabel MacKenna," Nick clarified.

"Isabel?" the nurse said, smiling. "I know her." She turned back to Walsh. "She's been very concerned about you. She came to see you, and she calls often to check on your progress. She's going to be so pleased to hear you're awake."

"MacKenna." Walsh's voice was suddenly infused with a burst of energy. "I remember. Donal asked me to talk to her. He was concerned for her safety." He took a deep breath, then winced in pain, squeezing his eyes shut. He opened them again and squinted up at the ceiling as though searching it for answers. When at last he returned his attention to Nick, he said, "Donal couldn't get hold of her, but she had told him she was flying to Boston and staying with the Buchanans on Nathan's Bay. He knew I was in Boston, so he contacted me. When I tried to reach her at the Buchanans', I was told she was going to the Hamilton Hotel."

"And you went there?" Samuel asked, urging him to continue.

Walsh nodded. "Yes, I did go to the hotel," he said, pleased he remembered. "I pulled my badge out and hooked it to my belt. I wanted the staff to talk to me. I asked at the front desk to call her room, but she didn't answer. According to the valet, Grace went for a walk along the Freedom Trail. He told me he gave her directions and watched her walk to the corner, but then she turned the wrong way. He said she was wearing jeans and a navy blue windbreaker, and if I hurried I might be able to catch her."

"You were pretty far away from the hotel when you were shot," Noah remarked.

"I must have walked a long time. I finally saw her. She was a couple of blocks ahead, and I tried to catch up. Then I lost sight of her and I figured she must have taken another route back to the hotel because I had made a wide circle and couldn't find her, and then suddenly I spotted her. I was hurrying to her when a man came out of nowhere right in front of me. He was staring at Grace and heading for her. When I saw he had a gun, I ran at him. I knocked him down and we struggled." Walsh stopped talking and looked bewildered, then said. "I don't remember anything after that."

"Do you want to take a minute and rest?" Samuel asked.

"No, I want to keep going."

"Okay, then. Let's move to something else and maybe what happened will come back to you," Nick said, his tone brisk, anxious now to find out as much as he could before Walsh faded. "We know that Donal Gladstone is Isabel's solicitor in Scotland."

"Dunross," he answered. "He only just moved there a month ago from Edinburgh. Donal and I have gone fishing a couple of times, and he fell in love with the area. Fishing's always good, but it's bitching cold," he said with a smile.

Noah laughed. "Bitching cold? That doesn't sound like fun to me."

"It's actually exhilarating. It's a beautiful nook just north of Inverness. Donal wants to retire there." He looked at Samuel and said. "I doubt he knows I've been shot."

"We'll tell him," Samuel assured.

Wanting him to concentrate on what had happened, Nick pressed on. "Do you remember a flash drive?"

"A what?"

"A flash drive," Nick repeated. "We think you had it in your hand and that you put it in Isabel's pocket."

"You had a gun in your other hand," Samuel said.

"The weapon wasn't mine," Walsh said. Frowning as though unsure of what he had just declared, he asked, "Was it?"

"No, it wasn't," Noah said.

"You were shot twice while you wrestled with him to get his gun away. It's possible that, somewhere in that struggle, you got the flash drive from him," Samuel said.

"And then you got up and staggered around the corner while you were losing copious amounts of blood," Noah added. "We know that's a fact because you left a blood trail."

Walsh grimaced.

"You really don't remember getting shot twice?" Samuel couldn't seem to wrap his mind around the idea of someone losing all memory of such a traumatic event.

"It's coming back, but it's hazy . . . except Grace Isabel MacKenna. I see her as clear as ever. I don't know why."

"Maybe because she saved your ass," Noah said.

Samuel pulled out his phone. "I'm going to show you a video. Hopefully watching it will jar your memory."

Opening the video on his phone, he held it so that Walsh could get a clear view. Walsh watched intently, flinching when he saw himself fall into Isabel's arms. The entire video lasted less than a minute, and after it ended he asked Samuel to play it again. At the spot where the assailant rounded the corner and Isabel shot him, he asked Samuel to pause the action. This time he sat forward and studied the screen.

"That's not him," he stated.

"What do you mean it's not him?" Nick asked.

"That's not the man I was fighting. I remember now. The man I took down had red hair. It was the color you don't often see, and I guess that's why it stuck in my mind. This is some other guy."

"And you've never seen this man before?" Samuel asked.

"No."

"Was there anyone else around when you first saw the man going after Grace?"

"I don't think so. He seemed to just step out of the shadows. Maybe there was an alley. I don't recall."

Samuel turned to Nick and Noah. "Isabel said she saw a redheaded man at a distance. None of the witnesses saw him, so I was certain she just imagined him, or he was a bystander who didn't want to get involved. I should have dug deeper."

"So the man Isabel shot was not the man Walsh took down," Noah said.

"Apparently not," Samuel admitted. "There were two coming for her."

Nick's reaction to the news was a mixture of anger and worry. "And that means one is still out there."

AS SOON AS THEY WALKED OUT OF WALSH'S ROOM, SAMUEL HEADED back to his office to begin the hunt for the second man. Nick turned to Noah. "We need to talk to Gladstone."

They went into an empty waiting room, and Noah shut the door for privacy. It didn't take long for Nick to get Gladstone's office and home numbers. Checking his watch, he calculated it was late afternoon in Scotland, and he made a call to the solicitor's office.

A woman with a thick brogue answered. "Mr. Gladstone is just finishing up with a client. Would you like to wait on the line, or may he call you back?"

Nick wasn't in the mood to be patient. "This is Special Agent Nick Buchanan, FBI. It's important I speak to Mr. Gladstone now."

"Oh," the woman said, as though startled by the authority in his voice. "I'll just put you through."

A few seconds later Gladstone was on the line. Nick introduced himself and then Noah.

"We have you on speaker," he explained.

"Two FBI agents. What is this about?" Gladstone asked.

"Detective Craig Walsh," Nick answered.

"What's happened? Is Craig all right?"

"He will be," Noah said. He then told him about the shooting and explained that Walsh had only just awakened. "His memory is still cloudy."

"Walsh told us you sent him to talk to Grace MacKenna," Nick said. "Is that right? And if so, why?"

"Yes. I didn't expect there would be any danger for him there in Boston . . . I shouldn't have asked him . . ."

They could tell Gladstone was rattled and gave him a moment to calm down. Then Noah repeated his question.

"I was concerned about her coming here and wanted my friend . . . Detective Walsh . . . to talk to her face-to-face and impress upon her the need to be on guard. I didn't want her to come up here alone." He added, "It might not be safe."

"In what way?"

"I haven't lived here long, and it takes time to build trust with your neighbors. The people around here tend to keep to themselves and are hesitant to talk to outsiders. One night I received a call from a man who wouldn't give me his name, but he said he was concerned. He told me he was in a pub late one night and heard three men talking about Grace MacKenna. One of them said that she was an interloper, and that no one wanted her here. The man on the phone said he was worried for her safety and that I should tell her not to come. It could be dangerous. I asked him why he called me, and he told me he knew I was handling the MacKenna estate. He also knew I was taking over for another solicitor and wanted to move to another building. He knew he could trust me because he had heard from several others that I was nothing like MacCarthy and that I was honorable and would look out for Miss MacKenna. He disconnected the call before I could ask him more questions.

"I had spoken to Grace about making arrangements for her to come to Scotland and she told me she was heading to Boston and would be there for a week. Then I got the anonymous call. I couldn't reach her so I called my friend, and he tracked her down. I feel terrible that I've caused him all this trouble. And I hope Miss MacKenna got the message and isn't planning to come to Scotland just yet."

"I'm afraid it's too late. She's already there."

"Oh no. Grace will be walking in blind. No one up here is going to tell her anything. I doubt they'll even talk to her."

TWENTY-FOUR

ISABEL COULDN'T GET THEM TO STOP TALKING. WHEREVER THEY went, shopkeepers and restauranteurs, customers and diners were eager to tell her all about their beautiful village or town and the colorful and charming people who lived there. They were fiercely loyal to one another—a trait she greatly admired—and were proud of their country and their heritage.

By the end of Monday Michael and Isabel had fallen into a somewhat comfortable routine, but it took a while to get there. Before they had even started their journey, they had an argument. They were in his car, parked down the street from the auto shop. Michael had taken the key to Isabel's rental inside and had a lengthy conversation with the owner. When he came out, he was smiling.

"You were inside a long time," she commented. "What were you talking about?"

"Cars." He didn't embellish with the fact that they discussed her car in particular, and maniac drivers.

"I have our route figured out. As I've mentioned before, I want to stay off the highways and take back roads to Ballyloch. We could spend the night somewhere around there, finding a hotel where we could look out at the North Sea."

He reached over, opened the glove compartment, and pulled out a map. Flipping it open, he handed it to Isabel. "Inverness and Dunross, you'll notice, are northwest, and Ballyloch is northeast. You want to go in the opposite direction?"

"Yes, I do."

She could tell he was going to be difficult, so she rushed ahead to explain her plan. "I want to get the lay of the land and a feel for the people."

He didn't understand. "For God's sake, Isabel, we're not on a sightseeing tour."

"I need time," she admitted with a sigh.

"You what?"

"I need time to absorb what has happened. I know I'm going to have to deal with it soon."

Michael rubbed his brow. "Sweetheart, do you need to read what was on that flash drive again?"

"Why?"

"So you'll remember there are people here who want to kill you?"

He couldn't be more blunt than that, she supposed. She decided she would have to be honest with him, and if he then thought she was weak, that was on him. "So I'll remember? I haven't stopped thinking about it, and inside I'm freaking out. I need time to calm down and come up with a plan. I don't want to go there scared. I'd like to get my fear under control first and if that means we have to take a roundabout way to get to Dunross, then that's what we should do.

"You said you'd give me today and tomorrow, and you'd drive me wherever I wanted to go," she reminded. "Don't you want to know what's going on up there, or would you rather walk in without a clue? I don't even know who's living on Glen MacKenna. I'm not going to rely on what Donal Gladstone tells me. I need to have all the facts before I make any decisions."

"Who you're going to sell the land to?"

"Yes," she said. "People like to tell me about themselves. If, after they tell me what's worrying them, I can steer them to talk about the MacKennas, I might find out what's really going on."

"Okay, we'll do it your way, as long as you follow the rules. Remember, you don't go anywhere without me."

"I know," she said. "I have a ground rule, too."

Folding the map, he acted as though he hadn't heard her.

"Michael?"

He reached over and put the map back in the glove compartment. "Yes?"

"I said I have a ground rule."

"Okay. What is it?"

He was about to start the car when she said, "No hanky-panky."

He burst out laughing. He didn't think he had ever heard anyone say those words. He wanted her to say them again.

"Could you repeat that?"

Isabel cringed. *Hanky-panky?* She couldn't come up with anything better than that? What was she? Ninety? She was beginning to think that her aunt Nora might have had a bigger influence on her vocabulary than she'd realized.

"You heard me. No hanky-panky, and that means no messing around. Do you agree?"

"Absolutely."

Before she realized what he was going to do, he reached over, cupped the back of her neck with his hand and pulled her toward him. Then he stopped and waited.

"What are you doing?"

"I want to kiss you."

"Okay."

The kiss was fast but amazing all the same. He made her want more, much much more. He pulled back, turned the motor on, and started driving. He couldn't have looked more unaffected by the kiss. She wouldn't have been surprised if he'd started whistling.

Okay? She said *okay?* What was wrong with her? She was the one with the problem, not Michael. Apparently a kiss didn't mean much to him, but now all she wanted to think about was how to get him to kiss her again.

She was such a fraud. The same old dilemma was once again staring her in the face. The only way she was ever going to get over him was to get away from him first, then concentrate on other things. Like a career. She knew she was never going to stop caring about him, but eventually she hoped she could move on. She didn't want to be miserable for the rest of her life. She could only imagine how depressing the songs she would write would be. Songs of heartache, heartache, and more heartache. She made a promise to herself. No matter what happened in the future, she wasn't going to write any whiny, my-man-done-me-wrong songs.

She turned her thoughts to more important matters. She pulled out a smaller map from her bag and spread it across her knees. She had highlighted the villages and towns on the way.

She never had to go to anyone seeking information; they all came to her. As soon as she walked into a shop and said hello and mentioned how much she loved Scotland, Michael found a wall or a counter to lean against, crossed one ankle over the other, folded his arms across his chest, and patiently waited. It became his go-to stance. He thought he looked relaxed and nonthreatening. Isabel thought he looked as though he was ready to pounce at the first provocation. She also thought it was a comfort to have him close, though she was loath to admit it to him.

Michael wasn't fazed by their openness with Isabel and their nervousness with him. He stayed just far enough away from her that her new friends—and they all considered themselves her friends after spending ten minutes with her—would focus on her and not worry about him.

She was recognized several times, and he admired her clever way of turning it around and deflecting the would-be fan.

The first time it happened they were in a shop crowded with what Isabel called knickknacks. She walked up to the register with some postcards she wanted to purchase. The teenage salesgirl behind the counter, wearing a tag with the name "Heather" clipped to her blue apron, did a double take the second she saw Isabel and blurted, "You're that famous singer, aren't you? Oh my God, it is you, isn't it?" Her voice rose to a squeaky shout. "You're really her, standing right here in front of me—"

Isabel interrupted. "I do look a little like her, don't I?" she said. "I was just thinking that you look like that beautiful actress . . . I can't remember her name . . ."

Heather's hand flew to her chest and she blushed. "You think I'm beautiful?"

"Yes, I do. You look so surprised," she added. "Surely others have complimented you . . . haven't they?"

Heather took a strand of hair and began to wind it around her finger while she thought about the question. "I've been told I resemble that famous French actress with the pouting lips, Monique."

"Yes," Isabel responded enthusiastically. "That's who you look like. Honestly, I think you're prettier than Monique."

And the issue of Isabel being a famous singer was forgotten.

Their next stop was at a shop in Kilcory. Isabel learned that a group of outsiders were trying to purchase Glen MacKenna, and there was a fight going on over ownership. The clerk of the woolens shop, after describing his worries about his son's lack of ambition and his wife's need to coddle the boy, said that ownership of Glen MacKenna could be tied up in court for years.

At one other stop she learned that someone was running people off Glen MacKenna and claiming the land for himself.

By the time darkness had fallen Isabel and Michael were starving. They stopped at the nearest market and purchased items they would need to remove Isabel's stitches, then went to the restaurant next door for dinner. They sat at a back table and ate salmon cakes and steak pie that tasted suspiciously like lamb but was still quite tasty, mounds of whipped potatoes, and biscuits with sweet butter. She didn't touch the side dish of mushy peas.

It was cold and rainy when they walked out of the restaurant and headed to a nearby hotel. Isabel didn't realize how tired she was until they checked into the Gleann Inn for the night. It was a small hotel the owner advertised as cozy. It wasn't. The manager assured them that their room had a brand-new king-size bed. It didn't. The size was somewhere between a queen and a double. There were square tables with lamps on either side of the bed, a saggy upholstered chair in the corner, and a small round table, which was all the tiny room could hold. The bathroom had been newly remodeled and was almost as large as the bedroom. Isabel showered first, then put on her blue pajama shorts and camisole. She walked back into the bedroom with the tube of body lotion her sister Kate had given her. Isabel loved its scent of camellias because it reminded her of her mother's flower garden.

Michael barely glanced her way. He had removed the floral coverlet—which matched the floral drapes and floral tablecloth—and now was on the phone having an intense conversation. How was she going to sleep in the same bed with him and not touch him? Ignoring him was impossible in such a tiny room, but she would give it her best try. She sat on the bed, propped a pillow against the headboard, and took her time rubbing the lotion into her arms and legs.

He was on the phone a long time. With his back to her he was speaking so quietly she couldn't make out the conversation, but she heard him utter agreement several times. Once he finished, he put the phone on his charger and turned to her. "Just as a precaution, I don't want you to turn your phone on. You can use mine to make calls."

"But I . . ."

"I don't want anyone tracking you."

"Can they do that?"

"We aren't taking any chances."

She agreed with a nod. "Who were you talking to?"

"Nick," he answered. He picked up his shaving kit and headed to the bathroom. "I'll fill you in after I shower. And Isabel . . ."

"Yes?"

"Put some damn clothes on."

She looked down at herself. Her clothes hadn't disappeared.

Closing her eyes, she folded her hands in her lap and tilted her head back to rest on the headboard, trying to clear her mind of everything but happy thoughts. That proved impossible because Michael kept getting in the way. She could hear the shower running and naturally pictured him naked with warm water cascading down his muscular shoulders and arms. She wondered what he would do if she stepped into the shower with him. Probably let her seduce him again. She tried to erase the image from her mind, but it was impossible. Thankfully, the shower ended.

She had the discipline of a nymphomaniac. She told herself to think about tomorrow and what she wanted to accomplish. She came up with a few ideas, but then Michael walked out of the bathroom, and every thought in her head vanished. He was wearing a white towel around his waist and nothing else. She could barely catch her breath.

"Put some damn clothes on," she demanded.

His reaction wasn't what she expected. He laughed.

How could she be coherent with him looking that good? This wasn't fair. And it didn't get any easier when he dropped the towel, pulled out a pair of boxer briefs, and put them on. Was that supposed to squelch her lust? She took a long deep breath and slowly let it out before she could talk again.

"Are we both sleeping in this bed?" she asked.

"Yes, we are."

"It's a small bed."

"Yes, it is."

"We could ask if they would bring up a cot," she said. Her voice sounded as though she had laryngitis.

"No."

She wasn't sure why he was being so stubborn. In an effort to get along, she decided to acquiesce, knowing it was going to be a long, tense, sleepless night for her. "Okay, then. We'll share the same bed."

"Damn right."

"You're in a mood, aren't you?"

He didn't answer her. Changing the subject seemed the prudent course of action because she didn't want to get into an argument. "I'm glad we had the chance to talk to some people today, but we didn't really find out very much about Glen MacKenna. I think we should head west tomorrow, like you said. I'm ready. I've had time to calm down. I'm still angry, but I think that's a good thing because it will keep me on edge."

Michael walked over with the paper bag from the store. She couldn't stop staring at his chest. All muscle, she knew from kissing and touching him. And the heat radiating from him . . . the way the dark hair tapered at his navel . . .

He had to move her legs out of the way so he could sit down next to her. "I know you want to take some time to get information about Glen MacKenna, so okay, we'll do that. We'll just have to be careful." He gestured toward her arm. "Okay, let's get those stitches out."

She shook herself out of her stupor. "What did you say?"

"I said it's time to take out your stitches."

Michael dabbed alcohol on her arm and gently clipped and removed the stitches. She grimaced a couple of times.

"It stings."

"I like that you don't hide what you're feeling."

"Why would I? I don't need to be tough with you."

"No, you don't," he agreed. "Okay, all finished. The surgeon did a good job. Remember what he called you?"

"No."

"Yes, you do. Greek goddess, right?" He laughed then. "The look on your face . . . You didn't like it."

"No, I didn't," she admitted.

Michael was sitting so close to her his leg rubbed against hers. It was odd, she thought. As sexy as Xavier was, she hadn't reacted to him the way she reacted to Michael. Even his scent aroused her. Who knew a whiff of soap could be so seductive?

He looked into her eyes, and she suddenly felt as though he could read her thoughts. Thank God he couldn't because then he would know how sex-crazed she became when she was near him.

"It seemed like it all happened such a long time ago. Shooting that man, getting stitches, performing with Xavier." *And you*, she silently added. *You happened, too.* "It has all blended together."

"You're handling it with grace."

He was wrong, but she didn't tell him so. Inside she was constantly struggling to keep it together.

He put the supplies away, grabbed a white T-shirt from his duffel bag, and put it on.

Isabel fluffed the pillow, pulled the sheets back, and lay as close to the edge of the bed as possible so that Michael would have a little room.

"Are you tired tonight?" she asked.

"Yes, I am."

Maybe that was why he was acting as though sleeping with her wasn't going to be a problem. He was exhausted from the long flight from Boston and the long day he'd spent with her. He probably hadn't had any sleep in thirty-six hours.

Was being with her a chore? she wondered. Had he drawn the short straw in the Buchanan family and got stuck with her? Maybe she should just ask. She didn't have to hide her real reactions and pretend everything was all right when it clearly wasn't. She could be honest with him.

So why hadn't she talked to him about that viper Amanda? Might as well get it out in the open now.

"Michael, Amanda asked me to sing at your wedding."

A scowl crossed his face when he responded. "Yeah, I know. Regan told me."

She waited for him to say something more, and after a minute or two realized he wasn't going to. Who was he angry with? Her? For telling him about Amanda's request. Or Amanda? For asking.

She broke the silence. "I told her no."

He nodded as though she had just given him some serious news he needed to mull over. She felt like shouting at him. *Why does she think she's going to marry you?*

Michael's words were measured when he finally answered. "Sweetheart, I was never going to marry her, and she knew that. We haven't been together in a long time. I saw her when I was in Boston, which wasn't all that often. I was convenient for her, and she was convenient for me. That's all there was to it."

She couldn't stop herself from asking. "Am I convenient?"

He laughed, surprising her. "No, you're not convenient. You're a pain in the . . ."

She smiled. "Thank you." *For lying*, she silently added.

Michael turned the bedroom lights off. With the drapes closed, the room was pitch black. He opened the bathroom door a crack to shed a sliver of light on the floor, then got into bed. Rolling to his side, he quickly pulled her up against him before she went flying to the floor, and anchored her with his arm around her waist.

"Will you be able to sleep like this?" she whispered. "I could move to the chair. It doesn't look too lumpy."

"I won't be able to sleep unless I know you're close."

"Do you think I'll leave during the night?"

"No," he answered. "I need you close," he repeated curtly. "Now go to sleep."

She tried. She really tried to relax and drift off to sleep. Counting sheep, relaxation techniques, replaying boring speeches she'd had to sit through in college . . . counting sheep again. Nothing worked.

She knew what the problem was. Michael, of course. She wanted him, and the longer he held her in his arms, the stronger the craving became. She wasn't going to feel guilty about it. She was an adult, and she didn't think there was anything wrong with having sex with a man she cared about. But she would not be the aggressor again. If he wanted her as much as she wanted him, he would have to make the first move. Maybe he was fighting the same battle she was and was just as miserable. That pleasing possibility was snatched away a moment later when his breathing became deep and even. He had already fallen asleep.

Gritting her teeth, she began counting sheep again. One little sheep . . . two little sheep . . .

She reached forty-two sheep and stopped counting long enough to vow that Michael would have to beg her before she let him touch her again. Beg, no matter what, and even then she just might say no. She started counting again, sincerely hoping that by the time she reached two hundred little sheep, she would be ready to fall asleep.

"Isabel?" Michael whispered as though he didn't want to wake her.

She rolled over in his arms. "Yes?"

"I want you."

Did he beg? Close enough, she decided. She kissed the side of his neck. "I want you, too."

She loved the way he kissed her. He tugged on her hair to get her to tilt her head back, and then his mouth covered hers in a scorching kiss. His tongue penetrated and stroked hers, receded, and penetrated again and again in the mating ritual that drove her wild. He held nothing back.

Keeping her tightly against him, he rolled and pinned her beneath him. Each kiss was hotter, wilder. He lifted his head and let out a long raspy breath in an attempt to slow down.

The passion ignited so quickly and became so intense, she didn't know how he got her clothes off and then his. Their bodies melded together, clinging to each other. The hair on his chest rubbed against her breasts when he moved, sending the most erotic sensations rushing through her body.

He slowly moved down her body, kissing every inch of her. He caressed her breasts, and when his tongue stroked her nipples, she cried out and nearly came off the bed.

She moved restlessly against him, pushing up against his arousal. She wanted to touch him, to drive him crazy, but Michael wouldn't let her. His mouth covered hers again in a wet, hot kiss, and then he lifted up and held her gaze as the palm of his hand slid down between her thighs. She was ready for him. But that wasn't enough. He wanted her out of her mind with desire for him.

"Michael, please," she begged. She thought she would die if he made her wait any longer.

He pushed her thighs apart, hesitated until she looked into his eyes, and then thrust inside. "You're so tight, so perfect . . ."

Her body was throbbing for release. She barely understood what he was saying to her. He started moving, slowly at first, but his need soon overrode his desire to make it last. He thrust again and again, harder and faster, spurred on by her demand for more.

Her arms were wrapped tightly around him, her nails digging into his shoulders, and she cried out his name as her orgasm burst upon her. It was magnificent.

Michael was there with her, though he didn't shout her name. He whispered it over and over as he climaxed deep inside her.

Spent, he collapsed on top of her and for several minutes all that could be heard was their harsh breathing as each tried to recover. He could feel her heart beating under his. He finally found enough strength to roll onto his back, but he kept Isabel wrapped in his arms. He couldn't stop touching her, stroking her shoulders, her back, her amazingly perfect backside.

It took a while for Isabel to recover. She had never been so overcome by an emotion. It scared her a little because she couldn't control it, and God help her if she became dependent on Michael loving her.

Crazy thoughts, she decided. She didn't want to worry about anything right now. Lying there with him seemed the most natural thing in the world. Although it didn't make any sense, she was feeling content and wonderfully lethargic.

"Isabel, baby, are you all right?"

"Yes," she answered. The side of her face rested against his chest.

Michael stacked his hands behind his head. When she sat up and straddled his hips, his breath caught in his throat. He thought she was the most beautiful and provocative woman he'd ever seen. Her hair was in wild disarray around her shoulders, her lips were swollen from his kisses, and her cheeks were pink from rubbing against his day's growth of whiskers. He pulled her down for a long kiss.

"You're insatiable," she said, her voice a husky whisper.

"For you, yes," he agreed. "And you're insatiable for me, aren't you?"

"Yes," she admitted.

He looked arrogantly pleased with her honesty.

"Michael?"

"Yes?"

"I have two words for you."

"Thank you?"

She laughed. "You think I was going to say 'thank you'?"

"You should. I was pretty spectacular, and I do believe you screamed my name a few times."

The smile in his eyes distracted her for a second. He was such a handsome devil. "That's not what I was going to say."

"Then what?" he asked. "What two words?"

She slowly trailed her fingertips down his chest. "My turn."

TWENTY-FIVE

THE FOLLOWING MORNING SHOULD HAVE BEEN AWKWARD FOR ISA-
bel, but it wasn't. Michael didn't give her time to be embarrassed or
have regrets about all the wild things she had done when it was her
turn to drive him out of his mind.

He woke her kissing her neck. She was still in his arms, and his
warm breath against her ear was giving her goose bumps.

"Wake up, Isabel," he whispered, his voice rough from sleep. "We
need to get going."

"All right," she said softly, and snuggled closer to him.

"Come on. It's time to get up."

"All right," she repeated on a sigh.

She finally moved. She put her arms around his neck and kissed
him. There wasn't anything timid or quick about the kiss. She put her
heart into it and was trembling when he pulled back.

Michael told himself to get out of bed, but he couldn't make
himself do it. He was too hungry for her. Her warm body pressed
against his made him ache to be inside her.

"Isabel, we need to get up."

Those were the last coherent words he said. He kissed her again,
and that kiss led to another and another, and before he could stop himself, he was kissing and caressing nearly every inch of her beautiful

body. His desire for her was completely out of control, and he couldn't seem to care. All she had to do was smile at him or look at him, and he wanted her.

"Are you okay?" he asked as he rolled out of bed and headed to the bathroom. He didn't wait for an answer.

Isabel was slow to float back to reality. Making love with Michael had been the most wonderful experience, and now she was in the mood to cuddle. Apparently, he wasn't. She wasn't upset that he was in a hurry. She knew what she was getting with him. There hadn't been any words of love after, but then she hadn't expected that there would be. He loved having sex with her. That was the only thing she was absolutely sure about.

Pushing those thoughts aside, she grabbed one of Michael's T-shirts and put it on, then sorted through her suitcase looking for something to wear today. She ended up choosing a pink V-neck T-shirt, khaki pants, and flats.

While she was in the bathroom, Michael dressed, packed, and made two phone calls. The woman was taking forever to get ready. As he was waiting, he had time to think. And Isabel was first on his mind. He loved being with her, but, once again, he couldn't avoid the reality of how ill-suited they were for each other.

He was fast and methodical in everything he did. He never took his eye off the target, and he always sought perfection. Ironically, he took his time only when he was making love to Isabel.

Everything Isabel did was slow and haphazard, and yet she seemed to find order in her chaos. Dylan told him she left old flash drives and notebooks all over the house. Writing songs was an important part of who she was, and yet it could be dangerous. When she had a song on her mind, she became distracted and wasn't aware of what was around her. She became so distracted in Boston, she got hopelessly lost and nearly got herself killed.

Once he focused on a goal, he went after it with a vengeance. Failure wasn't an option. He was disciplined and methodical, which was why the law appealed to him. He liked order. Until Isabel came along, he wouldn't let anything divert his attention.

Isabel did have other, what he considered endearing, strengths. For one, she had tremendous empathy for others. She took time to listen to strangers.

Those same strangers were suspicious and nervous around him. Isabel claimed it was because he was such an imposing figure and he never smiled. He could hold a grudge, even when he couldn't do anything about it. Revenge made sense to him. His only excuse was that he was a Buchanan male, and it was in his DNA.

She was an optimist.

He was a cynic.

She saw the good in people.

He looked for the bad and usually found it.

He had to admit she was a hell of a lot more fun than he was, and he was happy and content when he was with her, even when she was driving him nuts.

She had her flaws. She was stubborn, unreasonable at times, had a fierce temper, and was a maniac behind the wheel.

Simply put—they were all wrong for each other. He would make her miserable, and she would drive him crazy.

Isabel stood by the foot of the bed watching Michael. He had his hands in his pockets, his stance was rigid, and he was staring out the window with the most intense look on his face. She couldn't imagine what he was thinking.

It was drizzling outside. She put on her rain jacket and was ready to take on the day. She called his name twice before she got his attention.

"I'm ready to go."

"Do you have everything packed?"

"Yes," she replied. "I double-checked."

He looked around the room. "Do you have your phone?"

"Yes," she answered, trying not to be irritated. He was the one who left his things behind—like the shaving kit he left in her hotel room—not her. "I have my phone."

"No, you don't. It's on the floor next to the table."

Damn it. Now she felt like the bonehead. Without a word she picked up her phone and stuffed it into her bag with her charger.

Fifteen minutes later they had checked out of the hotel and were on their way. Michael backtracked a couple of times to make sure they weren't being followed. It seemed to Isabel that there was a round-about every other mile. She thought the circles were dangerous because she had had several near misses when she'd driven her rented car around them. Sometimes there were as many as six entrances into the circle. Michael wasn't having any trouble, though.

"I heard you ask the manager at the front desk for directions to the Edinburgh airport," she said.

"That's right."

"We're going north, not south."

"Right again."

"I'm assuming you wanted him to think we were going to the airport.

"Yes."

"You thought he recognized me, didn't you? That's why you lied. I thought he recognized me, too."

"No, I didn't think that," he countered. "I lied because I don't want anyone to know where we're headed. We've been lucky so far, but that isn't going to last."

"I do think that manager knew who I was. He kept staring at me."

"He's a man, and you're a beautiful woman. Of course he stared."

Did Michael just give her a compliment? She wasn't about to ask. He'd probably say something to ruin it.

"What's our first destination?"

"Food."

They stopped in a charming hamlet north of Inverslie and ate in a café attached to what Isabel called an all-in-one store. There were souvenirs of every sort: maps, both of olden days and modern, plaid hats, scarves, and blankets of the different clan colors. Nestled in the corner of the shop with a window overlooking an arched bridge was the café. There were only four small square tables with chairs.

They were the only customers in the store, probably because of the early hour and the rain. It was coming down in torrents now.

After the waiter took their order, an older gentleman came over to the table to introduce himself. He was tall, bulky through his sloped shoulders, and had a thick salt-and-pepper beard and a nice smile. He was also quite affable.

He welcomed them and said, "My name is Lachlan, and I'm the owner's father. How are you liking the weather?" he asked as he pulled out a chair and sat. He chatted with them while they ate and answered all of Isabel's questions about the area.

"Lachlan, will you help me find a map or two showing where all the clans are?" she asked.

"Old or new? Do you want to know where they are now or where they were back when?" He smiled then and said, "It's about the same. Borders haven't changed in centuries in some areas." He went to a wall with a display of maps and postcards. He returned to them with four different maps. "As soon as you finish your scone, I'll open them up and let you decide which ones you want."

"Did you grow up around here?" she asked.

"No, no," he answered. "I was born and raised in a tiny hamlet no bigger than a thumbprint not too far away from the Moray Firth." He pulled the chair out and sat again. "I'm a Highlander through and through," he boasted. "My job took me to Glasgow, and that's where I met my wife and where our son and daughter were born. We still live there," he added. "I'm only here for a few more days while my daughter and her husband attend a wedding in London. Why are you folks here?"

"We wanted to see all the placcs we've read about," Isabel explained.

Michael was watching Lachlan. He could see the worry in his eyes and knew he wanted to talk.

He was right. As soon as the dishes were removed, Lachlan angled his chair closer to Isabel. *Here we go again*, Michael thought.

"I've been trying to talk my wife into moving to my hamlet. I miss it, and that's where all my relatives are. I talk to my cousins, Hamish and Rory, almost every day, and they keep me up on all the news. I recently inherited my mother's cottage," he continued. "But my wife has been ill . . ."

He gave Michael a furtive glance. Lachlan was a little reticent to talk in front of him, but Michael wasn't about to leave Isabel's side, and so he pulled out his phone to answer his texts. He pretended not to hear the man tell Isabel his problems.

"She's been ill?" Isabel said, her voice filled with sympathy. "I'm so sorry."

"For a while it was bad, real bad. It's her blood," he explained. "She has great doctors in Glasgow." His voice shook with emotion, and there were tears in his eyes. Isabel reached over and put her hand on top of his. He grabbed hold and held tight as he continued. He talked for almost fifteen minutes, and when he was finished, Isabel gently pulled her hand back and said, "It sounds like you're doing a wonderful job of taking care of her."

Tears cluttered his eyes again. He pulled a handkerchief from his back pocket and wiped them away. "I don't know what I would do without her," he whispered.

Michael had been listening, of course. He realized that while Lachlan talked, he was actually working out his own solutions and getting rid of any guilt he harbored. Isabel had made a connection with this man because she understood his pain and his loneliness, for she had experienced both when she lost her mother and didn't have anyone to help her get through it.

"Of course, I can't ask her to move. Leaving doctors she has such faith in would be wrong." He took Isabel's sympathetic smile as an approval. "You know what? We could use the cottage for a getaway every now and then. It's not such a long drive. My wife would like that." He took a deep breath and slowly let it out. Having worked out the problem, he was ready to move on. "Let's get to those maps," he said. "I'm going to be making marks with this red pen, so I'll be giving you this map for free."

Isabel objected. "No, I'll be happy to pay . . ."

Ignoring her offer, he continued. "As you can see, this is a map of the Highlands. Now, the Kincaid clan and the Maitland clan lived way up here," he said, marking the area with an *X*. "Quite a few of their descendants live there even now. It's their land, after all." Hunched over the map, he looked at Isabel. "The Highlands are beautiful. No, that's not the word I'm searching for."

"They're majestic," Isabel offered.

"Yes," Lachlan agreed. "Majestic."

Michael noticed that Lachlan was far more relaxed now. The talk had obviously helped him.

"Bordering the Maitlands to the west are the Buchanans. There are still quite a few descendants living up there, too. You'll want to stay away from them on your travels," he warned. "Far away." He affected an exaggerated shiver for effect and said, "They can be mean and crazy. The least little thing sets them off. They enjoy fighting. Yes, they do," he added, nodding. "The Buchanan men like to frequent the Lazy Pig Pub in Kinley, which isn't far from here, and I'll admit the pub serves some of the best kidney pie in all of Scotland, but I'm warning you not to go there. It's too dangerous."

Lachlan must not have thought she and Michael understood just how ornery and mean the Buchanan men were, for he felt the need to give them yet another warning. "If one of you looks at one of them funny-like, he'll punch your man right in the face."

"Oh my," Isabel whispered.

Michael, she noticed, was trying hard not to smile. Did he think having the reputation of being the mean and crazy Buchanans was a good thing? And what did looking at someone funny-like mean? She didn't dare ask him, fearing she might start smiling, or worse, laughing, which she worried would offend him.

"Did I mention the MacHughs? They were way up there, too, and the edge of their property touched Finney's Flat, a coveted piece of land. Way, way back, ownership of the land bounced between the MacHughs and the Buchanans. Then the Dunbars got into it. They were almost as mean and crazy as the Buchanans."

With a sigh, he leaned back in the chair, stretched his legs out, and told them several stories he'd heard from his cousins about the Buchanans and the Dunbars. All the stories ended with someone getting punched in the face.

The goings-on of the clans fascinated Isabel. "You know your history," she praised, even though she suspected most of the stories were exaggerations.

"I like to think I do. Some things are always changing, and other things are never going to change. A Highlander never forgets a slight. Let me tell you about some of my favorite feuds."

Isabel couldn't help but notice that each feud he told them about always began with the same word, *sneaky*. The sneaky Kearns, the sneaky MacPhersons, and the sneaky no-good Monroes were just a few.

After he described feuds—some that went as far back as only God knew—Michael pointed to an area of the map that didn't have an *X* on it. He knew that was where the MacKenna land was, but he wanted Lachlan to assume they didn't know anything about the clan. If Michael came right out and asked about the MacKennas, Lachlan might want to know why they were interested.

"What clan lived here?" he asked.

"The MacKennas," Lachlan answered. "How could I have forgotten." He leaned over the table and made another bold *X*. "There's quite a bit of turmoil going on with some of the MacKennas who live there now. Quite a bit," he repeated, nodding for emphasis. "My cousin Rory says it's all anyone can talk about."

"I'd love to hear about it . . . if you have the time," Isabel said.

"Of course I have the time, and I enjoy talking about the feuds. It keeps them fresh in my mind." He scratched his cheek as he continued. "The MacKennas have themselves a giant feud percolating now."

Carefully folding the map, he handed it to Michael. Then he motioned to the waiter, who was hovering in the doorway. "Bring it on in now, Harry," he ordered.

The tray must have already been prepared because seconds later a fresh tea service was placed on the table. Besides the silver teapot, sugar and creamer, there were also little tea sandwiches, tea cakes, and scones with clotted cream, lemon curd, and raspberry jam.

Michael noticed that Harry couldn't take his eyes off Isabel. When Isabel looked up at him and smiled, the teenager nearly dropped two bottled waters Michael had requested. The waiter's obvious infatuation with Isabel irritated Michael. In the past he'd never been overly possessive, but with Isabel it was different. He was different.

Isabel nudged Michael under the table with her knee to get him to stop glaring.

"Here you are, lass," Lachlan said as he handed her a full cup of hot tea. The last thing she wanted was more tea, but she knew she was going to have to take a sip or two so that she wouldn't offend the man. She wanted him to keep talking about the MacKennas.

"The rain hasn't let up," Lachlan remarked as he reached for a scone. "My daughter owns this store, and she swears she makes a nice profit," he said, shaking his head. "I don't know how she could. Since I've been here the last couple of days, only a dozen or so customers have made purchases. Of course, the weather hasn't helped." He popped a bite into his mouth, washed it down with a gulp of tea, and then asked, "Now, where was I?"

"You were telling us about the MacKennas," Isabel reminded. "What clan is fighting with them? Could it be those ornery Buchanans?"

Lachlan chuckled. "No, not the Buchanans. According to Rory, the MacKennas aren't fighting with any other clan. It's infighting that's going on."

"They're fighting with one another?" she asked, trying to clarify.

"Exactly so. There's a lot of gossip flying around, but this is what I know to be true. A man named Compton MacKenna owned the land for nearly fifty years. He never married, and when he died, he willed the land to a relative.

"Compton moved to America when he was a young man, and he only returned to the Highlands a couple of times."

"He left his land all those years without knowing . . . ," she began.

"Oh, he knew everything that was going on. He had hired a groundskeeper, a man named James Gibson, and my cousin Hamish, who I'll admit likes to poke his nose into everyone else's business, told me Gibson was paid handsomely to keep his eye on the property and to let Compton know if there were any problems. James died a while back, and the job of groundskeeper has been handed down to his son." He thought to add, "That's what Hamish tells me, anyway."

Isabel still couldn't discern what the fighting was all about. Michael was as impatient as she was to get to the root of the problem.

"Who's making the trouble?" Isabel asked.

"Is someone contesting the will?" Michael asked a second later.

"I was just getting to that," Lachlan said, reaching for a cake. "There's a man named Clive Harcus who's claiming to be the legitimate son of Compton MacKenna. He insists he's the rightful owner."

"Does he have proof that he's the legitimate son?" Isabel asked.

"Not so far, according to Hamish and Rory. I hear new stories about Clive Harcus nearly every day. I swear his name is etched in my memory. Word is, he moved into a cottage on MacKenna land and is pushing all the other tenants out until they're willing to pay him a high rent. Rory says people are afraid of him. He's a bully, and mean, real mean."

"Is that gossip or the truth?" Michael wanted to know.

"It could be gossip, but from all the incidents I've heard about I'm thinking it's true. Rory says one day Harcus is going to kill someone. He's got a temper big enough to do it."

When he saw the shocked look on Isabel's face, Lachlan reached over and patted her hand. Then he sought to lighten the conversation and launched into a humorous story about one of the MacHughs.

"Were there any clans living above the MacHughs?" Michael asked. He already knew the answer, for he'd looked over the map, searching for his cousins the MacAlisters, out of curiosity. That clan did live above the MacHughs, and Michael was interested in what Lachlan would have to say about them.

"Oh my, yes, there were other clans living up there. Some descendants still are." He named several clans, added a few spicy tidbits about each one, and then said, "Way up there, hanging on the water are the MacAlisters." He smiled when he said their name. "Now, there's a rowdy bunch to rival the Buchanans."

For another fifteen minutes Lachlan regaled them with colorful stories about different clans while he devoured every bit of food on the tray.

Michael paid cash for the food and left Harry a handsome tip. Isabel also purchased three maps. Lachlan insisted on giving her his address and phone number. Should she run into any problems or need directions, he wanted her to call him.

Once they were back in the car and on their way, Isabel said, "You wanted to laugh when Lachlan was talking about those rowdy Buchanans."

"I wanted to tell him who I was."

"I'm glad you didn't. You would have embarrassed him."

She wasn't paying attention to where they were headed. The rain had slowed to a drizzle, but there were still heavy clouds overhead, chasing after them. It was dark and gloomy, and she knew they were in for another downpour.

TWENTY-SIX

ISABEL'S THOUGHTS KEPT GETTING AWAY FROM HER. SOME OF them were about the threats against her, the rest were about Michael. What would he be doing in a year, and who would he be with? She was pretty sure she knew the answer. He would be saving the world, and the woman at his side would be brilliant with a gazillion degrees, and she'd also be quite beautiful. Isabel already hated her.

Did he wonder what she would be doing in a year? Did he ever think about telling her how he felt about her? Or if they had a future together? He was a Buchanan male, so no. Sensitivity was the one gene the males in that family were missing.

After a couple of detours on back roads, they passed through a small village, and Michael spotted a stone house with the first floor converted into a restaurant. A large chalkboard by the front door touted the best fish and chips in Scotland.

"Are you hungry? Or did watching Lachlan eat all that food fill you up?" He pulled to the curb and pointed to the sign. "What do you think?"

"Sounds great," Isabel answered.

The entire restaurant was no bigger than a living room, with half a dozen tables scattered about. Since it was midafternoon, the place was empty except for three older gentlemen at a table against the wall.

In front of each was a cup of coffee. One could easily assume they had been sitting there for quite some time discussing matters of importance. Their conversation stopped as they watched Michael and Isabel walk in and take a seat at a table in the center of the room.

The waitress, a plump woman with a mass of brown curls on top of her head and round cheeks that looked like ripe apples when she smiled, emerged from the kitchen, holding menus in her hand.

After turning in their orders, she returned and said, "I can tell by your accents. You're Americans, aren't you? I've always wanted to visit America, but it just never worked out."

"Have you lived here long?" Isabel asked.

And thus began the life story of Moira the waitress.

From past experience Michael knew this brief stop for lunch was going to take longer than expected, so he sat back in his chair and watched Isabel do what she had done before. She let Moira talk. The woman had lost her husband of thirty years in a fishing accident, and Isabel sympathetically listened to her tell several stories about her dear, dear Dorian. Moira then veered into the problems she was having with her extended family, who wanted her to move to a village north of where she was currently living so she could be closer to them.

"It's beautiful up there," she admitted, "but it's just different."

As she described the area in detail, Isabel began to recognize that she was talking about a place that was very close to Glen MacKenna. She waited patiently for the right time, and then she nodded and said, "I think we heard some people talking about problems in that area. A dispute over some land, maybe?"

"I don't know anything about that," Moira said.

Before she could continue her story, one of the older men interrupted. "That's right. There's trouble brewing up there."

Isabel turned to face him. "What kind of trouble?"

"It's all got to do with a man named Harcus," he explained. "My son's place is up in Dunross, and he tells me the fellow is a real bastard. He says he's made a lot of enemies."

Michael straightened in his chair. "How so?"

"One of my son's friends was hired by Clive Harcus to put in new windows in his mother's cottage. They were double-thick panes and very expensive. After the work was done, Harcus refused to pay. He said the windows rattle during a windstorm and that it was shoddy work. The cost nearly put my son's friend out of business. There were other workmen who were never paid. I don't know the details," the man said. "All I know is that my son is trying to stay as far away from him as possible."

Isabel and Michael exchanged glances but didn't comment.

With the break in her conversation, Moira had gone to the kitchen and come back with their food. As Michael and Isabel ate, the three men opened up and began talking about themselves and their views on everything from the younger generation to world politics. The topic never returned to Harcus or the land, and Isabel was being careful not to appear too interested in either. The men had confirmed what she had already learned from Lachlan, and that was enough for now. She spent the rest of the meal letting the three men talk. By the time she left the restaurant, she knew each of their names, their ages, their marital status, and just about everything else about them.

There weren't many cars on the roadway. "That stop took longer than I had planned, but we're actually making good time," Michael remarked.

"Where are we going?"

"North," he answered. "I'll know exactly where we need to be when Nick calls."

"Okay. Would you like me to drive for a while?"

He acted as though she'd just told him a funny joke. "Good one," he said, laughing.

The clouds opened up again. Isabel looked out the side window but couldn't see much of anything because of the rain. She leaned back against the headrest and let her thoughts wander, replaying in her mind what Lachlan and the man in the restaurant had told them about Clive Harcus. If only half of what they'd said were true, this Harcus was a terror and needed to be dealt with. She made a mental list of all the things she wanted to say when she confronted the man.

She made the mistake of telling Michael her plan.

He gave her his *are you out of your mind?* look and said, "Isabel, you aren't going to get near Harcus. If anything happened to you . . ." He took a deep breath and then said, "The authorities will take care of him."

"If I have to drag that man off my land, I will." She hoped Michael wouldn't ask her how she planned to accomplish the feat because she didn't have the faintest idea . . . yet.

She expected an argument but didn't get one. She couldn't take the silence long. "Michael, are you pouting?"

The question jarred him. "Am I what?"

"Pouting."

"What the . . . Men don't pout."

He acted as though she had insulted him. "Some do," she said.

"I don't."

She decided to wait until later, when he was in a more reasonable mood, to talk about getting Harcus off her land.

The rain had finally slowed down. Shards of the sun, like iridescent glass, were shooting out from the dark clouds, bringing hints of light to the day. She wiped the condensation off the window and saw chimneys in the distance.

"Where are we?" she asked.

"Blackgoran Village."

"I don't remember seeing it on the map. How do you know—"

"I read the sign."

Michael drove through the village, circled around, and parked on a quiet side street. Tired of waiting to hear from his brother Nick, he pulled out his cell phone and called him.

While Michael was talking to Nick, Isabel scanned her surroundings. There was a church across the street. The beautiful building had a regal bearing, with a steeple that reminded her of a bishop's miter. She wondered how old it was. Age had given the structure a greenish-blue patina. She pushed the button to bring the window down so she could read the name etched in stone above the doors: THE MAGDA-LENE.

Isabel wasn't paying any attention to what Michael was saying to his brother. The church held her full attention. She wondered if the doors were locked. She could run up the steps and find out. She really wanted to see inside.

Michael must have read her intention because he grabbed her hand and shook his head. The message was clear. She wasn't going anywhere.

He ended the call a minute later after assuring Nick that Isabel was fine.

"Noah and my brothers are worried about you," he remarked as he started the engine.

"Why?" she asked, genuinely perplexed.

He laughed. "There's a killer out there searching for you," he reminded. "They think you might be worried about your situation."

"Why would I worry? I have you."

It had been a quick automatic response on her part, and it was only after she said it that she realized once again how true it was. She didn't have any reason to worry as long as she was with him. She hadn't said anything he didn't already know. Michael would watch out for her just as she would watch out for him. As far as she was concerned, it was a no-brainer.

His reaction to what she said was surprising. He looked stunned, but only for a second or two, and then his expression changed to arrogant satisfaction. "Damn right."

She rolled her eyes. "What's the plan, Einstein?"

"We're changing cars."

An hour later, following directions Nick had texted, they pulled into a garage tucked behind an auto repair shop, parked their car, and carried their bags to an older SUV. The car key was under the floor mat along with a room key to the hotel where they were staying for the night. Nick's connections had come through again. There was also a key to the hotel's back door. They could go in that way, take the back steps to their room, and hopefully no one would see them.

"We've been lucky so far," Isabel remarked. "I don't think anyone has been able to track us."

"We've had a lot of help. Nick has a friend with MI5 who hooked him up with an inspector in Inverness. His name is Knox Sinclair, and he's now the man in charge."

"In charge of the investigation?"

"In charge of finding the bastards who want to kill you."

"There's more than one?" She was stunned. Everything was escalating, and she was having trouble dealing with it all.

"That's just it. We don't know. The redhead you saw is involved . . . but how? Our best guess is that he and Jacoby were hired to see that you didn't get Glen MacKenna. We know the redhead is still out there, but we don't know if there's someone else behind him. Nick's heading up a team working on it."

"Then I guess we'll find out soon enough." She tried to sound as though she were taking it all in stride and knew she'd failed miserably. Even she could hear the panic in her voice. She took a deep breath. She was not going to let this horrible situation overwhelm her. No matter what. She was a strong capable woman, and she could handle whatever came her way.

The pep talk didn't help much. "I'm betting Harcus is behind this. It would be easier for him to claim ownership of Glen MacKenna if I weren't around."

The tension was getting to both of them. Neither one spoke for a long while as they drove through the countryside. He kept picturing Isabel walking into that police station covered in blood. Then he once again replayed that god-awful video in his mind. It was a miracle she was still breathing.

What in God's name were they doing? He should have put Isabel under lock and key surrounded by guards until Wednesday, when she would walk into Donal Gladstone's office, open the damn envelope, sign the papers—after he read them, of course. What they shouldn't be doing was driving all over the Highlands talking to people. It wasn't safe, but that didn't seem to matter to her.

They were pushing their luck to the limit. It was only a matter of time before the bastard . . . or bastards . . . caught up with them.

It was as though she had just read his mind. "At least no one knows we're here."

"Yes, they do know," he countered. "At the airport you signed autographs and those teenage girls took photos with their phones. By now they've posted your photo all over the Internet. I'm sure they're searching for you."

"Is there a chance they might have given up?" It was a stupid question, but she felt compelled to ask.

"You're worth a hundred thousand. They won't give up."

"Don't you mean dead I'm worth a hundred thousand?"

"Yes."

Isabel felt responsible for every bit of this mess, and she couldn't understand why she felt that way. None of this was her fault. But dragging Michael into the middle of her problem had been a huge mistake. If anything happened to him while he was protecting her . . . the mere thought made her sick to her stomach.

All this time she'd been thinking she needed to get away from him to protect her heart. Now she realized he needed to get away from her so he could keep on breathing.

If she told him what she was thinking he would become angry and get his back up. Then they would argue, and she knew exactly how it would go. Didn't she have any faith in his ability to protect her? he'd ask. Sure she did, she'd respond. She just didn't know how she could protect him. That answer was sure to rile him.

Michael glanced at her, took in her dark expression, and asked, "What's going on with you?"

"We're having an argument."

"We are?"

"Yes, and I'm winning."

"Of course you are. What are we arguing about?"

She didn't want to explain. "Nick seems to have connections all over the world. Is it because he's FBI?"

"Partly," he answered. "Since we were kids, Nick and Alec had a knack for collecting friends and making connections. Nick is more experienced now and has more"—he paused for a second while he searched for the right word—"finesse. Yeah, he has more finesse, but even so, Alec has him beat. Name a city anywhere and he'll tell you he knows a guy. Nick has had to ask Alec for help on more than one occasion."

"What about you? Did you have a lot of friends growing up, or were you a loner?"

He laughed. "It wasn't possible to be a loner in my family."

She tried to imagine what it would be like to be part of such a big, boisterous family. It would be loud and chaotic, she supposed, but fun, too.

"If you got into trouble, or ever got scared, you could lean on your brothers and sisters. That must have been nice." She smiled as she added, "You were never alone."

That thought led to lyrics for a song, but she wouldn't let herself be pulled away. She needed to focus on the task at hand, as Michael loved to tell her. Yes, she needed to do that now. Writing songs would come later.

"When are we scheduled to meet Inspector Sinclair?"

"I'm not sure yet. He'll text and let us know," he answered. "According to Nick there are police in Dunross now. Hopefully they'll soon have some suspects."

"We have time to make two more stops, and I think we should go to a pub. A lot of locals go there to catch up on the latest news and see old friends."

"How about we don't make any more stops." He thought he'd sounded agreeable, which was a real stretch for him, considering the fact that he wanted to lock her in the car until they got to the hotel.

"Oh no," she said. "You promised to drive me wherever I wanted to go as long as I followed the rules, and I've done exactly that, so two more stops, then the pub for dinner, and that will be the last of it."

"Isabel, we need to get the hell out of here. It's a miracle no one's taken a shot at you yet. Luck runs out, babe."

In the end it didn't matter what he said. He had given her his word, and she wasn't going to let him break it. He finally conceded.

"All right, but we aren't going to spend more than fifteen or twenty minutes at each place."

"I can't promise that."

He felt like growling. "If you aren't finished in twenty minutes, I'm throwing you over my shoulder and getting out of there."

From the set of his jaw she knew he'd do it, too.

"I'll try to keep it under twenty minutes."

They had just driven into Lockbridge Village. Michael parked in front of a fabric store at the top of a long, narrow street. Pretty shops lined both sides and Isabel couldn't decide where to stop first. There was Campbell's Flowers, the Cheese Factory, Cowan's Bakery, a tearoom, and a gift shop.

"You choose," she said.

"Anywhere but the gift shop. We've done enough of those."

"Tired of knickknacks?"

"How about the whiskey shop on the corner?" he suggested.

"Let's go to the flower shop first."

He put his arm around her shoulders as they walked along.

A bell over the door jingled when they walked inside. Millie and Alasdair Campbell, the owners, greeted them with a smile. The elderly couple's shop wasn't much bigger than a galley kitchen. The scents were wonderful. It was like walking into a perfume bottle, and the array of flower colors was beautiful. There were bright yellow lilies in full bloom, pink and purple hyacinths, white and red roses. The heather was her favorite, but purple thistle was a close second.

After Isabel asked a few questions, Millie told her a little something about each flower in between her whispered comments about her ailing father-in-law, while her husband, Alasdair, sat at a table in the corner, sipping tea. He kept a watchful eye on Michael.

After a few minutes, Alasdair motioned to Michael. "You might as well sit and take a cup of tea with me while we wait."

Michael took him up on his offer. He drank strong hot tea but kept his attention on Isabel while Alasdair sorted through a stack of orders.

Millie had a lot of frustration stored up inside. She went into a long tirade about her ungrateful, downright mean father-in-law, but by the time she finished, she accepted the fact that she was going to have to take care of him because he needed help. "He's scared because he feels helpless," she concluded, grabbing Isabel's hand. "Thank you so much for listening to me go on and on about family," she said. "Would you like a spot of tea?"

"I'd love some."

Five minutes later the four of them were crowded around the table with tea and scones in front of them.

"Are you and your mister on holiday?" Millie asked.

"Yes," Isabel answered.

"We're thinking of driving farther north and west," Michael said. "See the countryside."

"I'd be real careful if I were you," Millie said.

"Why is that?" Michael asked.

"There's turmoil up there. Isn't that right, Alasdair?"

Her husband had looked half-asleep but as soon as Millie pulled him into the conversation, he became animated. The floodgates opened and he poured out every fact he knew about the different fights going on. He didn't get around to the MacKennas for a long while, but when he did, he had a lot to say. Since Isabel and Michael were the only customers, Alasdair didn't have to curb his opinions.

"I don't want to talk out of turn," Alasdair said. "But there's a man named Clive Harcus boasting he's the legitimate son of the man who owned Glen MacKenna. Clive thinks he's the rightful heir, though everyone is guessing he wasn't named in the will. As far as being the legitimate heir . . . we know better, don't we, Millie?"

"Yes, we do, Alasdair."

"Why do you know better?" Isabel asked.

"Like I said, I don't want to talk out of turn, but Freya Harcus, Clive's mother, was friendly when she was younger. Real friendly, if you know what I mean, with quite a few men." He wobbled his eyebrows for emphasis. "Any one of at least a dozen men could be Clive's father."

"Is Freya Harcus still alive?"

Millie nodded. "She's adamant that Clive is the rightful heir."

"For the money, you see," Alasdair said. "Folks are whispering that he already has a buyer. Gonna pay him a lot of money."

Isabel was trying to hide her anger. The Patterson Group, she decided. Clive had probably already made a deal with them once he got rid of Isabel.

"None of the other men who were friendly with Freya would claim Clive, though, because he's such a mean son of a . . ."

"Snake," Millie rushed to say.

Alasdair rolled his eyes.

"We need to get going," Michael said.

"In just a moment," Isabel promised.

She wasn't going to leave without purchasing something. She

chose a large white vase and asked Millie to fill it with a variety of flowers. Millie was quite an artist, and when she was finished, the arrangement had every color of the rainbow.

Alasdair turned Michael's attention. "It's a might stuffy in here. Would you mind propping the back door open to get a breeze? Right around the corner," he directed, pointing the way. "There are some heavy boxes you'll have to move to get to the door. In fact, I sure would appreciate it if you could lift them and put them on the metal shelves. They're too heavy for me, and you look like you could handle it without any strain."

"No problem," Michael said.

While he couldn't see Isabel, he could hear her. She was asking Millie to send the flowers to the nearest hospital and insisting she didn't need a receipt.

"These flowers are beautiful, Millie. They'll cheer someone up."

Michael heard the bell signaling someone was coming in. He finished with the last box when he heard girls shrieking.

Oh, hell no.

There were four teenage girls cornering Isabel, and they all knew who she was. They had their phones out and were clicking away while Isabel kept shaking her head, trying to get to Michael.

Isabel had never seen anyone move as fast as Michael did. He had his arm around her, and all but carried her out the back door. Alasdair followed and locked the door so the girls would have to go around the block to catch up with them.

She waited until they were back in the car and on their way and then said, "One of those girls asked me if I was engaged to Xavier. She said she read it on the Internet, so it must be true. I shook my head, but I didn't talk to her." The muscle in his cheek flexed. "We aren't going to make any more stops today, are we?"

"That's right. No more stops."

"It's just as well. I'm plain sick of hearing about Clive Harcus. If you hear something terrible about a person, you have to wonder if it could be true. But when you hear the same thing over and over again from different people in different villages, you have to conclude there's more than a grain of truth in what they're saying."

"Uh-huh." He wasn't really listening. He was trying to figure out how he was going to get Isabel in and out of Gladstone's office. Inspector Sinclair would have all the details. The first thing he was going to do when they were in their hotel room was call Nick and find out why Gladstone couldn't meet them somewhere outside of Dunross.

"Millie's a lovely lady, isn't she?"

The question jarred him out of his thoughts. He nodded but didn't have anything to say about Isabel's newest friend. How did she keep track of all of them? he wondered.

"You know what we should do?"

"What?"

"We should drive to Kinley and eat at the Lazy Pig Pub. It's not that far from here," she said. "You'll get to meet some of your relatives, have a pint or two, and if you're lucky, you might get to punch someone in the face. That might lighten your mood."

"We aren't going to go into any pubs, remember? And nothing's wrong with my mood. I just want this to be over. I want you to be safe back in Boston, and I want to get on with my life."

He saw the look on her face and said, "Don't take what I said the wrong way."

"You want to catch the people who are after me so you can drop me off in Boston and get on with your life. How could I take that the wrong way?"

And just like that, Michael was back to being a bonehead.

TWENTY-SEVEN

MICHAEL WAS FEELING GUILTY BECAUSE HE KNEW HE HAD HURT Isabel's feelings. He probably shouldn't have been so blunt, but he had told her the truth. He did want to get her safely back to Boston, and he did need to get on with his life. He was expected at Quantico the end of August, where he would begin training to become an FBI agent. Once he achieved that goal, he planned to work his way into the department he was most qualified for and go after homegrown terrorists and power-hungry deviants, put them away before they could come up with bigger and better ways to blow up the world.

It was all mapped out, but he couldn't go anywhere until he was certain Isabel was safe and those who wanted to hurt her were behind bars. Only then could he move on.

But a future without Isabel at his side driving him crazy? He couldn't imagine anything more depressing.

Isabel watched Michael remove the map from the glove compartment and study it for a minute. Then he folded it, put it away, and started driving again. She didn't ask any questions. She was too angry and frustrated to talk to him now. She needed to get her temper under control before she said something she would regret. She was a lady, she reminded herself, and wouldn't use any of the foul words racing through her mind.

Michael really was a bonehead. Did he have any idea what he was giving up when he moved on with his life? She was all a man could ever want, damn it. Why couldn't he see that?

She reasoned it through. Michael wasn't only a bonehead. He was also dense, which in her opinion was just another word for *stupid*. With all his degrees and awards and only God knew what else, when it came to relationships Michael was almost as dense as she was. She had no business falling for such a stupid man. Someone should have warned her. She thought about it a minute and then decided she needed to write a song about it.

Michael was just about to apologize for hurting her feelings, but then he glanced at her. She looked serene and happy. What was that about? He told her he was going to get on with his life and she's happy? He expected a little pushback at the very least.

Then she smiled at him. He couldn't explain why that made him mad.

Isabel was much calmer now and enjoying coming up with lyrics she thought were funny but true about men in general and Michael in particular. Unfortunately, they were too inappropriate to sing. She even had a couple of titles in mind. "Men Are Jerks" was one. "Michael Buchanan Is a Colossal, Insensitive, Obtuse Jerk" was another. That was way too long for a title, of course. She'd have to shorten it to "Colossal Jerk." Yes, that would work.

She knew she would never write the song or sing it, but it made her feel better to think about it.

She continued to ignore Michael as they drove through the countryside. It had been another rainy day and the dark sky cast a gray shadow on the land, but when they reached the top of a particularly steep hill, the sun suddenly broke through the clouds and a golden orange light billowed out over the valley below. Michael parked between two Scots pines to face the view. Then he turned the motor off and sat back.

"Do you know where we are?" he asked.

"Glen MacKenna," she guessed.

"Yes."

"Is it safe to be here?"

"I took back roads. There was very little traffic, and I made sure no one was following us, so yeah, we're safe for now. What do you think of your glen?"

She was in awe. She had a panoramic view, and it was perfect.

"Isabel?" He said her name after a minute when she hadn't answered him.

"It's beautiful . . . pristine."

She wasn't exaggerating. The view was spectacular. There were gently rolling hills in the distance and black-faced sheep in the meadow, grazing on grass so green it looked like velvet. More sheep dotted the hills beyond. A clear wide stream flowed down from the highest hill and curled like a ribbon across the valley floor. Squinting against the sun she thought she caught a glimpse of a waterfall near the peak of that same hill. She was probably wrong, but it was a fanciful hope all the same. There were some stone cottages as well, but only a few dotting the hills.

The longer Isabel studied the landscape, the stronger her determination grew to keep it out of Patterson's hands. She wasn't going to let anyone destroy this magnificent land. She was going to sell it to someone ethical who would value it. Finding the right buyer would be difficult but not impossible. She would put stipulations in the sale to make sure they would protect the land and keep it as beautiful and unspoiled as it was now.

"It's almost too perfect to be real," she remarked. "Like paradise."

"Almost?"

"There's a serpent living in one of those cottages."

"Ah . . . Harcus."

As they sat quietly gazing over the beautiful scene, Isabel began to daydream. What would it be like to live here? she wondered. She could go hiking up the hills, she supposed. She had never hiked before, but there was always a first time for a new adventure. And fishing. She could go fishing, too. Though she'd never attempted it, she was sure she would enjoy it.

Michael's cell phone rang, pulling her back to reality.

He looked at caller ID and said, "Inspector Sinclair."

The conversation was quick, and when Michael ended the call, he told Isabel, "The inspector wants us to meet him at Rosemore Police Station."

"Where's Rosemore?" she asked, reaching for the map again.

He scratched his jaw. "I'm not sure. His assistant gave me directions, but he was talking so fast, and his brogue was so thick, I only caught a couple of words, 'past Garve.'" He laughed and added, "At least that's what I think I heard. I speak five languages, but I didn't understand any of what that man was saying. I'm not even sure it was English."

"I love their brogue. The sound is musical."

He could come up with a lot of words to describe their brogue. *Musical* wasn't one of them.

Getting to Garve was easy, but finding Rosemore took work. The GPS on Michael's phone wasn't any help, and there weren't any signs. They could have stopped and asked someone, but Michael was a Buchanan, so that wasn't going to happen. Men in his family didn't ask directions.

When they finally found Rosemore, they were surprised by how large the village was.

"Someone really needs to put up a couple of signs," Isabel said. "Isn't it pretty here with all the flowers blooming?"

Michael noticed two teenage boys, one with a bloody nose, fighting over a package, and a drunken older man throwing up in a trash bin. And yet Isabel noticed the flowers blooming. She always saw beauty in everything. Even people. She looked for and usually found some good in them. No wonder he was drawn to her. She had a sweet pure heart . . . with a bit of vinegar in her attitude . . . toward him, anyway.

The building they were looking for was painted white with blue trim. If there hadn't been a police sign on the lamppost out front, they would have thought it was just another house.

INSPECTOR KNOX SINCLAIR GREETED THEM AT THE DOOR. HE WAS a handsome man and terribly polite. Tall and thin, he was impeccably dressed in his dark blue uniform and starched white long-sleeve shirt with a navy blue tie. Isabel thought he looked quite stylish. His hair was blond and trimmed in a buzz cut. His mannerisms reminded her of Detective Samuel, though the inspector was much younger, perhaps in his late thirties.

There were two other men waiting to meet them. The older of the two told her his name was Matthew. He shook her hand, then turned to answer the phone. The younger man's name was Danny, and he looked as though he had just gotten out of school. As soon as he opened his mouth she knew he was the fast talker who had given Michael directions over the phone. She had to seriously concentrate on what he was saying to understand him.

Once the introductions were made, Sinclair led them into an office around the corner from the entrance and asked them to take a seat.

"I'm borrowing this office," he remarked as he walked behind the desk and sat in an old chair that squeaked.

"Your offices are in Inverness?" Isabel asked.

"That's right, Miss MacKenna."

"Please call me Isabel."

Matthew called out from the other room, "Inspector, they're waiting for you whenever you're ready."

"We have a suspect in custody we believe is the man who was with Jacoby."

"Where is he?" Isabel asked, astonished by the unexpected news.

"In one of the rooms down the hall."

She jumped to her feet. "Here? He's here?"

"There's no reason for alarm," the inspector said. "He's handcuffed to a table and can't get near you. Don't worry."

Michael saw the look on Isabel's face, took her hand, and tugged her back into the chair next to him. "I don't think she's worried, Inspector. I think she probably would like to have a minute alone with him."

"I don't believe in violence," she said. *Unless someone tried to shoot me*, she thought. 'Who is he?" Michael asked.

"Oscar Ferris," he answered. "We caught him up here. We'll be transporting him to Inverness soon," he added. "Thanks to some quick work by the FBI, we know he flew to Boston from Inverness and was met by Leon Jacoby. Surveillance cameras show Ferris and Jacoby at the airport, leaving together. Ferris used his own passport," he thought to add.

"Has he told you anything?" Michael asked.

"Not yet, but he will," the inspector promised. "Ferris isn't a stranger to trouble. He's got quite a long crime sheet."

"You're certain he's the man I saw?" she asked.

There was a large computer monitor on the desk. He turned it toward Michael and Isabel and pushed the key. And there he was. Slouched in a metal chair, the suspect had a sullen look on his face. He had bright orange-red hair and when he looked directly into the camera, she could see how cold his eyes were. He didn't look all that old, but the years of crime had already hardened him.

"Is he the man?" the inspector asked.

"Yes, I think so. I only saw him for a second or two, so I can't say with absolute certainty that he's the one."

"We were able to send his photo to Detective Walsh in America. He has assured us this is the man he fought with and whose gun he took. It was Jacoby who shot at you."

"When are you going to question him?" Michael asked. "I'd like to go in with you."

Sinclair was amenable to the idea but said, "You may ask questions, but you can't touch him. I know you would probably like to strike him or give him a couple of jabs because he and Jacoby tried to kill your . . ." Sinclair glanced from Michael to Isabel and then back to Michael again. It was apparent he didn't know what their relationship was and therefore didn't know what to call her.

Isabel could have said something, but she remained silent. She was curious to find out what category Michael would put her in. Friend? Lover? Or distant relative? She shivered at that thought. Although her sister was married to Michael's brother, Isabel was in no way related to Michael. Thank God. She'd be breaking nearly every commandment if she were. He could call her a hookup, she supposed. No, a hookup was for one night, and she'd slept with Michael more than once, so that wouldn't work. Might as well call her what she was. Easy. She almost nodded but caught herself in time. That's exactly what she was with Michael. Easy.

"Isabel is a friend of the family."

Are you kidding me? A friend of the family? She could feel her face heating up. He couldn't say she was a close friend or just a friend? No, he had to make it even more impersonal. A friend of the family.

Okay. If that's the way he wanted it, then that's the way it was going to be.

"Inspector, may I go in with you?" she asked.

"No." Michael's voice had a real bite to it. Sinclair was more diplomatic. He told her no in a calm, reasonable tone.

"Then may I watch and listen to the interview?' she asked the inspector, completely ignoring Michael.

"Yes, of course. Just sit back and watch the monitor." He tilted the screen to her and walked out of the room.

Michael stood and followed him. "Stay in this room, Isabel," he said, and when she didn't immediately agree, he turned back to her. "Promise me."

"I'll stay in this room. May I borrow your phone? I'd like to text someone."

It wasn't like Michael to show her any affection in public, and Sinclair was standing right there in the doorway, yet when Michael leaned toward her, she thought he was going to kiss her.

"Oh no, you don't," she whispered. "Since I'm just a friend of the family you can't kiss me good-bye."

Michael laughed. The second the words, "a friend of the family," were out of his mouth, he had known they were going to come back to bite him.

Isabel was disappointed by his amused reaction. She was being a real smartass, but he didn't seem to mind.

"Sure I can," he said as he leaned down, clasped her chin, and kissed her. After rattling her, he said, "Actually, I was just handing you my phone and was going to suggest that you call Dylan and catch him up on what is going on, but then you asked me to kiss you . . ." He walked out of the room and pulled the door shut behind him, leaving her speechless.

TWENTY-EIGHT

IT SIMPLY WASN'T POSSIBLE TO SHAME HIM. SHE THOUGHT HE
would at least apologize for his lame answer to the inspector. But did
he? Of course not. And yet, after the way he kissed her, it was difficult
for her to stay angry.

She called Dylan, got voicemail, and left a long message catching
him up on the latest development. Then she texted Lexi and Damon
to let them know where she was. She didn't mention the mess her life
was in at the moment. She told both of them how much she missed
them and promised that, as soon as she was back in Boston, she would
call them.

When she ended her texts, she could hear the inspector and Michael standing right outside the door talking. Sinclair was asking
legal questions, and Michael's quick responses showed he knew all
the answers. Why wouldn't he? Like his father and his brothers, Michael loved the law.

A few minutes later the two men walked into the makeshift interrogation room, pulled up chairs, and sat down facing the suspect.
Sinclair placed a thick manila folder on the table in front of him.

The sullen look that had been pasted on Ferris's face changed
the second the door opened. He straightened in his chair, forced his

notion of a serene expression, and tried to sound sincere when he said, "I don't understand why I'm here. I would appreciate an explanation."

"Weren't the charges explained to you when you were arrested?" Sinclair asked.

"Yes, they were. I thought I heard 'attempted murder,' but I knew that couldn't be right."

"You have the right to free legal advice."

"I don't need it," Ferris insisted. "I want to clear this up. It's all a huge mistake. You have me confused with someone else. I tried to explain to the officers that they had the wrong man, but they wouldn't listen."

"I'd like to establish a timeline," Sinclair said, ignoring Ferris's plea of innocence.

"That's fine with me. I'll be happy to help."

"Where have you been the last two weeks, and what have you been doing?"

"I've been taking it easy . . . relaxing," he said.

"What's your occupation."

Smiling, Ferris said, "I'm a jack-of-all-trades. A handyman. I can fix most anything that isn't electrical. I'm in between jobs now." He thought to add, "But I've got a big job coming up. A real big job. It's guaranteed and great pay."

Sinclair nodded, then asked, "Have you taken any trips in the past two weeks?"

"No, I just lazed around. I went to pubs every night."

"You didn't take a flight to Boston, Massachusetts?"

Ferris shook his head. "No," he scoffed, as though it were a ridiculous question.

Sinclair opened the folder and placed on the table a photo of Ferris getting off the plane at Logan Airport in Boston.

"Oh, that," Ferris said with a shrug and a shaky laugh. "It was just a quick trip in and out. I only stayed a couple of days."

"Do you know a man named Leon Jacoby?"

"No." Ferris looked from Sinclair to Michael and back again. "Why do you ask?"

Sinclair placed another photo in front of Ferris. "Isn't this you greeting Jacoby?"

"Why, yes, that is me," he answered.

Ferris didn't seem fazed that he had been caught in his lies. The man oozed confidence and acted as though he really believed he was soon going to be walking out the door a free man. He must have thought Sinclair didn't have sufficient evidence to keep him locked up, and these questions were nothing more than a fishing expedition in the hope of discovering information.

Sinclair was about to rip Ferris's confidence out from under him. "Do you know a young lady named Grace Isabel MacKenna?"

"Who?"

"Grace Isabel MacKenna," he patiently repeated.

"No."

Sinclair stacked his hands on top of the folder. "We have a witness who will testify that you and Jacoby were following Miss MacKenna from the Hamilton Hotel in Boston."

"No, I wasn't following anyone."

Sinclair continued. "The witness is Detective Craig Walsh. He's the man you shot."

"No, no," Ferris stammered. "That's not true. I didn't shoot anyone."

"There's also another witness."

"Who?"

"Miss MacKenna saw you standing on the corner, watching her."

"She's mistaken. She must have seen someone who looks like me."

Sinclair didn't seem bothered by Ferris's denials. "And, of course, there's other evidence."

Ferris sat up a little straighter. "Like what?"

"We have your gun."

"My gun? I don't own any guns."

"The gun Miss MacKenna used to kill your friend Leon Jacoby had her fingerprints on it, but there were also Detective Walsh's fingerprints, and . . ." Sinclair paused to let the tension build.

"And what?"

"And yours, Ferris. They found your fingerprints on the barrel, the back of the grip, and on the magazine release. You were all over that gun."

Ferris wiped a bead of sweat from his brow.

Sinclair tapped the folder. "I've got enough in here to put you away for a very long time, and we haven't even started talking about the flash drive yet."

The color left Ferris's face. *He's in a panic*, Michael thought. He must have finally realized, with all the evidence stacked against him, he was in deep trouble.

Clearing his throat, Ferris said, "Flash drive? What flash drive?"

Finding the charade tiring, Sinclair turned to Michael. "What do you think?"

Michael stared at Ferris when he answered. "I think you're wasting your time. He's done nothing but lie since we sat down."

"Lie? I have not lied," Ferris protested. Pointing to Michael, he asked, "Who is he? I have a right to know."

Michael's distinct Boston accent told him that Michael wasn't from around these parts, and it made Ferris all the more guarded and anxious.

"I've been remiss in not introducing you sooner," Sinclair said with mock courtesy. Tilting his head toward Michael, he told Ferris, "He already knows who you are. Oscar Ferris, this is Michael Buchanan. He's an attorney from Boston. Now, why don't you tell me about the flash drive."

"What flash drive?"

Ferris's phony innocence was wearing thin. "The flash drive that fell out of your pocket on the street in Boston, the same one Detective Walsh picked up. That's the flash drive I want to talk about."

"I don't know anything about it."

"Yes, you do," Sinclair countered. Looking to Michael for help, he said, "Do you have any questions for him?"

"I'm not going to answer—" Ferris began.

Michael deliberately interrupted him. "I should probably tell him what's going to happen to him. He's not going to like it. Unless you think I shouldn't tell him. You're in charge here."

"It's quite all right," Sinclair said, leaning back in his chair and gesturing toward Ferris with a wave of his hand. "Go ahead and tell him."

Michael shrugged. "I might as well. He's going to find out."

Highly agitated now, Ferris wiggled his way to the edge of his chair. "Just tell me."

"You know, Ferris, you're not helping yourself," Sinclair said.

"What do you mean?"

"If you want any consideration or leniency, you'll start cooperating before it's too late."

"When is it too late?"

Michael answered. "When the Feds get hold of you. Once that happens, there isn't anything Inspector Sinclair can do for you."

"What? That can't be true. The Feds don't have any power here."

It was apparent that Ferris had a less than rudimentary knowledge of the law, and Michael used that to his advantage.

"Here's what's going to happen to you. Inspector Sinclair will take you to Inverness, where he will complete the necessary paperwork and sign off on the case. He will then hand you over to two US marshals. They will escort you to Boston, Massachusetts, where you will be charged with attempted murder. The federal prosecutor will ask for the death penalty because it was a murder for hire," he said. "And he'll get it, too."

"Yes, he will," Sinclair agreed, going along with whatever Michael said.

"Wait . . . just wait. I'm not American," Ferris reminded. His gaze kept bouncing back and forth between Michael and Sinclair.

"The crimes were committed in Boston," Sinclair pointed out.

"You might want to start preparing yourself for life in an American federal prison," Michael told him. "I understand the treatment by the guards is brutal if a prisoner gives them any trouble."

Nodding, Sinclair added, "I've heard stories."

"I know all about the federal prisons in the United States," Ferris said. "I heard from a reliable source that they chain prisoners to the wall in their cells with their hands above their heads."

What the hell? Chain prisoners to walls? Maybe during the Spanish Inquisition . . . or in cartoons, Michael thought.

Sinclair didn't refute Ferris's ideas. "So you have an understanding of what it's going to be like."

"Yes," Ferris agreed. "And I'm not going—"

Sinclair interrupted him. "I'm not promising anything, but perhaps an arrangement can be made with the federal agents. You could be tried here and serve your sentence here."

Ferris leapt at the possibility. "Yes, I want to be here, but I'm not going down for attempted murder. I didn't try to murder anyone."

Now that Ferris was more cooperative, Sinclair said, "If you want my help, you're going to have to start answering my questions. No more lies." He added, "And you can begin by telling us where you got the flash drive."

"No one gave it to me. It's mine. There were papers inside an envelope with a lot of information about a young woman."

"Grace Isabel MacKenna," Sinclair supplied.

"Yes," Ferris answered. "I read all the pages, made a photo of them, and put them on a flash drive. I didn't want to carry the papers around with me. Someone could get hold of them and read them, and I couldn't think of a safe place to hide them. I knew if I tried to memorize all the information, I would forget something by the time I told Jacoby."

When Ferris didn't continue, Sinclair prodded, "So you copied them?"

"Yes, I did. Then I burned the papers. I thought it would be safe for me to travel with the flash drive. Still, I didn't want to leave it just anywhere, like in a hotel room. Too dangerous if the wrong people got hold of it. Laptops get stolen all the time."

"Was there anything else in the envelope?"

"Yes," Ferris answered. "Money."

"Who gave you the letter?"

"You mean instructions?"

"Yes."

"Don't you want to know how much money?"

"Answer my question," Sinclair demanded.

"I was getting to it. There's no reason to snap at me. I'm cooperating."

Sinclair's neck was turning red. It was obvious he was close to losing his patience. Michael, on the other hand, was as calm as a soft breeze. Cretins like Ferris didn't faze him.

"You still haven't answered my question," Sinclair said.

"What was the question?"

Since Sinclair looked as though he was about to shout, Michael decided to help out.

"Why don't you start at the beginning. Who gave you the envelope?"

"A solicitor in Dunross."

"The name?" Sinclair snapped.

"MacCarthy. Walter MacCarthy. I was one of his clients. He got me out of several legal problems . . . none of which were my fault," he rushed to add.

Even though the interview was being recorded, Sinclair pulled out a pen and a notepad and began to take notes.

"MacCarthy hired me to do a job," Ferris continued. "He knew he could count on me. He called me and asked me to come to his office. He said he needed a favor, but I'd get paid. He gave me the envelope and told me what he wanted me to do."

"And what was that?"

"I was told to fly to Boston, meet Jacoby, and give him information. I was just the messenger," he repeated.

"Who wrote the kill—" Michael caught himself in time. "Who found her itinerary? Was it MacCarthy?"

"I asked him that very question. He said no. It was one of his clients, but he wouldn't tell me who. He promised me he would pay me the full amount once the job was done. I stopped worrying about the money then because I trusted MacCarthy."

"MacCarthy knew what was in that envelope, didn't he?"

Ferris didn't hesitate. "Yes. The papers in the envelope he gave me were copies. He kept the originals, and he told me he was keeping them in a safe place just in case."

"In case what?"

"He didn't say."

Sinclair looked up from the notepad. "Let's move on. I want to talk about that day in Boston. Tell us what happened."

"I want you to understand. I was never going to kill anyone. I couldn't take another person's life. Jacoby was in charge. He decided I would drive the car and be the lookout. That's all I was supposed to do, but after I parked, Jacoby wouldn't let me leave. He insisted that I go with him and watch out for trouble." Ferris looked anxiously from Michael to Sinclair. "I tell you, I didn't want to hurt anybody. I was just supposed to give the information. It was Jacoby who made me go with him. He handed me a gun. I tried to get out of there, but Jacoby was mean, real mean. He could have killed me. He promised he would take care of everything. All we had to do was follow her until she was alone, and that turned out to be easy because she walked from the hotel and kept on walking. She damn near wore us out. She never noticed us following her because we kept to the shadows. Then the trouble started."

Michael wasn't so calm now. Once Ferris started talking in such a cold detached voice about Isabel, every muscle in Michael's body tensed for a fight, and all he could think about was putting his fist through Ferris's face.

Ferris went on. "She stopped, then turned around and started back. We had to scramble to stay hidden. Jacoby went ahead to find a spot, and I found what I thought was the perfect place, and all of a sudden this guy gets in my face."

"That *guy* is Detective Craig Walsh," Michael informed him.

"Which one of you shot him?" Sinclair asked. He already knew the answer but was curious to find out if Ferris would tell the truth.

"He shot himself," Ferris said. "And that's the honest truth. He grabbed my gun and shot himself while I was trying to get it out of his hands. I knew Jacoby wanted his gun back. I'd have to pay him if . . ."

"You were saying there was a struggle," Sinclair stated, once again trying to bring him back on track.

"Yes, that's right. There was a struggle, which he started. I didn't want him to shoot me, but he got hold of my gun, and he wouldn't give it back."

"What would you have done if he had given it back to you?" Sinclair wanted to know.

"I would have run away. It all happened so fast. The guy—I mean the detective I was fighting with—hit me hard and knocked me down. I don't know if he knocked me out or not. It was a pretty hard hit for someone who had just shot himself. I could feel him pulling on me, but I couldn't do anything about it because my head was spinning, and my eyes wouldn't open. I think the detective was looking for another gun. My flash drive must have fallen out of my pocket and he picked it up." Shaking his head, he looked down at the floor and exhaled a long slow breath as though telling his story was physically draining.

"When I got my wits about me and looked around, I was all alone. I thought Jacoby had taken off and left me, but then I heard gunshots.

I knew it couldn't be the detective who took my gun. There was so much blood on the ground, I figured he was on his way to dying. I got up and went to the corner, and I saw Jacoby on the ground, and that girl was still alive. He didn't get it done."

"'It'?" Sinclair asked. He wanted Ferris to spell it out.

Ferris began to squirm in his chair. "Look. I didn't have anything against her. Handing over information about her was just a job, and I needed the money."

Michael could feel his control slipping. Losing his temper in an interrogation had never happened before. When he worked, his focus and discipline were absolute. This was different, though, and he wasn't even running it. He wanted to destroy the man sitting across the table. Ferris was talking about Isabel as though she had as much value as a speck of dust.

Sinclair glanced at Michael, saw his expression, and rushed to finish the questioning.

Ferris also noticed Michael's expression. Tilting his head toward Michael, he lowered his voice and said, "The way he's watching me . . . it's . . ."

"It's what?" Sinclair asked.

"Scary," he blurted. "He looks like he wants to kill me."

Michael's smile didn't quite reach his eyes. "I'm a law-abiding man," he said.

"In other words, he can't kill you," Sinclair said. "Isn't that right?"

Michael nodded. "Do I think the world would be a better place without you taking up space, Ferris? Yes, I do. Inspector Sinclair is correct," he added. "I can't and I won't kill you because murder is against the law. I can make your life damned miserable, though, and I plan to do exactly that."

"Why?" Ferris asked, genuinely perplexed. "I didn't do anything to you."

"Oh, dear God," Sinclair murmured. Turning to Michael, he said, "I'll help you bury the body."

That comment took the edge off Michael's anger. "Thanks."

"Scaring me won't get you anywhere," Ferris said defiantly. "I've been cooperating, and I've been honest with you."

"Yes, you have been cooperating," Sinclair admitted. "Just a couple more questions. How did MacCarthy know Jacoby?"

Ferris shrugged. "I don't know. Maybe he got the name from one of his clients. Some of them are criminals. Not me, but some."

"The evening after Jacoby was killed you went to the Hamilton Hotel. Miss MacKenna saw you in the lobby."

"I know she saw me. It really put me in a panic. I just thought I could find out how long she was booked at the hotel and then call MacCarthy and tell him. Maybe I could still get paid."

Michael didn't show any reaction, but he wondered if Ferris had any idea how close he was to flying through the wall.

"Looks like you won't be getting that sweet job now. What was it?" Sinclair wasn't really interested, but he wanted to keep Ferris talking while he went through the folder to make sure he had covered everything.

"I was going to be on the crew building a lot of houses. Big, fancy houses," he stressed. "With a hunting club and a golf course. It's going to be real exclusive. That's what MacCarthy told me anyway. He was always in a chatty mood when he drank."

"Where are those houses going to be built?" Michael asked.

"I'm not sure. It's somewhere up around Dunross. MacCarthy told me one of his clients is selling the land to some big development company out of London."

"The Patterson Group?" Michael suggested.

"Yes, that's the one."

Michael half expected to hear a roar coming from the other room if Isabel was listening, and he was sure she was. She had to be furious.

"I'm in trouble, aren't I?" Ferris asked.

He was just now figuring it out? Michael slowly nodded.

"Yes, you are," Sinclair said.

Ferris looked as though he was going to cry. "If MacCarthy was still around he'd get me out of this mess. He'd tell you I was just delivering information."

"What do you mean, if he was still around? Where did he go?" Sinclair asked.

"He died, two or three days ago. I don't know exactly when. I had just gotten back from Boston and I was at the pub when I heard. Everyone was talking about it. They said his heart just gave out. It was a shock, though some people said they weren't surprised. He was a glutton for women and whiskey."

MacCarthy had been the next to be hauled in for interrogation. With enough pressure, they'd hopefully have gotten the lawyer to give up the name of his client. Sinclair couldn't hide his disappointment. He was now going to have to figure out another way to hunt down the man who wrote the instructions or, as Michael called it, the kill order.

"You know, Inspector, the more I think about it, the more convinced I become that I didn't do anything wrong." Ferris sat back in his chair and crossed his arms. His smug confidence had returned. "I didn't break any laws. I was just the messenger. I think, with a good solicitor, I'll be let go."

Michael couldn't listen to another word. He had had enough. He quietly got up and left the room.

TWENTY-NINE

ISABEL WAS READY TO PITCH A FIT. YET ANOTHER EXPRESSION SHE had picked up from her aunt Nora, but in this instance it definitely worked. She had heard every word Ferris said, and she was beyond furious. Someone was selling land near Dunross to the Patterson Group. What land could it be but Glen MacKenna? And what was Reid's involvement? Was he playing both angles? Was he also trying to broker a deal with someone else, some weasel who evidently thought he owned the land and could sell it? And just who was the weasel? Only one name came to mind. Clive Harcus, the Terror of the Highlands.

She was the one little glitch in their fantasy plan. They would have to get rid of her in order for their scheme to work, and that just wasn't going to happen.

Michael found her pacing around the desk in the small office. He motioned for the officer with her to leave, closed the door behind him, and then went to Isabel and pulled her into his arms. He needed to hold her close, to know she was safe, for he was still reeling from hearing Ferris so casually talk about the plan to kill her.

Isabel relaxed against him and closed her eyes. A long minute passed without either of them saying a word. She was thinking how secure she felt with his strong arms around her.

He was thinking about doing bodily harm to the bastard who wanted to kill her.

"Michael, you're squeezing me."

He lessened his hold but wouldn't allow her to step back.

Her lips touching his neck, she whispered, "That was some interview, wasn't it?"

"I wanted to throw Ferris through the wall."

"I would have helped."

"Yeah?" he said, smiling. He let go of her.

"Could we leave?"

"Not yet, but soon," he promised. "I have to go over a few details for tomorrow with the inspector. It shouldn't take long."

"Shouldn't take long," she'd learn, was code for "at least an hour." Danny kept checking on her and finally sat with her and told her all sorts of interesting and horrifying facts about Clive Harcus, including one that involved Danny's own family. His brother-in-law had ended up in the hospital because of Clive Harcus's temper.

When Michael and Isabel left the station, a chill had settled in the air, and it was so dark they could see only as far as the headlights on their car allowed.

"How do people walk around out here at night?" Isabel asked. "You can't see your hand in front of your face."

"Flashlights and phones."

"I suppose," she agreed. "Are we staying close to Dunross tonight?"

"No."

She waited for him to elaborate, and when he didn't, she asked, "Where are we staying?"

"Away from here."

Exasperated, she said, "That's helpful."

"There's a place about an hour away from Dunross. Nick's working on it."

"Working on finding a different place to stay? What about Inspector Sinclair? Will he know where we'll be?"

"He thinks we're going to stay at the Dorn."

"But we aren't going to stay there?"

"No. It's too easy for someone to get in and out."

"Will you tell the inspector where we are?"

"No. I don't want anyone to know."

She understood. It wasn't a matter of trusting the inspector, but the more people who knew their location, the bigger the chance of that information getting out.

Michael seemed preoccupied. She watched him for a minute and then remarked, "You're working something out in your mind, aren't you?"

"Just going over tomorrow's schedule."

"The only appointment we have is with Donal Gladstone."

He nodded. "I'd like to go to MacCarthy's office either before or after your appointment. Sinclair has officers there. He's probably on his way to MacCarthy's house now."

"Danny told me Dunross is a tiny village," she said. "MacCarthy's office can't be far from Gladstone's."

"Danny's the fast talker at the police station, right?"

"Yes, Danny had firsthand knowledge of what a mean bully Harcus is."

"How's that?"

"Danny's brother-in-law, Tim, and his pregnant wife, Laris, have lived in a small cottage on Glen MacKenna for several years. They were just sitting down to supper one night when Clive Harcus knocked on their door and told them that he was the owner of Glen MacKenna and that their rent had been doubled. They had five days to pay up or a late fee would be tacked on. Can you believe it?"

She didn't wait for Michael to answer. "Tim stood up to Clive and said he wasn't going to pay him anything."

"Who did Tim usually pay the rent to?" Michael asked.

"Graeme Gibson, the groundskeeper."

"What did Harcus do when Tim refused to pay him?"

"He told him he'd be sorry and left. The next evening Tim was walking home alone and Clive ambushed him. Danny said Clive's a big man, and he beat Tim near to death. He broke his jaw, Michael. Tim ended up in the hospital and had surgery. His jaw is still wired shut. Can you imagine how painful that would be?"

"Was Harcus arrested?"

"Yes," she answered. "He's out on bail now, but he's bragging to anyone who will listen that he never touched Tim and he has witnesses who will testify on his behalf. It was dark out and Danny told me Tim's wife is begging him not to testify against Harcus. She's terrified of him."

"I wonder how many other complaints there have been."

"Danny said Harcus's temper is explosive. He must not have impulse control."

"Apparently not."

As he drove through the darkness, looking for road signs to navigate his way, he thought about their plans for the next day. "We need a map of Dunross."

"You might be able to pull up directions on your laptop. I know Gladstone's office address. It was easy to remember. His office is at 3 Lickey Lake Road."

"Lickey Lake?" Smiling, he said, "Yeah, that would be easy to remember."

He pulled over and called Sinclair to get MacCarthy's office address. When he ended the call, she said, "I'll bet it isn't too far from Gladstone."

He laughed. "Not far at all. MacCarthy's address is 3 Lickey Lake Road. They're in the same building."

"Could they be partners?" she wondered. "And if so, should we trust Donal Gladstone now that we know MacCarthy hired men to kill me? Could he be in on it?" She continued without letting Michael respond. "Still, he asked Detective Walsh to talk to me because he was worried about me, and why would he do that if he was in on it? If he trusts Donal Gladstone, then maybe I should, too."

Isabel tilted her head back and stared up at the vast night sky, catching glimpses of the moon through breaks in the clouds. An old song she'd composed came to mind, and she began to softly hum it.

Michael liked the melody and asked, "Did you write that?"

"Yes, I did. It's a romantic song about everlasting love and commitment. I call it, 'What a Crock.'"

He burst out laughing. "I swear I never know what you're going to say. 'What a Crock'? When did you become so cynical?"

Since I figured out you're going to break my heart, she thought but didn't say. "It's just a song."

"Sing it for me."

For some reason she was embarrassed to sing with just him in the car and darkness all around them. It seemed too intimate. She shook her head at first, and then, with a little coaxing from Michael, she gave in. She sang the song but wouldn't look at him until she was finished.

"That wasn't cynical at all," he said. He wasn't one to give a lot of praise, and she was surprised when he added, "That was really beautiful, Isabel."

They passed through one village and then another, the only light coming from the cottages along the route. It seemed they had been driving a long time, but when she checked her watch, less than half an hour had gone by.

A short time later they pulled off the main road onto a side road almost too narrow for two cars to pass. Tall trees hovered on both sides for a short distance until there was a clearing and they drove into a lighted circle, the grand entrance to a huge stone manor house that had been turned into a luxury hotel. Nick had pulled off another impossible feat, securing a room for them at this exclusive, out-of-the-way resort.

Though the manor had been modernized, it still displayed the elegance of a past century. Even more appealing to Isabel, it offered twenty-four-hour room service. There was a charming pub at the back of the main floor, and they could have stepped in for a quick dinner, but all she wanted was a hot shower.

Their room was quite large. The king-size four-poster bed seemed enormous after the beds she had been sleeping in the past couple of nights. In this one, Michael would have room to move around. There was also a long plush sofa across the room, should he decide to sleep there.

"What do you think? Will this be okay?" he asked.

"I'm never going to leave."

He laughed. "I guess that's a yes."

A small alcove led to a large newly renovated bathroom around the corner. There was a huge shower enclosed in glass and a large marble vanity with two sinks, but what drew Isabel's attention was the old-fashioned claw-foot tub in front of a stained-glass window.

A hot bath was just what she needed to help her decompress. Her mind was filled with worries. James Reid, the Patterson Group, Harcus . . . All of them were motivated by greed, and all would love to have her gone.

On a marble shelf adjacent to the tub were bottles of various bath salts. One of them was called Wild Flowers. The scent was divine. She sprinkled some into the water, got in, and with a sigh settled back and let the water wash away some of her stress.

There wasn't anything she could do about that problem tonight, she reasoned. Tomorrow would be soon enough to take on the vultures. Her concern now was for Michael.

What was going to happen when they returned to Boston? Most likely Michael would leave her as fast as possible. The image of the cartoon character Wile E. Coyote taking off at warp speed came to mind and actually made her smile.

She hadn't told Michael how she felt, and he hadn't told her. Why was she playing the waiting game? Probably because she was the one who had started all this. She had seduced him, not the other way around.

Time for some honesty. This was more than attraction. As scared as she was, she couldn't ignore the truth any longer. She was hopelessly in love with Michael. Now, how in God's name had she let that happen?

She made up her mind. When they returned to Boston, she would tell him she loved him. At this point she didn't care if he crushed her because he didn't feel the same way. At least she wouldn't be in limbo. She would know the truth.

Isabel took her time soaking in the tub, then removed the hotel's thick cotton robe from the hook on the far wall and slipped it on. As she was tying the belt around her waist she heard the doorbell ring. Their dinner had arrived. She walked into the bedroom and was just about to tell Michael she wasn't hungry, but then he lifted the silver domes from the plates, revealing the grilled salmon with brown rice and root vegetables, along with thick crusty rolls and sweet butter, and she couldn't resist. She ate every bit . . . with one exception. Again there was a side dish of mushy peas. She didn't touch them.

As soon as the table was removed from the room, Michael locked the door and turned to her. "I want you to stay right here. Understand? Don't go anywhere."

He disappeared into the bathroom before she could ask him where he thought she would go.

Isabel removed her robe and draped it over a chair, then put on a pair of baggy sweatpants and an oversize red Kansas City Chiefs T-shirt. She had no intention of trying to seduce Michael tonight. She was exhausted, and comfort won out over attempting to look desirable. The bed had already been turned down and, after her long hard day, she couldn't wait to sink into the soft white comforter and pillows. But first she needed to talk to Michael about tomorrow. She didn't want any surprises—though she expected there might be one or two. After rubbing some lotion on her arms and legs, she sat back against the headboard and patiently waited for him to return to the bedroom.

Unlike Isabel, it didn't take Michael any time at all to shower. He knew he looked scruffy, but he didn't feel like shaving tonight. He brushed his teeth, put on a pair of old boxer shorts, and was ready for bed.

Rounding the corner into the bedroom, he took a couple of steps and came to an abrupt stop. He couldn't move. Isabel's face was scrubbed clean, and her hair was wet and brushed back. The clothes she wore were shapeless. And yet he couldn't take his eyes off her as she swung her legs over the side of the bed, walked across the room, and picked up the television remote. The way she moved was so sensual.

Isabel had turned everything upside down. Sex without any kind of emotional commitment used to be his standard. He wouldn't allow any complications or expectations. What had he called it? Oh yeah. A pleasurable activity. What a cocky bastard he was.

He was nearly overwhelmed by his need for her tonight. He closed the distance between them. She was still holding the remote when he took her in his arms and kissed her warm soft lips.

Her clothes, the remote, and his shorts were on the floor before they reached the bed.

Their passion was blissful and beautiful.

When both were breathless and spent, Michael raised up on his elbows. He could feel her heart pounding under his. He didn't have enough energy to move. He wanted to savor the feeling of her against him. "Are you okay, baby?"

Isabel couldn't make herself let go of him yet. "If we keep this up, it's going to kill us. You know that. Right?"

He gave her a heart-stopping smile, and said, "Yeah."

"You're pretty pleased with yourself, aren't you?" she asked as she trailed her fingertips down the side of his cheek.

He slowly nodded. There was a seductive glimmer in his eyes. "Give me a minute, and I'll try to kill us again."

She sighed. What a wonderful way to go.

THIRTY

ISABEL WASN'T A SUPERSTITIOUS PERSON, AND SHE DIDN'T GET spooked easily, but walking into Walter MacCarthy's office she felt as though she were entering Satan's waiting room.

The walls were painted a garish red, which would have been okay, she supposed, except for the large painting of a clown with a freakishly manic grin on his face hanging on the wall. Looking around she noticed the other clowns, too. There was a clown coffee mug and two small stone statues of clowns being used as paperweights on Mac-Carthy's desk. Large clown bookends sat on a shelf against the wall, and a clown key chain dangled from a hook next to a large paper shredder.

When Isabel was a little girl, clowns frightened her, but now that she was an adult they just creeped her out.

She and Michael had arrived for their appointment with Gladstone a half hour early. Sinclair had notified them that he had secured a search warrant and would be looking through MacCarthy's personal records. Michael was hoping he could help. Client files were off limits . . . unless Gladstone was MacCarthy's partner. Then he could look through those papers. Michael would soon find out.

The law offices were in an old two-story stone building. Only the first floor was occupied. They were greeted warmly by Nessie, a plump middle-aged woman wearing a blue knit cardigan over a floral blouse. Her cropped brown hair was swept back on both sides and held by simple black barrettes, and a pair of reading glasses hung from a chain around her neck. She sat behind a desk in the middle of the reception area.

"I'm sorry. Mr. Gladstone isn't here yet," she told them apologetically.

"We wanted to have time to talk to Inspector Sinclair first, perhaps take a look at Mr. MacCarthy's office ourselves," Michael explained.

Her smile faded and was replaced with a worried frown. "Oh yes, Inspector Sinclair," she said. "He and one of his officers are upstairs. He has a search warrant and is going through Mr. MacCarthy's personal things. I'm not quite sure what they're looking for, but I think I heard one of them say something about a contract for murder." Shaking her head and raising her hand to her chest she added, "I must not have heard that right."

Nessie then pointed out that MacCarthy's office was on her left, and Gladstone's office was on her right. There was a third office behind her that wasn't occupied. Down a short hall there were stairs that led to the second floor, which was used for storage.

"There are boxes and boxes of Mr. MacCarthy's personal papers stored in plastic containers up there," she said. "Some of them go back ten, fifteen years. The man never threw anything away until recently. The last couple of weeks before he died, he got into a shredding frenzy. I'm not sure why," she admitted. "It's going to take the inspector and his team a long time to go through everything." She pointed up to the ceiling. "You'll find him up there now."

While Michael had gone up to talk to Sinclair, Isabel stayed behind and slipped into MacCarthy's office. As she stood there gazing around the room, she couldn't help but wonder what sort of person would feel comfortable in such a bizarre environment. She also thought it might be a good idea to get a tetanus shot before she touched any-thing.

MacCarthy's proclivity for hair-raising art was disturbing, but the appalling condition of his office was disgusting. The man was a slob. There were papers stacked everywhere. The piles on the floor were so high, one pile of papers had spilled down into another pile, which spilled into another and another, mimicking the domino effect. The room appeared to have been ransacked, which is what Isabel had concluded until Nessie walked in to join her and explained it was always disheveled.

"I begged him to let the cleaners in, but he didn't want anyone moving his files around. He swore he knew where everything was in the clutter. All those stacks by the window are to be shredded. I've been helping him get it done."

"I doubt he could find anything in this mess," Isabel remarked.

"That rug under his desk hasn't been vacuumed or swept in years, and the air is so stale. When Inspector Sinclair arrived, he let me open the door to the reception area, but I didn't dare open any windows. Paper would be flying everywhere."

"MacCarthy's decorating choices were certainly different," Isabel said, tilting her head toward the clown monstrosity on the wall. The painting was huge, and the clown's eyes seemed to follow her around the room, and that, she decided, went way beyond creepy.

"Mr. MacCarthy told me the painting was a gift, and he had to hang it so feelings wouldn't be hurt."

"He must have had a soft heart to be concerned about someone's feelings."

"Oh no, no, no. There wasn't anything soft about him." Nessie shook her head and said, "I know it's wrong to speak ill of the dead, but I have to admit Mr. MacCarthy was difficult, impatient, and distrustful. He locked his door even when he went to the washroom or lunch. I think he thought I would sneak cleaners into his office while he was gone. He didn't want anyone touching anything. He was terribly secretive and yet he was also quite nosy. He had to know everyone's business."

Once Nessie started talking about MacCarthy, she didn't hold back. She had a lot to say and none of it was complimentary.

"If Mr. Abernathy hadn't been here, I would have quit. He and Mr. MacCarthy were partners in the firm, but as different as night and day. Mr. MacCarthy's behavior didn't bother me because Mr. Abernathy was so nice to me. He always said 'please' and 'thank you,' and he praised me for doing a good job. I hated to see him go."

"Where did he go?"

"He was ill," she said. "He never complained, but I could tell he wasn't feeling well. He cut down to two days a week, and he referred most of his clients to other solicitors, but there were several clients he kept. His friend Mr. Gladstone took over the office and his remaining clients. Mr. Abernathy was able to retire then. He was quite pleased with Mr. Gladstone stepping in for him. He felt guilty, though, because he deliberately failed to mention that his partner, Mr. MacCarthy, was so difficult."

"Are you pleased with Mr. Gladstone?"

"Oh my, yes," she said. "Mr. Gladstone is a prince to work for. He never raises his voice like Mr. MacCarthy did."

"That's good to hear."

Nessie folded her hands as though in prayer and said, "It's so odd to me. Life is full of surprises, isn't it? Nothing is ever what you expect. Mr. Abernathy looked so pale, and he was so thin and slow on his feet. Mr. MacCarthy was the complete opposite. He was robust and full of energy. He kept liquor in his office. He claimed it was for his clients, but I knew he drank with them. He closed down Jolly Jack's pub nearly every night. I heard that he had a heart problem, but I didn't give it any substance. He looked as healthy as an ox. Though I really shouldn't speak ill of the dead, Mr. MacCarthy was quite the womanizer."

Since Nessie was looking at her expectantly, Isabel said, "Is that so?"

"Yes," Nessie said. "And look at them now. Mr. Abernathy is still walking around, and I hear he's feeling better since he's retired. And Mr. MacCarthy? He keeled over dead. I don't think he had any warning."

"How did he die?"

"Heart attack," she answered. "He was slumped over his desk with a full glass of whiskey in his hand. The coroner said it must have been quick because he didn't spill a drop."

"Who found him?"

"I did," Nessie said with a slight shiver. "I came in the other morning, and there he was. He gave me quite a fright, and I had a good scream before I called for help. I thought he might have passed out from whiskey or fallen asleep, but when I nudged him and called his name, he didn't move. I touched him, looking for a pulse, and he was stone cold."

"Then he died the night before," Isabel concluded.

Nessie nodded. "That's what the coroner thought. I'll tell you, it was difficult to walk in his office after he was carted away, but I felt I should at least straighten his desk. I put the papers in two stacks and left everything else alone. I would have locked the door, but I don't have a key."

Nessie stopped talking when Michael and Sinclair appeared in the doorway.

Isabel raised her hands as though she expected to be chastised for being there without permission. "The door was wide open," she explained. "Don't worry. I didn't touch anything."

Michael surveyed the chaos of files and papers in front of him. "There's a lot here to go through, but so far Sinclair hasn't found the original copy of the orders MacCarthy gave Ferris. However, he has discovered a great deal of other incriminating evidence against Mac-Carthy in his personal files. Evidently, he had a secret side business protecting some pretty shady characters."

"MacCarthy didn't just bend the law. He ignored it," Sinclair stated.

Isabel didn't press them for details. She would wait until later to find out what MacCarthy had been up to . . . besides taking on a client who wanted to kill her.

Sinclair leaned against the desk and asked Nessie, "What is it you do here?"

"I answer the phones and take messages. I also do computer work and filing. I assist both of them."

"Do you book appointments?"

"Yes. I make all the appointments for Mr. Gladstone, but I only scheduled some of Mr. MacCarthy's."

"Why is that?" Sinclair wanted to know.

"He was very private about a few of his clients. Most of those came to see him after work hours. I always left at five."

"Did you ever get any names of these later clients?"

"They rarely gave their full names. If they happened to call during the day when I was here, and if Mr. MacCarthy was in his office, I put them through. If Mr. MacCarthy wasn't here, John or Harry or Matthew, or whatever name they gave, would ask for him to call back. No last names and no phone numbers, which made me think some of these clients were up to no good." She was quick to add, "Though I never had any proof. I was left out of those dealings."

She rushed back to reception to answer the phone.

Sinclair moved to MacCarthy's desk and scanned the papers that Nessie had neatly stacked. One of the documents caught his attention and he bent lower to examine it. He silently read for a few seconds then lifted up and said, "Michael, I think you'll find that first document quite interesting. I believe MacCarthy may have dropped dead on top of it. It's just a guess, but I wouldn't be surprised."

Michael picked up the paper, read it, and smiled. "You're right. It is interesting."

"What is it?" Isabel asked.

"It's a petition to the court stopping you from taking ownership of Glen MacKenna until Clive Harcus's case as the rightful heir can be heard." He added, "He's contesting the will."

"Why does that make you smile?"

"MacCarthy died before he could present it."

Isabel rushed to his side and read the paper. "This will enrage Harcus, don't you think? May I be the one to tell him?"

"Let him figure it out on his own."

Looking around the office, she said, "How will we ever find out if it was Harcus behind the kill order? The original has to be somewhere."

"We'll keep searching," Sinclair assured. "It's not in his house. We've already looked top to bottom."

"Then it has to be here . . . if it exists. Ferris could be lying. I don't think he was, though."

"Donal Gladstone will have to go through each file."

"May we help?" Isabel asked.

Michael shook his head. "Gladstone was a partner and can act as solicitor for all of MacCarthy's clients. Nessie was MacCarthy's assistant, so she can help Gladstone. We can't."

"That's right," Sinclair agreed. "We'll have Gladstone and Nessie sort out any privileged information. And now that we've discovered the other activities MacCarthy was involved in, we'll pack up everything else and take it to Inverness for investigation."

Isabel leaned into Michael's side and whispered, "Will they take the painting, too?"

"Why? Do you want to buy it?"

"Good God, no." She looked up at him with a twinkle in her eyes. "Then again . . ."

"What?"

"It might be a nice housewarming gift for Kate and Dylan."

He had a good laugh. "You wouldn't."

"No. It's fun to think about, but I'm not that cruel."

"Excuse me for interrupting," Nessie called out. "Mr. Gladstone is here."

DONAL GLADSTONE WASN'T AT ALL WHAT ISABEL EXPECTED. THE solicitor had a nice smile and a quiet voice that was at odds with his size. The man was at least six feet seven or eight inches tall and built like a linebacker. He was younger than she had imagined, probably in his early to midfifties. His cheeks were ruddy, his handshake firm, and his piercing gray eyes didn't seem to miss much of anything.

Compared to MacCarthy's cluttered pigsty, Gladstone's office was austere and squeaky-clean. There was an old weathered desk polished to a glossy shine. Two captain's chairs upholstered in dark blue leather faced the desk, and another chair sat by the window. An old-fashioned beige metal file cabinet was on the opposite wall. There weren't any paintings or photos on the walls or on the desk, and there weren't any clowns, which told Isabel that Gladstone wasn't a nutcase.

After the introductions were made, Gladstone motioned to the chairs and said, "Please make yourselves comfortable, and we'll get right to this." He paused for a few seconds and then said, "There is much to discuss."

He rounded the desk and pulled out his swivel chair. It groaned when he sat down. He tapped the thick folder on his desk. "This is Compton MacKenna's last will and testament. When I was informed you would be coming in to sign the papers, I took it home with me and read it without interruption. I went over the disbursements and conditions."

He leaned forward and stacked his hands on top of the folder. "At that time, along with the will, there was a sealed envelope addressed to Grace Isabel MacKenna. A note attached to the will explained that Compton had written a letter outlining his stipulations. You were to open the envelope in front of witnesses here in my office on your birthday or any day after." He thought to add, "There's also a certified copy of your birth certificate in the file."

"You said the envelope *was* in the file? It isn't there now?" Michael asked. "Or did I misunderstand?"

"There is a problem," Gladstone said. "The envelope is missing."

"Missing?" Isabel repeated.

"How did that happen?" Michael wanted to know. He tried to keep the irritation out of his voice. He knew he shouldn't react until he had all the facts.

"The next morning, after I made sure everything was in order, I put the folder back in the file cabinet. Every night when I leave my office, I lock the door. Every night," he stressed. "It's a habit I've gotten into since I moved into this building." He drew a breath and continued, "Someone came in here and took the envelope out of the folder. After talking at length to Nessie, I believe I know who did it. It was MacCarthy. I can't prove it, though."

"Who had access?" Michael asked.

"Nessie is the only person who has a key to my office. She's very trustworthy." Turning to Isabel, Gladstone said, "I'm so sorry. I never thought anyone would look in my files."

Isabel acknowledged his apology with a nod. Was Gladstone at fault? He had kept the file under lock and key. What more could he have done?

"When did this happen?" Michael asked.

"I'm not sure. I didn't look in the file again until yesterday. I've been going back and forth to Edinburgh to finish up with some clients and also help get my flat ready to sell. Each trip I've stayed five or six days."

Michael moved on to another question. "Inspector Sinclair told us that you received an anonymous call about Isabel?"

"Yes. That's right. I was in Edinburgh when I got the call on my cell phone from the stranger telling me he had overheard talk about Grace MacKenna. The man on the phone was fearful. I could hear it in his voice. I don't know how he found out, but he knew I was in charge of the MacKenna estate, and he pleaded with me to convince Grace to stay away. He was concerned about her safety. Before I could ask any questions, he ended the call."

"What did you do then?" Michael asked.

"I got hold of my friend Craig Walsh. I had talked to Isabel when I took over for Mr. Abernathy and notified her that I was her solicitor and would facilitate the terms of Mr. MacKenna's will. She told me she was going to Boston for a week and then coming here. After that disturbing call from the stranger, I had to do something. I knew Isabel was probably on her way to Boston by then, and so was Craig. I had spoken to him a couple of days before and knew he was flying up to Boston to visit family. I told him about the call and my worry for Miss MacKenna, so he agreed to look in on her and talk to her about the possible danger. I thought I might be overreacting. There wasn't an actual threat, but I felt compelled to warn her all the same. You can imagine my distress when I was contacted by the FBI and was told that someone was trying to kill Miss MacKenna. I now know I should have immediately gone to the authorities. It was a terrible mistake on my part. I didn't know any of this was happening until I was contacted by the FBI a couple of days ago. I gave them all the details, and they assured me, with the date and time of the call, they'd be able to track down the caller."

Isabel's back began to ache, and she realized she was sitting ramrod straight on the edge of the chair. Any straighter and her spine would snap. She forced herself to sit back.

"What do we do now?" she asked. "Do I still sign the papers?"

"The terms of Mr. MacKenna's will specifically state that you must read the letter he wrote to you before you take possession of the property."

Gladstone's statement was discouraging, but Isabel wasn't ready to admit defeat just yet. "If the letter can't be found, you'll have to go to court and start the process of straightening this out, won't you? It could take years, and by then Harcus will have made himself king of the manor, drive everyone off the land, and make a deal with the Patterson vultures to build hotels and water slides and only God knows what else." Turning in all directions she scanned the office. "We have to find it."

"If MacCarthy hid it, chances are it's with the instructions that were given to Ferris," Michael said.

He didn't know how much Gladstone had been told about the flash drive his friend Craig Walsh had slipped into Isabel's pocket. He gave him a quick summary and then said, "We believe MacCarthy kept the original kill order, but we can't look through the client files. You can. And, while you're looking for the letter Compton wrote Isabel, you could also look for the instructions MacCarthy gave the killers."

"My God, what was that depraved man into?" Gladstone asked as he pushed his chair back and stood. "Fortunately, I know that MacCarthy didn't have many clients. Most of them moved on to other solicitors, so this shouldn't take long."

Shouldn't take long? Had he been inside MacCarthy's office lately? Isabel wondered.

No matter what, she was determined to stay positive. Maybe Gladstone was right. Maybe it wouldn't take long to find what they were searching for.

Gladstone and Nessie immediately set about searching through files while Michael and Sinclair went back upstairs to complete their examination of MacCarthy's personal records. Isabel couldn't go through client files, but that didn't mean she couldn't help. As soon as Nessie finished checking all the stacks on the floor, Isabel put them in boxes and labeled them.

"Why was he shredding all those papers?" she asked Nessie as she closed the lid on the last box.

"Most are old reports he didn't use anymore. From comments Mr. MacCarthy made I got the feeling he was expecting a windfall and was going to retire. I don't believe he liked the law much."

At that moment Michael walked in and heard what she said. "He sure knew how to manipulate it."

Isabel looked at her watch and was shocked at the time. They had been there all day. She stood by the door and watched two officers carry out the remaining boxes. Where hadn't they looked? The desk was completely empty; every paper in the file cabinet had been examined, and even the papers in the shredder had been bagged and tagged. She'd done that on her own. Her thought was that maybe someone would take the time to tape the shredded pieces back together. She'd do it if no one else would.

Isabel realized she was becoming desperate. She couldn't help it. She had such a strong feeling those papers were hidden somewhere in this office. Where else could they be?

Reality eventually smacked her upside her head. All of this searching could be futile. What they were looking for could be in any of a hundred places. MacCarthy could have mailed them to someone to hold for him. He could have placed them in a security box at the bank. He could have buried them in his backyard. The *He could have* went on and on.

Sinclair seemed to be as frustrated as she was. "Maybe he did shred them."

Michael shook his head. "I don't think MacCarthy destroyed the kill order or the envelope with Compton MacKenna's letter. Keeping them gave him leverage."

Gladstone picked up a pile of folders. "I'll take these and put them in my file cabinet. I have a client coming in for a late appointment, so I'll be in my office."

Nessie stood and brushed the pieces of shredded paper from her skirt. "I'll be going home, if that's okay."

"Of course," Sinclair said.

Isabel took Nessie's hand. "Thank you so much for your help. We couldn't have looked through any of this without you."

Nessie blushed at the praise. "I hope you find what you're look-ing for."

Isabel stayed with Michael and Sinclair in MacCarthy's office. She wasn't quite ready to give up.

"Did you look behind the bookcase? Were there any loose panels he could have tucked the papers behind?"

"We looked," Sinclair assured her.

"What about the empty office? Did anyone look there?"

"Yes," Michael answered. "It's empty. No built-in cabinets. No safe."

"What about the desk? Any false drawers or hiding places?"

"I checked," Sinclair said.

Feeling defeated she said, "I don't know where else to look."

Michael could see that Isabel was wilting. Disappointment showed on her face.

"I think we're done here," Sinclair conceded with a resigned look around the room. "Are you hungry? I'd like to take you to dinner."

The mere mention of food made her stomach grumble. She and Michael hadn't eaten since breakfast.

Michael was apprehensive. "Whoever wrote the kill order is still out there. We've been pushing our luck, Isabel. It isn't safe for you to go into a pub." He rushed to add when she started to interrupt, "By now everyone knows you're here."

"I couldn't be safer," she argued. "I've got you and Inspector Sin-clair protecting me."

Sinclair agreed with her. "I have a couple of officers at the pub now, so that's four watching out for her, and when you leave, I'll make sure no one follows you. You'll be as safe there as anyplace." He turned to Michael. "I think you'll want to be there when Archie Fletcher shows up."

"Who's Archie Fletcher?" Isabel asked.

Sinclair explained. "Fletcher is the man who called Donal Glad-stone to tell him you were in danger. He used his cell phone. We tracked the call and have been trying to talk to him, but thus far he's been avoiding us. He hasn't answered any of our calls and he hasn't been at his house when we've gone there, but we know his habit is to go to Jolly Jack's on Wednesdays. It's their Cullen skink night."

"Cullen skink?" Michael questioned.

"That's a fine fish chowder. And Jolly Jack's is known to make the best in all of Scotland. Fletcher's friends say he never misses, and we are likely to find him there tonight."

Michael gave in, but once again went over the rules.

Isabel knew them by heart now. "I'll stay by your side. I won't go anywhere without you, not even the washroom, et cetera."

"Et cetera?"

Smiling, she said, "I'm saving time."

"Fletcher usually comes in around eight and stays for a couple of hours, according to two different sources," Sinclair said.

"That gives us a little more time to search," Isabel said.

"Search where?" Sinclair asked. "Where haven't we searched?"

Isabel circled the room, inspecting every surface, every crevice, searching high and low. When she stopped at MacCarthy's desk, she turned to Sinclair. "Did you move the desk and look under the rug?"

"The desk weighs a ton," Sinclair said. "It's going to take the movers a full team to get it out of this office. I'm not sure where it will go. MacCarthy didn't have any relatives or a will."

"Nessie told me MacCarthy wouldn't let anyone vacuum the rug. I think he may have put something under there. It's worth a look, don't you suppose?"

Sinclair moved MacCarthy's chair back and squatted down to look at the rug. "I don't think he could slide anything under it. The desk covers most of the rug." He looked up at Michael. "Want to give it a try?"

Sinclair removed the drawers to lighten the weight. The two men each took a side. Gripping the edges of the desk, they bent down and, throwing all their strength into it, hoisted the desk just high enough to inch it off the rug. Dust flew up as they rolled the rug back, and there it was, a large yellowed envelope. For a few silent seconds they just stood there amazed. None of them could figure out how Mac-Carthy got the envelope under the massive desk.

Sinclair opened the envelope and emptied the contents on top of the desk. Several folded pieces of paper fell out. The first paper he opened was the kill order. Instructions and Isabel's itinerary were printed in black ink on plain white paper. Sinclair carefully placed the paper into a plastic evidence bag and sealed it to take to the lab.

"Too bad it wasn't signed," Isabel said.

Sinclair's indrawn breath sounded more like a gasp. He had unfolded another piece of paper and whatever he was reading shocked him.

"What is it?" Michael asked.

"You wouldn't have heard about the Wiley Croft case here in Scotland . . . all about theft of government funds. With all the evidence against Wiley, he was convicted and sentenced to a long term." He looked at the officer holding the evidence bags and said, "He didn't do it. The proof is right here. My God . . ."

Those papers went into another evidence bag. Compton Mac-Kenna's letter was on the bottom. The seal on the envelope was torn, but the letter was intact. Michael used his cell phone to take a photo of the letter. Gladstone returned in time to hear Isabel read what Compton had written.

The letter was as cold and unfeeling as Compton MacKenna had been. There wasn't a salutation.

Grace Isabel MacKenna,

I have been watching you and your sisters for a long time, and I have been surprised and even shocked by your progress and success. I find it amazing that you have flourished in spite of the unrefined environment you were raised in. Of the three sisters, I thought that you, the youngest, would have the most difficulty pulling yourself up and getting out of an abysmal home life under the control of a backward, uncultured, common woman.

But you have surpassed my expectations. In the latest quarterly report it was noted that you had decided to put the singing nonsense aside. It was also noted that history was your passion, and that is why I have given you Glen MacKenna. I would have left it to my nephews, but they have not proven themselves to be worthy of such a bequest and would only squander it. Scotland is rich with history, and I believe you will appreciate it.

I have created a financial endowment for the upkeep of the land. This will ensure that its beauty will be maintained and my legacy will be sustained for generations to come. You will find all the pertinent information on the enclosed page.

Your father and I had our differences when it came to preserving our family's heritage. There is nothing more important than upholding the prestige of our noble name, a name that has been highly respected throughout generations of our clan. It was my sincerest desire that your father would recognize his obligation to those who came before him. However, in choosing a wife of inferior lineage, with no breeding and no regard for the high honor given to her with the MacKenna name, he turned his back on me and all his ancestors.

I trust you understand the importance of the MacKenna clan.

I am giving you this land with just two stipulations, and the money designated to preserve the land is contingent upon your adherence to them. Both are equally important. First and foremost, you will not sell it. Second, to protect my bloodline, the land will always have the MacKenna name.

Compton MacKenna

THIRTY-ONE

COMPTON MACKENNA WAS A REAL PRICK.

Michael didn't share his opinion of Isabel's great-uncle. The narcissistic son of a bitch old man had said such awful things about her mother. The look on Isabel's face showed how upset she was.

He put his arm around her, leaned down, and whispered, "I could be wrong . . ."

"Yes?" she asked.

"I don't think Compton liked your mother."

His comment made her laugh.

"Compton wasn't a very agreeable man, was he?" Gladstone remarked.

"That's putting it mildly," Michael said.

Gladstone shook his head. "He certainly disliked your mother."

"My mother came from a poor family, and that was unforgivable," Isabel explained.

"Do you still want me to write those two letters for you? You could sign them, and I'll have them delivered before the night is over."

Within minutes the letters were composed and printed on Gladstone's letterhead. The first was addressed to Clive Harcus, giving him ten days to vacate the property, and the second letter was a notice of immediate termination to Graeme Gibson, the groundskeeper. Gladstone signed his name under Isabel's.

Weary from the long stressful day, Gladstone graciously declined their invitation to dine with them. As soon as the messenger picked up the letters, the solicitor went home.

Tying up odds and ends took another half hour or so. Isabel went to the washroom to freshen up, and then she waited with Michael in the reception room while Sinclair finished giving instructions to the officers he was leaving in charge.

Michael tried once more to reason with Isabel. "I'm still not comfortable taking you into Jolly Jack's pub. I've heard everyone in and around Dunross goes into that pub, including Harcus and his crew. It could get dangerous. You've done what you came here to do," he reminded. "You read the letter, signed the papers, and now it's time to leave."

"We've been over this," she said. "With you and Inspector Sinclair watching out for me, I'll be safe. Besides, don't you want to hear what Archie Fletcher has to say? I do."

Michael could think of a hundred reasons why they should get on the next flight back to Boston, but he knew Isabel wasn't finished.

"Do you know what you're going to do with the land?" he asked.

She looked defeated when she answered. "I did know. I was going to sell it. Now it looks like I don't have that choice. I so wanted something good to come from it."

Sinclair interrupted. "Are you ready to leave?"

They were going in opposite directions after dinner, so Sinclair drove his own car and led the way to the pub.

The entrance to Jolly Jack's was easy to spot. The door had been painted a bright, iridescent red and was like a beacon shining through the thick mist that had rolled in. They could hear music and laughter as they opened the door and went down the steps into the pub.

Isabel noticed a plaque on the wall stating that the pub opened in 1879. The old stone floors and the tall intricately arched ceiling confirmed the accuracy of the date. The bar took up the length of one long wall. Dark wood carvings on the front of it were works of art, and the varnished top had been rubbed smooth and shiny by the thousands of patrons over the years. Behind all the bottles sitting on glass shelves was a mirror that covered the back wall. No matter where you sat, if you looked in the mirror, you could see who was coming in. Several men were seated on stools drinking pints while they talked to one another, catching up on the day's news.

Padded booths lined the opposite wall, and scattered around the middle were round tables and chairs. In the back room was an open hearth. Two gentlemen sat in front of the fire playing fiddles, and a couple of patrons tapped their feet to the jaunty tune.

The noise quieted down to a whisper when they entered the pub, but after a few seconds the sound picked up again. Michael spotted an empty booth near the back and led the way. Isabel slid into the booth first and Michael sat next to her. She was protected by the wall on one side and a big hunk of a man on the other. She couldn't have felt safer.

Sinclair went to the bar to order drinks and came back with three menus. Since the pub's specialty on Wednesdays was Cullen skink, Isabel decided to give it a try. The waitress brought her a steaming bowl, and after one spoonful, she declared it the most delicious chowder she'd ever tasted.

There wasn't any heavy conversation while they ate, but as soon as the dishes were taken away, Sinclair checked his watch and said, "If he follows his routine, he should be here anytime now."

"What if he won't talk to us?" Isabel asked.

From the look on the inspector's face she surmised she'd asked a foolish question. She'd seen that same expression on Michael's face a time or two.

"He'll talk to us," Sinclair assured, just as the bartender caught his attention with a signal in the direction of the front door. "And there he is," he said, tilting his head toward the mirror.

Turning to the bar's mirror, they saw the reflection of a man entering the pub.

Fletcher was alone and he seemed nervous. He kept glancing to the left, then right, as though he expected someone to pounce on him.

Isabel thought he was rather odd-looking. He was of medium height and had a wiry frame, but with freakishly large biceps that didn't seem to fit the rest of his body. He spotted friends at the bar and headed across the pub to join them.

"I'll go get him," Sinclair said.

"If he sees your uniform, he might panic. Let me go," Michael offered.

Michael crossed the pub and tapped Fletcher on the shoulder. When he turned around, Michael shook his hand, acted as though they were old friends, and greeted him loudly enough for everyone to hear, then practically dragged him to the booth. Fletcher didn't want to sit until Michael offered to buy him a pint or two.

When Fletcher turned and saw Sinclair sitting there, he flinched and took a step back. "Wha . . . what's this?" he stuttered. "I didn't do anything . . ."

"You're not in trouble," Michael assured as he put his hand on Fletcher's shoulder and pushed him into the booth, next to Sinclair.

The waitress placed a full pitcher of beer and a glass in front of Fletcher. As soon as Sinclair filled his glass, Fletcher grabbed it and took a big gulp. He wiped the foam from his face with the back of his hand and said, "I have a good memory, and I don't remember meeting you."

"We haven't met," Michael told him.

"But you shook my hand and said it was good to see me again," Fletcher said, suddenly aware of a trap. "I don't understand. Who are you? And who are these two?" he asked, motioning to Isabel and Sinclair.

Sinclair ignored the question. "You called Donal Gladstone and told him that you heard some people talking about Grace MacKenna."

Fletcher looked shocked, but quickly recovered. "No, I don't know who you're talking about."

"Donal Gladstone."

Fletcher shook his head. "Never heard of him."

"You called him to warn him—"

Fletcher interrupted. "I didn't call him."

"We have proof that you made the call."

Fletcher was belligerent. He kept denying, as he finished one pint and began working on another. Sinclair looked ready to grab him by the throat and shake him until he told the truth.

When it appeared he was ready to bolt, Isabel looked at Sinclair and asked, "May I say something?"

"You still haven't told me who she is," Fletcher declared with a suspicious glance in Isabel's direction.

"My name is Grace Isabel MacKenna, and I want to thank you for calling Mr. Gladstone. Your concern for my safety overrode your fear. It was a heroic thing to do."

Heroic? That was going a little far, Michael thought. It was the man's responsibility to do the right thing and call Gladstone to warn him, and also to alert the authorities . . . which he had failed to do. Heroic? Come on. Isabel's notion of what was heroic was far different from his.

Fletcher's eyes widened when she told him who she was. He slumped back against the booth and scanned the room to see if anyone was watching him. He looked ready to bolt again.

Isabel drew his attention. "Have you had the fish chowder?" she asked. "I just had a bowl, and it was delicious."

Fletcher didn't respond. He sat silent for a minute, looking around the bar, and then returned his wary gaze back to Isabel.

She wasn't deterred. "Really, Mr. Fletcher, you should try it. I can't remember what it's called . . ."

"Cullen skink," Fletcher mumbled.

"That's it," Isabel said cheerfully. "Have you tried this one?"

"It's my favorite," he admitted. "I worry they'll run out before I order. The cook never makes enough, and it goes fast."

"We would like to treat you, wouldn't we?" she asked Michael. She had to elbow him in his side to get him to agree.

Sinclair motioned to the waitress and placed the order.

Fletcher was so nervous, his hands were shaking. He needed to calm down if they were ever going to get answers. Since he couldn't seem to stop staring at her now, Isabel decided to try to put him at ease with more casual conversation.

"This is such a beautiful area."

He nodded and continued to stare at her. After answering several more questions with a nod or a yes or a no, he finally began to loosen up.

"Do you live around here?"

"Yes, I do. It's walking distance from my flat to this pub, and since I'm not driving, I don't have to worry about how much I drink, though I have learned not to overdo because of the morning-after hangovers."

Isabel smiled. "I'm familiar with those. They can be brutal, can't they?"

He chuckled. With her encouragement he started talking about his life in Dunross and how he never wanted to live anywhere else. By the time he finished two large bowls of chowder and four slices of bread, she knew quite a bit about him. She also knew that no one had taught him to chew with his mouth closed and to speak only in between bites. His manners were deplorable, but he certainly had enjoyed his meal. Quite a bit of the chowder was on his chin and on the front of his shirt. She placed a clean napkin in front of him. When he didn't take the hint, she added another one.

As soon as the dishes were removed, Isabel said, "Mr. Fletcher, won't you please answer some questions for Inspector Sinclair? It's very important."

"You can call me Archie if you want. You sure are a stunner."

Before she could respond—and frankly she didn't know what to say to get him on topic—Fletcher leaned forward and blurted, "They hate you."

Sinclair had been sitting back against the booth, but he leaned forward at that statement. "Who hates her?"

"Lower your voice," Fletcher pleaded. "It's bad enough that I'm sitting here with an officer of the law wearing his uniform so everyone knows it, and now you're yelling at me."

"Who hates her?" Sinclair repeated, though he lowered his voice. "Who are they and what did they say?"

Michael had been sitting quietly, but his patience had run out. "You are going to tell us," he said.

"And if I don't?" Fletcher blustered.

"You will."

Fletcher looked from Michael to Isabel and back to Michael. "Who is she to you? Is she . . ."

"She's with me," he snapped. "Now answer the question."

Michael was getting testy, and Isabel feared his temper would cause Fletcher to stop talking. She reached under the table and put her hand on his thigh. She was either going to pat him or pinch him. Before she could make up her mind, his hand was on top of hers, and he wasn't letting go.

Fletcher kept his attention on Isabel when he answered. "Harcus and his crew. They don't want her coming in here and ruining things. They have big plans. Clive Harcus says he's the real heir and she's trying to take the land away from him."

"Does he have proof?"

"I don't know," he said. "Clive says that, from the day he was born, his mother, Freya, has told him that MacKenna was his father. Maybe her word is all the proof he needs. From what I hear, it's probably true."

"Do others living around here believe Clive's the rightful heir?"

"They aren't going to admit it if they don't. Clive tells everyone who will listen that he owns Glen MacKenna, and no one dares argue with him."

"Are you afraid of him?"

Fletcher's voice dropped. "Anyone with half a brain would be afraid."

Sinclair continued to question Fletcher while Isabel and Michael quietly listened.

"Were you in here when you heard people talking about Grace?"

"Yes. I was sitting in the last booth nursing my drink. I wasn't ready to walk home just yet, but my friends had already left, so I was relaxing by myself, hunched over my drink."

"Could they see you in the mirror?"

"I don't think so. I was tucked in the corner with my back to them."

"Can you identify who you heard?"

"Walter MacCarthy was one of them. He was sitting right behind me. They must have seen my friends leave. They go out the front door, but I always leave by the back because it's closer to my flat."

"How many were in the booth with MacCarthy?"

"There were two others," he said. "One of them was Graeme Gibson. He has a real nasally, whiny voice. I'd know it anywhere. He has made a lot of money doing absolutely nothing as groundskeeper. Sometimes when Clive gets into trouble with the law, Graeme is his alibi."

"Graeme Gibson and MacCarthy," Sinclair said. "Who was the third man?"

"I don't know who he was. I didn't recognize his voice. MacCarthy did most of the talking. He'd been drinking for a while, and Graeme had to tell him to be quiet. I wasn't paying much attention until I heard him say that Grace MacKenna wasn't going to cause any trouble. He said he'd made sure she'd be taken care of and wouldn't be coming to the Highlands. I guess he was wrong about that since she's sitting right here."

"Did he explain how he had made sure? "

"No, and they didn't ask. Graeme wanted to know what would

happen if the plan failed. Then the stranger asked MacCarthy if he had a contingency plan."

"And?" Sinclair prodded when Fletcher didn't go on.

"I'm getting parched. Any chance you could order another pitcher?"

Michael motioned to the waitress, and a couple of minutes later Fletcher was gulping another pint. He seemed to be in a hurry to get drunk.

"Did MacCarthy have a contingency plan?" Sinclair asked impatiently.

"Yes. He said the land couldn't go to Grace until she read some kind of letter, and she wouldn't be able to do that. Graeme asked him why, and MacCarthy laughed while he admitted he took the letter. He said it would slow things down and give him time to make other arrangements to get rid of the problem."

"The problem being Grace?" Sinclair asked.

"I think so. Then the stranger said they'd be able to move forward with their development plan. He sounded real happy."

Isabel and Michael said his name at the same time. "James Reid."

Michael still didn't have the answers he wanted. He assumed that Clive Harcus had written the kill order, but he wanted confirmation. MacCarthy hadn't been doing this on his own.

"Was Clive Harcus aware of MacCarthy's plans? Did he hire him?"

"I don't know about that," he said. "Clive was one of MacCarthy's clients. He'd gotten him out of several messes in the past. Of course, it was easy work for MacCarthy because witnesses wouldn't dare testify against Clive."

"Were the arrests for fighting?" Isabel asked.

Sinclair had looked at Clive's record and answered. "Most were. Harcus can't or won't control his temper."

"If he kills someone, he'll probably get away with it," Fletcher said. He downed the rest of his drink and wiped his mouth with the back of his hand. Isabel couldn't stop herself from pushing another napkin toward him. There were now three in front of him and he hadn't touched any of them.

"He'll have to find another corrupt solicitor when he starts another fight and breaks someone's jaw," Sinclair said.

Michael looked at the bar and then turned to Sinclair. "I think the bartender is trying to get your attention."

Sinclair immediately got up and crossed the room, zigzagging his way around the tables. The bartender stopped wiping the counter with his cloth while he spoke to Sinclair. Whatever he said surprised the inspector, who turned to look at Michael and Isabel and nod.

"It's all right, Annie. You can ask," the bartender called out before speaking to Sinclair again.

The waitress appeared with their bill. She was blushing and seemed flustered. Michael paid and gave her a large tip. As she tucked the money into her apron, she leaned in and said, "You're Isabel, aren't you? You're really her." Needing confirmation she asked again, "You are her, right?"

"Yes, I am."

Annie's hand flew to her throat. "I love your voice," she blurted.

"Thank you."

"Could you give me your autograph? My boss said it was okay to ask."

As soon as Isabel agreed, Annie tore one of the blank pages from her order pad and handed the paper and her pen to Isabel.

"Sign it 'to Annie,' please, and you can say how nice it was to meet me if that's all right. You don't need to write your full name. Just sign 'Isabel' because that's what XO calls you."

"Yes, of course," Isabel said, and quickly wrote the message and signed her name.

"This is so exciting," she whispered. "Could I ask something?"

"What is it?"

"Are you going to marry XO?"

Michael was more surprised by the question than Isabel appeared to be.

"No, I'm not going to marry XO."

"All your fans say you are."

She had hoped the Internet chatter would have died down by now. "You read that I was going to marry him?"

"Oh yes, it's everywhere. It's all over social media. I turn on my laptop first thing in the morning and read the latest news while I have my tea. You're all that everyone is talking about. Tomorrow will be awesome. I'll get to brag that I met you." Annie started to walk away, then stopped. "Wait. You're not already married to XO, are you?"

Isabel smiled. "No, we're just friends."

Michael muttered something under his breath. Isabel was pretty sure it was a blasphemy.

"Are you famous or something?" Fletcher wanted to know.

She shook her head. "No."

The front door suddenly flew open with such force it bounced against the wall. The whole pub fell dead silent.

And the Terror of the Highlands stormed in.

THIRTY-TWO

TERROR CERTAINLY WAS A FIT DESCRIPTION OF THE MAN WHO WAS standing at the door surveying the pub's crowd as though he were hunting for prey. With fire in his eyes, the ugly brute then headed to the bar.

"That's Clive Harcus." Fletcher whispered his name and hunched down until his forehead was almost touching the tabletop. "Graeme Gibson is with him. They're both mean as rabid dogs."

Isabel didn't think she had ever seen anyone this angry. Harcus's body was rigid and his clinched fists shook with his fury. He was a big man, about Michael's size, but the comparison stopped there. Clive had more flab than muscle through his middle, but his shoulders and beefy arms were those of a weight lifter. He had a double chin and a thick neck that all but disappeared in his sloped shoulders. The hateful expression on his face could give children nightmares. Their parents, too. He looked exactly like what he was. A bully. And he was out for blood.

Graeme trailed behind him. The look on his face jarred her, as though he might start laughing at any moment. His expression wavered between a smirk and a smile, and how creepy was that? Was he eager for the blowup he knew was coming?

An older woman called out to Clive as she entered the pub behind them. She looked worried.

"Mr. Fletcher, do you know who that woman . . ." Isabel's voice trailed off when she realized he was gone.

Michael explained before she could ask. "He flew out the back door."

"I was about to look under the table," she said as she turned around and saw no sign of the man.

Annie rushed over to their booth. "You should get out of here. It isn't safe. Go out the back way," she whispered. "And be careful. They're here for you."

"You don't need to worry about me. I'm with him," she said, nudging Michael. "He won't let anyone get to me. Tell me, Annie. Who is the woman pleading with Clive Harcus?"

"Freya," she answered. "Poor thing. She looks like she's going to cry. She's Clive's mother, and that's reason enough to weep, I suppose. Now go, both of you," she begged before she hurried away.

The crowded pub was rapidly emptying. Customers couldn't seem to get out of there fast enough. One man tripped on the steps, and another man, clearly inebriated, fell on top of him. The two were a sight, staggering to their feet and helping each other out the door.

Clive was arguing with his mother, who was clinging to him. He pulled her along to a table in the corner and all but pushed her into a chair.

"Stay calm," his mother called out. "Try to stay calm."

The woman looked so anxious. Who could blame her? Her son, after all, was a monster. Did Freya realize it, or did she wear blinders?

Isabel noticed the paper in Clive's hand then.

"Uh-oh," she whispered. "The paper Clive is waving around is the eviction notice, isn't it?"

"It would seem so," Michael said. "Gladstone did say he would have both letters delivered by the end of the day."

Graeme was also holding a paper. His termination letter, no doubt.

He obviously wasn't upset about it because he was grinning. What was that about? These people were crazy, Isabel decided. And violent, she added when Clive started shoving chairs out of his way to cross over to Isabel and Michael's booth.

Sinclair intercepted him in the middle of the pub. With an obstacle suddenly standing in front of him, Clive got into Sinclair's face and began shouting at him.

Isabel was impressed by the inspector's calm demeanor. "Does Clive think Sinclair wrote the eviction letter?"

Michael shook his head. "From the look in his eyes I don't believe he's thinking at all. His anger is controlling him."

"Get out of my way," Clive shouted at Sinclair.

Unfazed by the madman screeching at him, the inspector held his ground. Twice Clive tried to get around him, but each time he was blocked.

"I told you to get out of my way," Clive shouted again. "You can't stop me from getting to her. Now move. I'm not going to tell you again."

Sinclair drew Michael and Isabel's attention when he looked in their direction and tilted his head ever so slightly toward the back door.

The bartender reached for a phone on the shelf behind him and ducked behind the bar, undoubtedly calling for backup.

"The inspector is giving us the nod. He wants us to leave, doesn't he?" Isabel asked. Not really wanting an answer, she rushed on. "No, I'm not going to run away. I want to stand up to Clive and let him know he can't bully me."

Michael wasn't going to argue with her. He'd like nothing better than to knock the smug look off Clive Harcus's face, but Isabel's safety came first. He was determined to get her out of harm's way, and if that meant throwing her over his shoulder and going out the back door, then that's what he would do.

"Sinclair can handle himself," Michael said. "And he's in uniform. Clive wouldn't dare touch him. He's not that stupid."

Apparently he was. The plan to get Isabel out of the pub changed when Clive shoved Sinclair. Knocked him clear off his feet. The back of Sinclair's head struck the edge of the table as he fell to the floor.

"Stay in the booth, Isabel."

Michael moved fast. One second he was sitting beside her, and the next he was nose to nose with Clive Harcus. Clive would have to go through him to get to her or Sinclair.

Both fists raised to strike, Clive lunged, but he was no match for Michael's speed and agility. He blocked Clive's left arm with one hand and slammed his fist into Clive's face with the other. Clive howled as he went flying back and down, landing on his backside. Blood spurted from his nose, and Isabel was certain Michael had broken it. She found herself hoping he had.

Isabel heard Freya cry out.

Clive's sidekick, Graeme, got up from the table where he'd been sitting with Freya and headed toward Michael. Seeing him coming, Michael shook his head and said, "You'll want to go sit down." There was something in his voice that got through to Graeme because he hightailed it back to Freya.

Both Sinclair and Clive staggered to their feet. Sinclair rubbed the back of his head and, when he saw the blood on his hand, muttered something Isabel couldn't hear.

"Put him in a chair," he told Michael.

Clive wiped his nose with the back of his hand, smearing blood all over his face. "I don't have to sit down," he muttered. "And I'm going to sue you, you bastard. You broke my nose."

"Sit down," Sinclair snapped.

Clive acted as though he was going to cooperate. He turned to pull the chair close, then spun around with clinched fist and tried to punch Michael again.

"You're a slow learner," Michael remarked as he twisted Clive's arm back and shoved him into the chair.

Clive squinted up at Michael. "I'm not going to forget what you just did, Buchanan. I'd watch my back if I were you."

Michael didn't seem surprised that Clive knew who he was.

By now, Sinclair was standing next to Michael, staring at Clive. "You put your hands on an officer of the law."

Clive shrugged. "I just gave you a little nudge to get you out of my way. Are you going to arrest me for that?" he scoffed.

"Yes, I am," Sinclair answered.

Clive grabbed a couple of napkins from the table and wiped his face. Then he tossed them back on the table. He leaned around Michael to look at Isabel. His face was turning red with fury again. While he stared at her, he slowly tore up the eviction letter. "I'm not going to let you steal what belongs to me," he bellowed. "If I have to, I'll . . . ," he began, then suddenly stopped.

"If you have to, you'll what?" Michael demanded, pressing in on him.

Clive shook his head, refusing to answer.

"Miss MacKenna signed the papers and is now the sole owner of Glen MacKenna. If you have a problem with that, take it to the courts. In the meantime, leave her alone."

Two police officers rushed into the pub. One of them pulled out a pair of handcuffs. Sinclair took them aside and gave them instructions while Michael stood over Clive. Twice he tried to get up, and twice Michael shoved him back into the chair.

Annie handed Sinclair a wet cloth, and he used it to wipe the blood seeping from the cut on the back of his head. She took the long way around Clive to get to the kitchen and grab a carry-out plastic bag Michael had asked her for.

Powerless to intervene, Freya had remained in her chair, looking frightened and distressed by what was happening to her son. When the officers began to put handcuffs on him, she jumped to her feet.

"He didn't do anything wrong. Please don't arrest him," she begged. She pointed at Michael. "That man assaulted him."

Her pleas were ignored.

It took both officers to get Clive's hands behind his back and snap the cuffs on.

"You won't be able to keep me locked up for long. I'll be out by tomorrow night," Clive boasted.

As he was being dragged out of the pub, he pulled away from the officers long enough to say good-bye to his mother. He told her to get him a solicitor and be damned quick about it.

"Who should I call, Clive? Tell me who to call," she pleaded.

The door closed before Clive could respond. Graeme answered her. "I'll find someone better than MacCarthy. Don't you worry." He paused to glare at Isabel and added in a shout, "You aren't going to get away with this atrocity. I'm going to make sure you can't cause trouble."

Shoving his chair back, Graeme stood and said to Freya, "The car is several roads over. I'll go get it and pull up to the door. Stay here until I come back inside for you."

With the pub quiet now, Annie returned and gave Michael the bag. He opened it and used it to scoop up the bloody napkin Clive had used and tossed on the table. He sealed the bag and handed it to Sinclair.

Isabel's attention went to Clive's mother. Freya held a lacy handkerchief up to her eyes, dabbing the tears away. Isabel couldn't imagine the distress she would feel watching someone she loved being handcuffed and taken away. She had an insane urge to go over to the woman and apologize, which didn't make a lick of sense, she knew. She wasn't going to do it, but she knew being Clive's mother had to be hell for her. Approaching Freya would probably upset her even more. Besides, Michael would probably tackle her if she took one step in the woman's direction.

She slid out of the booth with the intention of going to Michael, who was in a quiet discussion with Sinclair, but then she saw Freya stand and make her way over to her. They met a few feet from each other, with a round table between them. Isabel pulled out a chair and sat. Freya nodded to her and sat down across from her.

Neither one said a word for a minute while they studied each other. Freya was a surprise to Isabel. She wasn't at all what she had pictured. Her erect posture gave her an almost regal bearing. Isabel couldn't tell how old she was. Her dark hair was pulled back. The only hints of her true age were the few silver strands in her hair and the fine lines around her eyes. She was slender and dressed in a black sweater and slacks. Her simple attire was not matched by her accessories, though. The woman obviously had a fancy for jewelry. Large silver teardrops hung from her ears; several strands of beads circled her neck, and at least a half-dozen bangles surrounded her wrists. When she folded her manicured hands on the table, the bracelets made a clanking sound.

Freya spoke first. "Life hasn't been fair to my son. He is trying to get better control, but he has lapses, especially when someone has wronged him. He has his father's temper." Then, as though stating the obvious, she said, "Compton MacKenna was Clive's father. I was in love with him, you know."

"No, I didn't know."

"It was so many years ago, but I remember it like it was yesterday," Freya began with a wistful sigh. "Compton came to Dunross to make arrangements for Glen MacKenna. I was working as a waitress." She raised her hand to gesture around the pub. "Here at Jolly Jack's, actually. I met Compton the first night he arrived. We took to each other right away. I guess you could say it was love at first sight. I know he loved me. He told me so many times. We were together almost every minute that he was here. He made promises to me, and then he left. He just left me." She stopped for a second, shaking her head as though the insult was still fresh in her mind. "No warning at all. He made me look like a fool, and I was devastated by his betrayal. When I found out I was pregnant, I tried to get hold of him. I expected him to do the right thing."

"What was the right thing?" Isabel asked.

"Marriage," she answered. "I expected him to marry me."

If Freya really believed that Compton would marry her, she hadn't known him well at all, Isabel thought. He was all about titles and blue bloods. Freya was what Compton would have called common.

"Did you ever talk to him?"

"No," Freya answered. "I must have called him fifty times. He would never talk to me. I did speak to one of his assistants, who told me to stop harassing Compton or there would be unpleasant consequences. I told the assistant that I was pregnant, but I don't know if he ever told Compton. I guess I always expected him to return to Scotland, especially since he loved Glen Mackenna so much . . . but he never did. I was all alone with a child . . . his child."

"That must have been very difficult for you," Isabel said sympathetically.

"It was terrible. I didn't know where to turn. I had to support us both. Then, when Clive was three, I met Malcolm Harcus. We married, and Clive took his name, but the marriage only lasted a couple of years, and he left us. I raised that boy on my own without any financial help. It was especially hard on Clive. Surely you can understand what it was like for him . . . to be abandoned twice. That would make anyone angry.

"I never lied to him. From the time he was very young, he knew who his real father was. Over the years we would hear bits and pieces about Compton, and we knew he never married or had children. Clive was sure that Glen MacKenna would be his someday. So, you can see why he would want to oversee the management of the land in the meantime. Compton had left James Gibson in charge as Glen MacKenna's caretaker. When James died, his son Graeme took over. He's been Clive's right-hand man the last few years.

"I'm telling you all of this so you'll realize that your claim to the land is groundless. Just because there's a piece of paper that says it's yours doesn't make it so." She raised her voice defiantly then. "Glen MacKenna belongs to him. What will you do with the land? Go back to America and forget all about it?"

Isabel could see how distraught the woman was, so now was not the time to tell her that her son may well be going to prison for his role in attempted murder. It was obvious she was protective of him and would be defensive. Isabel would let any accusations come from the police.

She tried to sound understanding when she said, "I'm sorry for all you've gone through. I truly am. But that doesn't change the legality of Compton's will. It's final. I've signed the papers and I own Glen MacKenna now."

"So my son is being cheated out of his inheritance," Freya said as though the very thought were incomprehensible. She then straightened in her chair and looked straight into Isabel's eyes. "I suppose Clive may have to take you to court, then, to get what's rightfully his."

"Even if that happened, he can't ever sell it. Compton's will is specific. And it's obvious that Clive's only interest in the land is the profit he would make by selling it to developers."

"Why would you keep what doesn't belong to you? You selfish bitch," Freya hissed in a whisper.

"Selfish? I don't agree," Isabel said quietly, hoping her tone would calm the woman. "The Patterson Group, James Reid, and your son have big plans for the land. Simply put, they would destroy it. I'm making sure they can't."

Graeme interrupted. He called out to Freya and waited for her at the top of the steps.

Freya stood but kept her attention on Isabel. "Is it done? Have you already signed the papers?"

"Yes."

Freya didn't say good-bye. She put her purse over her arm and walked out of the pub with her head held high.

Isabel watched her leave. She didn't feel guilty. She was thinking about future generations. She believed it was her duty to protect the beauty of God's gift. The glorious Highlands belonged to the people, and whatever she could do to preserve the land she would do.

It came to her in that instant. She had her answer. She immediately turned her phone on and called Donal Gladstone to tell him what she wanted to do. He was so excited by her proposal, he promised to do everything in his power to make it happen.

Michael had kept his eye on Isabel while he'd been talking to Sinclair. She walked over to join them.

"How are you feeling, Inspector?" she asked.

"I'm fine," he assured her.

Isabel insisted on looking at the injury. "It's not bleeding anymore, but you might need stitches."

"Are you ready to leave?" Michael asked her.

"In just a minute." She hurried over to the bartender and asked him to put some ice in a plastic bag.

"Does the pub always clear out when Clive Harcus comes in?" she asked him.

"Pretty much," he said. "He's bad for business. The locals are afraid of him and for good reason. He's quite the bully. Word will spread that Clive is locked up, and there will be a crowd here tomorrow night."

Isabel thanked him for the ice bag and handed it to Sinclair. "This will help reduce the swelling."

Once again the inspector assured her that he was fine, but from the way he was smiling at Isabel, Michael could tell he was appreciative of her concern.

He shook Michael's hand. "I'll talk to you soon," he promised.

Isabel was suddenly in a hurry to get back to the hotel. After the brief interaction with Clive Harcus, she felt the need for a hot shower.

Michael was more relaxed now that Harcus was locked up, and yet he wasn't ready to let his guard down. Admittedly, he wasn't as desperate to get her on a plane back to Boston, though. Tomorrow they had another meeting with Gladstone, who had told Isabel he would have preliminary papers ready to go over. The meeting was set for four P.M.

An hour after the scene at the pub, Isabel was ready for bed, but she couldn't unwind. She was too revved up to sleep just yet. She thought about turning on her phone to check her emails and texts, but she couldn't make herself do it. She hated answering emails and texts almost as much as she hated talking on the phone. Realizing just how much she disliked the interruption actually made her smile. In high school her cell phone had been attached to her ear. It was the first thing she grabbed in the morning and the last thing she put away at night, but by the end of her college days she had developed a real dislike for the interruption of answering a call. She had certainly changed over the years.

"You look happy. What were you thinking?" Michael asked. He had just finished his shower and his hair was wet. She watched him turn off all the lights but her bedside lamp. He stretched out on the bed next to her, stacked his hands on his chest, and closed his eyes.

"I was thinking about phones. I realized that, except for a quick call tonight, I haven't turned my cell phone on for days. I put it in my charger every night, and every morning I put it in my purse, but I don't turn it on. It's been pleasant."

"I didn't want you to turn it on because they could track us, but now that everyone knows we're here, it doesn't matter if it's on."

"I haven't missed it."

"That's nice," Michael said on a yawn.

She knew he would be asleep in seconds. She wished she could do the same.

She saw a side of Michael tonight that shocked and surprised her. She had never seen anyone move as fast. The way he fought and controlled Clive was impressive. She knew he was strong, but seeing him in action was jaw-dropping. His Navy SEAL training came out in full force. He made it look so easy. He was almost nonchalant about it. In fact, he probably didn't think it was much of a fight at all.

Isabel wasn't an advocate of ever using violence, but the image of Michael punching Clive was quite gratifying. If anyone needed a good punch, it was him.

"Damn it," Michael muttered, opening his eyes and rolling toward her.

"What's wrong?"

"I forgot your birthday. I'm sorry. Guess it was pretty awful. We'll have to celebrate later."

"Awful? It wasn't awful."

"Then what was it?"

Once again she pictured Michael's fist connecting with Clive's ugly face.

"Best . . . birthday . . . ever."

He pulled her into his arms. "Yeah? It's about to get even better."

THIRTY-THREE

ISABEL COULD NEVER TELL ANYONE WHAT MICHAEL GAVE HER FOR
her birthday. To say his "gift" was X-rated was an understatement.
She didn't wake up until nine. She sat up in bed, her hair hanging in
her face. She brushed it over her shoulder and found Michael across
the room. He was working on his laptop.

He didn't look up. "Good morning."

He was dressed and ready to go. "How long have you been up?"
she asked. Her voice was as croaky as a frog's.

"A couple of hours. Get moving," he said.

"Yes, all right." She continued to sit there, staring off into space.

Isabel closed her eyes, and after a minute or two Michael realized
she had gone back to sleep. Sitting up, no less.

His laughter startled her. She wanted to curl up and go back to
sleep for a couple of hours, but she knew she couldn't. With a groan
she slid out of bed and went into the bathroom.

After dressing, she returned to the bedroom to find Michael still
on his laptop. She watched him reading the screen for several minutes
and then said, "I thought you were in a hurry to leave."

"I was just checking our route to Inverness. I booked our flight
to Boston, and we need to be at the airport by five tomorrow."

"Tomorrow? You want to fly back to Boston tomorrow?" She

hadn't expected his abrupt announcement. "Couldn't we stay an extra day or two? I like it here. There's so much I want to see."

"No."

No? The refusal came a little too quickly. "I know you want to get back to your life . . . ," she began.

"Yes, I do."

His curt response made her angry, but she was determined to stay calm, and yelling wouldn't accomplish anything. She began to straighten the room just to have something to do while she worked on getting her emotions under control.

"What are you doing?" he asked.

"What does it look like I'm doing? I'm making the bed."

"The maids will strip the sheets," he said.

"I know."

She didn't say another word until she had finished the task. Okay, her temper was under control, and her breathing was normal again. "Now that Clive Harcus is locked up, there isn't any reason to be worried about my safety. You go ahead and fly home. I'm going to stay here awhile longer."

Michael tried to be reasonable. "What about all of Clive's friends? You think they won't come after you?" Before she could think of a logical answer, he said, "A lot of people don't want you to ruin their plans for Glen MacKenna, and aside from that obvious threat, there's also the fact that you're a celebrity."

"What does that matter?"

"You don't remember what it was like getting out of the arena in Boston?"

Oh yes, she remembered. It would have been terrifying if Michael hadn't been with her. "Not all that many people know who I am," she argued.

"You're wrong. They know who you are. They just haven't been able to find out where you are, and that's because of all the help we've gotten from Nick and Alec and Noah with cars and hotels . . ."

"I can handle a crowd." It was a blatant lie, but she thought she told it well.

Exasperated, he said, "They'd run right over you. I'm not going back to Boston without you. It isn't safe for you here. You're going home with me."

He walked over to her, tilted her chin up so she would look at him, and softened his tone. "Do you honestly believe I would leave you?"

He didn't give her time to answer. He leaned down and kissed her. When he pulled away, she looked a little dazed.

"Come on," he said. "Let's get out of here. We'll stop at the front desk and let them know we'll be staying one more night."

She grabbed her rain jacket, shoved her wallet into a pocket and zipped it closed, put her cell phone in her pants pocket, and followed him out the door.

IT WAS A BEAUTIFUL DAY. THE SUN WAS OUT, BUT ISABEL KNEW rain clouds could sneak in at any time. The weather was fickle in the Highlands, but—hot, cold, wet, dry—it didn't matter to her. She still loved it.

"I've read books about this country, and I've seen hundreds of photos, but nothing compares to actually being here."

She was leading up to making him understand why she wanted to stay. He cut her off.

"Then we'll come back."

She was surprised that he had included himself. "It would be nice to roam around without people trying to kill me."

He laughed. "Yeah, I guess that would be nice."

On their way to Dunross they talked about the FBI and Michael's decision to enter the academy.

"You'll start the end of August?"

"Yes."

"Will the training to become an agent be as brutal and intense as it was for you to become a Navy SEAL?"

"No."

She waited for him to tell her more, and when he remained silent, she asked, "Care to explain why it won't be as difficult?"

"No."

"Michael? Do you know what people skills are?"

"Yes, I do."

"You ought to get some."

He just shrugged and smiled. It wasn't the reaction she wanted.

"What are you going to do when you get back to Boston?" he asked a few minutes later.

"Spend the night, then fly back to South Carolina, I suppose. I honestly don't know where I'll end up. I can work on my songs anywhere," she added.

Odd though it was, thinking about leaving the Highlands made her emotional, probably because she was trying not to admit leaving Scotland meant leaving Michael, too. He had his future all mapped out, and it didn't include her.

"We have a lot of time. Do you want to drive around Glen Mac-Kenna? We've only seen a tip of it."

"I'd like that."

Only when they'd taken the tour of her land did she realize just how big it was. It had everything a national park envied. There were streams, lakes, hills, and valleys, all places to fish, hunt, and hike. For an outdoorsman Glen MacKenna was Utopia.

They had circled around to Rosemore when Sinclair called. Michael put him on speaker. The inspector sounded ecstatic with his news. They were beginning the investigation to connect Harcus to the kill order given to Jacoby and Ferris, but in the meantime, the investigators going through MacCarthy's records had found proof that Harcus had received large sums of money to do MacCarthy's dirty work, including framing Wiley Croft for stealing government funds, the case Sinclair had mentioned earlier. They had enough hard evidence to put Clive Harcus in prison for at least twenty years. There wouldn't be any talk of bail. The Terror of the Highlands was finished.

There was also evidence implicating Graeme Gibson, and Sinclair was on his way to Graeme's cottage to arrest him.

Michael finished the call and parked in front of a little café down the street from the Rosemore Police Station.

"We have plenty of time to grab something to eat before we head over to Dunross for your meeting with Gladstone."

Another call came in for Michael—this one from his brother Nick—and while he talked to him, Isabel decided to turn her cell phone on and find out how many calls she'd missed and how many texts she needed to read.

The number made her groan. She would take the time to go through them all later. She turned the ringer to vibrate and dropped the phone back in her pocket.

Her stomach was growling. As soon as he had mentioned food, she became hungry. The power of suggestion. The café was small, but they were the only customers. They sat by the front window so that Michael could watch the street. While they ate, she told Michael what Freya had said to her.

"I can't imagine why she would believe Compton would marry her," she told him.

"I'm surprised she would talk to you."

"She was . . . almost pleasant until I mentioned I own the property now."

"Almost pleasant?"

"No, not really."

"Then why did you say she was?"

Michael was coming to the conclusion that figuring out how her mind worked was impossible. She was a constant contradiction. She kept him on his guard, he admitted, because he never knew what she was going to say or do. Life with Isabel would never be boring.

Isabel was trying to be compassionate toward Freya. The woman had been forced to raise a difficult boy on her own, and really believed that Compton would leave Glen MacKenna to Clive.

"Freya became very angry. She called me a selfish bitch. After she left, I realized how important it was to protect the land from people like Harcus, and so I knew then what I should do with Glen Mac-Kenna."

"And what is that?"

"You'll find out when we get to Gladstone's office."

Intrigued, he said with a smile, "Okay. I can wait."

When they arrived at the law office, Nessie was sitting at her desk and greeted them. "Mr. Gladstone will be right with you. He's just finishing a phone call."

As soon as they were seated in his office, Gladstone told Isabel he had been making phone calls since last night.

"Then it is possible?" she asked.

"Absolutely."

She couldn't contain her excitement. She turned to Michael to fill him in. "Compton wouldn't let me sell Glen MacKenna. He also prevented me from removing the MacKenna name. I don't think this is what he had in mind, but, since I can't sell it, I'm going to protect it by donating it to the National Trust for Scotland. It's a conservation organization that preserves Scotland's natural beauty. I want to make sure no one will be able to build shopping centers and amusement parks on the land. The name's going to change, too. It's going to become Glen Leah MacKenna."

"I'm not surprised," he said, nodding his approval. "Kate and Kiera gave away the millions they inherited to build a medical center addition with your mother's name on it, and you are their sister. So I figured you would do something as generous."

"This is going to take some time," Gladstone warned her. A few minutes later he repeated his concern. "This won't happen overnight."

Michael interpreted. "He wants you to be patient."

She nodded her understanding.

The meeting lasted an hour, and when all the details had been discussed, Gladstone turned to Michael. "Catch me up on Clive Harcus. I heard there was a fight."

"It wasn't much of a fight."

"It was more of a ruckus," Isabel said. Another Aunt Nora word.

"Now tell me, Michael. Is it true?" Gladstone asked. "Did Clive Harcus strike Inspector Sinclair? And you struck Clive?" The idea obviously appealed to him, judging by his wide smile. Before Michael could do more than nod, Gladstone said, "Oh, I wish I had seen it. I've run into Clive a time or two here in the offices since he was one of MacCarthy's clients, and he was a nasty bit of goods."

Nessie appeared in the doorway to let Gladstone know she was leaving for the day.

"Have a good night," he called out.

The two men continued their conversation, but Isabel noticed Nessie was still hovering at the door, as though there was something on her mind. Isabel got up, excused herself, and walked over to the woman. Before she could ask how she could be of help, Nessie said, "May I have a word with you?"

Isabel followed her into the next room.

Nessie was blushing when she said, "I hope this isn't too presumptuous, but my friends and I have heard you singing with XO, and we were wondering if we could have your autograph. We may be older, but that doesn't mean we can't appreciate good music."

Isabel was so touched by the sincerity in her voice, she couldn't help but say yes. Nessie handed her a pen, and she began signing a dozen papers placed in front of her, personalizing each one with a name on Nessie's list. When she was finished, Nessie thanked her profusely.

Isabel said good-bye, and as she was walking back into Gladstone's office, she almost stumbled over a couple of boxes sitting next to Nessie's desk.

"Oh, I'm sorry," Nessie exclaimed. "I was just about to take those to my car. It's mostly junk to be donated. Knickknacks. Someone will want them," she said, picking up one of the boxes.

"I'll help," Isabel offered. Bending down, she picked up the other and walked behind Nessie to the back door, which had been propped open with a brick.

"I don't have a key to get back in if the door's closed," Nessie explained.

They loaded the boxes in the trunk of her car, and Nessie thanked Isabel again as she slid behind the wheel.

Daylight was slowly fading as Isabel watched her drive away. She took a deep inhale of the clean fresh air. She reached for the doorknob and used her foot to push the brick out of her way, but just as she was going inside, someone grabbed her arm and wrenched it back, knocking her off-balance. She was so surprised, she yelped.

Isabel twisted around and came face-to-face with Freya Harcus. The look in the woman's eyes was chilling. Isabel was so shocked to see her she froze, but only for a second. Then she tried to get free of Freya's grip. My God, she was strong. Her hand felt like a vise clamped around Isabel's arm, squeezing the bone.

What was happening didn't make any sense to Isabel. Why had Freya latched on to her arm? What did she want? And where had her superhuman strength come from?

"Let go of me," Isabel demanded. She made a fist with her other hand, and was about to punch Freya to get free when she saw the gun Freya had pressed into her side.

"If you scream or shout a warning, your man, Buchanan, will come running and I'll shoot him. He struck my boy, made him bleed. He shouldn't have done that." Her voice was filled with loathing. "He deserves to die."

The heavy back door had already closed. Even if she could get away from Freya, she couldn't run inside because the door had automatically locked. If she tried to run the other way, she would never make it to the street before Freya shot her in the back, and Isabel didn't have any doubt that she would. Freya's rage was terrifying.

"What do you want?" Isabel asked, trying to stay calm. She was in such a panic now, knowing Michael would grow impatient and would come looking for her. He wouldn't suspect Freya had a weapon, which gave her the advantage. She'd kill him before he took a step outside.

"You're coming with me," Freya said as she jerked Isabel ahead of her. "You give me any trouble, and I'll pound on that door so Buchanan will come running. Do you understand?"

"Yes, I understand."

"Do you want to watch him die?"

"No, no, I'll do whatever you say."

Freya shoved Isabel forward. "Then move."

"Where are you taking me?"

"You'll find out soon enough."

Isabel's instinct was to refuse, but she couldn't do that. She was going to have to cooperate until they were far enough away from the building, and she knew Michael was safe. Then she would figure out how to get the gun away from Freya without getting shot.

Freya kept her gun trained on Isabel and held tight to her wrist as they rounded the corner to the side of the building where Freya had parked her car. She shoved Isabel ahead of her.

"You drive."

THIRTY-FOUR

ISABEL HAD VANISHED.

Michael searched the building looking for her, then went outside and circled the area, thinking she might have wanted to stretch her legs and get some fresh air. No, he knew she wouldn't have done that. Still, he had to look.

They had made a pact. She had promised him that she wouldn't go anywhere without him. She gave him her word, and she wouldn't break it. So, what happened to her?

He was not going to panic. He had to stay calm and clearheaded so he could find her. She hadn't been gone long. He had seen her just a few minutes ago. She was in the lobby talking to Nessie. And now? Gone?

Someone had taken her. It was the only possible explanation.

Michael wouldn't allow himself to think she might be hurt. He had never been this scared before. If anything happened to her, if he lost her forever . . .

When he walked back into the office, Gladstone was on the phone trying to find Nessie. He thought she might know where Isabel was. He tried her cell phone first, but it immediately went to voicemail. He called her home phone next. Her husband, William, told him that

Nessie had planned to stop at the local bakery to pick up some sweet cakes. Gladstone caught her there just as she was leaving.

Nessie was rattled. "Did something happen? Did I forget to do something? Do you need me to come back in? What's wrong?"

When Gladstone could get a word in, he said, "We can't find Isabel."

"What? What did you do with her?"

"No, no, we can't find her," he repeated. "We hoped she might be with you."

"No," Nessie answered. She sounded calmer now. "Isabel helped me carry some boxes to my car, and she stood outside the door as I drove off. I waved to her." She added the insignificant fact before continuing. "I did notice a car parked on the side of the building when I made a U-turn to get out of the lot. I don't know who the car belonged to."

"What kind of car was it?"

"A sedan, a dark blue sedan. I don't know the make."

Michael had already called Isabel's cell phone. No answer, but it didn't immediately go to voicemail. He called Inspector Sinclair next for help. The second he answered, Michael asked, "Did you arrest Graeme Gibson? Do you have him in custody?"

Sinclair could hear the urgency in Michael's voice and knew something was wrong. "No," he answered. "I've got officers out looking for him. One of his neighbors said she saw him throw a bag in his SUV and take off. She said he was in quite a hurry. I think he must have heard we were coming for him."

Graeme Gibson was Clive Harcus's partner in crime. Michael remembered what Gibson had shouted at Isabel: "I'm going to make sure you can't cause trouble."

"Isabel is missing," Michael said. "I think Gibson has her."

Saying the words out loud sent a chill down his back. The hatred Michael had seen in the man's eyes should have been warning enough that he would do something.

Where would he take her? It would have to be someplace private where no one would see or hear. The Highlands were perfect for him, with the mountains and the rugged, unexplored terrain. There were a hundred places he could hide her and not be seen.

Sinclair pulled him back from his dark thoughts. "Meet me at the Rosemore Police Station. We'll hear calls coming in. I'm going to put a bulletin out on Isabel right now. And Michael . . ."

"Yes?"

"We're going to find her."

THIRTY-FIVE

FREYA STARTED SCREAMING BEFORE THEY HAD DRIVEN OUT OF THE village.

"Turn left down that road between the trees. I said left. Not now!" she screamed. "Wait until that truck gets out of the way."

The truck driver was honking and shouting at Isabel. Even though the window was closed and Freya was yelling at her, Isabel could still hear the truck driver. She thought he was telling her to move over. The way he was wildly waving his arms suggested that's what he was saying.

With all the chaos—Freya screaming and cars honking—it was difficult for Isabel to concentrate on driving. She kept forgetting that they drove on the left side of the road in Scotland. She swerved to get over and narrowly missed hitting another car. The owner of that vehicle was now honking at her. She must have been driving too fast because she made the turn on two wheels.

She knew that by now Michael would have noticed she was missing and called the police, and they would be looking for her. She still had hope. But once she turned onto the isolated dirt road, hope vanished. The area was desolate and wooded, and she didn't think they would ever find her here. The only building she passed was an old, burned-out shell of either a cottage or a barn.

They bounced along the broken dirt road, twisting and turning with the curves. God, she was scared. She gripped the steering wheel with all her might. The gun was pointed at her, and every now and then Freya would jam it into her ribs. Isabel couldn't tell if the gun's safety was on or not. If it went off . . .

She was so afraid she could barely think. Horrifying images of the gun going off flashed through her brain, but she squelched them. She couldn't let fear control her. She needed to figure out a way to escape even though the gun in her side was running the show now. If she could get it away from Freya . . . but how?

"Slow down," Freya ordered. "Pull over and park in that clump of trees. Back in so we can see the road."

Isabel slowed the car and looked at the trees Freya was pointing to. The pines were so close together Isabel didn't know how she was going to fit the car between them.

Backing up was a challenge. The steering wheel was on the wrong side of the car, and Isabel couldn't quite adjust to that change. She was also having trouble shifting the gears. After several grinding tries she finally got it in reverse, but while she was backing up, a tree trunk got in her way and scraped the length of the car. It clipped the side mirror, which broke loose and was now hanging by a couple of wires. As she persisted, the mirror dropped to the ground.

"Stop here. Stop right here. You're destroying my car."

Isabel put the car in park but kept the engine running.

Freya never took her eyes off Isabel as she picked up her phone from the console. "If your hands move from the steering wheel, I'll shoot you. Do you understand?"

"Yes."

Whomever she was calling must have been waiting to hear from her because only a couple of seconds passed before there was an answer.

"I've got her. Yes, she's right here in the car with me. I was looking for an opportunity . . . I thought I'd have to follow her for at least a day or two, but she made it easy. How long will it take for you to meet us?" There was an annoyed bite in her tone. "Where? At the spot you chose. That's where."

Freya ended the call, checked her watch, and said, "We'll wait here until it's time."

"Who were you talking to?"

"You'll find out soon enough, now shut your mouth."

Panicky thoughts raced through Isabel's head. What was she going to do? How was she going to get away from this maniac? Her mind bounced from one idea to another. She had her seatbelt on and thought about unclipping it and jumping out of the car, but where could she run that Freya wouldn't have a clear shot at her? Besides, she was pinned in by the trees and probably couldn't even get her car door open. She'd have to climb over Freya to get out, and that was ludicrous.

She noticed that Freya didn't have her seatbelt on. Once they were on the road again, Isabel could drive real fast, then slam on the brakes. Hopefully Freya would go through the windshield or at least knock herself out if her head hit hard enough. She could still shoot Isabel, though. If she didn't have the safety on the gun, it might go off.

It seemed hopeless. Every plan Isabel thought of ended with her getting shot.

As surprisingly strong as Freya was, Isabel thought she was stronger. Back at the lawyer's office her shock at being grabbed had given Freya the edge. That and the gun in Freya's hand. Maybe Isabel could grab the gun and twist it until Freya let go. And then what? Once Isabel had the gun, would she shoot Freya? Violence was wrong; it was a sin, and taking joy from it made it worse, but at the moment she was willing to take on the guilt.

Isabel came up with another idea. People liked to talk to her, to tell her their worries, and if she could get Freya to open up about her troubles and her son—or even brag about him—the woman would hopefully relax, sit back, and move the gun away from Isabel. Having it glued to her side and not knowing if the safety was on was terrifying. Any second it could discharge. But if it was in Freya's lap, Isabel could grab it, hold it down with all her might, and punch Freya with her other hand.

She thought the idea was a little better than the others. To get Freya talking, Isabel knew she would have to sound sympathetic, and that was going to be a real stretch.

"Until it's time for what?" Isabel asked.

"What?"

"You said we would wait here until it was time. Time for what?"

"Time to drive on. Now shut up," she snapped.

Freya was so filled with hate, it was eating away at her. No wonder Clive was such a mean bully. He had his mother to teach him.

When Freya jabbed the gun into her ribs this time, Isabel flinched. She could only imagine how horribly painful a gunshot to the stomach would be. The pain alone would probably kill her.

Stop thinking like that, she told herself. *Concentrate on getting away.*

The longer they sat waiting, the more impatient Freya became. "You've caused me a great deal of trouble. You should have signed the land over to my son."

"Why would I do that? Your son hired men to kill me."

"You stupid girl," Freya scoffed. "Clive isn't smart enough to plan a murder. He didn't know anything about it. That boy would have nothing if it weren't for me."

Isabel couldn't hide her surprise. Was Freya telling the truth? "If it wasn't Clive who hired those men to kill me, then who was it?"

The smirk on Freya's face gave her the answer.

"It was you, wasn't it?" she asked, and before Freya could admit it, Isabel said, "Did you do it alone or did you have help?"

"Walter hired men for me."

"Walter MacCarthy?"

"Enough talking. Shut your mouth."

Isabel ignored the demand. "You're right, Freya. I am stupid. Do you know, when I met you, I felt sorry for you? The poor woman who raised a difficult boy on her own. I got it all wrong, didn't I? Not that it matters."

Freya remained silent. Isabel decided to try praise to get her talking.

"It was very clever of you to convince your son and everyone else in Glen MacKenna that he was the rightful heir. So tell me. Is he?"

She still didn't answer. Isabel wasn't deterred. "If you were so certain that Clive is Compton's son, why didn't you get proof? I know DNA testing wasn't as sophisticated back then as it is today, but you could do it now. There are enough of Compton's relatives alive who would be a familial match, including my sisters and me. Why didn't you insist he get tested?"

"Walter said he could take care of it if it became an issue."

If it became an issue? Of course it would be an issue. "Is he Clive Compton's son?" she pressed again.

Freya shrugged. "He could be."

"You're a very smart woman. You manipulated everyone to get what you wanted."

Freya nodded. "Yes, I am smart," she agreed. Her expression was smug. She sat back and moved the gun a bit farther away from Isabel.

Isabel messed up then. She should have kept silent. "There's just one problem. Compton gave the land to me."

"In a couple of hours that won't be a problem. You're going to sign the land over to me. If you don't, you'll have a little mishap and disappear." To underscore her point she shoved the barrel of the gun into Isabel again.

Isabel knew Freya planned to kill her either way. Did she think Isabel would believe she'd let her walk away if she signed the land over? And killing her with a bullet wasn't a little mishap. It was murder.

Freya pulled the cuff of her blouse up to see the time on her watch. Isabel noticed the charm bracelet then. At first glance the cubes dangling from the bracelet looked like dice, but when she looked closer, she realized there were red clown faces on each side. Good God, Freya was the clown-loving freak. "You gave that painting of a clown to Walter MacCarthy, didn't you?"

The switch in topics must have confused Freya because she made Isabel repeat the question. "Yes, I gave it to him."

"Where would you find such a thing?"

"I didn't find it. I painted it."

That certainly explained a lot.

"You're very talented." Isabel almost choked on the words.

"Yes, I am," Freya responded condescendingly.

Isabel jumped topics again. "Where are you going to get the papers you think I'll sign?"

"Walter had everything ready. You were supposed to die in Boston, but Walter was a careful man, and he had a contingency plan." Freya glanced at her watch again. "All right. We can go now. Follow this road until we reach High Glen Way. It's busy with traffic, but we'll only be on it a very short while."

"Then what?"

"You'll turn onto a road that will take us up the mountain. You won't have to worry about traffic. There won't be any. Start driving. Now," she barked.

Isabel put the car in drive and pulled forward.

"Turn right. Not left. Right. What is wrong with you?"

Isabel was scared out of her mind. That's what was wrong with her. She was trying to concentrate on driving the car and at the same time block out Freya's annoying screams. She didn't deliberately try to hit every hole in the road; it just happened that way. Back on the main thoroughfare, there was a roundabout ahead, and Freya told Isabel to turn at the third exit. Isabel missed it several times, and at high speed they flew around and around the circle. By the time Isabel managed to make the turn, her head was spinning, and she nearly rammed another vehicle. It was an SUV, and the driver wasn't happy. Like the others before, he was honking and shouting at her, but this one was more explicit, giving her a couple of crude hand gestures.

Isabel inadvertently clipped another car as she sped past, but just barely.

They were on High Glen Way for only two minutes, but it was long enough to cause several near crashes. Cars were swerving to get away from her and pulling off to the side. Isabel noticed a couple of drivers were talking on their phones. She hoped they heard Freya screaming and were calling the police.

Isabel had had enough and made a decision. As soon as they stopped, she was going to lunge at Freya and get the gun away from her. She'd have to surprise her and be quick. Real quick.

She increased her speed. In a frenzied panic Freya started slapping Isabel's shoulder. Then she used her fist. It hurt like the devil. With all the shrieking and punching distracting her, Isabel could barely pay attention to the road or the other cars she was nudging out of the way. She shouted so Freya would hear her. "Stop screaming at me, and stop hitting me. You're making me nervous."

Freya continued to smack Isabel's shoulder. "Slow down. There's the turn. Take the turn," she screamed. "Slow down first, then turn. What is wrong with you?"

Isabel didn't take time to answer. She was busy trying to make the turn without flipping the car over.

She made the turn without killing them and proceeded to drive up a narrow dirt road. There weren't any cars around now. As they made the climb, the road grew even more narrow and wound in a spiral up a steep hill. On one side of the road was a sharp incline and on the other, a sheer drop. There was no room to turn around or to make a mistake. With each turn, the car drew dangerously close to the edge.

Freya shouted, "You're going to go over. Do you want to kill us?"

Isabel answered, though she doubted Freya heard her through

all the racket she was making, "If I'm going to die, I'm taking you with me."

Just as they were nearing a very sharp curve, Isabel stepped on the gas to make Freya think her threat was serious. If she swerved one more foot to the left, the car would plunge off the road and take flight. Freya's shrieks became even more high-pitched, and she grabbed the door handle. As they reached the bend, the car hit a bump and lurched slightly. The sudden jolt was all it took. Freya—giving one last shriek—suddenly flung her side door open and threw herself out. Isabel was so shocked she nearly took her hands off the wheel, but somehow she managed to keep control. Tightening her grip, she slowed the car and looked back to see Freya rolling down the steep hill, squealing like a tortured pig. There was a stream at the bottom, and Isabel couldn't tell if Freya rolled into the water or landed just short.

Pulling the car to a stop, she glanced down at the passenger seat and saw the gun. Freya hadn't taken it with her. There it was, sitting on the seat, the barrel pointed at her. She reached over, grabbed it, and lifted it to take a quick look. "Oh my . . . holy . . . ," she whispered. The safety wasn't on. With Freya jamming the gun into her side again and again, it was a miracle it hadn't discharged. Isabel flipped the lever and dropped the gun on the seat beside her.

She was shaking so, she could barely breathe. She reached into her pocket for her phone, but it wasn't there. Where was it? She was sure it was in her pocket when she got in the car. It must have fallen out while she was driving and dodging Freya's fist. She had to call Michael. She frantically patted the floor, but it wasn't there. Maybe it slipped behind the seat. The car was so close to the edge of the road she couldn't get out to find it, and looking at the road ahead, she knew she was almost to the top. She also knew someone was there waiting for her and Freya. There was no way she could back up. She'd drive over the side of the mountain if she tried, and if she stayed where she was, Freya's friend would come to her. Her only choice was to drive on. If she could just reach a safe place to turn around, she would drive back down the road, pull over, and find her phone. There wasn't any other option.

Okay, she had a goal. She drove the car slowly around one more curve to where the hill flattened out, and when she looked up, there he was, Graeme Gibson, waiting, with a rifle cradled in his arms. Had he seen Freya jump out of the car? He had surely heard her.

He was bringing the rifle up now, his aim on her. Without thinking twice, she increased her speed, racing up the last stretch. She hunched down so she wouldn't be an easy target and began to pray that Gibson was a lousy shot.

Gibson didn't dive out of the way. Instead, he shot at her twice. The bullets went through the windshield, narrowly missing her.

She didn't miss. She closed her eyes at the last second and hit him full on, propelling him into the air and sending him flying back toward the edge of a drop. He disappeared over the side of the mountain.

She slammed on the brakes, spinning the car and finally coming to a stop facing the road she had just come up.

Unbuckling her seatbelt, she twisted around and felt for her phone, ultimately discovering it lodged between her seat and the car door. When she dropped it into her lap, it was vibrating. She grabbed it with one hand, the gun with her other hand, and staggered out of the car. Her legs were too weak to stand, and she fell to her knees.

Michael was on the line. "Isabel?"

She was so relieved to hear his voice, she wanted to cry. "I did it again. Oh, Michael. I did it again."

"What did you do?"

"I killed another one."

THIRTY-SIX

WHILE ISABEL WAS BEING TERRORIZED BY FREYA, MICHAEL WAS going out of his mind worrying about her. He rushed into the Rosemore Police Station looking for Inspector Sinclair just as the first call came in from a frantic driver.

Danny, the fast talker, answered the phone and—as was his habit—put it on speaker.

"This here is Sheldon Piers calling. There's a young lady driving an older lady, and the older lady appears to be very upset. She's screaming something awful. The driver is weaving and swaying in and out of traffic, and she's going to kill someone if she isn't stopped. She shot out of the roundabout and nearly crashed into me. You'd best get her off the road."

The call was disconnected before Danny could ask which roundabout. There were quite a few in the Highlands.

Quick as a blink, another call came in. The woman didn't identify herself, but it was clear from her shaky voice that she was distressed. "A driver in a blue car just clipped the bumper on my brand-new Range Rover, and she didn't stop to see if she'd done any damage. There was another lady with the driver, and she was yelling. The driver kept drifting into the other lane. She was hitting her, too."

"The driver was hitting the other lady?" Danny asked, trying to clarify.

"No, the other lady was hitting the driver. You better do something before they crash. I think the driver might be inebriated."

From the description the caller gave, Michael suspected Isabel was the erratic driver. He felt a wave of relief because she was alive and, if she was driving, hadn't been hurt, but the feeling didn't last long. From past experience riding with her, he knew it was very possible she could accidentally kill herself by driving into a tree.

He needed to find her.

He had called her cell phone several times, but after several rings, it went to voicemail. He knew she had turned the phone on and assumed the ringer was off. He left a message in case she picked up.

"Where did this happen?" Danny asked the caller.

"On High Glen Way."

There was a map of the area pinned to the wall. Michael studied it for a minute and became more frustrated. High Glen Way curved around Dunross and intersected with a major road that intersected with A9, the longest road in Scotland. There were too many exits, and Isabel could have taken any one of them.

They needed more information if they were going to find her.

Sinclair grabbed his car keys and headed to the door. "We'll head over to High Glen Way. My car is equipped with a police radio, and hopefully Danny will call us with more information on Isabel's whereabouts."

Michael was right behind him.

Just then another call came in. Michael stopped in the doorway to listen while Sinclair ran ahead to get his car.

"This is Merlin Hopkins, and I just saw the damnedest thing. I had been fishing down at Lucky Nevin's stream," he explained. "I wasn't catching anything so I packed my gear and headed home. I had climbed up that steep hill, and when I was halfway up, I had to stop to catch my breath, and that's when I heard screaming. I looked up just as a woman came careening down the side of the hill. She was too far away from me to catch her—and going way too fast. She was rolling and screaming, and I think she might have bounced on into the water. I'm going to try to find her and fish her out, but I would appreciate some help."

"Yes, we'll send help," Danny promised. "Is there a road near you?"

"Backer's Road," he answered. "The police should drive up that road to get close to the stream."

"Is Backer's Road off of High Glen Highway?" Michael asked.

"Yes," Danny answered.

As he rushed out the door, Michael shouted over his shoulder, "Call and give us directions."

WHEN SINCLAIR PULLED UP TO THE DOOR, MICHAEL GOT IN AND told him what he had heard the last caller say. "We have to get to Backer's Road," he ordered.

Sinclair must have been in quite a few car chases because he drove like a pro. Still, Michael wanted to shove him out of the way and take over.

Within seconds Danny called and gave exact directions to Backer's Road. He added, "We have the license plate. The car belongs to Freya Harcus."

Neither Michael nor Sinclair was surprised. But how had Freya gotten hold of Isabel? Michael knew she wouldn't have willingly gone with Freya. Michael realized he was gripping his cell phone and once again called Isabel. She answered this time.

"Isabel, are you all right?"

"I did it again, Michael. I did it again."

She sounded as though she was in shock. "What did you do?" he asked, trying to keep his voice calm.

"I killed another one."

"You what?" He was having difficulty understanding what she was telling him. "Do you mean Freya?"

"Oh no, did I kill her, too?"

He didn't answer. "Where are you?"

"I'm on top of a mountain. I had to drive up this awful winding road—"

"The inspector and I are coming to get you. We're almost there. Sit tight and don't drive. Did you hear what I just said? Don't drive anywhere."

Michael didn't know how Isabel had made it up the road. Once Sinclair drove past all the trees with branches hanging down, there was a sheer drop on one side of the road and a steep hill on the other. It was a miracle she hadn't driven off or crashed into a tree.

"This road is so steep in places I feel like the car is going to flip over," Sinclair said.

"There she is," Michael shouted as they reached the top.

Isabel was standing next to Freya's car. Her hands were down at her sides, and Michael spotted the gun she held. Where had she gotten it? Sinclair hadn't even stopped the car before Michael was out and running to her. He wrapped her in his arms and hugged her, then gently took the gun from her hand.

He could feel her shaking, but then he was shaking, too. It took a minute for her to calm down. It was going to take him much longer.

"When I couldn't find you, when you disappeared and I . . . damn it, Isabel, you scared the hell out of me."

"I was scared for you, too," she whispered. "Freya told me she would shoot you if I didn't go with her."

Regaining control, Michael was finally able to let go of her and step back. Then he looked up and spotted the windshield.

"There are bullet holes in the windshield."

Inspector Sinclair joined them, and Michael handed the gun to him. Sinclair also spotted the bullet holes. "Isabel, who shot at you?"

"Graeme Gibson."

Isabel leaned into Michael's side. She needed to be close to him to feel safe right now. The adrenaline was gone, and the horror was catching up.

"Inspector, you are not going to believe what happened to me." She raced through her account and ended with her confession that she had deliberately hit Gibson with Freya's car. "I don't know if I sent him flying off a cliff. I'm not even sure how hard I hit him. I just know he disappeared over there," she said, pointing to a drop-off.

"We'll find his body," he said.

Michael caught the sudden movement on his left before the other two noticed. He saw a rifle swinging up next.

Isabel didn't know what hit her. One second she was talking to Sinclair, and the next she was flat on the ground. Michael had pushed her down behind Freya's car and at the same time grabbed Sinclair's arm and jerked him out of the way.

The first bullet whizzed past Sinclair's cheek. Had Michael not acted so fast, it would have killed him. The inspector's shoulder struck the car bumper hard when Michael shoved him down next to Isabel.

Gibson must have thought they were all defenseless because he kept shooting as he ran toward them.

"What the hell is he thinking?" Sinclair shouted.

Michael answered, "That he has nothing to lose."

Sinclair tossed the gun to him. "Kill the bastard."

As much as the idea appealed to him, Michael didn't kill Gibson. Rising up from behind the car, he took aim and shot the rifle out of his hands. Gibson dropped to the ground, howling in pain. Michael ran to him and grabbed the rifle. Sinclair followed him. Michael handed him the rifle, then patted down Gibson and found a pistol and a wicked-looking knife. The man had come prepared for anything.

Isabel stayed by the car. She was actually relieved she hadn't killed Gibson when she hit him. Holding his wounded arm, he was writhing on the ground and wailing, but she didn't have an ounce of sympathy for him. He had tried to kill all three of them. He deserved to be in pain.

Just as Michael and Sinclair pulled Gibson to his feet, Danny and another officer came running up the hill.

Isabel rushed over to him. "Danny, has anyone found Freya Harcus?' she asked.

"Two officers are looking for her."

A couple of minutes later, Gibson was in Danny's police car and heading back down the mountain.

Sinclair watched the car disappear down the steep road, then turned to Isabel. "Did you push Freya out of the car, or did she jump?"

Isabel was still so angry with Freya, she was sorry she hadn't pushed her. "She jumped out," she said. "It happened so fast. One second she was there, and the next she was gone. She was screaming at me and hitting me, and when I was driving around a sharp curve, she opened the door and jumped. She was in such a hurry she left her gun on the seat. She had been jabbing it in my side . . . and she didn't have the safety on."

Michael shook his head, imagining the worst. "You could have been killed."

Isabel was so relieved to have Michael next to her, tears came to her eyes. She didn't want to be needy, and she usually wasn't, but after the ordeal she had just gone through, she was feeling vulnerable.

"It was Freya all along," Isabel told them.

"What?" Michael asked, still trying to sort out all that had just happened.

"She's the one who planned to have me killed. It wasn't Clive. She told me she and MacCarthy plotted the whole thing."

"If Freya is alive, she's going to be spending the rest of her life in prison," Sinclair said.

"She painted that freaky clown hanging in MacCarthy's office, and that should tell you everything you need to know about her."

"That was some fancy driving, Isabel," Sinclair praised.

"Fancy?"

"Driving like a race car driver, zooming in and out of traffic lanes to get other drivers to call the police. That was very clever of you."

From Isabel's puzzled expression, Sinclair realized she didn't know what he was talking about. Now he looked puzzled. "It was on purpose, wasn't it?"

The inspector's phone rang, saving her from attempting to explain how difficult it had been to drive a car where the steering wheel was on the wrong side. Trying to stay in the correct lane turned out to be a whole other challenge.

Sinclair finished the call and said, "Freya is crawling up the hill. According to Danny, she went into the water, pulled herself out, and is soaked through. She's howling and cursing you, Isabel."

Isabel was exhausted and ready to leave. "Where is your car?" she asked Michael.

"Back at the station."

"I'll drive you back," Sinclair said.

"I left the keys in Freya's car."

Sinclair nodded. "Don't worry about it."

The three of them drove down the steep road but were stopped midway. Danny's car blocked them from going any farther. He was out of the car and looking down at the bottom of the hill where Freya stood with two officers on either side of her. They were offering assistance, but she was having none of it. Lashing out at them, she cursed and tried to jerk her arms free of their grasp.

She really was a mess. Her thick eyeliner had dripped black lines down her cheeks, and her hair was standing on end. When she looked up and spotted Isabel, her obscenities intensified.

"She kinda looks like the clown she painted, doesn't she?" Michael remarked.

Isabel couldn't resist. Wanting to let Freya know that Gibson hadn't succeeded—that she was alive and well—she took a step forward, waited until Freya looked at her again, and then waved. Another round of profanity followed her gesture.

Unfazed by the onslaught of insults, Isabel merely smiled and said, "Shall we go?"

THIRTY-SEVEN

MICHAEL AND ISABEL WATCHED THE INTERROGATION. DANNY HAD set up the monitor in the adjoining office and had pulled up two chairs for them to sit while the inspector questioned Freya.

They had been back at the station for a couple of hours. While Freya was being told the charges against her, Isabel, in another room, was giving a statement detailing the events from the time Freya showed up at the law office to the arrest of Gibson. It had been a long, trying day, but when Sinclair offered to let Michael and her observe the interrogation, there was no way Isabel was going to miss seeing Freya try to manipulate her way out of the mess she was in.

Michael thought the interrogation was hilarious at times; Isabel found it infuriating.

Everything out of Freya's mouth was a lie. Michael had to block Isabel with his arm several times to keep her from bolting out of her chair and storming into the interrogation room to give Freya a blistering for telling so many lies.

Freya blamed everything, including her miserable life, on Isabel. None of what happened today was her fault. According to Freya, it was Isabel who forced her at gunpoint into the car and proceeded to "scare her to death" by driving like a madwoman. She was certain

Isabel was going to shoot her because she kept waving her gun and poking it into her side, and when they had almost reached the top of the treacherous road, Isabel had reached over, opened the passenger door, and pushed Freya out.

"I pushed her out?" Isabel gasped. "Did you hear what she said?"

Michael once again arm-blocked her to keep her in her chair. "Yes, I heard. I'm waiting to hear where you got the gun."

"I didn't get a gun. It's hers."

He laughed. "I know it's her gun. I want to hear the spin she puts on it."

They both looked back at the monitor just as Danny walked into the interrogation room and handed Sinclair an envelope. The inspector opened it, read the paper inside, and told Danny to make a copy and give it to Michael Buchanan. "Then bring the original back to me," he instructed.

Freya continued to glare at Sinclair from across the table. She had been given a change of clothes, a long-sleeve, lime green T-shirt and sweatpants. A considerable amount of makeup had been wiped from her face, and she now looked fifteen years older than Isabel had previously estimated. Being as mean as a rabid rottweiler had obviously aged her.

"That MacKenna woman is a greedy bitch," Freya grumbled. "She knows the land belongs to my son. She tried to kill me to shut me up because I've been telling everyone the truth."

Sinclair looked at the camera and shook his head. "Compton MacKenna was never going to marry you or claim Clive for his son. I've done a little research, Freya," he said as he opened his notebook. "You already had somewhat of a reputation before you met Compton."

Freya crossed her arms defiantly. "Oh? And what was that?"

"According to the people I've spoken to, you've had quite a few— shall we say—*intimate* relationships with men."

She reached out with her hand to strike him but stopped herself in time. "How dare you," she shouted.

Sinclair decided to be more direct. "You had sex with a lot of men back then, didn't you?"

Freya scoffed as though Sinclair's question were absurd. "I like sex. There isn't anything wrong with that."

"Did you ever take money for sex?"

She shrugged. "Men like me, and they like to take care of me. I let them."

"Did Compton like you?"

"He must have. He got me pregnant."

At that moment Danny walked into the room where Michael and Isabel were watching and handed Michael the copy of the paper Sinclair had given him. Michael quickly scanned the page.

"What is it?" Isabel asked.

Instead of answering, Michael pointed to the monitor and said, "Watch. You'll see."

Isabel turned back to the screen to see Danny hand the original back to Sinclair.

"The land doesn't belong to your son, does it, Freya?" Sinclair asked as he held the paper up in front of her. "Compton MacKenna isn't Clive's father, but you knew that already, didn't you?"

"You're wrong. Compton is his father," Freya argued.

Sinclair handed the paper over to Freya. "DNA doesn't lie."

"What is this?" Freya asked, glancing at the paper suspiciously.

"That's proof that Compton couldn't be Clive's father. There's no DNA match."

Panic crossed Freya's face. "But how . . . No. This isn't real." She threw the paper back at him. "You manipulated the results."

Surprised and puzzled, Isabel turned to Michael for answers.

"We took the DNA from Clive's bloody nose after the pub fight. As luck would have it, there were DNA results on record from Compton's great-nephew, who happens to be doing time in prison back in the States, so we were able to get the lab to do a rush analysis. There was no connection to the MacKenna family."

"So, Clive never had a claim," Isabel said. "Do you think he knew?"

"I doubt it. I think Freya kept that little secret to herself . . . with one exception."

"Who's that?"

"Walter MacCarthy. The analysis shows a genetic match to him."

"So that's why MacCarthy was so involved in stopping me. He was Clive's father. He and Freya had big plans, didn't they?"

"Yes," Michael said, turning his attention back to the monitor.

Sinclair was shaking his head. "Lying comes easy to you, doesn't it?" he asked Freya. "Do you ever tell the truth?"

Freya didn't have anything to say to that. Her chin came up a notch, and her eyes all but glowed with her hatred.

"Graeme Gibson has already confessed," Sinclair said. "He told us you hired him to kill Isabel MacKenna."

Freya slammed her fist on the table. "He's lying. He'll say anything to save his own skin."

Once again, Sinclair tried to get Freya to come clean, but when she wouldn't budge, he called a halt. "I'm finished here," he said as he shut his notebook.

He called out to another officer, who immediately entered the interrogation room and pulled Freya to her feet.

"Where are you taking me?" she demanded. "I haven't done anything wrong."

Sinclair muttered something under his breath, then once again gave her a summary of the charges against her. She homed in on the charge of attempted murder, acting as though she were just now hearing about it, though the inspector had spelled out each charge two or three times already.

"Attempted murder? You can't be serious. I didn't attempt to murder anyone. That MacKenna woman attempted to murder me. Do your job," she snapped. "Go arrest her and let me go home."

Isabel couldn't watch any longer. "I'm beginning to think she really believes what she's saying."

Michael disagreed. "She knows what she did. I doubt she'll ever own up to it, though."

"I'm ready to get out of here." She stood, arched her back to work out the stiffness. "It seems we've been sitting for hours."

Sinclair looked worn out when he joined them, and Isabel didn't want to keep him, but she still had a few questions.

"Inspector, what made you decide to test MacCarthy's DNA? And how did you get it?"

Sinclair took a seat and leaned back, folding his hands behind his head before patiently explaining. "Freya has been with any number of men, but her connection to MacCarthy seemed to be stronger than most. I guess it was just a hunch. But a pretty strong one, so I sent a man to MacCarthy's house to find something—hair, skin, blood—anything we could send to the lab." He smiled. "Lucky for us, Mac-Carthy was going bald and there was hair everywhere—on his pillow, in his comb . . ."

"With all the proof against her, I can't believe Freya still denies everything."

"She can deny all she wants," Sinclair said. "Facts don't lie."

Before letting them leave, he told them he had all the information necessary to contact them, but he didn't think they would have to return to the Highlands anytime soon. He would keep them informed of the progress—the courts were glutted with cases now—so it was going to take a while before Clive Harcus, Graeme Gibson, and Freya Harcus had their day in court.

THIRTY-EIGHT

IT WAS TIME TO GO HOME. ISABEL HAD MIXED FEELINGS ABOUT leaving the Highlands. It was such a beautiful land, and the people who lived there were kind and gracious—except for the few who tried to kill her, of course, but they were the exception.

She and Michael met with Donal Gladstone one last time to go over details of the transfer of Glen MacKenna. He had hired a new groundskeeper and told Isabel he knew the man, that he was honest and hardworking and would do a good job. Isabel agreed to stay in contact with Gladstone by email and phone, and told him, if any problems developed, she was confident he could handle them.

After the meeting they drove to Inverness, returned the car to the rental agency, and headed to the airport. Once again Noah came through for them and arranged for two seats in first class.

A teenage girl waiting to check in recognized Isabel and asked for an autograph and a photo. Isabel was happy to accommodate her and was pleased because the girl didn't make a big deal about it and didn't scream.

As she and Michael were walking toward their gate, she said, "I told you my so-called fame would be fleeting and that it would all calm down." Grinning, she added, "And I was right. Only one person asked for my photo. In another week I'll be all but forgotten."

Michael had stopped and was looking over her head. "Uh-huh," he drawled.

"I did say it would go away. Don't you remember?"

"I remember," he said with a hint of a smile.

"What are you looking at?" She turned around, gasped, and took a hasty step back. In front of her was a small kiosk filled with bottled water, juice, and soft drinks. There was also a rack filled with a popular weekly rag magazine, and there Isabel was, smack-dab on the cover. Xavier was by her side. He had his arm around her waist and the two of them were staring into the camera. The photo must have been taken at the concert.

"Oh no, no, no," she whispered. She wanted to run to the gate, but Michael took her hand and kept walking. With her head down, she reached their gate just as the first-class passengers were welcomed aboard. "Okay," she exhaled. "Now I'm calm again."

Michael put his arm around her shoulders and gave a reassuring pat. Her face looked as though it were on fire. "Sure you are," he agreed.

MICHAEL DIDN'T WANT ANY SURPRISES WHEN THEY REACHED BOS-
ton. He knew that Nick and Noah were back home in Boston to attend a seminar and would be happy for a break. He texted both of them and asked for help when he and Isabel got off the plane. He was concerned there might be a crowd waiting for her.

Thanks to Nick and Noah and their connections, Isabel and Michael were ushered through the terminal to a private door and got out of the airport without much fuss at all.

Isabel had planned to spend the night at the Hamilton Hotel—she had made the reservation from Dunross—but all three men insisted she stay on Nathan's Bay. No one could get to her there.

Isabel was quiet on the drive. How was she going to get back to Silver Springs? Flying commercial was out of the question, for now anyway.

Michael noticed her worried expression and asked, "What's the matter?"

"I'm trying to figure out how I can get home. I shouldn't fly to Silver Springs tomorrow."

"No, you shouldn't," he agreed.

"I'll cancel the reservation. I suppose I could rent a car and drive . . ."

All three men shouted, "No!" at the same time. Neither Nick nor Noah had driven with Isabel, but they had both heard enough hair-raising stories to know she shouldn't drive anywhere.

Nick was diplomatic. "It's not safe when you're exhausted. You just came back from a long stressful trip."

Noah nodded. "He's right. Driving such a long distance would wipe you out. Take it easy for a couple of days."

"And then what? I'm not ninety. A good night's sleep and I'll be fine."

Michael was blunt. "You're a terrible driver, Isabel." He took hold of her hand and squeezed, letting her know he didn't want an argument.

"But I . . ."

"Terrible," he repeated forcefully.

She was beginning to think he might be right, but she would go to her grave before she admitted it to him. There had been signs, she supposed. Passengers tended to scream when she was driving. Even calm, in-control Michael had done a fair amount of shouting while she was driving him to Nathan's Bay.

Maybe she needed glasses. She thought about that possibility for a couple of minutes and decided she just might. She couldn't remember the last time she had an eye exam. She did pass the driving test. Still, she decided that, when she got back to Silver Springs, she would make an appointment.

Like it or not she was going to have to fly home. Hopefully, she could find a very early or very late flight when the airport wouldn't be so crowded. It was a foolish wish because Boston's Logan Airport was always buzzing, but it was the only choice she had. She pictured herself running the gauntlet to her gate and cringed. Then she gave herself a pep talk and decided she could handle anything or anyone who got in her way.

"I'm tougher than I look," she announced.

"Yes, you are," Michael agreed.

A few minutes later she asked, "Why would anyone want to be famous?"

She sounded so bewildered Michael wished he had a good answer for her. "Some people crave fame," he said.

Noah concurred. "They love the adulation."

"I don't."

"We know," Nick said. "That's yet another reason we all love you."

BY THE TIME THEY REACHED NATHAN'S BAY, ALL ISABEL WANTED was a big glass of water and a bed.

Michael had decided to sleep in one of the larger bedrooms with a king-size bed, but Isabel chose to sleep in the room on the third floor. It was cozy and comfortable.

She fell into bed, closed her eyes, and was sound asleep seconds later.

Following breakfast the next morning, Isabel had just opened her laptop and was looking for flights to Silver Springs when Judge Buchanan walked into the kitchen and invited her into his office for a "sit-down." She knew what that meant. Dylan would say those very words whenever he wanted a private conversation with Kate or her, and once they were alone, he would begin by insisting that he wasn't going to tell her what to do, when, in fact, he ended up doing exactly that.

The judge was much more diplomatic. He asked her questions that made her reevaluate her decision to fly home right away. He suggested she stay for at least a week, preferably two, meet with the entertainment attorneys on Nathan's Bay—they should come to her, not the other way around, he insisted—and if she wanted, he would read the contracts before she signed anything. It was an offer she couldn't turn down.

The day was productive. She talked to Xavier for over an hour. He knew the two attorneys Nick had recommended and told her they were both honest and ethical. Which was a rarity in the business, he claimed. He wanted to record one of her songs as soon as possible, and she gave him permission to go ahead. They would work out the details later. They settled on an amount—she thought it was way too much—and within the hour the money was deposited in her account.

It seemed to Isabel that every minute in Xavier's life was scheduled. He couldn't work on recording with her for at least ten, maybe twelve, weeks, but she promised she would be available. All she needed was the time and the place.

Xavier didn't seem to be in a hurry to end the call. He explained before she could ask. "Talking to you helps me relax."

"Aren't you getting any sleep?"

"Not much," he admitted. "I've been working hard lately. I'd like to think about something other than music for a few minutes. Tell me, are you involved with Michael Buchanan?"

The question jarred her. "What makes you think I would be involved with him?"

"The way he looked at you and the way you looked at him the night of the concert."

"But you were only with him . . . with us for a few minutes."

"So, are you?"

She laughed. "I don't know."

Before he could ask any more probing questions, she changed the subject. "Want to hear about my trip to the Highlands? It might put you to sleep."

"Sure. Tell me all about it." He didn't sound enthusiastic, and she thought she heard him yawn.

"Do you like clowns?"

"What?"

She repeated the question and then told him all about her encounter with Freya Harcus and the freaky-looking clown painting that resembled the woman. When she described the drive up the mountain and how Freya had jumped out of the car screaming profanities. Xavier couldn't stop laughing.

"It really wasn't funny at the time," she insisted.

When he calmed down, he said, "It's the way you told it. The next time I'm feeling wiped out, I'm going to call you and ask you to tell me about the clown look-alike."

"Glad I could help."

After talking to Xavier, she was in a great mood. Then Michael came along and ruined it. She was sitting in the sunroom writing questions she wanted to be sure to ask the attorneys she would be interviewing when Michael walked in and said those four dreaded words.

"We need to talk."

She guessed there was no getting out of it. She knew this was coming. They were back in Boston, and Michael needed to get on with his life. As to that, so did she.

She wondered how he would react if she declined, then decided to find out. "Maybe later."

He smiled as he pulled her to her feet. "Let's go for a walk."

He didn't let go of her hand, and he didn't say another word until they had walked all the way down to the shore and were headed back. They stopped beneath the giant tree with the arched branches she loved. The sun was setting, the breeze was light and warm, and Isabel thought it might be a perfect evening if Michael wasn't glaring at her.

"You and I . . . ," he began, then looked across the bay as though searching for his words in the distance.

"Yes?"

His eyes returned to hers. "It's been real intense."

She nodded. It had been intense. But wonderful, too, she thought.

"We were thrown into a situation where it was just the two of us . . ."

When he paused again, she thought he was waiting for her to agree. "Yes, we were thrown together, and I was constantly throwing myself at you." She smiled as she added, "You really didn't stand a chance."

"But now that we're back in Boston . . . I what?"

"You didn't stand a chance."

After making that statement she turned and tried to walk away. She didn't want to continue the conversation because she knew where he was heading. Same old, same old. He was breaking up with her again, but this time with more finesse.

He grabbed her hand and pulled her back. "Isabel, what I'm trying to say is that I have my future all mapped out, but I don't think you do. You're just starting. You need time to figure out what you want, to know what's real and what isn't."

"I need time away from you?"

"Yes," he said with a firm nod.

"You need time away from me, too, don't you, Michael?"

"Yes."

As much as she wanted to argue, she knew he was right. They did need time apart. She knew her feelings for Michael weren't going to change, but he definitely needed time to realize he was in love with her.

She took a deep breath and said, "When are you leaving?"

"Soon. I've got to finish up a couple of things with the Navy, and one of my SEAL brothers needs some legal advice."

They walked side by side to the house, "I'll be staying here for a week or so and then on to Silver Springs."

Michael opened the door, turned to her, and kissed her. She thought maybe that was his good-bye.

Dinner was a quiet affair. Mrs. Buchanan had gone to a book club meeting, and Michael was also absent, so Isabel dined alone with the judge. Since Lucy wouldn't let her help with dishes, Isabel headed to her room, but first she wanted to find Michael and ask him how long she was supposed to take to figure out her future. Would he call her, or did he expect her to call him? Hell would freeze before she did.

She checked his room and there was no sign of him. Even his travel bag was gone.

He really had left, hadn't he?

Later that night she stood at the window in her bedroom. The moon was bright and she could see the waves dancing against the rocks. She was going to miss Nathan's Bay. She was going to miss all the Buchanans, too. Most of all she was going to miss Michael.

Parting is such sweet sorrow. The line from Shakespeare's *Romeo and Juliet* came to mind. In the play, Juliet tells Romeo good night and says their parting is sorrowful, but it is also sweet because the two lovers can look forward to the next time they will be together. Shakespeare's words made parting seem so romantic.

Shakespeare was a schmuck.

THIRTY-NINE

WHAT WAS THE PROTOCOL AFTER A BREAKUP? IF, IN FACT, IT WAS a breakup.

Isabel's chaotic thoughts were bouncing back and forth like a tennis ball. Did he break up with her or didn't he? She had loved only one man and had possibly been dumped by him, but Isabel wasn't experiencing the heartache, outrage, melancholy, or depression—to name a few of the emotions her friends had gone through. She supposed everyone's reaction was different. Some were extreme. One of Lexi's sorority sisters had stalked her ex-boyfriend for months before she moved on, and there was another woman who recently made the news when she tried to run over her ex with her SUV. She was going to spend the next ten to twenty getting over him.

Isabel wasn't feeling any of those emotions. She wasn't weepy like Lexi when Jason broke up with her, or melancholy like JoAnn when Ryan, the man she thought she loved, dumped her.

Isabel was irritated with Michael, but that was it. She didn't want to run over him with her car. Not yet, anyway. Maybe it was because a part of her believed he really was giving her time to think about her future and her feelings.

He was going to think about his feelings, too. Yeah right. Michael thinking or talking about feelings. Not possible.

WHILE SHE WAS AT NATHAN'S BAY, THE TWO ENTERTAINMENT AT-torneys she'd contacted came out to talk to her. The men couldn't have been more different. One of them was full of ideas on how to make her a huge star. He talked a mile a minute and had the energy and enthusiasm needed to get her to the top. She wouldn't soon forget the look on his face when she explained she didn't want to become a star. He appeared flabbergasted.

Nick liked him because he was a great attorney with a stellar reputation. He was also part of a large agency in Los Angeles with offices in New York and Miami. It was so prestigious, talent fought to get in.

The other attorney she talked to was Jason Westerfield. His agency's only office was in Los Angeles. There were four other agents in the firm. He talked to her for a long while, explained what he could do for her, and listened to what she wanted. Really listened. Nick had gone to law school with Jason. He told Isabel Jason was brilliant, and he highly recommended him.

It didn't take long for her to make a decision. She chose Jason Westerfield. She needed calm in her life, and he fit. He would guide her in her career, but he wouldn't pressure her to do anything she didn't want to do.

GETTING BACK TO SILVER SPRINGS TURNED OUT TO BE TRICKY BUT doable. She flew out of a small airport outside of Boston and landed at an even smaller airport halfway between Savannah and Silver Springs. Kate and Dylan were waiting for her. She fell asleep in the backseat of their car while Dylan talked about the remodel on the house. The events of the last few weeks had been exhausting, but she hadn't realized just how tired she was until she was back home.

As soon as she caught up on sleep, she went to work. She had made a list of what she wanted to get accomplished before she met with Xavier. Her priority was to get all her songs uploaded. She would have to listen to each song and make necessary changes first, which meant she was going to be kept busy and wouldn't have time to think about Michael.

She didn't expect him to call her for at least two weeks. He was giving her time to think, and yet with each day that passed, she became a little more annoyed.

After three full weeks without a word her irritation reached its peak. Was she fooling herself? Had he moved on, and if so, shouldn't she do the same thing? Her misery was her own fault. She never should have allowed herself to fall in love with him.

Luckily, there was plenty for her to do. She had talked to Donal Gladstone several times about the progress with Glen MacKenna. He told her he was working with the National Trust, and the negotiations for the donation of the land were going well. He also told her she had become somewhat of a hero in Dunross. According to Gladstone, the people of Dunross were crediting her with ridding them of the Harcus menace. Now that the Harcus duo and Graeme Gibson were behind bars, the entire area was breathing a sigh of relief. Isabel tried to downplay her part in the arrests, but he insisted she was being modest.

"Nonsense," he told her. "Without you, people here would still be under their thumb. Everyone, especially the tenants of Glen MacKenna, hope you'll return soon so they can thank you properly." She promised she would just as soon as her life settled down, though she didn't know how long that was going to take.

She finally got around to going to the ophthalmologist for an eye exam and discovered she was nearsighted and didn't have much depth perception. She picked out a pair of black frames and another pair of tortoiseshell frames. The specialist explained she didn't have to wear them all the time, just when she wanted to drive . . . or read . . . or see.

When she wasn't working on her songs, she spent a lot of time on video chats with Damon, Owen, Lexi, and JoAnn. They caught her up on their lives, and she told them all about Scotland, but she didn't say anything about her relationship with Michael. It was too raw. Besides, she didn't know what the relationship was.

Despite her determined efforts to forget, Michael was never far from her thoughts. Four full weeks and not one word from him. What was the matter with that man? She knew he loved her. Why was it taking so long for him to realize it?

Maybe he was never going to realize it.

As soon as the thought wiggled its way into her head, she erased it. She had faith in Michael, maybe more than he had in himself. Eventually he would realize he loved her and would come to her. Meanwhile, she was going to keep busy writing songs.

Late on a Tuesday evening Isabel was working on polishing an old song and changing some of the lyrics. Dylan and Kate had gone out with friends, and she had been at it for hours. As she sat at the piano in the living room singing the new version, she was unaware of the audience behind her. Dylan was leaning against the doorway with his arm around Kate. Her head was on his shoulder, and her eyes were closed as she listened to the captivating melody.

"That was beautiful, Isabel," Kate said. "I love it."

Startled by the voice, Isabel spun around. "You do? I thought it was good, but then I started doubting . . ."

"It's perfect," Dylan commented as he started up the stairs. "I'm going to bed. You coming, Katie?"

"I'm right behind you," she promised. "Isabel, you should go to bed, too. You look exhausted. Have you been working on this song all evening?"

Isabel nodded. "And most of the day. I wanted to finish it before I left for Los Angeles."

"Why are you going to Los Angeles?"

"Damon is going to propose to Mia. He wants me to come to the engagement party. I wouldn't dare miss it. He's already booked a ballroom at the Sienna Hotel."

"That hotel is pretty exclusive and elegant. Is he planning to propose at the party?"

"No, before."

"She better say yes."

"She will. They love each other."

"When are you going?" Kate asked, jumping into worry mode.

"Thursday."

"That's the day after tomorrow. Who's going with you? You should have security."

"I've got it covered."

"You're sure?"

"Absolutely."

Lying to Kate was easy because Isabel knew if she told her sister the truth, she would worry all the more. Isabel didn't plan on taking anyone with her. She was going by herself, and she didn't expect any trouble. If she were going to L.A. to perform with Xavier, she would need bodyguards to get to and from the venue, but this was a simple trip to see friends. She was certain no one would bother her.

She was excited to see everyone. She packed enough clothes for a week, adding two dresses her aunt Nora would call too racy. She couldn't make up her mind which dress she would wear to the party, so she took them both. One was the black dress from the Buchanan party. That had been a disaster. Maybe this time, if she wore it to Damon and Mia's party, she'd have better luck and the night would end on a happier note.

Wednesday her L.A. attorney called and asked to meet with her at her hotel on Friday. He wanted to hire a security team to watch out for her while she was performing. There was one agency he considered superior to all the others, and he wanted her to meet with the CEO, Steven Carr. Although she agreed to talk to him, she hoped she would never need his team. She wanted to stay out of the public eye and off the stage, and if she was to accomplish that, it wouldn't take long for her fans to move on. There was only one problem with her plan:

Xavier. He had done at least a dozen interviews before leaving for his European tour, and in each interview he mentioned Isabel or was asked about her.

Despite her discomfort with all the notoriety coming her way, Isabel felt she was coping quite well. But that all changed on Wednesday night when Lexi sent her a link with a note: *Have you seen this?* Curious, she watched the interview. The particularly nosy reporter asked Xavier one last question: "If Isabel asked you to marry her, would you?" Xavier looked into the camera, smiled that killer smile of his, and said, "In a heartbeat."

Isabel was neither thrilled nor flattered. She was mortified. Were the paparazzi, with their cameras flashing in her face, going to be chasing her along with all the crazy fans now? Would everyone want to know if she was going to marry Xavier, and if not, why not?

Because of Xavier's latest interview, attending the party took on an extra degree of planning. She was going to have to get security for the trip after all, she supposed, and that meant bringing in the big gun. She was going to dump it all on Dylan.

Fortunately, Kate was out for the evening and wouldn't interfere with the arrangements. If she had her way, Isabel would be surrounded by armed guards, and she'd be wearing a bulletproof vest. She was tenacious, and Isabel knew she would eventually wear her down. Nagging was Kate's superpower.

Since Isabel was going to stay at the newly expanded Hamilton Hotel, Dylan called their head of security. Come to find out, Regan had already talked to security and hired a driver for Isabel. They were all quietly taking care of her, and she was humbled by their thoughtfulness. She didn't know how she could ever repay them. All of the Buchanans had stepped forward to help her.

Had Dylan talked to Michael about any of this? Probably not, she decided. Four weeks and five days. Michael had left her exactly four weeks and five days ago, not that she was counting. She hadn't asked Dylan or any of the other Buchanans what Michael was up to, but she thought it was odd that Dylan hadn't mentioned him to her, not once in all that time. Why was it taking Michael so long to figure it all out? Loving someone like Michael took patience and stamina, and she was running out of both. She vowed she wasn't going to worry about him while she was in L.A.

She was ready to have some fun, even if it killed her.

FORTY

MICHAEL'S STAY IN SAN DIEGO HAD LASTED LONGER THAN HE EX-
pected. The trial that had resulted from a SEAL brother's PTSD
episode had dragged on, but in the end had come to a favorable conclusion. Michael was grateful his friend's wife had called him for help
and legal advice. His friend was now going to get the treatment and
support he needed.

Michael was finally ready to pack up and head back to Boston—
but first things first. Isabel. He had let her have these last few weeks
to think about what she wanted. He had had time to think, too, and
there was no way around it. He couldn't see a future without her.

He called to schedule a flight, and then he called Isabel. There
was no answer. He waited a few minutes and tried again. Still no
answer. Impatient, he called Dylan.

His brother answered immediately. Michael didn't waste time on
pleasantries. "I need to talk to Isabel."

"Hi, Michael," Dylan said. "Where are you?"

"San Diego. I'm taking a flight back to Boston this afternoon."

"Did you finish helping with that legal—"

Michael interrupted. "Yes. I did. I need to talk to Isabel."

"Why did it take you so long?"

"A friend needed some help. I really need to talk to Isabel."

"She isn't here."

"When will she be back?"

"I honestly don't know. Hold on. I'll ask Kate." He came back to the phone a minute later. "She doesn't know."

"What the hell."

"I've got a crazy idea. If you want to talk to Isabel, why don't you call her?"

"Her phone's turned off. Do you know where she went?"

"Los Angeles."

"Los Angeles?" he repeated.

"That's right. She's staying at the Hamilton Hotel. Regan made the reservation for her. She's such a sweetheart, isn't she?"

"Yeah, yeah . . . sweetheart," he said impatiently. "But why?"

"Why what?" Dylan was deliberately being obtuse. He could hear Michael's frustration coming through the phone.

"Why did she fly to L.A.?"

"The party."

"Dylan, quit screwing with me."

"There's a party tonight at the Sienna Hotel."

"She flew all the way out there for a party?"

"Yes."

"Why?"

"Damon's going to propose—" It was as far as he could get.

Michael shouted, "He's what?"

"He's going to propose—"

Once again Michael interrupted. "The hell he is."

"If you'll let me explain—"

"She is not going to marry him."

"Listen," Dylan demanded. "Damon—"

Michael had ended the call.

Kate walked into the kitchen and asked, "How's Michael?"

Dylan was shaking his head. "Every time. Every damn time. He never lets me finish what I'm trying to tell him. I tried to warn him about Isabel's driving. Remember? I said, 'Isabel likes to drive.' Michael wouldn't let me finish. I would have added, 'But if you value your life, don't let her. She's a horrible driver.'"

Frowning, she said, "And now?"

"He thinks Damon is going to propose to Isabel."

Kate started to laugh. "Aren't you going to call him back and explain?"

Dylan grinned. "Now, why would I want to do that? He'll figure it out soon enough."

FORTY-ONE

FRIDAY MORNING ISABEL MET WITH HER ATTORNEY, JASON, TO discuss her contract, then spent the afternoon being pampered at the spa. She was massaged, plucked and waxed, and slathered with wonderful scented lotion. She got a pedicure and manicure, and while her nails were drying, her hair was washed and dried. When the stylist was finished, her hair fell in soft curls just below her shoulders. It all was completely indulgent, but after the last few depressing weeks, she was ready for a makeover and a brand-new outlook on life.

She paid for all the treatments then and there so it wouldn't go on the hotel charge and disappear. Regan had already been so generous. Isabel didn't want to take advantage.

Isabel was still in her robe when Damon called.

"We might have a problem."

"Uh-oh. Did Mia say no?"

Damon laughed. "She said yes."

"Then what's the problem?"

"I didn't tell Mia you were coming until a couple of hours ago. I wanted it to be a surprise," he explained.

"Okay," she said, wondering why he was dragging this out. "Get to the problem already."

"Mia has four younger sisters. Brigit, the youngest, heard us talking. Mia grabbed her and made her promise not to tell anyone so the guests attending the party will be surprised. Brigit promised, but she told one friend, then another and another. You get where this is going?"

"Yes."

"It didn't stop there. Brigit, wanting to be the first with such big news . . ."

"Why is it big news?" Isabel wanted to know.

"Brigit might have implied that XO was going to stop by."

"He's in Europe. His fans know that."

"I know," he agreed. "But as I was explaining, Brigit, wanting to be the first with big news, posted it."

"Where?"

"Everywhere."

The picture of overzealous fans crushing her in an attempt to get close to Xavier came to mind and she shuddered. She'd seen firsthand how wild and uncontrolled fans could get. They'd wanted Xavier. Now, apparently, they wanted her and Xavier.

"There's more."

"You're kidding."

"Brigit promised she would find out if you were going to ask Xavier to marry you. Then she planned to post the answer."

Isabel laughed. Xavier's fans were obviously getting worked up because of what he had said in the interview. The next time she saw him she just might put a gag in his mouth.

"How old is Brigit?"

"She just turned thirteen. The girl knows her way around a computer. She used Mia's laptop to post."

"I can't wait to meet her."

"You won't meet her tonight. She's been banned from the party."

Isabel remembered what it had been like when she was thirteen. Everything was monumental. "Damon, let her come to the party."

"But she posted . . ."

"I'd like to meet her. Let her come. It's not a big deal. I'll see you soon."

KNOWING DAMON AS WELL AS SHE DID, TONIGHT WOULD BE AN elegant black-tie affair. Damon came from a very wealthy family, and they dressed up for every occasion. Isabel decided to wear the black dress.

She called the concierge, followed his instructions, and took the service elevator to the garage. The driver Regan had hired was waiting for her. There was another man in the car with him who rushed around to open the car door for her. He was around six feet and solid. She guessed his job was bodyguard.

"Who are you?" she bluntly asked.

"My name is Conrad," the driver answered. "And with me is Jones. If you don't mind, he'll hang around with you at the party. He'll stay outside the ballroom but keep an eye on you. When you're ready to leave, he'll walk you to the car."

"I don't think I need a bodyguard at the party."

"Mrs. Regan Buchanan thought it was a good idea."

"I appreciate her thoughtfulness, but I really don't think I need you to escort me, Mr. Jones."

"Just Jones," he corrected. "Mrs. Buchanan thought it was a good idea, and we wouldn't say no to her."

Isabel gave in. They were following orders and weren't going to budge. She wasn't going to make their job more difficult.

"Thank you for your assistance, then," she conceded.

Guests at the party were going to think that Jones was her date. He was young enough—early thirties, she thought—and nice-looking. Not that that mattered.

Not as handsome as Michael, of course. The second that thought popped into her head she got angry. She reminded herself that she wasn't going to think about him tonight.

The Sienna Hotel was twenty minutes away from the Hamilton. The ballrooms were on the lower level, and Conrad pulled the car around to the lower entrance.

Isabel couldn't wait to see her friends. The party started at eight, and Isabel, with Jones at her side, strode through the people milling around outside the ballroom. She didn't think anyone noticed her until some young girls rushed over to her with notepads and pens and cell phones. They wanted photos and autographs. Four teenage girls multiplied to eight within a minute. Isabel tried to be gracious as she made her way to the doors.

Jones stayed outside the entrance. The party was in full swing when Isabel walked in. Lexi spotted her first and ran to her. Then Damon and Mia rushed over to hug her. Mia showed Isabel her beautiful engagement ring and demanded to know if Isabel would come to their wedding. Isabel promised she wouldn't miss it.

With all the introductions to Damon's and Mia's family and friends, it took a good hour before she was finally able to relax and enjoy the party. Damon brought her a beer, and Lexi carried over two plates of hors d'oeuvres. The two of them sat at the table, but before Isabel could take a drink, she was pulled to the stage to sing a song for the guests. She didn't want to sing, but she accommodated her friends and sang the song they had heard the last time they were together.

Wild cheering followed, and she was pressed to sing another song. Then she was done. For another hour Isabel was grabbed and pulled to pose for cell phone photos and answer question after question about Xavier. One brash young girl pushed her way to Isabel and asked if she was going to marry the love of her life. She held her cell phone up and was obviously recording. The girl had to be Brigit, Isabel thought. She was petite with freckles. Brigit resembled her sister but wore braces and, according to Mia, was going through an obnoxious stage.

"Hello, Brigit. No, I'm not going to marry the love of my life," she said. "And I'm not going to marry Xavier. He's just a friend."

"Are you mad at me? Mia's mad at me."

Thus began a fifteen-minute discussion on being mad and not being mad. It was exhausting.

When Mia's mother finally dragged Brigit away, Isabel asked a passing waiter for a sparkling water with lime. Then she walked to the back of the ballroom for a moment alone without people grabbing her. The band was playing a romantic ballad, and couples were swaying to the music. Damon was dancing with Mia. The way they looked into each other's eyes was so loving. They were lucky they had found each other. Damon was loyal and steadfast. He would stay by Mia's side in the good and the bad times. He wouldn't go away for four weeks and six days without calling. In fact, he probably wouldn't leave her at all.

Uh-oh, she knew where this was heading.

Standing there, drinking her sparkling water and feeling like a wallflower, Isabel made a decision. She would give him one more week to figure it out, and if she still hadn't heard from him, she was going to hunt him down and explain it all to him. She would very calmly tell him that he loved her. She was pretty sure she was going to call him a bonehead, too. It couldn't be helped.

The clock was ticking. Now that there was a deadline she felt better and was ready to get back to the party. She was here to celebrate Damon and Mia's engagement, and she was going to do exactly that.

She went up on the stage, picked up the microphone, and belted out a rousing old rock-and-roll song that made everyone rush to the dance floor and let loose. Afterward, the band continued to play old songs everyone could dance to. Isabel joined the fun. She danced and laughed and talked to old friends and met new ones. She and Lexi even did an intervention. They took JoAnn into the ladies' room and, as gently as possible, told her she had a problem. If she didn't stop coloring her hair a different shade every week, using bleach to strip the old color each time, her hair was going to fall out. It was a brassy blond tonight with streaks of orange, which JoAnn confessed weren't supposed to be there.

The party was still going strong after midnight, but Isabel was weary. She was standing in a room filled with happy people, and she was suddenly feeling alone again. Oh, how she missed Michael.

She heard a commotion, looked up, and there he was. She was so shocked she actually closed her eyes and opened them again just to make sure. He hadn't disappeared. Michael Buchanan was standing just inside the door, talking to Damon.

Hands shaking, Isabel pulled her glasses out of her purse and put them on. Michael was still there.

She could barely catch her breath as she made her way over to him. She saw the astonished look on Damon's face and stopped. Michael was furious and he wasn't making any sense.

"You can't marry her. She doesn't love you. She loves me."

Confused now, Damon asked, "She loves you? Did she tell you she loves you?"

"No, not yet, but I know she does. You're not going to marry her. Got that?"

"Do you love her?"

"Of course I do. Do you think I would be standing here yelling at you if I didn't?"

"Michael, what are you talking about?" Isabel asked.

Michael looked relieved to see her. He almost smiled, but then remembered he was angry. No doubt about it, Isabel had made him crazy. "For the love of God, Isabel, what were you thinking?" He tilted his head toward Damon. "This guy says he's going to propose, and you drop everything and fly out here so he can ask you? He can't even come to you? And keep your damn phone turned on."

"What . . . ," Isabel began. She was so discombobulated she didn't know what to say.

Michael glared at her. "You belong with me." He was going to add, *And I belong with you*, but Damon demanded his attention.

"Listen here," Damon said. "I don't know what your problem is—"

Michael resisted the urge to grab Damon by the neck. "I told you what my problem is. You're not going to marry her. Understand?"

Isabel moved to stand in front of Michael, and he immediately put his arm around her. His whole body relaxed. He had her now and he wasn't going to let go.

"Damon, he thinks you proposed to me," Isabel explained.

Mia chose that moment to join them. "Is everything all right? Damon, your face is red. Is it too warm in here?"

Damon shook his head and then laughed. Mia moved into his arms.

"Let me make the introductions," Isabel said. "Mia and Damon, I'd like you to meet the usually intelligent Michael Buchanan. Michael, these are my friends Damon and Mia. Damon asked Mia to marry him, and she said yes."

Michael let out a long sigh before he spoke again. "Yeah, I got that." He kept his left arm around Isabel but put his right hand out to shake Damon's. "I guess I owe you an apology."

"You guess?" Isabel whispered.

Michael wasn't used to apologizing, and it was difficult for him, but he managed a sincere one. His behavior had been appalling. It was unlike him to turn into a hothead. When Dylan had told him that Damon was going to propose, Michael instantly remembered the look on Damon's face in that video when he was watching Isabel sing. He'd looked entranced. Now Michael realized pretty much every man who watched her perform wore a similar expression.

He also thought that, as soon as he had time, he was going to kill Dylan. His brother had deliberately left out an important bit of information.

Damon's gaze bounced back and forth between Michael and Isabel. "Michael, did you tell me that Isabel loves you?"

"Yes."

"And did you also tell me that you love her?"

"Yes."

Damon laughed. The look on Isabel's face was priceless.

Isabel was immediately angry . . . and ecstatic at the same time. It was going to take an auditorium full of therapists to figure this one out. She pushed Michael's arm away, but then he took hold of her hand and wouldn't let go. Ignoring him, she thanked Damon and Mia.

"It was a great party. Thank you for inviting me. I'll call both of you tomorrow."

Since Michael was holding on to her, she couldn't hug Damon and Mia. She kissed both of them on their cheeks and said, "Tell everyone good-bye for me," before pushing Michael out the door.

Jones was waiting for her outside the ballroom. He barely glanced at Michael, his attention fully directed on a large group of teenagers running down the escalator. Another group was rushing toward Isabel from the corridor. Their number was growing exponentially.

"I'll go first," Jones said. "Isabel, you're right behind me, and Michael, you protect her back. Okay, let's move. Fast."

The men's long-legged strides were difficult for Isabel to keep up with, but Michael put his hands on her waist and all but lifted her through the door Jones held open. Fans screaming for attention were gaining on them. The car was right there waiting for them, and they were on their way seconds later.

Isabel sat in the backseat with Michael. "How do you know Mr. Jones?" she asked.

"Just Jones," the bodyguard corrected, looking over his shoulder. "Michael introduced himself on his way into the ballroom."

"I feel guilty I ran from those kids. I should have talked to them. There were just so many of them . . ."

"A crowd can soon become a mob, Isabel," Jones said. "And they could swallow you up."

"Yes, I know."

The rest of the ride back to the Hamilton was quiet. Isabel used the time to gather her thoughts. Michael showing up had certainly been a shock. She was so happy to see him, and yet she couldn't wait to shout at him for being thoughtless and insensitive. How could he ignore her for such a long time? Four weeks and six days? Come on. She had been miserable and wondered if he had given her a single thought in all that while.

Her heart skipped a beat when she looked up at him. Would she ever get used to him?

"Where are you staying tonight?" She whispered the question so Jones and the driver, Conrad, wouldn't hear.

Michael didn't whisper his answer. "With you, Isabel. I left my bag with the bell captain."

She didn't argue. She wanted him to stay with her. She had quite a lot to say to him, and when she was finished, he damn well better promise never to put her through this misery again.

She refused to think about the bizarre conversation Michael had had with Damon, fearing none of what she had heard had been true.

At the hotel Michael picked up his bag and followed Isabel up to her suite. He locked the door, dropped his bag on the floor, and as he was removing his suit jacket and tie, he slowly walked toward her.

Isabel was loaded for bear. Planted firmly in the middle of the room with her arms folded across her waist, she was ready to let him have it for making her wait so long. When she had said everything she wanted to say—and God only knew how long that was going to take, for she had quite a bit of anger saved up inside of her—she would calmly explain her expectations.

"Four weeks and . . ."

Michael had unbuttoned his shirt and was removing it, breaking her concentration. He had such a fine body. How could she not take the time to appreciate it?

"What are you doing?"

"Getting naked."

She could barely catch her breath. It was his seductive smile. The man mesmerized her. Nothing new about that.

She mentally shook herself. "Oh no, you're going to listen to me. Four weeks and . . . ," she began again.

"I love you, Isabel."

He didn't fight fair, she decided, a scant second before his mouth covered hers. Holding her tight against him, he said again, "I love you . . . even when you make me nuts." He pulled back, put his hands on her shoulders, and stared into her eyes. "Tell me you love me," he demanded. "I know you do, but I need to hear you say it."

She didn't make him wait. "I love you, Michael."

Neither could say who reached the bed first. It had been such a long time since they had been together. Their lovemaking was uninhibited and . . . magnificent.

Michael wanted to take her with him to shower, and after a couple of kisses she was more than willing. By the time the last of the soapy lather had swirled down the drain, there wasn't a spot on his body she hadn't kissed or caressed, and he was even more thorough with her.

Later, Michael entered the bedroom with only a towel wrapped around his waist. Isabel was already in bed and he smiled when he saw her in glasses. "I noticed you wearing them at the party. You looked damned hot."

She removed her glasses. "And now?"

Dropping the towel on the floor and sliding under the sheet, he grinned. "Still damned hot."

She was about to roll into his arms when he asked, "Why didn't you call me?"

Suddenly wide awake, she bolted upright. "Why didn't I . . . why didn't . . . ," she sputtered. "You were supposed to call me. Why didn't you?"

Michael sat up in bed and leaned back against the padded headboard. "I was helping out a friend with a legal matter. It was a real mess," he admitted. "I should have called you then. God knows I thought about you all the time."

"You did?"

"Yes," he said. He reached over and turned the bedside lamp off. The bedroom was cast in shadows from the streetlights below.

"I did think you needed time to figure out what you wanted and hopefully that your future would include me, but then I realized it didn't matter, because I was never going to let you go."

She laid her head on his shoulder. "I didn't need any time to know that I loved you."

"I wanted to tell you how I felt in person, not over the phone. I was in San Diego winding things up with the Navy, but then a friend with PTSD disappeared. His wife needed help finding him. She contacted me and the others who were part of his team in Afghanistan. Fortunately, we found him before he did anything too crazy. He's in the hospital now, getting the help he needs."

"Are you having second thoughts about leaving the SEALs?"

"No, I think, with my law degree and my training, I can do more in the FBI."

He started talking about what he hoped to accomplish and the path he had taken that led him to his decision. For over an hour he opened up and told her about his successes and failures and his future goals. He never mentioned the SEALs or talked about his time with them, and she knew not to ask.

It was almost three in the morning by the time he finished expressing all he wanted to do with his life and what was in his heart. She came first, he told her. Always.

Then it was her turn. He asked her what she planned to do about Xavier. "Are you going to tour with him?" He felt her shiver. "So that's a no?"

"I'll tell him I'll do one concert with him this year, and I'll record a few songs with him, but that's all. I'll continue to write songs because that's what I love to do, and Xavier will have first choice to buy or pass on every song. You like Xavier, don't you?"

"Yes, I do," he said. He yawned as he added, "But I'm going to have a little talk with him."

"About what?"

"I'm going to explain that if he ever kisses you again the way he did onstage, I'm going to put my fist through his face."

"You wouldn't."

"Yeah, I would." He kissed her bare shoulder, then her neck, then her earlobe, and whispered, "I want you to marry me."

When she didn't immediately agree, he nudged her. "Marry me," he insisted. "You do want to marry me, don't you?"

The worry she heard in his voice surprised her. "This is not the proposal story I want to tell our children."

"What's wrong with this proposal?"

"Children, your father and I were naked in bed . . ."

He laughed. "Okay, I'll propose when we're dressed and I have a ring. But know this. You are going to marry me. I love you, Isabel, and I want to spend the rest of my life with you."

She fell asleep smiling. Bonehead loved her.

FORTY-TWO

MICHAEL OFFICIALLY PROPOSED TO ISABEL ON NATHAN'S BAY.

This proposal was perfect, the one Isabel wouldn't be embarrassed to tell, should the subject come up.

Michael had gotten past the little incident that occurred on their way home from their appointment with Father O'Dowell at St. Michael's Church to lock in a wedding date. Isabel had insisted he give her another chance to prove she was actually a good driver. She wore glasses now and assured him her vision was perfect.

Michael decided to accommodate her. He found a huge, empty parking lot the size of a football field in front of a brand-new supersize We-Carry-Everything hardware and appliance store that hadn't opened yet, and then he let her get behind the wheel. There were a multitude of tall, round steel poles with giant numbers on top to help customers remember where they parked, but the poles were so far apart, Michael didn't think they would be a problem.

Isabel maneuvered around the poles with ease, and Michael was pleased—and relieved—to discover that her driving was no longer going to be an issue.

He was wrong about that.

He couldn't figure out how she had done it. One minute they were heading out of the parking lot, and the next he was examining the dent in his right-front fender. He didn't yell, and she didn't make any excuses. As he exchanged places with her, taking the driver's seat, he simply said, "Okay, now we know."

Neither one of them mentioned the damage, but after she snapped her seatbelt on, Isabel muttered, "That exit sign came out of nowhere."

"Uh-huh," he replied.

IT WAS SUNSET WHEN THEY ARRIVED AT THE HOUSE. MICHAEL dropped their bags on the porch, took her hand, and walked with her to the old gnarled tree she loved, overlooking the ocean. The weather was lovely, warm and balmy with just a tinge of humidity and a gentle breeze. There was a golden blaze of color filling the sky as the sun slowly eased away for the night. After he slipped the emerald-cut diamond ring on her finger, he kissed her passionately and told her how much he loved her.

The family was happy about the news of their engagement, but no one was surprised. Apparently, they all had known that Michael and Isabel belonged together.

TWO WEEKS LATER JORDAN AND REGAN HOSTED AN ENGAGEMENT party for the couple. Isabel didn't want them to go to any trouble, but they insisted it wasn't going to be anything fancy.

"We're keeping it small," Jordan promised.

"Only the family and a few close friends will be invited. There will be food and beverages . . . and maybe a couple of tables with linen tablecloths and candles sprinkled around the lawn. People will want to sit, after all," Regan explained. "Don't you agree, Laurant?"

"Absolutely," she said.

Jordan and Isabel were on a conference call with Regan, who was in her office in Chicago, and Laurant, who was at her home in Boston.

"Have I left anything out?" Regan asked, and before anyone could answer, she remembered, "Oh, and a little music, too, and maybe a make-do dance floor so couples can dance to the band."

"Band?" Isabel asked. "What band? It's supposed to be a casual party . . ."

"It's just a small band," Jordan explained. "You know how Regan is. She's quite the organizer, and she's planning all of this from Chicago. She's so impressive and amazing, isn't she?"

"Yes, she is, but . . ."

"She wanted to throw the party at the Hamilton, but Judge Buchanan wouldn't hear of it. He said it was safer for you on the island so crazy fans will leave you alone."

"There's going to be a buffet," Jordan interjected. "Nothing fancy. By the way, Isabel, you should probably get a bit dressed up . . . for the photographer. Maybe wear one of your new outfits."

"Photographer? This doesn't sound like a small get-together," Isabel protested. "You're going to a lot of work."

"The food is being catered, so we won't have to lift a finger. It's going to be so much fun," Laurant said. "I love a good party."

Isabel stopped trying to squelch their enthusiasm. They were hell-bent on throwing Michael and her a party, and she wasn't going to object any longer, though she couldn't understand why they wanted to go to all this trouble for what they were calling a little get-together with family and a few close friends.

AS IT TURNED OUT, THERE WAS QUITE A CROWD—AROUND SIXTY at last count. When she and Michael walked outside, Isabel was astounded by the number of guests. This was considered a small get-together?

"I didn't realize . . . I should have invited Damon and Mia and Lexi and JoAnn, and Terry . . ."

"Who's Terry?" Michael asked.

"The nurse at the hospital who took such good care of Detective

Walsh. Oh, I should have invited him, too . . . and his lovely daughter, Kathleen. She and I became good friends."

"Everyone you meet becomes your friend." He was smiling, so she knew he wasn't criticizing her.

Throughout the evening Michael never let Isabel out of his sight. His brothers noticed, of course, and took great delight in ribbing him. Michael didn't mind the razzing, but he didn't like that he and Isabel kept being pulled apart by friends.

Isabel was heading to the porch when a valet rushed to her with two strangers following behind.

"Miss MacKenna, this man said he's a business associate, but he doesn't have an invitation. He insists he'll only take a minute of your time."

"It's all right," she said.

She didn't recognize either of the two men. One looked like a bodybuilder. The other man was short with a stocky frame. He held papers in his hand, and when he spoke to Isabel in that nasally, whiny voice, she knew exactly who he was.

James Reid had crashed her party with a man he called his driver at his side. He thrust the papers toward her and said, "This is your last chance for the deal of the century. One signature, Miss Mac-Kenna, and you will become a multimillionaire. Here, I even brought a pen."

She dodged the pen he was waving in her face. She was having difficulty believing he had come all this way to give one last sales pitch. The man didn't understand what the word *no* meant.

"Is there someplace quiet where we could talk? I'll only take you away from your party for a few minutes," he promised.

"I am not interested in selling the land to the Patterson Group. Now please leave."

Reid made a big mistake then. He grabbed Isabel's arm and jerked her toward him, inadvertently drawing the attention of Michael and his brothers.

Isabel pulled her arm away and took an intimidating step toward the rude man.

"Mr. Reid, I don't know if you've been in a cave the last few weeks and aren't aware of what's happened with Glen MacKenna, or you think you can play ignorant and act like you've done nothing wrong— but either way, if I were you, I'd forget about Glen MacKenna and be more interested in staying out of prison."

"I promised Patterson I would get you to sign . . . Wait, why would I worry about going to prison?"

"Apparently you and a few of your friends discussed getting rid of me. I believe Mr. McCarthy had it scheduled, and you were an eager participant."

"What? Where did you hear such a crazy story?"

"You were sitting in a booth in Jolly Jack's pub with your friend, or rather your coconspirators. A man named Archie Fletcher was sitting in the booth next to you. He heard the conversation and reported it. Inspector Knox Sinclair is in charge of the investigation, and he's looking for you now. I think it would be a good idea to stay away from Scotland."

"They don't have any real proof . . . do they?"

What a stupid question to ask her. No denial, though.

"I know the inspector is looking for you."

Reid's face turned white, and she didn't have any doubt at all that he was in that booth with MacCarthy.

Michael walked over to her, and when she turned, she saw his brothers standing behind him. They looked ready for battle.

Reid swallowed loudly. "I was just explaining to Miss MacKenna that, as soon as she signs these papers, I'll be on my way."

He wasn't giving up. Michael started forward but stopped when she said, "I've got this." Turning to Reid, she shook her head. "I can't sell the property because I don't own it. I probably should have mentioned that to you sooner."

"I don't understand."

"I gave it away."

"You can't be serious. You would throw away millions of dollars?"

"Yes."

Reid finally believed her. He looked devastated. Isabel thought he might start crying.

"I think you should leave now," Isabel said.

Reid saw the look on Michael's face and couldn't get out of there fast enough. He and his driver all but ran to their car.

"I probably should have offered him a beverage," Isabel said.

Michael laughed as he took hold of Isabel's hand and said, "Let's get out of here."

"We can't. It's our party."

"Let's go to our tree."

It took them quite a bit of time to circle the yard and get to the tree where Michael proposed. He sat, leaned back against the tree trunk, and pulled her into his arms.

"The next year is going to be busy," he warned her. "I'll be in training for half a year, hopefully graduate, and then be assigned. We won't know where we're going to live until then. Your life is going to be busy, too, recording with XO and dodging fans."

"Are you ready for all that, Michael?"

"Absolutely. The next year may be uncertain and crazy, but there's one thing I know for sure. Life with you, Isabel, will never be boring."